NOMENCLATOR
IMPERIUM

BILL O'MALLEY

Nomenclator Imperium is the second book in the Nomenclator series of novels.

PROLOGUE

To my dear friend Nicarcus, from Lucius Annaeus Seneca:

I must add my regrets for not sending this sooner. I did not fail to forward you my further recollections of that most interesting man, Polybius Tychaeus, the lifelong nomenclator and friend of that great statesman, soldier and now god, Gaius Julius Caesar out of neglect. Rather, I refrained to send it out of caution. Times are not safe, and our current Caesar distrusts most who serve him, including me. Shortly after I sent you that last packet of material, I was approached by Nero Caesar's mother, Agrippina. In a very odd conversation, she mentioned it would not be wise to be spreading inaccurate histories of the Imperial Family. In recent months, the suspicions swirling around court have subsided and it now seems safe, as long as we are both cautious, to continue to share with you the remarkable tale that old man shared with me so long ago. Polybius spent many years first as a slave in the close company of Julius Caesar and then later as a freedman of Augustus, who is now also a god. I can assure you, however, my account is quite accurate. Polybius had no reason to lie, and, at least in those years, it was possible to check the veracity of much of what he told me.   I do find one thing quite curious that I mentioned to you in the postscript of our previous correspondence. Long ago, Polybius gave me a very similar warning to be cautious as to how I present my history because Tiberius, our Caesar in that time, and his mother Livia, were careful to allow the publication of only those histories which conformed to the story they wished the world to remember. It is curious how with the passage of all these years, things have not much changed. That is why I believe the time of Julius Caesar was a golden age for the recording of history and will probably be remembered as such for a thousand years or more.

I look forward to learning your thoughts on the material I now present during your next visit to Italia.

Affectionately, your friend Lucius Seneca.

LIBER I

Even after these many years, I can still recall the morning an invitation came from Polybius, asking me and my brother Mela to join him. This invitation arrived more than a month after he fell ill and I was overjoyed by it. After believing our friend was going to succumb to his most recent illness, it was sweet relief to be invited back to hear him continue his recounting of the time he spent as a slave of Julius Caesar's. When the invitation arrived, my family had moved from our home in the city to our villa on the far side of the river. The fever season had arrived and the city was an unhealthy place to live. My father readily gave us permission to spend time with him, but instructed us to return home at the end of each day so as to not overtax Polybius as he recovered from his illness.

Upon our arrival at Polybius' villa, we were brought up to the room on the second floor that had the balcony overlooking the vineyard. Polybius was sitting in a chair, but chose, with my help, to make his way to the couch on the balcony. After exchanging the usual pleasantries of friends who had not seen each other for a time, Polybius resumed his telling of the long past events.

"You will both recall, I assume, that we left off with Caesar and his men, myself among them, all gathered in a courtyard, preparing to set out for the province of Hispania Citerior, where he had been appointed Praetor. He knew he had only a year to govern the place, and he wanted to establish a name for himself, so we were leaving behind the political troubles of the city of Rome, for very different troubles in that distant land. So, I will begin.

After a quick breakfast, the entire party was summoned to meet in one of the spacious courtyards of the villa to finalize our plans. The slaves were the only ones surprised by the announcement of our sudden departure from Italy; it seems Caesar had already discussed his plans with the rest of the group. When I realized this had all been plotted well in advance, I was quite angry with Caesar. Since I was often treated as though I was a free man, I had grown accustomed to Caesar's trust. I wasn't sure whether I was angrier about his lack of faith in me or about not being allowed time to say a proper goodbye to Cornelia and our son. The plan was to circle around the city by some of the minor roads and link up to the Via Cassia several miles north of Rome. In this way, it was hoped word would not reach the Senate that Caesar had departed until it was too late to summon him back to Rome to explain his actions.

The plan worked, but to make it work Caesar decided we must move quickly. As a result, my mode of transport was upgraded from mule to horse. This occurred on the second day at the villa of one of Caesar's clients about thirty miles north of Rome. I was roused early, before the sun, so I could be instructed as to how to ride a horse. I am a fast learner, and in the two hours of training, I found I could grasp the basics of horsemanship, but I must confess it would be a long time before I became proficient at riding. The rest of the trip was perhaps the most uncomfortable forty days of my life. The other slaves were relegated to traveling in relative comfort with the baggage train, but I was needed with my master as Caesar worked constantly. He produced a nearly endless river of correspondence and each day, every time we stopped for food or water or to give the horses a brief rest, Caesar would dictate a letter or make a list of goods to procure or people to seek out once we got to the next town. I was also required to make note of anything interesting that occurred. It was Caesar's plan to produce regular reports of his activity to be published and distributed in Rome. He wanted to ensure the Roman people remembered him and appreciated what he was doing for them in far off Hispania Ulterior. At the end of the second day of travel, we stopped just before sunset at an inn sixty-five miles from Rome."

"How did you know the distance," Mela asked. I knew the answer to this question, so I used the opportunity to clean my stylus.

"You have not yet traveled any distance, young man," Polybius answered with a smile, "or you wouldn't need to ask. At regular intervals along the major roads, large stones have been planted in the ground. They are most often cylindrical or square, and on them, the distance to the nearest town is inscribed. Most of them have the distance to Rome also listed. You can now know how far you are from Rome anywhere in the empire, from far off Lutetia (Paris) to some small town far south of Alexandria along the Nile River. In those days, of course, much of what is now under Roman dominion was just being settled, so the markers only existed on the main roads. At any rate, the inn was just a few hundred yards past the sixty-five-mile marker.

I was in a foul mood. Every part of my body ached from riding that accursed beast that was assigned to me. To this day I believe an evil spirit sent from the underworld by one of the infernal gods possessed the monster. When I wanted it to go faster it would slow to a walk. When I wanted it to stop it would break into a gallop. Each time I tried to mount the animal it would attempt to shake me off. My traveling companions found my predicament most amusing. I did not.

I assumed Caesar would want to work well into the night, but he was tired and we went straight to our rooms. Caesar and his party shared two rooms on the upper floor of the two-story structure. Rather than embarrass his companions by having them share the small cramped space with a slave, I was assigned a corner of the stable as my place of rest. I was glad of it though because I was still quite angry with Caesar and I was upset by the journey and really didn't feel like spending time with others. I chose instead to brood on my own misfortunes.

The following morning we started out early. It was a bright warm day for Januarius (January) and the ground beside the road was dry so we made good time." Polybius anticipated Mela's question and raised a hand to quiet him. 'We rode alongside the road because that's what one does while on horseback. The roads were built, at least at first, to facilitate the movement of armies and for that purpose they are ideal, but no matter how carefully fitted the stones are, the spaces between them and the fact that the road bows down to each side to allow water to drain off makes them difficult for horses to keep their footing. Each road has a separate dirt path along the side for horses to follow, while foot traffic and wagons, drawn by oxen or men move on the road surface proper. By midday, we were some seventeen or eighteen miles from the inn. I broke from the group so I could urinate in a clearing beside the road. I tied my horse to a low tree branch and found a convenient spot by another tree. While I was relieving myself I briefly considered running off and finding some farm nearby where I imagined I could find employment. I had a very full bladder so I was pissing for some time. About midway through I heard the sound of someone else pissing. I looked to my left and saw Caesar, his back turned to me, urinating on a bush. At first, I feared he had somehow read my thoughts and came to stop me from escaping. Soon it became apparent he wanted to talk to me about other matters.

'You should be careful. There could be bandits around. Or, there could even be wolves.'

Bandits didn't frighten me. I had nothing they could steal and I figured they would have no reason to kill me. On the other hand, wolves did frighten me. "I'm sorry master. I really needed to piss.'

Caesar finished first and waited for me. We walked back to the horses together. Once on the path, Caesar set a slow pace and I rode to his right. The rest of the party was close enough to be seen but far enough where we could talk without being overheard. 'You're angry with me,' he said. I didn't respond, so he continued. 'That's fair enough. I suppose I would be too. It's not that I don't trust you, but I do not trust the slaves that came to me with the Domus Publica. I don't know them, and they don't yet know me.'

I looked over at him. 'I wouldn't have told anyone.'

'You would have told your woman.'

I knew he was right. I also knew he was right not to trust her. She almost certainly would have told another slave or two and within an hour the whole house would have known; within half a day all of Rome would have known.

He took my silence for agreement and went on. 'I'll be candid with you Polybius. More candid than I've been with any slave save Demetrius.'

I looked at him while he collected his thoughts. I was grateful my horse had chosen this moment to behave.

Caesar sighed. 'You are not like most other slaves. Most slaves are content with their lot, but you're not. You burn with some slow fire in your heart. I suspect this is because you're more intelligent than most of the others. Maybe it's just something your parents passed to you. Just don't do anything foolish. Stick with me and you can have a good life.'

I didn't know what to say, so I just recited the formula, 'I am loyal to you master, in every way.'

We rode on in silence. The rest of the party had stopped to wait for us, and when we had almost caught up, he spoke again. 'You know you can write to her regularly, I've arranged for an exchange of letters each month between Rome and our fort. My mother is in charge of it, so you know it will be done right.'

Once again, I didn't know what to say, so I said nothing. I could have pointed out to him that Cornelia couldn't read, but I didn't.

Caesar continued. 'She will be cared for, and your son will be cared for. In a year's time, you will return to Rome with great stories to tell and money in your purse.' With that, we had rejoined our group.

LIBER II

Just before sunset, we came to a small town. We stopped at an inn but we didn't spend the night there. Caesar spent a short time talking to the proprietor of the inn and we moved on. I assumed there were no available rooms, and I was afraid we would need to spend the night outdoors. Instead, we made our way to a comfortable home just inside the wall of the town on the north end. This was the home of one of Caesar's many clients, and since I wasn't in a mood to talk to my master, it was not until the next morning I learned the real reason we had stopped at the inn. I spent the night in the small stable attached to the inn just down the way from the home while the rest of the party enjoyed the hospitality of the master of the house. I was fine with the arrangement, as it added to my misery, and as one often does, I was in a way enjoying my misfortune. I was bathing in my resentment. Just after sunrise, Sypax the Numidian who was traveling with us for reasons I did not fully understand, came to the stable. He had no real reason to visit the stable and made the excuse of wishing to see an Italian town before moving on. During the course of our quite pleasant conversation, he happened to mention he had hoped I would have stayed at the inn, so he could have visited me the night before. I found this odd but asked him why we stopped at the inn but stayed in the private home.

'Caesar bribed the man at the inn to say we had been there the night before but left that morning. He wants to be certain that anyone trying to follow us to summon him back to Rome won't catch up with our party.'

I wasn't surprised. Caesar was a master of improvisation when the situation warrants it, but he was always careful to see that he didn't need to improvise too often. 'Why,' I asked, 'would you have visited me last night?'

Sypax was sitting on an inverted pail, and he looked shyly down at his shoes. This was an odd way to talk to a slave, but I found people often treated me with greater respect than the average slave. 'I have heard you sometimes like to have sex with men.'

I wondered how I had acquired such a reputation, but then I realized slaves talk and like to curry favor with their masters and the friends of their masters so, just as I knew the secrets of others, my secrets were not so secret after all. I nodded and smiled. I was flattered that such a handsome and cultured man would find me attractive. I was drawn not only to his good looks but also to his strangeness. In those days, foreigners were still considered exotic. That morning we started our sexual relationship and that was the only thing that sustained me for the many days of our long journey. Each day, when the cold wind was making my hands chap and my lips dry, I could think of those few moments of passion Sypax and I would share later that day, and take some consolation that the trip wasn't entirely miserable. He was a man of great appetite and was capable of having sex two and sometimes three times a day, so we frequently ran into each other on the way to a latrine, or while I was packing away our gear in a stable loft, or carrying our laundry to the local washer. I found the fact that he wanted our relationship to remain secret only added to the excitement. I'm sure others in our party must have suspected what was going on. Caesar had the ability to take in a situation and understand it better than anyone I have ever met, with perhaps the exception of Livia Augusta, but neither he nor anyone else ever said a word.

Several days after leaving Rome we came to the city of Ariminum (Rimini)."

"At this point, I had to clear up what I thought to be an important discrepancy. 'Ariminum is to the northeast of Rome, on the Adriatic Sea. It is opposite the way to Hispania."

"Quite right," Polybius answered, "we traveled that direction for several reasons. First and foremost, Caesar wanted to confuse anyone who might be sent out to bring him back to the city. Secondly, Caesar was doing a favor for Sypax and allowed him to collect some money due to him. The third reason demonstrated how far in advance Caesar was plotting his career. While over dinner that night at a taverna in Ariminum, I too asked Caesar why we traveled in the wrong direction.

His answer was swift and to the point. 'There is little money to be had in Hispania, and Pompeius has squeezed most of the glory from that province. Someday I intend to govern Transalpine Gaul, where there are still opportunities for wealth and glory. If we take the road to the north I can introduce myself to many of the most important men of that province.'

It was in Ariminum, a town over two hundred miles from Rome, Sypax came into enough money to rent a separate room in the local inn. A merchant in that town owed him a sizeable debt, and when he learned Sypax was traveling with the propraetor of Hispania Ulterior he paid what was owed. Upon collecting the debt, he offered half the money to Caesar out of respect and gratitude for protecting him all those months he was in Rome, but Caesar declined, telling the man to keep his money. Caesar turned down the offer, saying, 'I appreciate the gesture, but that money will do you much more good than it will do me. With my debts, that sum would be like pissing in the sea. Keep your money and use it to enjoy the trip. Besides, at some point, you will need to purchase passage across the sea to Numidia.' I was always surprised Caesar could laugh at the staggeringly large debt that hung over his head.

After that, whenever we stopped at an inn Sypax would inquire whether an extra room was available. Often times I was able to sneak into his room late at night and after having sex as quietly as we could, I could sleep in his warm bed. It was a pleasant change from a bed of straw in the inn's stable.

Four or five days outside of Arminum, and some four hundred miles or more from Rome, we came to the city of Placentia

(Piacenza). This was a pleasant town in the foothills of the mountains that separate Cisalpine Gaul from Transalpine Gaul. It was here we caught up with the baggage Caesar had sent ahead. To that point, the wagons carrying Caesar's things were always a couple of days ahead of us. The four wagons traveled slower but had the advantage of being able to travel farther on most days, since there were tents and supplies with the party that traveled with it. We frequently needed to stop long before sundown, knowing there would be no place to sleep if we found ourselves between villages or roadside inns. The party with the wagons could simply erect a tent and sleep in the countryside.

After joining the baggage cart, our party would also sometimes travel right up to sunset and sleep in tents alongside the road, but whenever possible, Caesar tried to find an inn. I took advantage of the opportunity and as frequently as I could I found an excuse to ride on one of the wagons. The wagon ride was almost as unpleasant as riding the horse, as it jostled and bounced with every imperfection in the road, but I felt better knowing there were four wheels under me rather than a crazed beast determined to kill me.

The day after we met the party traveling with the wagons, I first saw Caesar dressed as a general rather than a senator. As usual, I was waiting with the horses, just outside the stable of the inn where we had stayed the night before. I heard the group of men laughing and joking with one another before they rounded the side of the building. I was surprised to see they had all dressed in military tunics and cloaks. As general, Caesar's cloak was dyed deep red, matching the belt around his tunic. To a man, each had a sword hanging from his belt. One of the slaves, Myron I think his name was, came from behind the group and ran into the stable to fetch another two horses. I was to later learn these extra horses would be used to carry the rest of the groups 'kits,' those military supplies every soldier brings with him on campaign.

That evening, just after sunset, Caesar was sitting picking at the remains of the meal he and the officers had just finished. At this time he said something that is still cited as an example of his ambition. The subject of Pompeius' success came up in the conversation. I was a bit nervous that Caesar may get annoyed, but all he said was, "I would prefer to be the first man in this small town than be the second man in Rome." What is not quoted, however, is what he said next. He quickly laughed and added, "But I have no intention of being either." I believe some of the men thought he was being modest, but I knew he meant he would do whatever it took to supplant Pompeius in that place. The following morning we turned south toward the town of Genua (Genoa)

LIBER III

A few days after that we arrived at Caesar's villa just outside the port city of Massilia (Marseilles). This came as a real relief to our traveling party and we enjoyed a rest of two full days and nights. It was good to take a proper bath and find clean, fresh clothing. This was the first time Caesar had seen the villa, as it was purchased through correspondence by Demetrius some months before. Being his usually efficient self, Demetrius had arranged for the villa to be well-stocked and supplied and the freedman who oversaw the estate was prepared for our arrival. Rather than open onto a garden, the rear of the villa opened onto a rocky beach overlooking the sea. The view was quite pleasant and the sound of the waves crashing on the shore lulled me to sleep those two nights.

Our stay in the villa was, for me, the high point of the journey. After Massilia, the region became less civilized. The inns were smaller and dirtier and the food was of strange varieties I was not accustomed to. It was at this time I developed my aversion to eating fish, as for days fish seemed to be the only sort of meat the locals ate. I did enjoy seeing the strange and exotic merchants and traders from the parts of Gaul beyond Roman reach. These men were rough and large, but not fat, with long hair. To a man, they all wore their beards long with equally long mustaches. They spoke Latin with a strange accent that is unlike any other I've heard since my time spent with Caesar in Gaul.

When we reached the city of Narbo (Narbonne), located where the Atax (Aude) River meets the sea, I knew we had reached the halfway point of our journey. In using the term city, I am being generous. While this town was a fairly prosperous port with well-built homes and the rudiments of Roman culture, it was in every way inferior to Massilia. In all, Narbo was a pleasant town to spend two days in. We spent one full morning being shown around the local garrison by Fulvius, commander of one of the legions stationed there. Caesar was very keen on forming new connections with the leaders, both military and civil, in Gaul, but at the same time, he went out of his way to ingratiate himself with even the most common soldier. He later explained to me that he saw these connections as the more important. The commanders would come and go as the political winds in Rome shifted direction, but the soldiers of a legion were often together for years. Therefore, he reasoned, it is essential he develops a strong rapport with the men so they remember him well should he ever have the opportunity to lead them.

The following morning the leader of the local senate gave us a tour of the town and its port. The afternoon was spent at the local bath, getting to know the community leaders and the local merchants. Since I wasn't allowed in the bath proper, that evening Caesar and his associates supplied me with all the names and particulars of as many of the men they could remember meeting that day. Between them, they were able to provide a good deal of information.

From Narbo there was a fine view of the Pyrenaei (Pyrenees), that range of mountains that separates Hispania from Gaul. I found the view quite beautiful, but it also made me anxious. I was not looking forward to leaving behind the pleasant climate of southern Gaul and crossing the rugged mountains along what I was certain would be little more than a goat track. As it turned out, the road was wide and well-constructed. The roads that cross our empire were constructed for the rapid movement of large armies and, for the most part, the armies themselves built them. When not occupied with war, Roman soldiers often prove to be some of the finest engineers in the world, and the men are a ready source of willing labor. As we crossed the mountains we were offered splendid vistas; to our right were the even higher peaks of the chain of mountains, while on our left we had views of the vast Mediterranean Sea in the distance. Because the uphill climb slowed us down, on the first night in the Pyrenees, we were forced to build a fort on a flattened area along the side of the road. From the looks of it, travelers had been camping at the spot for years. There were the remains of numerous fires and the bones left behind from the cooked carcasses of a wide variety of local game.

For much of the four days we spent crossing the mountains I felt light-headed and slightly dizzy. Sypax said this was because the mountains reached into the heavens and we were breathing the beginnings of the rarified air reserved for the gods. At this Caesar simply smiled and shook his head.

The next town we encountered was Barcino (Barcelona). The locals of this town told us a legend that had Hercules founding the town during his travels some four centuries before the founding of Rome. From the looks of it, I chose to believe the competing account that had Hamilcar Barca, the father of the great Carthaginian general, Hannibal as the town's founder. This town has since been established as a Roman garrison. From there it was just a few days to the city of Colonia Iulia Urbs Triumphalis Tarraco, or as the locals called it then, simply Tarraco (Tarragona). Being the capital of Hispania Citerior, Tarraco was truly a city built on the Roman model with all the amenities, including free-flowing clean water from a fine aqueduct, a theater, a circus, and a bath. Unlike Rome, the streets were much more regular, resembling the grid pattern of a Roman military encampment. I suppose this is because the city was built by soldiers on top of the ruins of the old town.

Weary of our travels, by unspoken consent, the party decided to increase our pace. We traveled farther each day, staying on the road later and moving faster whenever possible. In a short time, we came to the town of Valentia (Valencia). This town had been destroyed by Pompeius Magnus in his pacification of the province and was still in the process of rebuilding itself. There was construction occurring on nearly every street and with it the dust and grime and noise. We only stayed one night in this unpleasant town before moving on. In a few days, we made it to Carthago Nova (Cartagena). While there we spent the night and the following day at the villa of one of the two town magistrates. The villa was just outside the city itself and the garden in the back opened right onto a smooth sand beach. I was given the freedom of spending a few hours playing in the surf and salty seawater.

Later that night I engaged in passionate sex, for the last time, with Sypax. The following morning our entire party saw him off to the port and watched him embark on a merchant ship that was headed across the sea to one of the port cities in Numidia. I was sad to see him go, but I knew our connection was one of the body and not of the heart, so I was ready for this day.

It was another five days before we reached the border between Hispania Citerior and Caesar's province of Hispania Ulterior, and another two days after that before we reached the capital city, Corduba (Cordova). We first saw the white wall of the city six days before the Calends of Februarius (January 24). Corduba was one of the hottest cities I have ever visited, but I didn't yet know this, as it was still springtime when we arrived. As we crossed the mountains and the warm dry coastal areas, members of our party frequently warned me to expect Hispania Ulterior to be a wild and lawless place filled with bandits, but when we entered Corduba's main gate, we encountered another small but fairly sophisticated

Roman city, also boasting a bath, a theater, a circus, and a proper forum. We were met by one of the legates of the former propraetor.

As he swung his leg over and dismounted, Caesar said to the man, 'where's Decius, I'd expected him to meet us?'

'Your predecessor has already left on the return journey to Rome,' the man answered with a smile. 'I've been left to run things.'

Caesar seemed angry, looking hard into the man's eyes. 'What day did he leave?'

Having worked for an older and more experienced governor, the legate was clearly not impressed with Caesar and shot back, 'It's not at all unusual for a man to get an early start on the return trip. This province was left in good hands.'

What day did he leave?' Caesar repeated, ignoring the man's comment.

'Decius left on the calends.'

With that, Caesar burst into a laugh and turned to the legate who had just dismounted and was standing beside him. Caesar slapped the man on the shoulder.

'You were right,' the man said, flipping a coin he had fished out of his belt at Caesar. 'You win.'

Still laughing, Caesar said, 'I told you he wouldn't wait around here one more day than was legally required,' as he caught the coin and stuffed it into a fold in his own belt.

I was set to work immediately. It was my task to meet Caesar's temporary lictors and arrange their schedules. Men carefully chosen from his clientele for their trustworthiness would be joining us in a month or less, but until then we would have to deal with local equites who would be acting as praetorian lictors. That was when I first met your grandfather, Lucius, and Mela."

"You knew our grandfather?" Mela was genuinely surprised.

"Yes." Polybius took a moment to take a sip of wine and wipe his chin with the cloth before going on. "He was just a young man at the time, barely older than I was. He was very keen on ingratiating himself with whomever the Propraetor of the year happened to be. Your grandfather, young Senecas, wanted to go to Rome. It was through his association with Caesar that he got that chance."

"Tell us about him!" Mela was eager to hear about the grandfather he had never met.

"That story will have to wait for another time, but we will get to it should the gods grant me enough years. For now, we need to stay with Caesar's story as that's the one I promised your brother."

Mela was clearly disappointed, but there was nothing to be done. Polybius continued his tale. "I also had to immediately organize the festival honoring Tellus (Mother Earth). The Roman citizens of Corduba were very excited to have the Pontifex Maximus as their Propraetor and wished for him to personally lead the festival, which started on the following day. To assist me in this I was turned over to Anastius a young and quite handsome, temple slave. We became fast friends that spring and he turned out to be a valuable asset in explaining the local variations to our festivals. Unfortunately, he was strongly attracted to girls and had no interest in me. I was able to have him transferred to the slave staff attached to the Pontifex, and he continued to work for me for several years.

The Propraetor's villa was a rather small but comfortable house on the Baetis (Guadalquivir) River. I'm certain the house was chosen for its topography more than its architecture. It was situated on a rise of ground beside the river with a high wall on two sides and the river to its back. The western edge of the property ended with the inner wall of the city itself. Just outside the western gate of the city, the Legions had their fort. There was a small quay attached to the property, jutting out into the river. The rise of ground and the walls made it easily defensible, while the river allowed for a quick escape. Until quite recently, the area's native population had been prone to revolt against Roman governance.

The city itself was situated at a bend in the river with the newer Roman part of the city butted up against what was said to be the older Carthaginian city. I believe the older city dates much farther back, as the location was ideal for a settlement and was most likely settled around the same time the city of Troy was founded. Some locals even claim the city was founded by Hercules, during his travels. This seemed to be a common belief in the area, but I could see no reason to trust it. Even the most recent additions to the city had extremely narrow streets, narrower even than the streets of the subura in Rome, and the insulae built on these streets usually had balconies that nearly touched one another. As a result, there was frequently a permanent feeling of twilight as one moved about the city. Of course, open plazas at regular intervals allowed the sun to shine through. It wasn't long before I discovered why the city was designed in this way. Corduba, as I said, is nearly as hot as the deserts of Africa. On summer afternoons, the narrow streets provide small respite from the intense sun. designed in this way. Corduba, as I said, is nearly as hot as the deserts of Africa. On summer afternoons, the narrow streets provide small respite from the intense sun.

LIBER IV

Almost immediately upon arrival, the locals began to press upon Caesar petitions for the redress of various complaints. For the first few days, Caesar ignored them until he could establish his administration. The first order of business of the morning after our arrival was for Caesar to meet with the legion and to place his men in command. This was my first real encounter with a Roman legion and I was sufficiently impressed.

If you've not yet seen legionary soldiers parade before their commander, you have missed an inspiring sight. The fresh legions were all dressed in their clean and freshly dyed red tunics and every bit of metal they wore was polished to reflect the sun. However, what was most impressive is how they moved in formation as if they were one giant living organism. But, this digression won't help this history along.

That same day, Caesar issued an order calling for military recruits. The Tribunes were not only instructed to bring the legions up to full strength by raising ten new cohorts and reorganizing the legions to fit the new recruits in as was usual for a new Propraetor, but to increase the strength of the auxiliaries and support staff. These actions effectively boosted the size of his army by fifty percent within a matter of a month or so.

On the evening of the third day after our arrival, Caesar called me into the tablinum of the villa. 'Polybius, prepare an announcement to the effect that I will be making a speech from the platform in the forum the day after tomorrow, followed by a meeting of the Senate in the Curia. We will then meet with the local pontiffs and magistrates.'

I was surprised when I wasn't required to help Caesar compose the speech. I had plenty of work to do so I certainly didn't mind not having to participate, as Caesar sat up late into the night writing his speech. I was equally surprised to be awakened by the very early arrival of Caesar's staff of men, including not only those who accompanied us on the journey but several new arrivals from Rome and even some locals. I had not even been made aware there would be a meeting. I quickly splashed water on my face and hurried to the latrine, expecting to be called in to take notes, but when I made my way toward the tablinum, the meeting had already begun. I returned to my work cubicle and tried to look busy. Unfortunately, my workspace in this villa was too far from the tablinum to clearly hear what was being said, but I did have a clear line of sight. After nearly an hour, Caesar waved me into the room through the open front and introduced the new members of his staff to me.

I was once again surprised, and actually pleased when he said, 'anyone who wishes to meet with me, send to Polybius. He will be handling my calendar. I don't want to have people unexpectedly showing up and surprising me with a complaint or some irrelevant problem. I've only got a year here and I mean to make the most of it.'

From there, the first salutatio of the new Propraetor commenced. I was directed to go outside and make a list of only ten men who would be heard that morning. I told the others they would need to contact me for an appointment. The ten I chose were those who I had been able to determine in the short time we were there were the men who were the most influential. Without clearing it with Caesar, I told them I could be found in the small taverna beside the basilica in the forum, nearest to where legal cases were heard, and I would only be available when my master was judging cases or otherwise engaged. Of course, this didn't prevent men from approaching me any time they saw I was alone, so I began to take a separate tablet with me even to the baths, on which I would note the appointment and add it to the calendar when I returned to the villa.

Caesar's speech outlined a broad vision of uniting the entire peninsula under Roman rule. I assumed this was very nearly the same speech every propraetor appointed to the province gave, and my assumption was confirmed when I overheard one man in the audience say to another, 'They should just leave a copy of the same speech behind every year for the next man to read,' to which his companion replied, 'at least this Caesar delivers his words with conviction.' Then, about halfway through his speech, he moved in a different direction. Suddenly he was endorsing expanding the citizenship for the people of the province. He also promised to create a policy that would address the debt crisis. Like almost everywhere in the empire, the province of Hispania Ulterior was filled with ambitious men looking to advance politically. As a result, there was enormous debt. The province also shared the huge disparity in wealth between those with the most and those with the least. This led to borrowing on a massive scale. Of course, the poorer citizens who borrowed money simply to survive would never be in a position to repay the loans. I found it ironic that Caesar put himself in a position to address a debt crisis for an entire province when he hadn't found the solution to his own personal debt.

Naturally, I was left out of the meeting with the Senate so I asked Caesar's permission to retire to the taverna in the basilica to wait for him. Within a very short time of sitting at one of the tables under the portico (slaves were not allowed inside this establishment), men began to approach me looking for appointments. I had not thought out a strategy for asking for bribes but soon discovered I didn't need to ask. After telling me the pressing need he had to see the propraetor, the first man slid a coin across the table. Naturally, I made an appointment. I was soon to learn that every petitioner did the same thing, so I could be more selective about whom I allowed access to Caesar. A few days later, one of the more seasoned freedmen of an officer informed me of the proper procedure for these matters. The more pressing the reason for the appointment, the larger the payment should be. He said if I felt the payment should be higher I should scratch the tabletop and more coins would appear, but he warned me not to get greedy, as then men would go directly to my master and complain. I was actually disappointed when Caesar returned, as the morning had been quite lucrative.

Just before the Senate meeting was to adjourn, as I was placing my wax tablets and stylus case into the canvas sack I always carried, someone stepped in front of my table, blocking the sun. When I looked up I couldn't see his face, as it was in shadow, but I recognized the toga of a Roman senator so I immediately rose to my feet. From a standing position, I could see it was Lucius Lucceius. Behind him stood three slaves. 'You're Caesar's man.' It wasn't a question. I nodded a little fearfully, as he was far from home and I knew Caesar owed him a substantial sum. 'Your master is a slippery eel. He left Rome before I could meet with him. I have something very important I want to discuss with him. Tell him I'll meet him at the baths this afternoon.' I nodded and with that Lucceius turned, followed by his slaves and made his way into the crowded square. Needless to say, he did not leave me a coin. A short time later when I told Caesar about the encounter, I expected him to be upset by Lucceius' visit, but he seemed genuinely pleased. I was relieved.

We spent the afternoon at the baths, and as was the custom, I waited outside. Although there were fewer men than in the morning, several petitioners approached and coins were exchanged for appointments to see the propraetor.

After we returned home, I went to work listing in order the men Caesar would meet during the salutatio the next day. I also listed the appointments that would occur later in the day, either at the baths or in the forum. While I worked I could, once again, observe but could not overhear the meeting Caesar was having with his circle of associates. I was a bit jealous that I couldn't join them, as there was a great deal of laughing coming from the room. After about an hour Caesar called to me. 'Polybius, do you have my appointment list ready?'

I jumped from my stool and nearly tripped on my way across the atrium. 'Here it is, master.' I didn't really know most of the men surrounding Caesar, so I thought it best to address him formally. Caesar took the list and immediately began to scan it. When he came to Rufus, captain of the auxiliary archers, he stopped. Without looking up, he said, 'any military men I want to see late in the day. They have too much to do in the early hours and can't be away from the fort.' Then looking up from the sheet, 'Otherwise, this looks fine. Did you make a copy for yourself?'

I nodded and turned to leave. 'One last thing,' Caesar said.

I turned back. 'Balbus here tells me there are some local tribes of bandits north of here who have an annual tradition. They like to harass the military escort of each new Propraetor assigned to the province and try to steal something from him. The tribe who succeeds first enhances its prestige. Keep your ears open and maybe we can head off this little prank.'

'Yes, master.' Even as I said it, I didn't think it would be likely I would ever hear anything about the tribes living in the north of the province. 'What will you do if they succeed?'

'Nothing, I suppose. If I react at all, I will just give them what they want. Anything they could steal wouldn't be worth the expenditure or risk to our soldiers to get back. I won't even acknowledge the loss. I plan to address the issue of banditry in a systematic way, and I won't be prodded into going after some insignificant band of thieves. I'll get to them when I get to them.'

Since the region had become a province, there had been a steady but manageable problem with the tribes to the north raiding Roman farms and outposts. They would occasionally steal from a merchant caravan, but for the most part, they were more of a nuisance than anything else.

I was glad I didn't mix up any of the appointments and the next day's salutatio went perfectly. Later as we were walking to the forum Caesar casually said, 'you should keep the money you make in the strongbox. I'm not yet sure we can entirely trust the new slaves.'

I tried to look as innocent as possible. 'Money?'

Caesar simply smiled and said, 'you have something they want, and they should pay for it.'

'What do I have?' I knew the question sounded foolish as soon as it left my mouth.

'You have access to me and you should get paid for providing it to them. It's the way of the world. When we get home, put your money in the strongbox.'

I was kept extremely busy during this month or more. I made all Caesar's appointments, supervised a staff of seven secretaries, all slaves, and maintained a constant stream of letters to and from Rome. Caesar spent a good deal of each day with the garrison and often didn't return home until well after dark. It was then he would frequently dictate letters or orders that were to be posted around the province. On the infrequent evenings I wasn't busy with this sort of work, I spent my time memorizing the particulars of the most eminent locals and placing them into an empty room in a separate memory domus." "What is a memory domus?" asked Mela, causing Polybius to blink two or three times as he tried to make sense of the question.

He then grinned and answered. "Ah…you were not here when I first described this technique I used to remember all the people I had to hold in my memory. I was taught to picture a house in great detail, memorizing the layout of every room. Then, with my mind's eye, I would imagine the people in a room in the house, wearing something or saying something that would remind me of their name and characteristics. It is an effective way to recall more than you would think possible."

At this point in the story, Polybius cut us off, saying he was tired and needed a nap. Both Mela and I were disappointed, but we politely took our leave.

LIBER V

The following day a slave arrived at our villa to let my father know Polybius was ill again and would not be receiving any visitors for some time. I was rather worried when we didn't hear from him for eight days, but then on the morning of the ninth day, Pollux, one of the slaves Polybius relied on most, came to our villa and asked our father if he would allow us to go fishing with Polybius. He instructed me to bring my tablets and writing implements and suggested we would not need fishing poles. We were escorted to a very pleasant spot on the Tiber River south of and opposite to the emporium. Polybius had arranged for a couch, two chairs and a table to be set up under a bright yellow canopy tied between trees. Fishing, as he called it, involved Polybius' great-grandsons both young men already, and their father, Polybius' grandson Ajax sitting on a small dock along the river, doing the actual catching of fish while we ate fruit and drank wine nearly three hundred feet away on a flat area west of the river bank. Castor and Pollux, the two slaves who constantly attended to Polybius' needs, were off in the distance playing at dice. Just beyond where they sat were two small carts and two horses. Today, of course, that area is filled with houses.

Polybius was in good spirits and showed no signs of his recent illness. He wore a hat with a very wide brim, and rather than lay on a couch he sat in a heavily cushioned chair. "Welcome," he said extending a hand to each of us. "Excuse me for not rising, I'm feeling some weakness in one of my legs. Shall we continue?"

Mela and I arranged ourselves on the couch and I poured the wine before picking up my tablet. "Before we start, I have a question?" Mela had been thinking a great deal about the things Polybius told us. Polybius nodded at him. "Why were you and Caesar doing so much of the work? Couldn't the local magistrate's help, and what about the staff he brought along?"

"That is an excellent question. I will clear that up before we go on, as it speaks to Caesar's character in general, but particularly at this stage of his career." With that Polybius took a sip of wine, adjusted his hat to shield more of his face from the morning sun, and began our instruction. "When Rome was a republic in more than name, it was impossible to rule the provinces from the capital city. Propraetors and Proconsuls were sent forth to govern. Because of the slow communication and pressures from barbarians on every frontier, those sent to govern were given much more latitude than they have today. They ruled more like Hellenistic kings than Roman magistrates, In fact, the only thing that kept them in check and prevented many governors from behaving like Assyrian despots was the fear of prosecution when their year ended. Many men, when they were sent to rule a province did allow the locals and their staffs to carry much of the burden, preferring, instead, to use the power they held to provide themselves wealth and luxury. Caesar was not like that. While, contrary to what his enemies then and now might say, Caesar never behaved like a despot, however, he did crave great Imperium and reveled in the command of legions. I firmly believe it was his intention, once he was awarded Imperium to not only reach the top but also to never willingly relinquish power. He had always shown great energy, but from this time on, my master worked at a nearly constant pace. The one exception to this was some months he spent with Cleopatra, the queen of Aegyptus, but we shall get to that at its proper time. Caesar never ruled in an arbitrary manner, but this was due to his natural disposition and the fact that he wanted to enlarge his sphere of influence so he chose to not alienate anyone unnecessarily. It certainly wasn't a fear of prosecution that kept him in check, as he never intended to be without Imperium and therefore to be always immune to prosecution."

Mela announced he was satisfied with the answer. I didn't say a word, but in my heart, I felt this went a long way toward explaining what I already knew of Julius Caesar.

"Now, if I remember correctly, we left off in the first days of Caesar's Propraetorship. As soon as the new soldiers were organized into their proper cohorts and had the rudiments of training, Caesar desired to take his legion out to review the countryside of his province. This was my first experience seeing a Roman army on the march. Here in Rome, it was easy to look at a map and declare the entire peninsula of Hispania under Roman rule, but the reality is the effective extent of the two Roman provinces of Hispania was, in those days, only to the Tagus River. This long, wide river is said to originate in the western mountains of the peninsula and flow into the great Ocean, neatly dividing the peninsula into two nearly equal parts. Since I have little trust in geographers, having encountered as many inaccurate maps as I have those of any use, I can only say for certain the river does terminate in the ocean, having seen this myself. The portion of the peninsula north of this river had some towns that claimed to be and were accepted as Roman allies, but their allegiance was tenuous. The region was mountainous, and not conducive to farming. As a result, there were many communities who had, since the misty past, made their livings through banditry and plunder. It would take the force of Roman arms to make them change their ways.

Since the military exercise was just that, an exercise, Caesar wanted to continue working on matters involving the public interest in his province as well as back in Rome. Therefore, my presence was deemed necessary, and I had to, once again, mount a horse. This second attempt at horsemanship, either as a result of my improved skills or because the beast was of a gentler nature, went somewhat better than my first, but I was still very uncomfortable in the saddle. I had just recovered from the chronic ache in my thighs caused by trying to remain on the first animal's back when I was once again told I must sit astride another.

We followed the road west from Corduba about one hundred miles, before turning north at the city of Hispalis (Seville), another ancient town said by most to have been founded by Hercules. If this is the case, he must have been Carthaginian, because, as with so many other towns he is said to have founded he built in their distinctive mode of architecture and carved pediments and stelae with their indecipherable script.

Unfortunately, we had to remain with the legions, outside the city. I desperately wanted a proper bath, as the weather had turned hot and my horse and I had begun to take on the same rank odor, but when I complained, the other men merely laughed. 'Welcome to life with the army,' one soldier said to me. After that, I resolved to suffer in silence. We never spent more than one night in any one location. Up until this point, we were housed in preexisting forts with permanent structures for barracks and the auxiliary buildings. Once we took the road north, the legions would have to construct new forts and we were housed in tents. This was the main reason for this exercise; Caesar wanted to give the new recruits experience with marching across rough terrain and exposure to their required duties in constructing, guarding, and dismantling a fort before they encountered any real resistance.

In four days the road came to an end. In reality, what we would call a road came to an end a day earlier, but the dirt track that followed was still sufficient to move the army at their usual steady pace of twenty or more miles a day. After that, the progress slowed as the terrain became more difficult and the road became a mere trail. In twelve days we reached the Tagus River. Each night the legions would create a new fort and each night they prepared it as if we were on a wild frontier surrounded by barbarian armies, which everyone assured me was not the case. To me, it appeared as if we had ventured into a place that was just a few miles north of Rome.

It was a marvel to watch the men create a new fort each night. The new fort was always nearly an exact copy of the previous night's fort, which was a copy of the main fort outside Corduba. The only significant difference was the permanence of the structures. In constructing a marching fort, each soldier is assigned a duty. More often than not, the location has been chosen and the boundaries marked out by the surveyors and engineers who follow the covering force. If all goes well, the main column arrives just as they are finishing their work and the legionary soldiers can begin their own tasks. The lucky ones are posted as guards while the others separate into groups and set to work. Every soldier carries a small spade that is as essential as his sword and most of the men find their appointed place in the line and dropping their kit nearby begin to dig the ditch that forms the boundary around the fort. The dirt that is dug from the ditch forms the rampart. While it wasn't deemed necessary from a defensive point of view, Caesar ordered the construction of a wooden palisade around the entire fort. He did this to further the training of the new recruits in how they would construct the fort were the region home to a more daring and dangerous adversary. Some of the men would go to the baggage train and collect the mules carrying the tents. Each canvas tent was home to eight soldiers.

The next morning I awoke before sunrise to the smell of campfires and the sound of the hewing of wood. I and the nine other slaves were all housed in a tent that was situated right beside the line of horses near the center of the fort. On looking out I could see about fifty men, all of the legion's engineers, either chopping logs in the forum or preparing breakfast nearby."

At the mention of the forum, Mela felt the need to interrupt. "You said you were in the fort, not the city."

Polybius smiled politely and sipped his wine. "You are too young to have spent time in a fort. Each one is like a miniature city, with streets and workshops and yes, even a forum with an altar and the legion's standards. A permanent fort will even have a bath and a temple or two.

Now, let me go on. The men noticed but chose to ignore me, so I made my way to the latrine. This was probably the only place in the fort where slaves and soldiers were equal. On my way back from the latrine I could hear the trumpets announcing to the fort that the day had begun, so I immediately made my way to Caesar's tent at the center of the fort. He was already awake, standing facing west so the rising sun's light would illuminate the page he was trying to read in the dim light. Balbus was looking over his shoulder.

'Good morning, Master.'

'Good morning, Polybius. Can you make out this line?' He leaned over to me and indicated the words.

I carefully examined the line of text. 'I have asked the Senate to postpone the election until my return, so as to support my friend Piso, but I think they are suspicious of my motives. I sincerely do look forward to nothing more than a peaceful retirement, and I wish to reassure you of this. Thus far, Cato has blocked a vote on the matter.'

Caesar and Balbus looked at each other and laughed. 'Who isn't suspicious of his motives?' Balbus asked.

'Who is the letter from?' I was curious.

'Pompeius Magnus.' Caesar sighed. 'He is trying to convince everyone he wants to take a break from politics. 'No matter, we can deal with Rome later. For now, we need to get an army across a river.'

That was what the engineers were working on. There was a bridge nearby, across the Tagus, but it was badly in need of repairs if it was to support an entire legion. Those not needed for the bridge went back several miles and leveled and widened the dirt track we traveled on so it was more like a road. They also went ahead and surveyed the track on the other side of the river. Today, of course, those dirt tracks are now proper roads as good as any in Italy.

The day was spent on these things. The soldiers were kept busy guarding the engineers and foraging for food. It was still too early for the grain to be ripe and anyway, there were few farms in the area, but game was plentiful, so that night we dined on meat. Caesar trusted his Tribunes to oversee the work and his centurions to supervise the soldiers, so we spent the day writing letters to send to Rome. It was good to work in the open air, and the climate here was quite agreeable when compared to the heat of Corduba.

The following day we crossed the river. I was still frightened by the thought of bandits and said so during a stop to water the horses and the men. Caesar was sitting on a fallen log and as he spoke he looked down and kicked his toe into the dirt. 'I have only a year here. Putting down bands of thieves will never win me glory. I desperately need to celebrate a triumph. Pompeius is about to celebrate his third and he will have earned one on each continent. Winning a great victory this summer now will more than compensate for any trifling thing they can take from me. I have no intention of wasting even an hour chasing after some thief who got away with a piece of furniture from our baggage train, and Balbus tells me that's all they will do. They just want a trophy so they can earn the respect of their fellow bandits. There are much bigger fish to spear in Lusitania, to the north.'

That, of course, did little to ease my fears, but since he was confident there was nothing to worry about, I chose to be confident as well and I tried to put it out of my mind. That night the legion built a fort identical to the one the night before. I'm still amazed that every soldier knows his job and his place. I now suspected that Caesar was leading into the field to do more than just survey the territory. What he said about winning a triumph indicated to me he thought of staying into the summer. I also calculated the amount of grain we brought with us and realized it would be just enough to last until the first harvest of the summer.

At any rate, we broke down the fort in a slight drizzle of rain. The more experienced soldiers didn't even seem to notice, but I overheard complaints from some of the new recruits as I made my way to Caesar's tent. The weather did not improve and the legion picked its way along a muddy track through steep hills. The order of march was the same as each of the previous days, but as the road sometimes narrowed to a point where only two or three men could pass at the same time, our pace slowed and the line grew longer and more spaced out. Since you have not yet marched with a legion you are probably unfamiliar with the order of the column."

Polybius paused and took a sip of wine. "Would one of you young men mind changing places with me? I feel the need to lie down as it seems to help my memory, and what comes next is important. Sometimes when I lay on the couch and close my eyes I can see the events of my youth as if they had just happened this very morning."

Mela obliged him and took a seat in the chair while I helped Polybius to the couch. I sat at the foot of the couch to give Polybius more room to stretch out. "The column of march. The first to move out are always the scouts. These consist of auxiliary archers and foot soldiers. Sometimes cavalry accompanies them, but as the terrain was too steep for horses to be much use, there was no cavalry on that day. The infantry checks for ambushers and the archers are there to cover their retreat should it be necessary. The next part of the line is the covering force. On this day, this was an entire cohort of infantry. Behind them, the surveyors and workmen who will lay out that night's fort then follow. The engineers then follow them. These men are handpicked from the legions because of their skill at building and their experience at engineering. They are there to make the road passable. Over a flat plain, they will sometimes build a road as they go if the materials are available. On this day they were frequently clearing brush and felling small trees to lie over the muddiest and least passable parts of the road. The baggage train follows them. It is vital the army protects the baggage since it is there the supplies for the entire campaign are carried. The siege engines generally travel next, but this legion only had a couple of small catapults and they traveled in the baggage train. Behind them, the slaves and civilian workers travel. This is to give the general and his officers access to us should they need something, as they come next in the line. Whenever possible, the officers travel on horseback. Both officers and cavalry are in the middle of the column so they can move rapidly to either the front or the rear of the line as any crisis might demand. The legion proper follows next and this is by far the largest part of the column. They are, of course, followed by a covering rearguard."

After this description of the marching column, Polybius took another sip of wine and lay back on the cushion I noticed he closed his eyes as he paused for a long moment. I was on horseback, while the other slaves rode mules or walked. This caused some resentment, but I ignored it. I also placed myself between the other slaves and Caesar's place in the line. The rain began to fall harder and I had the hood of my cloak covering my head, so I almost missed hearing the distinctive triple whistle he used to signal me to come to his side. I turned my horse to check to see if I had heard correctly and saw him nod, so I kicked my horse into a trot and pulled up and turned it just as I approached his place, bringing the animal to a stop, allowing him to catch up. Caesar leaned over so he could be heard over the rain. 'You are becoming quite the rider, Polybius." I smiled in return. 'Ride ahead to that last cart in the baggage train and make sure it is covered with a tarp. That one has the maps and I don't want them to get soaked.'

I nodded and kicked my horse ahead. After passing the slaves and civilian helpers, I was surprised to not see the baggage train ahead of me. The column had slowed and been allowed to spread out to such an extent that the baggage train had gotten significantly ahead of those behind and had gone around a curve in the road. I was still nervous and did not like to be out in the open so I spurred my horse into a pace somewhat faster than a trot but slower than a gallop as that would have been unsafe in the mud. The road curved around the side of a wooded hill. On my right was a slope covered in brush and on my left the ground sloped down a short distance to a swollen stream. As I reached the last cart of the baggage train I heard a strange animal-like whooping. I looked around to see its source. Just as I turned my horse to the right the sky was split by a bolt of lightning followed instantly by a loud crash of thunder. My horse reared up, throwing me from the saddle. As I fell I looked to my right and saw the source of the strange whooping. It was a group of about ten strangely dressed men on ponies riding out from the trees. They had shields and spears except the one in the lead. He carried a sword. I hit the ground splashing hard into the mud, knocking the breath from my body. I scrambled to my feet. Realizing I would have no time to find my horse, I tried to leap onto the last cart that was, incidentally, covered with a tarp. I slipped on the oiled cloth of the tarp and fell to the ground again. From the baggage train, I heard cries and whistles signaling to the rest of the column that we were under attack, but that wouldn't help me. Just as I struggled to my feet the rider with the sword was upon me. I saw the crazed look in his eyes and watched as if the passage of time slowed, seeing him raise his sword and swing it at my head. I closed my eyes and all went dark.

LIBER VI

When I finally awoke it was night. It hurt to move my head so I wanted to lay still but I was being poked with something on my leg and body. I opened my eyes and saw that I was in a crude cage made of a wooden box fronted by a rusty iron gate. I immediately sat up and vomited out the front of the cage. That drove away the three small naked boys who had been poking me with sticks. They left screaming and laughing as they ran off somewhere behind my cage. I leaned back against the wooden wall behind me and tried to remember what had happened. I smelled smoke and saw the flicker of flames reflected on the ground in front of my cage. I noticed it was no longer raining. I needed to piss and I was hungry but more than anything else I wanted to sleep, so I lifted my muddy tunic and urinated onto the splash of vomit I left a short time before. Then I lay on the damp straw piled on the bottom of the cage and slept.

The next thing I was aware of was the sound of the cage door being opened. The bright morning light hurt my eyes and caused my head to ache. Reaching up to my forehead I felt a large bump and the crust of dried blood, but the cut that left the blood was not deep, and I was relieved a bit. The man who was unlocking the door was talking in some strange language to another man who held in his hand a bowl of some sort of soup. The two men had long shaggy hair and beards. They were shirtless but did wear leather breeches. I was in no condition to put up a fight so I simply took the bowl when it was thrust at me by the shorter of the two men and greedily drank it down, as the men walked away. In the light of day, I could better see where I was. Looking around I noticed I was in some sort of crude forum. The ground around me was covered in crushed stone and wet dirt and two of the three sides of the square that were visible to me were lined with buildings with mud-brick sides and thatched roofs. The third side led to a road that sloped down the hill to a high wooden palisade. I couldn't see over the wall, as the pickets had been built on an earth mound.

It wasn't long before a group of people had gathered in front of my cage. They all spoke the same strange language I heard the other men speak when they came to feed me and they all seemed intensely curious about me. One young girl began to toss pebbles from the ground into my cage with enough force to irritate me but not cause any pain. I turned away from them and faced the wall until they grew bored and, one by one, wandered away. At last, I turned back when I thought I was alone, but standing in front of me was the shorter man who had given me the soup earlier. We just stared at each other. Twice he opened his mouth to speak but stopped himself. On the third attempt, he said in heavily accented Latin, 'You are Roman? You are soldier?'

I moved quickly to the front of the cage. 'You speak Latin!'

'A little,' he responded hesitantly as if searching his mind for the right words.

'Where am I?' I asked. I had already pieced together what had happened. The man on the pony who charged me at the baggage train the day before had hit me on the forehead with the flat side of his sword. I was taken with whatever else they had managed to steal from the carts.

'Village,' was all he said.

'What village. What is this village called?' I don't know why this was important to me but at the time I needed to know the place. The man clearly didn't understand what I was saying, so I repeated myself speaking more slowly. He smiled and named a place. I couldn't understand what he said but realized it didn't really matter where I was.

I then remembered his first question to me. He had asked if I was a soldier. I thought I might have a better chance of living if I was not a member of the legion, so I answered him slowly and honestly. 'I am only a slave. I am no soldier.'

At that, he seemed to get excited and said something in his barbaric language and hurried off. A short time later he returned with two other men, each wearing proper woolen tunics, dyed blue. They also wore gold jewelry. One wore a necklace and the other had a band of gold around his left wrist. They stared at me for what seemed to be a very long time and first one then the other turned and walked away leaving me alone again with the Latin speaker.

'This is good,' the Latin speaker said.

'What is good?' I responded.

'You are slave.'

All I could say was 'I need to go to the latrine.'

For that, he couldn't help me. All my companion did was indicate the hole in the bottom of my cage. Looking through it I noticed my cage was on some sort of raised platform and there was a wooden pail beneath the hole. I was to squat over the hole when I need to relieve myself. What I was to learn over the next several conversations with my new friend was that he had been captured by a Roman scouting party as a boy and had spent three years as a slave in a Roman frontier town before escaping and returning to his native village. I'm sure his story would have been fascinating had he been more fluent in Latin. I also learned that the tribal leaders were elated that I was a slave. Had I been a soldier they would not have been the first to take something from the new propraetor and they would not have won the contest. As a slave, I was property and they could claim victory over the other tribes. I also learned that two of their men had been killed by the Romans and therefore, as soon as my status as a slave could be verified to the other tribal leaders I would have one of my hands removed and I would be stabbed to death as an offering to Cariocecus, or some such outlandish thing, their name for Mars.

That night, I grew very despondent. I knew there would be no rescue for me. I was the small piece of property that was stolen, and that Caesar would not acknowledge his loss, as that would prevent him from continuing on to the great victory that would earn him his first triumph. I knew that in a few days I would die a terrible death. I thought about Cornelia and my son, knowing they would probably never learn of my fate. I thought of Artemisa and how she too would never learn that her son had at least risen to the position of nomenclator to a member of an ancient patrician family. I thought about my boyhood friend Quintus and wondered if he was still a gardener at the Titus Villa. I also thought about Gaius Vitrius. I realized he and my son were the two I was most disappointed to be leaving behind. I wanted them to learn of my success and I wanted them to have some measure of pride in my accomplishments. I also secretly dreamt of one day gaining my freedom and living with him. Cornelia sometimes figured in these notions, but I came to realize that Gaius I loved more."

With that, Polybius opened his eyes and propped himself up on one elbow. Before he reached for his wine I saw him wipe a tear from his cheek with the back of his hand. After pausing a short time he lay back down and shut his eyes once again and continued his story.

"At long last, I drifted into a fitful sleep. That night I dreamt of Gaius. Men were coming to kill me and I was mired in thick mud up to my knees and found it impossible to move. I cried out for his protection, and when I did, he appeared on a hill in the distance, holding a sword and the long shield of a legionary soldier, but he wouldn't come to my aid. He looked around as if he couldn't tell where my cries were coming from and I was helpless to move toward him. I waved my arms but he simply looked confused and turned away, walking off into the darkness. I sat back and buried my head in my hands and cried.

It was then that, after so long, I once again heard the musical voice of Fortuna. 'He saved your life once, and he will save it again, but you don't need his protection this time. He is not yet strong enough but there is another who is.' I looked up and there she was standing before me, lighting up the area around her as I had seen in past dreams.

'Are you the one?' I asked her pleadingly.

'I will always be with you.' With that, she bent to the ground and picked up a red cloak. I recognized it as being the cloak of a Roman general. She draped it over my shoulders and said, 'go back to sleep.'

'But, I am asleep,' I answered. With that, she simply smiled and walked away.

The following morning I woke to the sound of feverish activity. Along the side of one of the buildings, I could see men were stacking spears, swords, and the round shields I had seen my captors carry. There was a line of ponies tied together being led up the road from somewhere down the hill and a group of women gluing feathers to the ends of arrows on the other side of the square. One of the men who came to my cage the day before walked by and noticed my intense interest in the activity. He glared at me and strutted off. A very brief time later the Latin speaker came to my cage with a large leather tarp and threw it over the front of the cage. Before covering my view I was able to briefly question him. 'What is happening?'

'We go to war,' was all he would say.

I was elated. If the tribe was too busy fighting another tribe, I might live a while longer. To a condemned prisoner, uncertainty is good. I held out hope that my captors would lose and the victors would free me. In a short time, I heard voices and could feel my cage being lifted off its platform. I was carried quickly into a building of some sort and my cage was set down again. The room grew quiet as the men who carried me departed, but a short time later the Latin speaker came in and removed the cover from my cage. Looking around I noticed I was in a round room, empty and without windows. 'You become gift for our god. We prepare.'

At that, my heart sank. My erstwhile friend left as another man entered the room. This new man was carrying a burning bundle of some sort of dried plant and he began waving it in front of my cage, the smoke stung my eyes. All the while he was chanting a strange melody of which the only word I recognized was the name of their war god. It was apparent that the threat of war sped up my sacrifice. They no longer cared about winning the competition, as they had a more pressing need for divine help.

Two more men joined the priest and opened the cage. I kicked and struggled, but the men were too large and they easily pulled me from the cage and forced me down on the stone floor of the room. My hands were bound behind my back with a rope made of some sort of twisted grass and my feet were bound with the same material. Another length of the rope was forced into my mouth and tied around the back of my neck, effectively stifling my cries. I remember it had a bitter taste. One man took my feet and the other grabbed me under my arms and they easily picked my twisting and writhing body from the floor.

I struggled fiercely as they brought me outside. A young boy in some sort of priestly clothing was standing beside a pole implanted in the ground and I was carried toward him. The boy was clearly frightened. The priest followed behind, chanting prayers. I, in turn, mumbled, through my gag, prayers as well. I prayed to the gods and goddesses of Rome. A loop of rope was put around my neck and tied to a metal ring projecting from the post. I needed to stop struggling at this point because each movement tightened the rope around my neck and I felt it starting to restrict my breathing. Suddenly, a strange calm came over me. I was still terrified, but it was as if I was an outside observer and I could see the events happen to someone else. The dreamlike quality of the situation made me think of my dream I had the night before and I began to pray fervently to Fortuna. As I started to pray, war trumpets began to blare from the palisade in front of the square. I squinted my eyes against the bright sun and could make out smoke rising behind the wall and archers standing on a platform near the top shooting down toward the unseen enemy. Then, first one and then a series of tremendous thuds rang out from outside the wall. The two men who had carried me outside ran off leaving just the priest and the boy. It was then I looked down at the tray he held in his hands. On the tray was a long silver dagger. The priest picked up the dagger in his right hand while waving the bundle of burning weeds with his left and the boy stepped back three or four paces. The priest began to walk in a broad circle around the pole, still chanting his prayers while the thudding sound continued at the palisade. Suddenly the priest stopped in front of me and leaned in close. I could see he was sweating and he looked pale. I could hear him breathing in short gasps. Suddenly he took a step back just as the sound of splintering wood from the palisade filled the air. The priest turned to look toward the wall behind him and I followed his gaze to hear another thud and see some of the sharpened logs that made up the wall crack and move. Two of the archers on the platform lost their footing and fell backward onto a group of men at the base of the wall. Just then first one and then several blazing arrows came over the wall. One found its mark on the thatched roof of a nearby building. Flames immediately erupted from the building sending a shower of embers and a cloud of smoke into the wind. The priest turned back toward me with a look of panic on his face. He tried to begin chanting once again but he couldn't seem to find his breath. In my mind I cried out, 'Fortuna, help me!'

Over the din and chaos of the situation, I clearly heard her gentle voice as if she was whispering in my ear, 'always.'

The priest stepped forward once more and pressed the dagger to my belly. He began to press, but he was hesitant and while I could feel the knife cut my skin he seemed to lack the strength to thrust it in. A groan came from his throat and he first dropped the bundle of burning weeds and then the dagger. Stumbling back a step he clutched his left shoulder and dropped to his knees and then fell hard, face-first into the dirt. I heard the boy scream and I looked up to see him running down the road.

The goddess had spared me, but I knew I was not yet secure. If someone from the village didn't kill me, the invaders almost certainly would. I took a deep breath to calm myself but the smoky air caught in my throat and I began to cough. I forced myself to concentrate my mind and I began to methodically twist at the rope that bound my wrist. It was of a very pliable and loose material so it was only a short time until it was loose enough to slip my wrists out and free my hands. I was then able to reach up and by leaning back against the post, loosen the noose and slip it over my head. I dropped down and grabbed the silver dagger and used it to cut the ropes that bound my feet and gagged my mouth. I kicked the priest over with my foot and looked into his dead eyes. His face had a bluish cast and his eyes were staring blankly. I stepped out into the square but didn't know where to go. Behind me was the battle; before me the village. I guessed all the men of the village were fighting at the wall, but if I ran into the village, there would be enough women to subdue me. I had heard barbarian women fight almost as fiercely as their men. I turned. In front of me was a wall of smoke. The flames had jumped from roof to roof and almost every building I could see was ablaze. From the sounds of battle behind the smoke, I knew the invaders had breached the wall and would soon sack the village. Just as I resolved to take my chances and run into the unknown behind me I heard a shrill whistle; two short tweets followed by one long one. That was one of the sweetest sounds I had ever heard."

Polybius paused to sit up and take a drink from his wine cup. I smiled, knowing he was being dramatic, just waiting for one of us to ask the question. I kept my mouth shut and waited for Mela who excitedly asked, "who was whistling?"

Polybius smiled and leaned back on the cushions and shut his eyes. "It was the signal whistle of a Roman centurion giving orders for his cohort to regroup. I moved closer to the main road running down toward the palisade, gripping the dagger tightly while peering into the smoke. Then I saw it, a flash of red from the feathered helmet crest of a centurion. The sound of caligae boots on the crushed stone of the street was followed by a parting of the smoke as a centurion and several Roman soldiers entered into the open square. They stopped and moved to the sides and I saw a figure step out from the smoke. In his left hand, he held a sword. I couldn't see his face because his helmet covered his forehead and nose and he was holding his cloak over his mouth as a protection from the smoke, but I didn't need to see his face for I knew who it was. The cloak while smeared with smoke and blood and dirt was clearly the red cloak of a general. Caesar had come for me.

He stopped about twenty feet from me and dropped his cloak. With his right hand, he undid his chin strap and pulled off his helmet and handed it back without looking, expecting someone to be there to take it. A soldier stepped up and did. Caesar then strode forward while I ran to him. We met in the middle and he threw his arms around me and kissed my forehead. I wrapped my arms around him and held him tightly. I'm uncertain how long we stood like this, but finally, Caesar released his grip and taking a step back held me by my shoulders, surveying me from head to foot. 'You are hurt.'

'It's just a scratch,' I said through my tears. 'I'm alive. You came for me.'

I looked into his face. It was streaked with smoke and sweat and his hair was pressed to his forehead. This was the first time I had ever seen him acting as a real Roman commander on a battlefield, as it were. 'Why did you ever think I wouldn't come for you?' He seemed genuinely surprised by what I said

'You said you would never waste the time to recover whatever property the bandits could take.' I reached up to steady myself by placing a hand on his breastplate. He put his right hand over mine and leaned in so only I could hear. 'You are much more than property; you are like my son.'

He then turned to the men behind him and began to shout orders. 'We have what we came for! See what else is worth taking. I want captives! Try and stop the fire from spreading. Look for their stores of grain!' There was more of this but I couldn't hear it for long as I was surrounded by a group of soldiers led by the centurion I first saw. He handed me a canteen full of water, which I greedily gulped down until it was empty. I was then escorted out through the front gate. From there, in the shadow of the battering ram in its protective testudo that had been used to break down the gate, I was turned over to a contingent of cavalry and pulled up on one of the horses in front of its rider. Each time the horse's hooves struck the ground it jarred my head and caused me some pain, but I took this pain as a reminder I was alive. The fort was only a few miles from the village and very soon I was in a medical tent getting my wounds treated while I simultaneously tried to eat a stew that was thrust into my hands by another slave.

LIBER VII

It was a few hours later when the legion returned to the fort. First, the injured came in. There were less than twenty men with injuries and each was able to walk in under his own power. One of the injured soldiers was Balbus. He came limping into the medical tent with an arrowhead protruding from his left thigh. He was followed by several other legionary soldiers with various injuries. Because of his high rank, a medic rushed over to treat him first, but Balbus waved him off, saying, 'take care of the boys who are still bleeding first, mine's stopped and isn't getting any worse.' I was about to leave to make room for others when he waved me over. I sat next to him on the bench he had sat down on.

'You are a very lucky young man.' He looked at me strangely.

'I know. I could have died. The gods favored me today.' I smiled uncomfortably.

Balbus snorted. 'Gaius Julius Caesar favored you today. And, that's something.'

'I'm grateful my master came for me.'

'You know, we all advised him not to, but he wouldn't listen.' This made me even more uncomfortable. 'We told him it was a waste of time. We told him you were almost certainly already dead. We told him he could replace you soon enough, but no, he wouldn't listen.'

After an uncomfortable pause, I asked Balbus, 'tell me what happened. After I was hit, I mean.'

Balbus sat back against a tent pole and touched the part of the arrowhead sticking from his thigh and winced. 'We heard the alarm sound from the baggage train and knew instantly it was a raid. Caesar called your name and then kicked his horse into a gallop. Naturally, we followed him, as did the contingent of cavalry behind us. When we got to the baggage train the veterans who were guarding its flanks were already engaged with some of the bandits, but since the raiders were on horseback, our men were mostly acting defensively. One old guy did manage to pull one of the bastards from his horse and wounded him pretty badly. Our cavalry drove the rest of them off, killing one in the process, but at this point, you were already taken. The bandits disappeared into the woods. Caesar gave orders for us to fan out and find you, but they knew the terrain and we didn't, so after about an hour we were called back.'

'Did the wounded man die?' I asked.

Balbus laughed a little. 'He wasn't hurt that badly. That is until he refused to tell us where you'd been taken. The longer he held out the more banged up he became until he finally told us what we needed to know. It was after that he died from his wounds. As I said, you are a lucky young man.' With that, a medic came to remove the arrowhead and I excused myself and walked over to the forum. I lay on one of the benches near Caesar's tent to await the return of the legions. I saw the column of dust rising from the ground and heard the singing of the soldiers before I actually saw them. The village where I was held captive was on the level part of a rocky hill and there was a small valley between that hill and the rise of ground our fort was on, so it was easy to see the line of soldiers as they approached. The men were in good spirits. The returning legion followed the same order as the marching column, but instead of the baggage train, there were carts and wagons filled with the loot from the village. There wasn't much in the way of valuables as the village was poor, but there was some loot and they did have some grain stored away, no doubt captured from a farming community on the nearby plain.

That night I learned from a centurion that once Caesar made it clear he was determined to get me back it was the consensus of the Tribunes that a message would be delivered to the town demanding my release. Caesar vetoed this. He reasoned if the village leaders knew I was important to him they would never release me alive. Instead, he had a message delivered demanding they quit their village and resettle on the plain in the valley below and take up farming as a living. He knew full well they would refuse as they had been bandits for several generations and pride would keep them from agreeing to any suggestion coming from Rome, no matter how practical, Their refusal provided the pretext to take the village by force. His message to the village leaders made no mention whatsoever of me.

Before retiring for the evening, Caesar called me into the private area of his tent. You must understand, the general's tent is much more than the cramped sleeping quarters of the legionary soldiers or even the somewhat more spacious tent of a Tribune or quaestor. The general's tent serves as a command center. A large table in the center, covered in maps and documents, dominated Caesar's tent. A few feet from the large table was a smaller table with stools. This served as the work area for the secretarial staff and me. Another similar table was set up just outside the tent. I chose to work outdoors when the weather permitted, and to this day that is still my preference. There were several chairs in the tent as well as hanging oil lamps and two beds in the main area, one for two other slaves and one for me. The other slaves grumbled about sharing a cot, but I tried to not notice. Later I would welcome sharing a cot. By this time my sleeping quarters had been moved to Caesar's tent and I no longer had to spend the night with the horses. A smaller area was curtained off to form Caesar's private area. This space contained his bed, a chair, a small table, and his personal strongbox. Outside this area, to one side of the curtain's partition were two stands for armor; one stand held battle armor and the other parade armor. On the other side of the curtain's opening stood a rack for his toga, which was almost never worn at this time.

Caesar was sitting at the smaller table as I approached. In his hand was a document he had been reading. 'While reading this and others like it, I noticed a curious thing, Polybius.'

"What is it?' I was tired, and the stress of the day and my injuries caused me to crave sleep.

'It's an old document I had copied out many years ago from Sertorius' report on the fighting tactics of the hill people of Lusitania. I'm not sure how much of it is still relevant, but I thought it might be useful to review.' Caesar handed me the scroll. 'The writing looks familiar.'

I took the scroll near the hanging lamp and opened it. I only needed to scan a couple of lines before saying, "I wrote this.'

'So it would seem, but it has me puzzled since I don't know how that could be. I've had it for nearly ten years.'

I smiled and handed him the scroll. 'Many years ago, before leaving for your quaestorship you came into Titus' copying shop and had some work done. I was assigned to copy many of the documents. This, and no doubt several others are my work.'

Caesar looked hard at me as he searched his memory and then the light of recognition came on his face. 'I remember! Well, that clears up the mystery.'

Assuming that was all he needed I began to move toward the curtain.

'There is one more thing, Polybius.'

'Yes, master?' I said, turning toward him.

'Well, two more things then. First, you don't need to call me "master" unless we are in front of common soldiers or provincials.

When we are alone, or with the staff, I am Caesar.' For some reason I did not understand, I started to call him "master" more often, since my rescue.

I nodded waiting for him to tell me the other thing when he got up from his chair and walked over to his strongbox and opened the lid. I was surprised it wasn't locked. While we were in the fort he always kept it locked with one lock. When we were on the move or when the legion went out to battle he used three locks."

Polybius paused to adjust his cushion and eat another date, so Mela took the opportunity to ask, "Why three?"

"The reason is simple, my young friend. The key to the first lock Caesar kept on his person. The key to the second lock was held by Balbus, and the key to the third was in my possession, on a chain around my neck. That way, it would be much more difficult for anyone to either break into the strongbox while he was away or to steal his possessions should he be killed in battle.

At any rate, when he turned away from the strongbox, he held, gently across both palms, the dagger that had nearly caused my death. He held it like it was some sort of precious work of art. 'I don't know how this came to you, but you had it in your hand when I found you and I thought you might like to keep it.'

I took the dagger and examined it carefully. I had not looked at it so closely before. The blade was silver with a delicate design of interwoven lines and the handle appeared to be bone inlaid with gold and amber. I didn't remember dropping it, but I must have as

I didn't have it when I left the village. 'Slaves can't have weapons,' I said sadly, handing it back to him.

'I will keep it here in my box, but it is yours.'

'Thank you, Caesar,' was all I could think to say. I remember I had tears in my eyes as I turned to leave, but I stopped short of the curtain and turned back to him. 'Can I tell you what happened?'

Caesar nodded, so I told him the entire story. When I got to the part where the goddess struck down the priest and my life was spared, I noticed he smiled skeptically.

'It's true, I swear by the gods!' I wanted him to believe me.

'I'm sure it is,' he said, 'my father was struck dead in just the same way, and he was simply bending down to put on his shoes. Sometimes these things just happen.'

'That may be, but today I was very fortunate. Why can't the gods sometimes have a hand in such things?'

'I suppose you're right. How many great events turn on a stroke of fortune?' He dismissed me with, 'Sleep

LIBER VIII

The sacking of the village did not go unnoticed by the other Lusitanian towns in the hills around the area. Within a few days, we began to get word that other villages in the area were preparing for war."

I was curious about this. I'd often heard or read that commanders learn of the plans of their enemies, but I was never clear from whom they heard the news. "Who supplied this information? I'm sorry for interrupting, but I am curious."

Polybius dismissed my apology with a wave of his hand and took the opportunity to reach for a dried fig from the plate on the table. "An army on the march follows the same roads local travelers take. Every day the column encounters a merchant, or some itinerant craftsman or worker. While none of the towns in the area were large enough to support women who exclusively made a living as prostitutes, there were always enterprising girls and even matrons who took the opportunity to augment the family income by selling their favors to our soldiers. Information on the movements of the enemy was readily available, for a price of course, and I am certain intelligence of our plans was relayed back to the enemy by the same channels. The advantage a Roman legion has is its greater organization and discipline. In the rabble that passes for a barbarian army, every man with a spear and a shield fancies himself a general and needs to know all the details of the plan. Then, to demonstrate how important he is, he discusses the plan with every merchant or traveler he encounters. As a result, the plans of the barbarians are well known to many people. A Roman soldier though trusts his leaders and goes where they direct him without question, so it is easier to keep plans a secret or to even spread false information. However, sometimes the lack of organization of the barbarian proves to be his strength. Plans made one day and communicated to the Romans are often changed the next so the information is frequently unreliable.

At any rate, we knew they were making their preparations. Caesar didn't do anything out of the ordinary, deeming the abilities of a Roman legion could easily outmatch the barbarian forces. He did, however, order his commanders to be extra vigilant and to be prepared for ambushes. Ambushing an enemy's marching column was a favorite tactic of the indigenous peoples of Hispania, and indeed of barbarians the great world over. They realize they are no match for our soldiers in a pitched battle unless they have far superior numbers or the element of surprise on their side, so they will try to wear our numbers down by engaging in many small encounters or by trying to interrupt our supply lines. The tribes of Germania do this even today.

To avoid being ambushed, Caesar ordered his legion to take to less-traveled paths and by this tactic, he was able to sack two of their towns in four days. After that, the enemy's preparations were more serious and we were only able to take three more settlements in just less than a month. Four small villages were abandoned entirely, choosing to combine their fortunes and move their entire populations to neighboring towns to increase their fighting power. As food supplies diminished, the barbarians tried to entice the legion into an ambush by grazing their cattle nearby, but it was quickly discovered that enemy forces where hiding in the forest on the hill and this plot came to nothing. Realizing their towns would be sacked one by one and their women and children would become slaves of Rome, the barbarian leaders decided to risk all on a pitched battle. They were finally drawn out on a plain near the valley formed by the Munda (Mondego) River. I watched the battle from the palisade of the Roman fort on a hill overlooking the plain.

I thought the battle was something lifted from epic poetry. It opened with archers loosing their arrows, followed by the legions in perfect formation moving forward to clash with the rushing horde of barbarians. The cavalry swept in from each side and the barbarian army was doomed. What I didn't realize at the time was that I would see battles much greater than this in the years to come.

The enemy was crushed. Nearly seven thousand were killed and even more were taken captive, but a large number of forces escaped across the river into the rugged wooded area to the north. The cavalry pursued them, but the thick brush hindered the horses and most of the survivors were able to escape.

The legion returned to the fort in the same orderly way as it had left, and after visiting the wounded (there were only twenty-two), Caesar called the troops to the forum and made an impromptu speech from the platform, thanking the soldiers in the name of Rome, for their valor. The men cheered him wildly.

One cohort under the watchful eye of a Tribune was sent out to collect any loot from the battlefield but little of value was found. The legions then retired to their tents for a meal and much-needed rest. Caesar quickly washed and called a meeting of his staff to discuss his next move. It was decided to pursue the enemy, as Caesar saw this as an opportunity to conquer a people that had not yet come under the dominion of Rome. The following morning scouts were sent out to try and learn of the fate of those who escaped across the river and it was discovered they had joined up with a larger force of barbarians fleeing toward the protection of the Lusitani, living on the coast, with whom they had an alliance.

Because the enemy was more lightly armed and fleeing for their lives, they were able to reach the coast nearly three days before we did. We quickly learned from wounded stragglers left behind in an abandoned village that the enemy was moving northwest toward the Durius (Douro) River. While our destination was only some eighty miles away, it took seven days for the legion to arrive there, as they stormed and captured two villages that refused to capitulate and accepted the surrender of two others. This was all easy work but it took time.

When the legions arrived it was discovered the enemy with their protectors had fled to a small but heavily fortified island in the ocean, just north of the mouth of the river. The Gauls had used many boats for transport to the island and those that were left behind they burned, so there were no boats for many miles along the coast in either direction. Caesar set his men to the task of building boats, but the legion was clearly not equipped to build warships and it was the consensus of the staff that the boats that could be built were inadequate to the task. Nevertheless, boats were built."

At this point, we took a break to eat our midday meal. The men had returned from the dock with enough fish to feed us all, and Castor prepared the meal, cooking the fish over a small fire in the distance, while Pollux assembled a rough wooden table and benches from boards that he brought from one of the carts.

"Help me over to the table Lucius," Polybius said, pushing himself into a sitting position. "I thought we would dine like soldiers, as the army would provide the main topic of today's discussion." Both Mela and I supported Polybius, as he walked with a noticeable limp toward the table and our meal. While we ate fresh fish from the river, Polybius ate only cheese, nuts, and fruit. We spent a pleasant hour discussing literature with Polybius and his relatives. At one point a great-grandson named Alcaeus tried to turn the conversation toward current politics, but Polybius steered him away with, "I am much more comfortable in the distant past, so let us limit our conversation to those things, and to what you men have been reading lately."

After we ate, Polybius suggested we return to his villa and continue our conversation. Mela and I readily agreed and we finished the dates and wine as Castor, Pollux, and the great-grandsons disassembled and loaded the table and benches, the canopy, our small table, and finally, the couch and one of the chairs onto one cart, obliging us to stand. Castor and Pollux then carried Polybius, while still seated in the remaining chair over to the second cart. Once he was securely arranged in the cart, surrounded by cushions, the chair was loaded into the other cart. My brother and I were prepared to walk, but Polybius insisted we join him in his cart and off we went down the bumpy road. I'm certain Polybius would have been more comfortable were he carried in a sedan chair, but I believe he chose the setting and the mode of transportation to, in a small way, relive the experiences he described to us.

LIBER IX

Back at the villa, we arranged ourselves on the familiar upstairs balcony overlooking the vineyard. Polybius and I reclined while Mela sat on at the foot of Polybius' couch. Before Polybius could continue his story, Mela eagerly said, "Tell us about the great ocean!"

"The ocean is much like our sea. The water has the same salty taste and the waves crash continually against the rocks or rush up to beaches. At least in the north, the water is colder. When I've encountered the ocean further south, there is little difference except for the important facts that the limits of our sea are well known, whereas the ocean is vast beyond measure. There are some who claim there are lands beyond the horizon, but of that, I don't know. Since the ancients clearly demonstrated our world is a sphere, I suspect if one were to go far enough one would reach those kingdoms beyond the Indus River. No Roman, of course, would ever try, since as a people we tend to loathe sea and ocean travel and only do it when necessary."

At this, Mela interrupted. "My grammaticus has told me the world is a sphere, but I don't see how anyone can ever know that."

Polybius looked surprised. "My dear boy, this has been known since more than five hundred years ago. Aristotle gave many reasons why this must be so, and Eratosthese was even able to determine its circumference by measuring shadows at different places on the same date and time. Now, if you would like a more detailed explanation, we can delve into that at another time. For now, allow me to continue." Mela's face turned red and he nodded.

"Where we found ourselves facing the enemy on their island the beach was level and composed of sand. Further up it turned to rocks and finally rose up to low cliffs. It was on the higher ground that our marching fort was built. The island the barbarians occupied also appeared to have a smooth sandy beach. This was a tactical error on their part, but I suppose their choice of refuge was dictated by haste rather than careful consideration. An island with cliffs for sides could be held indefinitely if it was large enough to provide food and water. Smooth beaches allow a foe to land ships, and that is just what Caesar planned to do. Caesar also ordered the construction of a smaller beach fort to house the workers who were building the boats. I noticed the main fort was much larger than necessary and asked him about this. 'I have sent for the second legion. I want to gain control of the lands to the north and as you know, I don't like to do things halfway.'

I was surprised I hadn't had a hand in composing the order calling up the legion, but military orders were often issued without my knowledge. While he set the men to the task of building boats, he did have me put pen to parchment and write his orders for the outfitting and construction, if needed, of a fleet of warships. I also composed, in his hand, a series of orders to the cities and towns along the route to open their gates and welcome the delegation from the propraetor. As you will perhaps recall, when I worked slave to a copy shop owner as a boy I became quite skilled at mimicking anyone's writing style.

He then had the Tribunes select a group of soldiers who were close to retirement from the legion to act as an escort and sent Balbus and me to Gades (Cadiz) to deliver the orders. Balbus was chosen not only because his leg wound was taking longer to heal than he expected and he was not fit to be on his feet for too many hours a day, but because he was the legions chief engineer and a native of Gades. I was chosen, I believe, because Caesar saw that the military life was wearing on me and I needed a break from the constant marching from fort to fort.

At that point, Pollux the slave came into the room and, without saying a word to Mela or me, leaned over and whispered something in Polybius' ear.

Polybius, with assistance from Pollux, struggled to a sitting position. Looking at me he said, 'A matter that needs my attention has come up, so you will need to excuse me for the rest of today." I will send a message as to when we can resume my tale. With that, Pollux escorted us to the door.

As Mela and I were stepping out the door, Polybius called out to us. With Pollux' help he shuffled up to me. He looked into my eyes long enough to make me feel a bit uncomfortable, before reaching into the belt around his tunic and bringing out a small scroll of papyrus. "I want you to carry this with you on your way home today." His tone was most serious.

"What is it?" I asked.

Before answering, he waved Mela over. "It is a bill for my services. Should anyone ask, you are to tell him that your father has hired me to tutor you two young men in the art of rhetoric. This bill for my services will support what you tell him."

I had a suspicion as to what the reason was, but I asked, just to confirm it and to clear up the confusion my brother was having. His answer was quick. "Tiberius Caesar is a suspicious man, and he has, it would seem, turned his suspicions toward me. Because of my past connections with Gaius Julius Caesar and his successor of the same name who you know of as Augustus Caesar, he worries about my feelings toward him. I don't want him to begin to suspect you young men of anything, so you are learning rhetoric from me. Do you understand?"

We both nodded and, after saying our goodbyes we left him with Pollux.

LIBER X

Three days later, we received a message inviting us back for our next "rhetoric lesson." We were able to meet with him that very afternoon. Upon arrival we found Polybius sitting in a chair beside the fountain in his atrium. There were two chairs and a couch beside him.

After we exchanged greetings, we settled down and Polybius resumed his narrative.

'I have my notes from the other day, so I can resume right where we left off. We left off with Balbus and me moving on to take ship to Gades carrying orders from Caesar. We took the road, which was initially a wide dirt path down to the port city of Olissipo (Lisbon), stopping first at Talabriga (Aveiro), moving on to Aeminium (Coimbra), where the path became a proper road. We then reached Sellium (Tomar), and finally, Scalabis (Santarém), before reaching Olissipo. At Olissipo I was able to have a proper bath since there was nothing to make the locals believe I was a slave. I was grateful to Balbus for tacitly ignoring my status. At Olissipo we were able to board a merchant vessel destined for Gades. We were fortunate in that we arrived the evening before it was set to sail and the letter from the propraetor and a few coins gained us passage.

Since we were representing Caesar we were given a small cabin and spared the unpleasantness of sleeping on the deck. It was also quite useful that the ship's owner was on board and had been a friend of Balbus' father. Balbus had hoped one of his own family's ships would have been in port, so we could have had better accommodations, but this wasn't the case. We sailed with only one soldier as a guard, since space on the ship was very limited, and he dismissed the rest of our guard, sending them back to Caesar.

This was my first taste of traveling by ship and I took to it at once. I suppose it is in my blood since my mother was from the island of Lesbos and her ancestors were a seafaring race. Balbus was also quite comfortable on a ship since he grew up in the sea trade, and we both relaxed during our journey that lasted two days and a few hours. We arrived in the port of Gades, about the middle of the third day at sea. I found the ocean air refreshing and relaxing, and the reputed monsters that Balbus and Vatinus the legionary soldier assured me were swimming right beneath our vessel didn't at all frighten me.

Immediately after establishing ourselves in the Balbus family domus on the harbor side of the city, we presented ourselves to the local magistrate who knew Balbus well. This man was a Roman equite and had a degree of sophistication, so he immediately inferred that I was Balbus' slave and treated me accordingly. My telling him rather sternly that I was nomenclator and chief secretary to the propraetor, Gaius Julius Caesar did nothing to change his attitude and he dealt exclusively with Balbus. This suited me well and I suggested I could make better use of my time by making the necessary arrangements to have several letters and the military dispatches from Caesar forwarded to Corduba, where they would then be sent on to Rome. This was easily done since Gades was a prosperous Roman settlement and Balbus had furnished me with the names of several contacts who would likely be traveling to Corduba. When I asked him for money to pay the courier, he eyed me suspiciously, thinking I was perhaps planning to run away, but he relented and gave me a few coins. I must admit escape did enter my thoughts, but since my rescue from the barbarian village, my loyalty to Caesar had solidified. I began to realize that as long as I was a slave, I would never find a better master, so I did as I said I would and found the courier who was one of Balbus' clients and made the arrangements quite quickly. This gave me the opportunity to explore the city.

I must tell you something about this city. Gades is very ancient and existed well before it fell under the rule of Carthage. The Phoenician name for the city was Gadir, meaning 'walled stronghold' and that is what it is. The city itself exists on a finger of land that extends out into the ocean, with one side facing the horizon and the other facing the harbor. It is said to be some four centuries older than Rome and, like so many others, to have been founded by Hercules after he slew the monster Geryon. Of course, half the cities in Hispania are said to have been founded by Hercules. It is difficult to imagine he would have had time for his twelve labors with all the city building he was doing." At that, Polybius laughed, causing him to cough and he needed to take a moment and compose himself before going on. "The city came under Roman authority almost a century and a half prior to my visit, when Scipio Africanus seized it from the Carthaginians, and by the time of Caesar's propraetorship, it had become a thriving trade port and a fledgling naval base. Of course, our arrival would be the impetus that would increase the military presence significantly. The city had spread outside its original walls and the Balbus family domus was near enough to the Northwestern gate to allow easy access to the sea and the fisheries just outside the wall. I noticed a steady stream of people moving in and out of the gate so I went to investigate. When I passed out through the gate I was captivated by what I saw. To the north and to the south were fishing huts, but right before me was a stretch of sand and Ocean waves, and people were playing in the water! I returned to this place several times in the ten days we were in the city. Balbus was busy overseeing the final fitting of three quadriremes and the repairs needed by several triremes, so I enjoyed the feeling of freedom, being able to play in the ocean with the free people of the city.

Each day Balbus and I would visit the boat sheds and I would take down his dictations and later convert them into formal written documents. These were usually orders to make the fitting of the ships go more quickly. I noticed that he had the workers make some repairs, at public expense, on two ships of his own family's merchant fleet, but that is the way of the world. When not supervising the workers at the shipyard, Balbus was recruiting the crews to man the ships. Caesar had evidently been planning to use a fleet for some time, as rowers had already been recruited and had been training for many days. I was set the task of purchasing supplies for the trip and arranging the delivery of food and water for the fleet. Water was particularly difficult because, in addition to the support staff and officers, more than 2500 rowers manned the fleet, and each rower needed to drink fifteen to twenty sextarii of water (two to three gallons) each day. Of course, we would only need to bring aboard one day's worth of water, as the fleet would spend each night onshore meaning each ship needs to carry a minimum of fifty amphorae.

It is well known to sailors that our sea and the ocean have certain areas that flow like rivers in a particular direction. This sometimes changes depending on the time of the year, shifting direction with the seasons, often following the prevailing winds. Unfortunately for our rowers, the flow of water along the coast of Lusitania wanted us to travel in the direction opposite our destination and the winds agreed. Sails proved useless and the rowers had to work each day against the current. It was marvelous to watch them work maintaining a constant rhythm to prevent fouling the oars against each other, but in spite of their best efforts, it took just over eight days to reach our destination.

We left in the early morning of our tenth day in Gades, with Balbus and me on the Shark, the quadrireme that was the flagship of the fleet. The smaller, faster, Liburnian galleys went ahead of the fleet to scout for any trouble and to look for suitable landing sites. Each night we would beach the ships and the crew would set up a fort on the beach. Since we were, at least for most of the journey, traveling along a settled and civilized coast, there was no need to dig a ditch around the fort and there were a minimal number of tents, as most of the men slept on the ships. Seven nights were spent quite close to cities and we were able to purchase supplies. The last night was spent on a beach near the mouth of the Munda (Mondego) River and the wildness of the area and the uncertainty as to the loyalty of the locals led to the construction of a small but proper fort with a ditch and palisade. A beach fort, however, has only three sides, with the Ocean serving as the defense for the rear of the fort. Between our stop at Olisipo (Lisbon) and the Munda River fort, we spent the night on a delightful island several miles off the coast. The island had long stretches of golden beaches and a cliff covered in wildflowers.

LIBER XI

We arrived just before midday eight days after our departure. A larger beach fort had already been prepared so we immediately beached the ships and after the crew was fed they began to prepare the fleet for battle. All the fittings were checked and rechecked for soundness and the masts and sails were removed and stored in the small fort. Within the first hour of our arrival, Caesar joined us with a contingent of carefully selected soldiers to act as the rowers and marines for each ship. When they arrived their shields were lined along the sides of the ship.

I ran to meet Caesar as soon as he ended his conference with Balbus. He threw his arm over my shoulder and escorted me to the tent that served as the praetorium at the beach fort. While Caesar still divided his time between the beach and the fort further up the hill, he had the larger tent brought down to the beach; the beach fort now acted as his main headquarters.

'I trust you had a pleasant trip?' Saying it as a question indicated he wasn't sure how I would respond.

"I've learned I love to sail!' My answer was enthusiastic and quite true.

'Did you make any money in Gades?' I was surprised by the question.

'I made some, yes.' I actually made quite a bit. Supplying a

Roman fleet is a major undertaking, so there had been several wealthy traders competing for the opportunity to provide what we needed. Naturally, every proposal came with a 'gift.'

Caesar poured us both water from a pitcher on the table; he rarely drank wine while on campaign as he felt even a little can cloud a man's judgment and he wanted to keep his mind clear. 'Put it in my strongbox, and with it leave an accurate tally of that which is yours. Should anything happen to me tomorrow, I want to be sure you receive your money.'

This surprised me, as Caesar never showed anything but the highest confidence going into battle. I was in excellent spirits and risked overstepping my boundary a little and playfully asked him, 'are you afraid to sail?'

'Let's just say, I respect the titan Oceanus very much.'

'I'm sure nothing will happen. The island is just an easy swim away. You can probably walk half the distance. You can swim, can't you?' I could see he was apprehensive.

'I've had one of the sailors teach me while you were gone.' He abruptly changed the subject. 'Now, let's get to work. I need to dictate to you what we've been up to while you were busy in Gades.' Caesar had begun the practice of setting aside some time each day to compose a record of his actions. The plan was to put it into a proper narrative when we returned to Corduba and have it forwarded on to Rome to be read in the Senate and from the rostrum, it was then to be copied, read, and posted around the city.

Caesar was always very focused on the task before him, but he never lost sight of his political goals, and he aimed to be Consul the following year. Therefore, he felt it was essential the voters and his supporters in the Senate remain aware of his accomplishments.

I learned that using small boats, and rafts for the siege engines, Caesar attempted two landings on the island. Both attempts failed, because the walls of the enemy fortifications were too close to the shoreline, making it easy for them to repulse any landing attempt with arrows and slings. After the second attempt failed, the boats were kept at a distance each day and sentries were posted all along the beaches each night, to prevent anyone's leaving the island to resupply the fortification. As it was, the enemy had laid in a large amount of grain and there was a cistern on the island that was filled with rainwater. The island had been used as a place of refuge for the local tribe's women and children during a time of war for as long as anyone could remember, so they were amply prepared to hold out for longer than Caesar wanted to wait.

Also, while we were in Gades, the extra legions arrived. Caesar had sent for them while I was in captivity and I was not aware they were even coming to join us. It was apparent that once Caesar decided to act he was not going to be timid. He now had, counting the rowers for the fleet and the auxiliaries, more than twenty thousand men under his command. He kept the legions busy by leading them against the towns in the hills to the east and northeast. It was his plan to subdue the whole of Lusitania and

Callaicia and double the size of the province. A few of the towns offered some resistance and provided opportunities for looting, but most saw the futility of opposing the legions and opened their gates, agreeing to pay a tribute to Rome and avoiding the prospect of slavery or death.

The fort had gone to sleep, save those on watch duty. I had a strange dream that night. I dreamt that I was asleep and dreaming, which indeed I was, but in this dream, an unseen hand shook me awake. It felt so real it woke me both in the dream and from the dream. I could see a lamp burning in Caesar's portion of the tent so I lay still and listened for voices, but there were none. At first, I supposed Caesar might be entertaining one of the local women as he sometimes did, but this was not the case and strangely, I was relieved. I quietly rose from my bed so as not to wake the others and went to the far side of the tent, drawing back the flap to Caesar's private space. Seeing it empty I put on my shoes and went to look out through the tent's entrance. I didn't know why it was important to me to find him, but I felt Caesar might need something from me.

When I stepped out into the night air I felt a cool breeze hit me. It caused me to shiver. Turning to the soldier standing guard at the tent, I asked, 'Do you know where Caesar is?' The man pointed straight down the Via Praetoria without speaking. By the light of the moon, I could make out a lone figure on the beach just south of where the ships had been run up on the sand.

87

Even in the summer the north of Hispania Ulterior is somewhat cooler than Rome and on this night, it was cool enough for me to go back for my cloak, which I hadn't worn in many days and nights. After wrapping the cloak around me and putting on my shoes, I walked down toward the beach. As I got closer to the seaward side of the fort the earth under my feet turned first to small stones and then to sand. The sound of the ocean waves drowned out all the other sounds. Even before I was near enough to call out to Caesar, a soldier who, I surmised had been acting as a guard came toward me. 'Who approaches?' he asked, moving to block my way.

Before I could speak, Caesar turned around and, recognizing me in the moonlight said to the guard, 'let him through.' As soon as I was close enough to him to speak, I realized I had nothing to say. Caesar seemed to sense this so he began to walk and I walked with him. He led the way to the place where the sea met the land and we walked along on the damp sand.

'Are you worried about the coming battle?' I had finally found something to say.

'No,' he answered as if the battle was not important. 'We have made our plan and it's a good one.' Caesar stopped walking and looked out to the Ocean. 'I was thinking about Imperium.'

In those days, Imperium was the goal of every ambitious senator. Cicero was driven to achieve it to prove to the world that he could rise to the top in spite of his humble beginnings and he worked his entire life to become Consul until he achieved that goal. Pompeius was driven to earn military Imperium. He had little taste for politics and knew that military glory would bring him eternal fame and add luster to his dignitas. Pompeius also knew that military fame would earn him the Consulship in due course, but he realized he had little talent for governing. Caesar was, like many patricians, driven to have Imperium in both the civil and military realms. He was, however, different than any other man of his generation. Since he realized the republic was nothing more than a shadow of what it once was, he began to consider the idea that it was possible to not only gain the Imperium granted a man by the voters as Consul, or by the Senate, as Proconsul, but he could achieve a sort of permanent Imperium. This was the lesson he learned from the dark days of Sulla's dictatorship.

Just to the south of where we stood there was a boat overturned on the beach. In front of it, a small fire was dying. 'I had the boys build a fire for me,' he said. 'Let's go sit.' He led the way to the fire and we sat before it on the bottom of the boat. 'I will become Consul,' he said, adding driftwood from a small pile to bring the flame back to life. 'And, after that, I will be Proconsul of a province where I can earn a triumph or two.'

The intimacy of the moment made me bold enough to ask, 'what will you do with your Imperium?'

'You read my thoughts, Polybius. What good is Imperium if it is not put to use. It's like parade armor, fine to look at, but too good to wear into an actual battle.' I expected him to tell me what uses he could make of Imperium, when Caesar surprised me by saying, 'Tell me, Polybius, about the time you ran away from your first master.'

I slid down off the boat so I was sitting on the cool sand with my back to the boat. I didn't want him to see my face when I talked about sad memories. I told him of my unhappiness in the Titus house. I told him how my only friend was sent away and how my mother was sold. I told him of the cruelty of Titus' bride. He let me speak, but I sensed what I was saying was not what he wanted to hear, so I paused a moment to let him speak.

'I'm sorry to ask you to bring up painful memories,' he said, but he wasn't going to let me off with just that. 'Tell me about how you lived after you escaped. As I understand it you spent an entire summer in Rome, without a master's home to live in.'

I took a breath and told him everything. I told him of the good times and the bad. I let him know how I cherished those days because I was free and how I cherished the memory of my friendship with Gaius, but then I began to realize I had blocked out the bad memories so I shared those with him as well. I told him of Gaius' prostituting himself and I told him of how we often stole the food we needed to survive or scavenged through garbage. I told him of the people I knew and knew of who had to live as I had, as an animal lives. I told him everything I could remember about my days before he came to possess me. I told him of my time with abusive masters and my time as a runaway slave.

When I was finished I wiped my tears away with the back of my hand, hoping Caesar didn't notice I had been crying. He put his hand on my shoulder and said quietly, 'Thank you, Polybius.'

'Imperium can be like the parade armor or the death mask of an illustrious ancestor, but it should also be used to make things better for people. Roman citizens shouldn't live like animals.' Caesar sounded a little sad when he said this.

I too was sad. I had read enough of the history of Rome to realize the limits of Imperium. 'Those who have tried to make good use of their Imperium have most often failed. Look at the Gracchi. The problems are bigger than anything one man can do to solve them, and the senators don't care about the people I met that summer. If you try to solve those problems, your efforts will be blocked or you will be killed.'

'It's time to get some sleep,' Caesar said, rising to his feet. We walked back to the fort in silence. After polite goodnights, I went to my bed and Caesar went to his private area. Just as I was falling asleep, I heard Caesar push back the flap that separated his area from the rest of the tent. I opened my eyes to see his silhouette standing just inside the main room. He said, quietly but firmly, 'I don't accept that the problems are more than one man can handle.' With that he turned and retreating into his private space, let the flap drop behind him.

LIBER XII

The fort awoke well before sunrise the following morning. By torchlight, Caesar addressed the troops. He rarely composed speeches for such times, choosing to speak from his heart. He didn't display any of his own trepidation at the necessity of boarding a ship, as he wanted the men to feel confident on what would be for many of them a new adventure. The plan as he laid it out was simple. The fleet would split into three parts. He would be on the flagship to the Oceanside of the island with several ships while the other two parts of the fleet would move to the north and the south of the island. The ships were to move out under cover of darkness, using the fires on the island's hilltop to orient them. At the first sign of sunrise, the smaller ships and rafts would move out once again, pretending to engage in another landing attempt on the beach closest to the mainland. It was hoped this would draw the archers and slingers to that side so the rest of the fleet could move in without being seen and use the onboard catapults to overawe the enemy.

The plan worked perfectly. While the fort's defenders were all facing the east with the sun in their eyes. The opening salvos began. On the flagship, Caesar ordered the catapult to launch a large bale of hay that had been soaked in pitch and lit on fire over the west palisade. This was the signal for ships to the north and to the south to do the same. The catapults then began to shoot large stones into the walls and at times the nearer ships were able to launch them over the walls. The continuing barrage created panic within the fortification, causing many of the defenders to leave their posts on the east wall. This was enough to allow the small ships to land and lay logs in the sand to provide a platform on which to drag the raft with the battering ram up to the wall. The ram never needed to touch the wall though, as the defenders opened the gates. Some of our men rushed forward to enter the fort, but a Tribune and a centurion were able to check their advance.

It has been the long-standing policy of Rome that if a city or fort opens its gate before the ram first touches the wall, their lives and property will be spared. Technically this wasn't the case since the catapult missiles had struck the walls many times, and volleys had even struck within the walls, but Caesar wanted these tribes to become productive allies of Rome and not avowed enemies, so he practiced clemency whenever possible and in this case, he spared their lives. Of course, since this wasn't a proper settlement and was considered an enemy fortress, while those inside the walls were not killed, they were sent back to Corduba and then on to Rome to be sold as slaves. There were thousands of men, women, and children captured. I had a splendid view of the entire operation from a perch on the palisade of the main Roman camp. The entire engagement was over in less than two hours by my reckoning from observing how far the sun had risen in the sky.

The most populous and best-fortified city in the area was Brigantium (A Coruna). Today this is a prosperous Roman port, but in those days it was the capital of a tribe of the Callaeci called the Arrotrebae. Caesar immediately understood the importance of the site. This walled city sits on a port at the far north of the peninsula. From this strategic position, it can trade with the communities that dot the coast to its south and with those along the north coast, to its east. The area was also reputed to be a vast source of gold and other metals. Caesar was determined to take this city. We left the fort the following day and marched north along the coast with the fleet shadowing us just offshore far enough to avoid the dangers of the rocky coast. Word must have reached the Arrotrebae of our approach as the area for fifty or more miles south of the city was nearly deserted. The people had either retreated into the foothills or took refuge behind the walls of Brigantium. It took four days to reach the plain to the southwest of the city and from our fort on a rise of ground two miles distant, I was surprised to see that Brigantium truly was a city. Of course, it didn't compare to an Italian city, or even Gades, for that matter, but it had stone walls with towers on either side of the gate, rather than the wooden palisade of most of the settlements in Hispania Ulterior.

Caesar sent a messenger to the headmen of the place demanding they open their gates and submit to him. Trusting in the strength of their fortifications they naturally refused. Word was then sent to the beach fort some twenty miles to the northwest where the fleet was waiting, for the ships to launch at once and approach the city from the harbor side."

Mela, at this point, grew very interested. "It must have been a great battle from both sides, with the ships sending rocks and fire over the wall from the sea and siege engines battering the gate!" Mela loved to hear about famous battles. He instilled the same love of the arts of war in his son Lucanus who is in the process of completing an epic poem about the civil war between Caesar and Pompeius Magnus. Unfortunately for him, Polybius disappointed him this time.

"No my boy," Polybius said, without opening his eyes. "There was no great siege of Brigantium. You see, the city was well fortified on the landside, but the harbor side was only protected by a low wooden wall. Since the Arrotrebae, and indeed none of the natives living along the coast of Hispania, had perfected the art of naval warfare, a wooden wall was deemed sufficient to protect the city from an attack by sea. The largest warships these people had ever seen were smaller than our liburnian. The mere sight of our fleet of warships rowing into their harbor caused them to capitulate and open their gates. Our ships did engage and sink three of their small warships that had been caught protecting the harbor before they were even aware the enemy had surrendered. Caesar demanded a large tribute from the city not to enrich himself, as he had already made enough to pay off his debts, but instead to cripple the city's ability to make war. Later he was to send the city elders the order to tear down their wall and replace it with a more modest structure. From that point forward they were to rely on the protection of the Roman legions in the province. Inside the city were warrior leaders from several of the region's tribes and they also submitted to Rome.

That evening in the fort, Caesar addressed the troops from the platform. I have no idea what he said in his speech, as I was busy making copies of the list of villages and tribes who had submitted to Rome as part of Caesar's dispatch home. I sat in the praetorium tent, and as the evening was warm I placed my table and stool near the tent flap where had I chosen to, I could have heard everything Caesar said. As it was, I chose not to listen. I had heard many such speeches and I assumed this one would be much like all the others. I must have been right, as no one thought it notable to copy down even the most memorable line to later quote. What I couldn't avoid hearing was the laughter of the soldiers gathered in the forum in front of the platform. It was then, and still is, the practice of the legions to gather in the open space before the praetorium to be addressed by the legate both before and after an important event. After a great success, Caesar always played to the high spirits of the men by being most affable and telling jokes, often at his own expense. He gave the men license to banter back and forth with him, so the laughter was not unusual. On this particular occasion though, at some point, one of the men shouted out his commander's name, and others took up the shouting. Quite suddenly, thousands of men were chanting Caesar, Caesar, Caesar! It took some time to quiet them so Caesar could continue with what he had to say. He wasn't allowed to continue for very long though when a word was shouted from somewhere in the group of men that made me stop writing and look up. One of the men had shouted 'Imperator.' This was followed by a brief moment of quiet when several more voices also shouted the title. Soon the entire fort was chanting 'Imperator!' I slid off my stool and stood in the entrance to the tent watching this display, with the men chanting in time to the clapping of hands and the stamping of feet. This time Caesar did nothing to quiet the group and the chanting continued until the men were hoarse and their voices were exhausted.

This was exactly what Caesar wanted but seldom is a commander hailed as Imperator by such a spontaneous acclamation. More often than not it is initiated by the quaestors and Tribunes and seconded by the centurions only to be voted on by the men. There was no need for a vote on this night, as there was no one in the fort who had not made his will know. Later that night during a meeting with the quaestors, Tribunes, legates, and centurions, Caesar would dictate a dispatch that I would copy out onto a parchment scroll:

To the Senate and People of Rome: On this day of the nones or Aprilis in the Consulship of Q. Manlius Ancharius Tarquitius

Saturninus and P. Petronius Niger, the legions under his command have by spontaneous and unanimous acclamation hailed Gaius Julius Caesar as Imperator for leading them to victory over the enemies of Rome.

This brief message was signed and sealed by each of the men present; Caesar would have his triumph. He was elated. Late that night, after the praetorian tent emptied out and the other slaves were asleep it was just Caesar and me. While I was happy for Caesar, I too wanted to sleep, but Caesar was too excited to retire to bed and wished to talk so I sat near him and listened, struggling to keep my eyelids from drooping and stifling my frequent yawns.

About an hour into his monologue, Caesar slapped the table and said for the fourth or fifth time, 'I have my first triumph, Polybius!'

I looked over to see if this woke the others. I wanted someone to share in my suffering, but they both continued to snore. I was a little irritated that Caesar didn't see how exhausted I was, so I answered with, 'the Senate still needs to approve it, and you have many enemies.'

At that Caesar laughed. 'They will approve it! Why are you so glum? There will be plenty of men who want to piss on my triumph. You don't need to be the first.'

'I'm sorry master.' I truly regretted what I said. 'It's just that I'm exhausted. I don't have your vigor.'

'Then I'm the one who should be sorry. Find me parchment and a pen and you can go to sleep. I need to send a letter to Pompeius Magnus.'

Against my strongest desire, I said, 'I can stay and you can dictate it.'

Caesar simply waved me away with, 'get to bed, I can find the parchment and writing supplies.'

I gave a sincere 'thank you,' as I got up and went to my sleeping pallet.

LIBER XIII

The next several days were spent in constant work, settling the region. A propraetor has only one year to complete his work, and Caesar had learned from studying the mistakes of the past that it is vital he establish a firm settlement of the province so jealous rivals in the Senate cannot undo it. While he has absolute authority during his propraetorship, his Imperium is dissolved when he returns to Rome and lays down his office, and the Senate must confirm his acts. The first thing to be done was to divide up the tribute and the treasure that had been looted from the towns foolish enough to resist. Caesar kept just enough to break even and perhaps a little more. He then provided a substantial benefit for the treasury at Rome and divided the remainder amongst the legions. Levels of annual tribute were immediately established in treaties between the subjected peoples and Rome. He next worked to take control of the gold and iron mines of the region, using some of the slaves that had formerly belonged to the barbarians to continue working the mines. I felt sorry for those men, as all they received from the defeat of the barbarians was a change of masters.

When the most immediate military necessities were settled, and things were secure in the north, one legion was left behind to establish a permanent fort while the two others returned to Corduba. Caesar was eager to get on with administrative matters in Corduba, so in spite of his reluctance to board a ship, it was determined we would sail back to Gades with the fleet and take the road the rest of the way. On the return trip, the current and the winds were with us and we were able to make the trip to Gades in less than six days. Caesar was as much relieved to see the harbor of the city come into view, as I was disappointed. I had struck up a friendship with a deckhand of the same age as me, named Decius and had hoped the relationship would turn sexual, but I was disappointed. Still, I enjoyed his company and was sad to leave him behind. We spent only one night in Gades, leaving just after sunrise on the following morning, arriving at the gates of Corduba two days later. Once we arrived to the city there was no time to rest. Caesar worked harder than anyone I have yet to meet, save perhaps Livia, wife of the god Augustus and mother to our current Caesar. Once we had left our horses with the grooms at the propraetorian villa, I was instructed to quickly wash the dirt from the road off my body and gather my writing supplies. We left immediately for the baths, where Caesar had arranged to meet Balbus, Marius, Servius, and a couple of others. I took notes while the men bathed and discussed the most pressing needs of the province and established an agenda for meeting those needs.

As a result of that meeting, almost immediately, a new colony was established in one of the most fertile valleys north of the Tagus as a settlement for the veteran soldiers who had served their time in the legions. Of course, soldiers were not allowed to marry, but since some of these veterans were stationed at Corduba for many years, they had met local women and had families, and they were married in all but name. It was common practice for centurions to grant a rotating leave to many of the soldiers so they could spend at least a night or two each month with their families.

Another very pressing matter was the need to provide grain for the conquered people in Lusitania and the lands to the north of there. The war was devastating to the harvest in those areas and there would be widespread famine if nothing was done to provide for the people. Caesar's goal was to incorporate the cities into the province and he wanted to be certain that after the barbarians submitted to Rome they were given a clear understanding of the benefits of joining our expanding empire. Therefore, a plan was put into place to redistribute grain from the south and to import grain from Sicily. Fortunately, there were good harvests throughout the world that year and this was accomplished quite easily.

In addition to this, Caesar heard cases involving disputes between the various allied communities and even prominent individuals. This practice was very different from a hearing in a law court. In the provinces, both sides present their cases, but rather than a jury and judge, the cases are heard only by the propraetor and his closest advisors. This provides for much swifter justice, but the loser usually questions the fairness of the process. It is also the accepted practice for representatives from each side of a dispute to present a 'gift' to the propraetor. Caesar showed no reluctance to accept these blatant bribes but informed all the parties involved that the money would do nothing to influence his decision. Naturally, no one believed him and the bribes continued, but Caesar was being quite honest and judged each case on its merit. It quickly became apparent that many of the disputes revolved around individual and public debts. Like everywhere else in the empire, those in Hispania who wished to advance in society were forced to spend beyond their means. Ironically, Caesar found himself in a position where he had to force men to pay their creditors while he had spent most of his adulthood avoiding paying his own debts. His settlement was simple and favored the creditors. Debtors were ordered to pay two-thirds of their income each year toward their debts. Of course, this angered those who owed money but allowed Caesar to become quite popular with the men of wealth and influence in the province, which was much better for him politically.

This all took a great deal of time and left us quite busy, but Caesar found time for female companionship in the person of a woman named Aquila who was the wife of one of the city magistrates of Corduba. I, on the other hand, was quite frustrated. I found no one, either male or female, to alleviate my sexual urges. My position as chief secretary and nomenclator to the propraetor scared many potential partners away. As a distraction, I worked as much as I could. When I wasn't involved in the business of the province, which was in itself very substantial, or the correspondence with Rome, or the personal business with Caesar, I would work on adding names and faces to my 'memory house.' For the people from Hispania, I placed them in a replica of the praetorian villa, created in my mind. Caesar's propraetorship put many men, mostly equites, in debt to him and they were added to his clientele. I, of course, had to commit their personal details to memory and every day there were new men to put in the villa in my mind. Of course, all these contacts continued to fill my purse.

A propraetor's term is supposed to end on the first day of Maius but, once again, the appointment of new governors was delayed. Since it took nearly a month for orders from Rome to reach a province as distant as Hispania Ulterior, we waited for the arrival of the new propraetor completely unaware that Caesar would be asked to remain in his province nearly one month longer. When the notice did arrive from Rome, the reason given was that there were inauspicious omens each time the Senate was scheduled to vote on the new appointments. This was, of course, a complete fabrication. Signs from the heavens were being used more and more to obstruct politics in the capitol. The real reason was that Cato and the rest of the Optimate faction didn't want Caesar to return too soon. The longer he could be delayed in the province, the less time he had to canvass for votes in the upcoming Consular elections.

I was always surprised by how quickly Caesar was able to

assemble separate facts and bits of information into a coherent story. From the various letters, reports, and travelers' tales his inner circle and household staff had gathered, he knew he was being squeezed out of the election. Each evening the staff slaves and freedmen were required to report to me any gossip they had heard during the day. I would then sort it out to avoid duplication and leave the report in a box on the table in the tablinum. In the evening, when Caesar had his usual meeting with his prefects, Tribunes, and quaestors, he would scan the report and discuss what was being said. At first, I assumed this was sparked by vanity and a desire to be loved by the people, but I soon realized Caesar showed no reaction to either bad or good crumbs of information about him. In reality, he was using the information and any correspondence from Rome to have a full understanding of where he fit into the political situation in the capitol.

Finally, good omens were reported and we were allowed to return to Rome. Everything was set for our departure on the calends of Maius (May 1). Caesar had determined we would take the overland route to Narbo where we would board a merchant vessel of the Balbus family fleet. I suggested we save time and sail the entire journey, but Caesar truly disliked sea travel and certainly didn't want to travel outside the Pillars of Hercules if there was no military necessity to do so.

The evening before we were to leave, a messenger approached Caesar in the forum of Corduba and announced he had an important dispatch from the Senate in Rome. Caesar had, of course, already been warned that the Optimate faction in the Senate was taking measures to delay the awarding of provinces, but this message would have been the first confirmation that they had succeeded. I say it would have been because Caesar refused to accept the scroll in public. Instead, he walked the man over to a taverna on a nearby corner. The five lictors, seven slaves, myself included, and the eight or ten other men that now almost always accompanied him in public followed Caesar. The lictors scrambled to move to the front of the group, but not knowing where to go simply followed the road. Once we reached the taverna, the lictors and slaves were stopped at the door, but the rest of the staff continued inside. Since Caesar had not specifically told me to remain outside, I followed. It was early in the day and the place was nearly empty. The only people there were the proprietor, leaning on the counter talking to a customer who was obviously also a friend, but the place was otherwise empty. We entered the taverna, Caesar guiding the messenger by the elbow with me following. The taverna owner and the customer stopped talking and stood up straight as if at military attention. Caesar simply said to the owner, 'I need the room.' The taverna owner scrambled out past the group in the doorway with his one customer on his heels.

Caesar led the man to the back of the room and sat him down at a small table in the dimly lit corner. The only window in the place was high on the wall and the sun had not yet reached it. I stood nearby, trying to not be noticed. It was only then Caesar held out his hand and accepted the scroll. Breaking the seal and unrolling the papyrus, Caesar took some time to read the document by the light of the oil lamp on the table, before looking up and staring into the face of the messenger. Without taking his eyes from the messenger he reached back and held out the scroll for me to take. He said, in a tone low enough for only the three of us to hear, 'commit this to memory, Polybius. Especially the names of the men who signed off on it.' I correctly surmised that because Caesar wanted me to memorize the message, he had no intention of keeping the original. I took a step back where the light was better and read the document three times before stepping forward and leaning over Caesar's shoulder. I recited the message back to him quietly, handing him the scroll.

Leaning forward, Caesar then said to the man in almost a whisper, 'you will return to Rome and tell Cato you couldn't locate me, so you left the message with one of my men.'

'But I did locate you, and I sat here and watched you read the message.' The messenger was smiling conspiratorially.

'How much will it cost me for you to say you never saw me?' This was the first time I ever witnessed Caesar openly bribe someone.

'Six hundred denarii,' the man said, leaning back in his chair.

'Keep your voice low.' Caesar was clearly angry but tried to not show it. 'You will get five hundred.'

The messenger was not to be dissuaded from his original demand. 'I was paid to deliver this message directly to you. How will I explain handing it over to another? That will cost me.'

'Come back here tomorrow at this time. Do you know Vetius?' The man nodded. 'He will have your money! There is a door in the back,' Caesar gestured to the back of the taverna with the scroll. 'Use it.'

Caesar sat back in his chair not saying a word for a long moment after the man left. I stood silently behind him. 'They mean to deprive me of the Consulship, Polybius,' he said, at last, holding the papyrus scroll over the low flame of the oil lamp until it ignited. Caesar turned and held the scroll out so none of the ash would fall on his toga and watched it burn until just a small corner of the page remained. He shook what was left and looked at it closely, turning it with his fingers to be sure none of the writing remained before he stood and rubbed the ashes into the stones of the floor. 'When we get back to the villa send someone to find Balbus. We will be leaving as soon as he can arrange a ship.' Knowing my fondness for sea travel, Caesar managed to give me a smile."

Polybius paused to lean forward so I could adjust his cushions. Both Mela and I had come to expect this sort of thing. Polybius had a fondness for drama and would always pause after building suspense in his account. Sometimes he would even conveniently forget to fill us in on the missing details until one of us would ask, so I asked. "What did the message say?"

"The message was short and to the point and signed by the group of men selected by the Senate to arrange the lottery for assigning provinces for the following year. The gist of their message was that the auspices were bad and the selection of provinces would be delayed until the next lucky day, which according to the calendar was two days before the Ides of Maius (May 13). Caesar was required to remain in his province until the calends of Junius (June 1). Upon returning to Italy he could then apply for an exemption to seek the Consulship without entering the city."

This time, Mela didn't wait for the pause and asked the question. "Why couldn't Caesar enter Rome?"

Polybius took another sip of wine and continued. "A Propraetor or Proconsul gives up his Imperium when he crosses the Pomerium, the official boundary of the city. Once he does that, he can no longer celebrate a triumph. Since the elections are held in Quintilis (July), even if Caesar was able to return to Italy by mid-Maius, there would not be enough time to both celebrate the triumph and file for the Consulship before the election. Caesar was planning to have his friends in the Senate push through an exemption to the law requiring candidates to appear in the city, so he could run in absentia and campaign from outside the official boundary as a triumphant general. By delaying his return to Italy until near the end of Junius, the Optimates were hoping to be able to block his getting the exemption and force him to give up running for Consul that year."

I still didn't fully understand, so I asked, "Why was it so important to Caesar that he run that year?"

Polybius smiled. "I asked him the same question as we walked to the door of the taverna. 'I know this is your year, and that's important, but why not run next year. The people will still remember your triumph.'"

"What do you mean by 'his year,'" Mela asked.

"It was the goal of every ambitious senator to move up each rung of the ladder of honor by winning each election in the first year he was eligible. It seldom happened, and was considered to be a notable achievement and added luster to a man's dignitas,' Polybius answered. "I expected Caesar to tell me as much. Not wanting to have the conversation in front of the others, he stopped where we were, saying, 'If I don't win the Consulship I will no longer have Imperium. They can then try me for corruption and banish me to some colony in a province.'

'With Crassus' help you can beat them in the courts.' I tried to sound upbeat.

'I'll take that chance if I must, but that gamble is too rich for even me to take willingly,' he answered. Then, putting his hand on my shoulder, he looked me in the eyes. 'If I'm put on trial, you will be required to testify.' With that, he turned and walked to the door with me following. Halfway to the door, I became fully aware of what he said and this caused me to come to a stop. I felt a little sick and dizzy. Slave testimony can only be presented to a court if it is obtained by torture. At the door, Caesar turned back and said, 'we'll find a way out of this. Now let's go, we have work to do.' With that, I quickly caught up and stepped out into the sunlight at Caesar's   side.

LIBER XIV

The following day Balbus dispatched two of his freedmen to Gades with instructions to travel on horseback as quickly as possible and secure the fastest vessel available in the harbor. Balbus was then left in charge of getting two of the legions to Rome for the triumph. Since the preparations for the journey had already begun, this would be an easy matter and the speed of the plans was simply increased. On the morning of the third day after receiving the message from Rome, Caesar and a few close associates set out on the road with six lictors and only four slaves. We set out without even knowing there would be a ship waiting for us. When we arrived, the crew of the ship that had been obtained for us was unloading cargo to provide space for our party and our meager supplies and to allow the ship to travel faster. While the vessel was being readied we went to the Balbus domus and had a simple meal of bread, eggs, and olives. Without even bathing, we boarded the ship and less than an hour later we were underway.

The weather and currents were with us and we only made one stop, at the port city of Caralis (Cagliari) in Sardinia, to re-supply our ship. During our brief stop, I remained on the ship with the other slaves. As a result, we landed at Ostia nine days after our departure. A sizeable party met us at the quay. Caesar's daughter, his mother, and his niece Atia holding her nearly three-year-old son Gaius, (the future god Augustus), by the hand, and several others were all there. Word of our arrival in Caralis made it to Rome with a merchant ship that had left that city on the same day we arrived. Our ship carried the distinctive symbol of the Balbus family on its mainsail, so the slave that was sent each morning to watch for our arrival was easily able to spot us and run back and alert his mistress, Aurelia, in plenty of time for the party to meet us at the dock. Caesar walked down the plank first, wearing his military tunic and general's cloak. I watched from the deck as Aurelia embraced and kissed her son. I felt a brief twinge of sadness when that caused me to think of my own mother, but it quickly passed in the excitement of the homecoming. I was the last to walk down the plank, feeling a little wobbly after so long at sea. I remained at the back of the group, respecting my place when Aurelia caught my eye, waving me toward her. As I stepped forward to greet her, she surprised me by wrapping me in her arms. She broke the embrace while looking around. Suddenly she said excitedly, 'There they are!' When I looked in the direction she was looking I saw Cornelia rushing toward us with our son in her arms.

I looked to Caesar who was watching the scene for permission and he smiled and nodded. This sent me running toward my small family. I wrapped my arms around them both when we met. Cornelia didn't seem as eager to see me as I was to see her and our son, but I dismissed this as all my attention was focused on Tychaeus. Our son had been given my Greek name. I tried to take him in my arms, but he turned shyly away and buried his head between Cornelia's shoulder and neck. 'He doesn't know you, Polybius,' Cornelia said, smiling apologetically. 'He will get better now that you're home.' I marveled at how much my son had grown. I had left him a small, pink, wrinkled infant, and now he was a plump babbling baby with a full head of curly dark hair.

I looked at Cornelia. 'I missed you,' I said. As soon as I said it I knew it wasn't entirely true. I had not often thought of Cornelia as anything other than the mother of my son, and what I had missed was the sense of family. I realized I didn't truly love her, so I was grateful she didn't tell me she missed me too. We were glad to see each other, but neither of us felt the passion that lovers feel after being reunited. After a quick sacrifice at the temple near the small harbor, our party made our way to a domus owned by Gaius Octavius, Atia's husband, just a short distance from the quay. Once inside the domus, Cornelia set baby Tychaeus down and took his hand, allowing him to attempt to walk. The baby instinctively reached up with his other hand to grasp mine. This was the first step in my son and me getting to know each other. Unfortunately, circumstances would keep us far apart for many years and I wouldn't get to know him as a person until we met again, when he was nearly a man.

It was determined we would stay for three days at the domus

while Caesar's villa outside Rome was prepared for the large group that would now be living there. Caesar was to divide his time between his own villa and the Villa Publica. In addition to holding the records of the censor's office and acting as the office and base of operations for the censors, this public villa had a suite of rooms reserved for generals awaiting a triumph. It is, of course, no longer used for this purpose, as now the only generals allowed a triumph are members of the imperial family and they live in the palace.

The domus was equipped with a room where the slaves could bathe. I was happy to wait until the other slaves had taken their turns, as I was busy getting reacquainted with baby Tychaeus. He quickly warmed up to me and we spent about an hour playing with each other until it was time for my bath. Caesar spent the hour conferring with Demetrius about his now much-improved finances. When I had changed into a fresh tunic, we were off to the baths so Caesar and his party could wash away the dirt and body odor of travel and get a proper meal. As was usual, I waited in the courtyard of the bath with two of the secretaries, both slaves attached to the domus, while the men bathed. Demetrius bathed with the others, as he was now a free man, but he left the men early and came out to the courtyard to fill me in on Caesar's plans on the domestic front. We were to split our time between the villa on the far side of the Tiber and the Villa Publica, because the suite reserved for generals was too small and austere for any Patrician of our times to find acceptable, but Caesar wanted to use the symbolism of the place to remind the people of his position as a triumphant general.

Once the others had finished bathing, we gathered in a rather cramped room at the baths to have a conference on the current political situation. It became clear Cato and the Optimates were planning to deprive Caesar of the Consulship by whatever means possible. As the discussion went on, I began to feel sick, as the prospect of finding a way out of the trap seemed more and more hopeless. Caesar was firm that he intended to celebrate his triumph and every report from the city indicated the Optimates intended to stand firm on the law requiring him to announce his candidacy publicly within the walls of Rome. Finally, it was agreed we were at an impasse and Caesar adjourned the meeting and we returned to the domus for much-needed rest. What was settled was that each man agreed to dispatch his own loyal followers to the city to promote Caesar's cause. It was also agreed Caesar was moving to the Villa Publica immediately, whether it was ready or not. As it was within a short walk to the forum, residing in the villa would not only increase Caesar's visibility with the voters, but it would allow his political operatives to work more efficiently.

That night, with our baby sleeping in a cradle nearby, Cornelia and I made love. It was actually quite satisfying, in spite of the fact that our hearts were not really in it. When young people go too long without sex and then have the opportunity, they approach the act like animals, forgetting the more tender emotions, driven simply by physical desire. In a sense, that is probably a purer form of the sex act. When we were done, and I drew her body, moist with perspiration, close to me, she started to speak. In a hesitant voice, she said, 'Polybius....'

I cut her off by pressing a finger to her lips. 'I know, I know. We can talk about this in the morning. For now, let's just enjoy this moment.'

In the moonlight that filtered in through the two narrow windows along the sidewall, I could see her nod her head in agreement. We both drifted into sleep. When the morning sun woke me, I opened my eyes to see Cornelia sitting in the chair beside the cradle nursing our son. I watched the scene for a long moment before sitting up.

Cornelia spoke first. 'You will be called to work soon. We should talk, don't you think?'

I nodded. 'I will always love you Cornelia, but I'm not sure I love you enough for this to last. Caesar cannot sit still. He's already making plans for after he becomes Consul. I'll be away from Rome for at least another year, and I really can't imagine he will want to retire after that.'

'Did you meet someone else in Hispania?' Her question took me by surprise.

'For a short time I was involved with someone, but it was just sex.' I answered honestly, but I failed to mention the sex I had was with a man. I wasn't sure how she would react to that, so I politely omitted that detail.

'Cornelia bit her lip and looked down. 'I've met someone.' It was almost a whisper.

I was surprised at how her admission hurt me. I felt as if I had been punched in the belly. For a time, I even found it difficult to breathe. I tried to disguise what I was feeling because I was a bit embarrassed by my reaction and I didn't want to make Cornelia feel bad for causing me pain. I suppose it was disappointment I was feeling, at being so easily replaced in her heart, but the feeling was quite strong. It took me some time to recover and we both sat quietly.

Cornelia was the first to break the silence. 'We haven't had sex, but I think I love him, and he says he loves me. I'm so sorry Polybius.' There were tears in her eyes, I suppose as a reaction to the tears in mine.

I took a deep breath to recover my composure. 'Well, I'm glad this is in the open now. I said I'll always love you and I didn't lie. I intend to buy your freedom and that of our son. Whatever happens though, I want you to promise Tychaeus will always be mine. You can do nothing to prevent me from seeing him when I'm in Rome, and you cannot move from Rome without my permission. I was standing now, and pacing across the small floor, looking at the mosaic tiles so I didn't have to look Cornelia in the eye, fearing how she would react to my demands.

'Of course,' she answered. 'You're his father and that won't change. But, it's silly to talk about you buying us. I know that was our plan, but after you left, I came to realize it isn't possible. I'm a public slave, and I think our son is too. I suppose you could make an argument he belongs to Caesar since you're his father, but I don't know.

I had a plan in place and I'd done my research. 'Our son belongs to Caesar. I've checked the law.' Cornelia looked a little frightened when I said that, so I quickly added, 'don't worry, I won't ever separate him from you.'

'You are a public slave,' I continued, 'but I've checked into that too. The Pontifex Maximus can free you, so long as the Consul gives his consent. As you know,' I added with a smile, 'I have some influence with the Pontifex Maximus.'

At that, Cornelia smiled too. 'Good luck getting the Consul to approve that. We both know public slaves are only given freedom when they are too old or too sick to be of much use.'

At that moment, one of the other slaves stuck his head in the doorway and said, 'Master Caesar is asking for you.'

'Okay,' I said to the slave, turning to follow. I stopped at the door and turned back to Cornelia. 'Caesar intends to be Consul next year.' With that, I left her.

That morning we moved on to Caesar's villa near the Tiber allowing another day for the suite in the Villa Publica to be readied. A salutatio was held, but since we were still some distance from Rome the group waiting to be seen was smaller and almost all the clients outside the door that day were well-off equites who could afford slaves and litters and be carried to the villa. Cornelia was still with us, but she and our son would soon return to the city and to the Domus Publica. She spent the day preparing four toga canditae for Caesar. It was a long process to whiten the togas with bleaching and chalk, so they dazzled in the sunlight, and this kept her quite busy. I was surprised to learn that Caesar's daughter Julia volunteered to watch baby Tychaeus while Cornelia worked. Many patrician women don't like to even tend to their own children. It was unheard of, in my experience, for one to take care of a slave child.

Later that evening, after everyone was sent home, Caesar sent a slave to summon me to the triclinium where, when I arrived, he was picking at what was left of a chicken. The last meeting of the day was held over dinner. Aurelia rose from her chair and kissed her son on the head. 'I'm off to bed,' she said. 'There will be much to do tomorrow. Goodnight Gaius, goodnight Polybius.' When she left Aurelia pulled the drapery to cover the doorway.

I stood by the stool and asked,' May I sit?'

Caesar waved to an empty couch with a chicken wing. 'Lay down there, we're alone.' I was surprised. That was the first time I had ever lain on a couch outside of the Saturnalia festival. Setting down the three dice he was rolling around in his left hand, Caesar leaned forward and poured me a cup of wine. 'I hope you don't mind drinking from someone else's cup.' I noticed he picked up the dice again and began to absent-mindedly roll them around in his hand again.

I took the cup and leaned back almost spilling the wine. 'Really, Caesar, I think I would be more comfortable on the stool.'

'Nonsense,' he said, looking at the ceiling, 'you'll get used to it. I want to tell you what I've been thinking. If I ask you a question, I want your honest opinion and if you have something to add, say so, without hesitation.' I nodded, so he continued. 'A triumph will add greatly to my dignitas and show the world I'm a commander to be respected. Pompeius already has three. On the other hand, winning the consulship in my year will also increase my dignitas.'

When Caesar paused, I realized we were engaging in the same process he and Demetrius used and I knew it was my turn to speak. I thought carefully. My first thought was that I wanted to argue that he should seek the consulship, but realizing this was for personal reasons, I tried to think of another argument in favor of Caesar postponing the consulship and celebrating his triumph. I couldn't find one and told him so. 'I know you really want your triumph, but politically, it makes more sense to seek the consulship if you are forced to choose.'

'Why?' he asked.

I knew he must have been thinking I was saying so to avoid being tortured should he be brought to court, so I addressed that point first. 'Of course,' I said, pausing to sip my wine, 'I would like for you to hold Imperium so you aren't impeached in court, but this is about you and not me. If you forego the consulship this year, you will no doubt be put on trial, but I would guess you could get enough support in the Senate and among the Tribunes to give you even odds or maybe a bit better to win an acquittal. That, of course, would be expensive.'

'You know money doesn't mean much to me.' When he said this, I thought of a conversation I had with Demetrius that morning, where I learned he was involved in negotiations with a gem dealer to purchase a pearl, in Caesar's name, worth a fortune, as a gift for Servilia.

'I don't believe it would be worth taking the chance with those odds. Even if you win, the trial would damage your dignitas as much as the triumph would increase it.'

'What if I give up my triumph and fail to win the consulship. It's a gamble either way.' Caesar seemed truly puzzled by this problem. 'What difference will it make what I choose to do? I'm sailing between Scylla and Charybdis.'

I thought about it and took my time in answering. 'There's more to gain by winning the consulship this year than there is by celebrating a triumph, so it's wiser to gamble on the consulship. If you become Consul, you can influence the Senate to grant you a province where you will win another triumph and become very wealthy to boot. In spite of the fact that you don't care about money, it would be a useful tool in winning an acquittal in court when your Proconsulship expires. If you forgo the consulship you will need to spend everything you won in Hispania to keep from being exiled.'

Caesar sighed and said, 'let's see if we can't find a way I can do both.' With that, he changed the topic. 'Your boy has grown a lot in a year. He looks like you.'

It was uncharacteristic of Caesar to make small talk with a slave, or for that matter to discuss any man's infant son unless it was to ingratiate himself with a man of influence. I knew where he was steering the conversation, so I came to the point. 'He has certainly grown. I would like, one day, to buy him from you.'

'It's unusual for a slave to own a slave. Most masters don't even allow it.' Caesar was looking at me now. 'It would be cruel to separate him from his mother.'

'It will probably be some time before I have enough money to buy them both, but it would be my intention to set them free.'

'Cornelia doesn't belong to me. She's a public slave and as such, I can't sell her.' Caesar was choosing what he said carefully. I wondered whether or not the slave who had summoned me that morning had lingered near the doorway and listened to what I said to Cornelia.

'The Pontifex Maximus can sell any slave attached to the Domus Publica, provided the sale is authorized by a Consul.' I said, trying to remain calm, but I began to feel as if I had butterflies inside my belly.

Caesar swung his legs over the side of the couch and sat up, so I quickly did the same. 'Another reason for me to win the consulship,' he said as he rose to his feet. 'It's time for bed,' he added resting a hand on my shoulder. 'We'll talk about this again, I assure you.'

LIBER XV

Everyone in Caesar's inner circle worked at a nearly constant pace at this time. A formal request was sent to the Senate asking for a waiver to file his candidacy in absentia. Caesar pressed to have this voted on immediately, but Crassus made a strong case to arrange for a delay of nine days, with the Senate voting just one day before the filing deadline, so we could drum up more support for the proposal and shore up the support we already had. Caesar felt that it was worthwhile to take the risk and have an immediate vote and head off any tricks the Optimate faction may put into play. Crassus won the day on this one though, and it was decided there would be a delay of nine days. After this meeting, I remember as we stood at the gate to Caesar's villa watching Crassus carried in his litter down the path to the road, Caesar turned to Balbus and said, 'The vote will be dangerously close to the deadline for filing my candidacy. I hope I don't regret allowing Crassus to persuade me in this matter. I think he's losing his touch.' With that, Caesar sighed and turned back toward the villa with his dog Ajax at his heels, leaving Balbus and I watching Crassus and his associates move down the hill.

When the day of the vote came Caesar and his family chose to spend the time awaiting the news in the Temple of Spes, the goddess of hope, just outside the Pomerium close to the

Carmentalis gate. I arranged to have my small staff of secretaries arrive in the forum at dawn, so they could find places on the steps of the curia. I had hoped it would be possible for someone to get close enough to the doors to hear the proceedings, but I knew this was unlikely. As the crowd filled in, slaves would, naturally, be pushed to the side. I instructed them to pair up and record any news on wax tablets. At regular intervals, or if there was any news Caesar should hear immediately, one of the pair was to run to the gate with his tablet where I would be waiting. Those associates of Caesar who happened to be senators made similar arrangements with their own slaves, being able to report directly from within the Curia itself. Because of this, there was a constant flow of information coming from the forum to Caesar.

Balbus moved to introduce the measure, but Cato immediately moved to delay debate on the measure until all the business from the previous session was cleared. This was to be expected, but what was not expected was the way the Optimates took turns giving particularly long speeches arguing either for or against the legislation that was considered so inconsequential that the Senate had chosen to put off debate in previous sessions. It was obvious there was a coordinated plan in the works. When I could, at last, report to Caesar that the previous day's business had been cleared and the Senate broke for the midday meal, he asked me what I considered a strange question. 'I notice from your reports that the same six or seven senators are monopolizing the debates. Tell me, who is not speaking?' Caesar and Julia had been playing at dice, and he still held the dice in his hand when he rose to his feet.

'Many senators aren't speaking, Caesar. Your people are either not being called on to speak, or when they are speaking; they're being very brief, as we planned. There are many others who haven't joined the debate. That's why we all agree the Optimates are delaying the vote; their faction is making long speeches to slow the process.'

Caesar sounded cross. 'I know that, but I haven't heard Cassius, Piso, or Cato mentioned yet.'

I scanned my notes to verify his observation. 'You're right, they haven't yet spoken. Strangely, Metellus has not even called on them.'

Caesar scowled, but Aurelia who had been feeding grapes to little Gaius Octavius, slapped the table making the small bowl of fruit rattle and the baby burst into tears. 'Damn them to Dis!' This was the first time I could recall hearing her curse. 'They are saving their voices. You were right, Gaius, you shouldn't have listened to Crassus this time.'

Without looking at her, Caesar said, 'so it would seem, Mother.' With that, he walked out of the temple onto the portico and starred at the wall marking the Pomerium, lost in thought. I didn't dare ask him what it all meant, so I quietly asked Aurelia's permission to take a small loaf of bread and some cheese and made my way out to the temple steps. Caesar nodded in reply as I pointed to my place near the Carmentalis gate and I returned to my post to await the news that the Senate had assembled once again.

The Optimates were as well organized as we were, if not more so. Caesar's people in the Senate ate quickly, if at all, and returned to the Curia as soon as they could, hoping for a quorum before many of the Optimates returned, thus forcing a vote. The Optimates delayed their return until their own people reported that a quorum was imminent, and they arrived just before the debate was to begin on the measure to allow Caesar to run for Consul from outside the Pomerium. By this time it was well into the afternoon but I was not concerned as there were still several hours for the motion to pass. As it turned out, I should have been very worried. Through various procedural moves, the debate was delayed at least an hour longer. At last, the debate began. Piso and Gabinius both made long-winded speeches taking up another hour. When Cato, the last of the Optimate faction yet to be heard from, was called on to speak there was, by my estimation, at least six or seven hours until sunset would force the adjournment of the Senate. I never imagined he would talk for that long, but he did.

With time running out, I returned to the Temple of Spes to report that there was no break in the impasse, and Cato showed no sign of weakening his resolve to speak until darkness caused an adjournment of the Senate. I knew there was less time than there seemed to be from my vantage point, as the shadow of the Capitoline Hill brought dusk to the Curia well before it came to us on the west side of the hill. I found Caesar standing near the Temple of Janus, just to the north of the Temple of Spes, where he had a clear view of the sun as it sank in the western sky. I gave him the news without any emotion. He didn't say a word, merely looking down at the three dice he still rolled around in his left hand, sighing and shaking his head. I had never seen him look so despondent. He turned and walked back toward his family, waiting on the steps of the Temple of Spes. Not knowing what to do, I returned to my post at the gate. All day long, members of Caesar's clientela had been gathering in the area of the Forum Holitorium (vegetable market), where the Temple of Spes was located, so there was a considerable crowd. When a slave came to report that a motion had been made to adjourn the session without taking a vote on the measure, I was crestfallen. My hopes of buying freedom for Cornelia and my son were crushed, and I faced the prospect of being tortured to provide evidence against Caesar when he was brought to trial. I needed Caesar to win the consulship and now he couldn't even be a candidate. I dreaded forcing my way through the crowd to bring my report to my master, but I turned to face my duty. As I made my way forward along the street a murmur rose from the crowd, starting to the west and quickly moving closer to me. I heard a woman shout, 'Caesar is coming,' just as the crowd parted before me. The six retired soldiers who made up Caesar's unofficial bodyguard were clearing a path in the crowd. When they stepped aside, Caesar quickly swept into view, followed by his family and friends. Even though the sun had dropped below the roof of the temples in the market, I could see it was he, by the brightness of the toga candida.

When Caesar was about twenty feet from me, he said, with a look of resolve on his face, 'Let's go Polybius.' I was confused and paused just a moment, running to catch up, as he swept past.

'Where are we going?' As soon as I asked it, I knew the question was foolish.

'To announce my candidacy,' was his reply.

LIBER XVI

The following morning, having spent the night in the city, Caesar held his first salutatio at the Domus Publica, in over a year. There was a considerable crowd, so I knew the list of appointments would be long. As I was gathering the tablets I needed to make the list, Caesar stopped me. 'Leave at least an hour for Lucceius.' I knew from the way he said it that this was to be an important and confidential meeting, so I quickly made eye contact with Lucceius when I stepped out onto the portico, and with a slight nod let him know he should wait. I came to him in due course so as to not raise any suspicion and told him to be at the baths on the Esquiline Hill that afternoon. As he turned away, I noticed his nomenclator waiting in the background. We made the sort of eye contact that those of us who are attracted to our own sex recognize immediately. This, of course, caused me a bit of a thrill and it took me a moment to refocus. I looked forward to meeting him as we waited on our masters at the bath.

As was often the case, we had some religious ceremonies to attend to, and then it was off to campaigning. The campaign for Consul was much like the campaign for praetor, but with more at stake, the bribes being offered were larger and the intensity of the campaigning was greater. Caesar employed more of his clientela than I had ever seen in the city at one time to work toward his election and to each man, the message was the same; whatever the cost, get the votes. When I heard the amounts being bandied about I couldn't imagine how he planned to pay for it all, but I continued to faithfully keep my tally. When the sum finally topped fifty thousand denarii, I had to stop him. 'Caesar,' I said as we sat under a brightly colored canopy in front of a wine seller's shop in the Basilica Amelia, 'You have now promised just over fifty-seven thousand. Do you have a plan to pay for it?'

Caesar laughed as he stood up. 'You remind me more of Demetrius each day,' he said slapping me on the back as I stood. 'That is why I had you arrange a meeting with Lucceius this afternoon.'

I knew Lucceius was fabulously wealthy but I didn't understand how Caesar could get him to provide the funds and I said so. 'Why should he support your campaign?' I asked.

'Because, Polybius, he thinks I can make him Consul.'

'Can you?' I was genuinely curious.

'I doubt it, but one never knows. Fortuna can be quite fickle.' He was in a good mood. A political or a military campaign always buoyed his spirits and increased Caesar's energy at least fivefold.

Since he was in such good spirits I decided to playfully challenge what he said. 'I think Fortuna only seems to be fickle because we don't see the entire vista. I think she has a plan.'

Suddenly Caesar looked serious. 'You may be right. We should go.' With that, we returned to the crowds in the forum.

Later that afternoon we made our way to the baths on the Esquiline. Caesar always attracted a large following as he moved about the city, but since announcing his candidacy the crowd had steadily grown larger. He continued to use his retired legionary soldiers as unofficial lictors, but even with the six men clearing a path, it was slow going. When we arrived at the baths I noticed Lucceius' nomenclator sitting on one of the benches in the courtyard watching some of the men exercising. Caesar's entrance caused a stir and the man looked over to us and our eyes locked again in recognition. Caesar turned to me and said, 'I'm going into the cold room. Watch for Lucceius to arrive.'

'He's already here,' I said.

'How do you know?'

'His man is right over there,' I said, pointing with my stylus.

Caesar noticed Balbus chatting with some associates near the entrance to the bathing rooms. 'I'm going to talk to Balbus. Find out where Lucceius is and let us know.'

I gladly went over to Lucceius' man where he sat watching the exchange between Caesar and me. 'Hello,' I said, as my eyes met his and didn't stray. This was something Caesar had taught me. He always said, if you wish to charm a person, talk to that man or woman as if you are the only two people in the room. 'You are Lucceius' man if I'm not mistaken.'

'Yes.' He smiled. 'Please call me Marcus.'

'I am Polybius, Caesar's man.' I smiled back, not breaking eye contact.

Marcus looked toward the ground. I noticed he was blushing, 'I know who you are.'

I was afraid I had been a little too forceful and unnerved him, so I turned to business. 'My master would like to know where Lucceius is; they have planned to meet.'

'My master is in the cold room waiting for Caesar.' He still looked at the ground and I began to think I had misjudged our exchanges.

'Thank you, it has been nice meeting you.' As I began to turn away, to ease his discomfort I said. 'I'll leave you alone now.'

I had gotten maybe five feet when Marcus called out, 'Polybius?' I stopped and turned back to him. 'Please, come back when you deliver the message.' Marcus hesitated, his face turning red again, but this time he didn't look away. 'That is if you want to,' he added.

I smiled a genuinely broad smile and walked as quickly as decorum allowed to deliver my message.

I waited until Caesar and Balbus passed through the entrance into the bathing area before I quickly made my way to the bench where Marcus was sitting. The place was filling with people and I didn't want someone else to sit in the space beside him. When I did sit. Marcus was looking at his feet again. I realized the young man was just being shy, and I tried to make a joke about it, just to fill the uncomfortable silence. 'I've never met a nomenclator who is uncomfortable around people.'

'He looked up at me apologetically. 'It's not all people.' Marcus smiled. 'I'm just more comfortable when people ignore me. My master likes when I keep to my proper place.' He hesitated as if he was unsure if he should continue, but then he added. 'It is said you frequently cross the proper bounds for a slave, and your master tolerates it.'

I was truly surprised. I had never thought I acted differently than any slave in my position would, but on reflection, I had to agree. 'I suppose you're right.' I was also surprised others were talking about me.

We made small talk briefly, ignoring our mutual attraction as best we could. I took the initiative when a rather fat slave took the space beside me on the stone bench. I slid over and pressed my leg against his. I was happy to notice he didn't pull away. Leaning in, so the other slave wouldn't hear, I said quietly, 'would you like to go somewhere else? I know a taverna down the street that will allow slaves in if you don't bring too much notice to yourself.'

'I've never been into a taverna,' he answered. 'My master has me wait outside on the rare occasions he goes to such places. He always said the main advantage of being rich is that a man does not need to frequent that type of establishment. He can be a snob.'

'Caesar tells me he will be meeting with Lucceius for about an hour. That will give us plenty of time for a glass of wine. Does Lucceius allow you to drink?'

'Only at home, and only a little.' Marcus smiled weakly as if to say he was sorry.' I thought he was going to say no, when he added, 'our masters will be at least three hours, perhaps longer. My master never meets with anyone for an hour. He loves the sound of his own voice and is impervious to the boredom of others.' I shifted on the bench as if to rise when he hesitated again. He gave me an embarrassed look. 'I have no money.'

I smiled and said, 'don't worry about it, I have enough for both of us.'

Marcus hesitated yet again, before finally making up his mind. He rested his right hand to my thigh, giving me a small thrill, and then pushing himself up with the same hand, he said, 'alright, I'll do it.'

As we made our way toward the entrance to the baths, he stopped again. 'What if one of my master's friends sees us?'

I laughed, putting my hand on his shoulder to guide him forward. 'The place we are going is not the sort of place a friend of Lucius Lucceius would admit being in, so you are safe.'

We quickly made our way down the street. Marcus stopped at the taverna door and hesitated one last time as I playfully pushed him through the entrance. This was the sort of taverna that didn't have windows. The only light came in through the open front and the room was long and narrow leaving the back half mostly in deep shadow. You only got the use of an oil lamp if you asked for it, and the proprietor always made it clear he was reluctant to provide one without a coin changing hands. The front tables filled up first with men playing at dice; the back tables filled up with people not wishing to be seen. I found us a table in the back and quickly bought a flagon of wine. Over our first cup of wine, we each learned a bit about the other's life. At last, came the inevitable question. 'Do you have a woman?' Marcus asked the question as if he was just making conversation, but I could tell by his tone he was very interested in the answer.

'I did', I answered, 'but we have come to an understanding.' I laughed a little. 'What about you?' I added.

His answer was to the point. 'No.'

I decided to get everything out in the open and see where it led, so I said, 'actually I prefer men to women.'

Marcus then hesitantly slid his hand on my thigh. I placed my hand on his and guided it over until it rested on my growing erection. He leaned in close as I refilled our cups, and whispered, 'I wish there was someplace we could be alone.'

I quickly whispered to him, 'I'll be right back,' and slid from behind the table and went right up to the proprietor. I had never been so bold before, but I knew this opportunity might soon pass, so I did what I had seen men do many times in this taverna, mostly with women, but sometimes with other men. I bluntly asked the man how much it would cost to use his storage room. I didn't even try to negotiate a price and very soon we were locked in an embrace in the dusty storage room filled with jars and shelves stacked with plates and cups. The sex was quick but strangely intense; the long buildup and the inherent risk for two slaves having sex in a taverna closet heightened the excitement.

When we slid back the bolt and left the closet, we both walked out not looking anyone in the eye. I was sorry to leave two nearly full cups on the table, but Marcus was clearly not comfortable enough to stay any longer. I must admit I felt agitated as well.

As it was, we had returned to the bath with plenty of time to spare. Marcus was correct; the meeting took much longer than I had anticipated. We used the time to continue to talk about our lives. I learned that like me, he had been born a slave to a mother who was captured when a Roman army took the city in which she lived. She was nearly nine months along in her pregnancy when the city fell and he was born before the enslaved captives could be shipped to Rome. His father was killed in the war, but his mother continued to live and work in the villa owned by Lucceius, in the Alban Hills, and they saw each other often. I was grateful to the gods to have met an intelligent and attractive man who, like me, was born of a Greek mother. Before long, however, I piloted our conversation along a different course, talking about politics. Marcus seemed to have little interest in politics and, therefore, failed to look for connections between the activities of his master, and the events happening in the political world. I, on the other hand, was keenly interested in what Caesar and Lucceius were planning behind the wall to our backs. It was easy to get him to talk freely about his master's associates and I learned a curious bit of information. It seems Bibulus had been discussing an electoral pact with Lucceius. He too wanted to run alongside Lucceius, using his money to augment the political influence Bibulus had. This sounded to me exactly what Caesar was planning.

'How often has your master met with Bibulus?' I asked the question casually as if I was just curious about Marcus' master.

He answered just as casually. 'They have met on several occasions. The two met again just yesterday. They are becoming fast friends, though I can't for the life of me see why my master likes the man since master Lucceius drinks very little, and Bibulus seems determined to live up to his name and likes to drink wine as a fish drinks water. But who my master chooses to associate with is none of my business, and when they spend hours over their wine, it frees up my time, so I don't question it.'

I was glad I asked that question when I did because a short time later I heard Balbus' booming laugh and looked over to see Caesar, arm in arm with Lucceius coming through the archway into the courtyard with several associates of both men trailing behind. Before we both rose to return to our masters, Marcus and I clasped our hands briefly. That and a lingering look were the only signs of affection the circumstances would allow us.

As the sun was setting and we were walking down the Sacra Via returning from the bath, I realized the deal between Lucceius and Caesar had originated months earlier with the man's visit to

Hispania. Caesar arranged an exchange with Lucius Lucceius. They would run together for the two consulships and Caesar would use his political connections and popularity with the people to attract as many votes to them both as possible, while Lucceius would provide the money needed to bribe the voters Caesar could not bring over. I was happy to hear they would be cooperating in a run for the consulship; this would give me, at least until the election, frequent access to Marcus. I also knew Lucceius was planning a similar arrangement with Caesar's political enemy, Bibulus. I regretted having to tell Caesar that Lucceius was plotting against him, as this would separate me from Marcus, but I knew I would have to.

The revelation of what I had learned from Marcus was not a conversation to have on the street, so I waited until Caesar and I were alone in the tablinum of the Domus Publica. Caesar had just returned from the dressing room where a slave had helped him remove his toga candida. He was scanning over the summary of his religious duties I had prepared while he was changing clothes, and casually said over his shoulder, 'it's late, Polybius. Get something to eat and spend some time with your son.'

I paused and took a breath before I spoke to his back. 'Thank you Caesar, can I talk to you about something first.'

He turned to me with a look of concern. 'Of course. What is it?'

With that, I told him what I had learned that afternoon in the courtyard of the baths. I was shocked by his response. He simply laughed and shook his head. I pressed on. 'I am quite serious. I believe what he told me.'

Caesar laughed again and reached out to lay his hand on my shoulder. With a smile, he said, 'you truly are my eyes and ears in addition to being my memory. I'd heard you went for a walk with Lucceius' man. I should have known you were fishing for information.'

I wasn't too surprised that Caesar had learned of my movements that day. Everyone gossips and the slaves working in the baths are some of the worst gossips of all. I just wondered how the news found its way to Caesar so quickly. 'You're not concerned?' I asked.

Caesar continued to smile. 'Concerned? No, Polybius, I'm delighted. Lucceius is following my instructions to the letter.'

'I don't understand.' I truly didn't.

'Think about it, there has never been any doubt Bibulus would oppose me in the election. I want him to think he has no need to worry about money until it's too late for him to do anything about it. It also helps that the man gulps his wine nearly full strength, while Lucceius sips his water with just a hint of wine to give it color. Bibulus has already let slip several plans his Optimate associates have begun to cook up.'

'I'm glad Lucceius is not secretly against us,' I said, my worries lifted. 'I rather like his man.

With that, Caesar looked at me strangely and rather longer than

I was comfortable with, so I began to busy myself with collecting my writing kit while avoiding his glance. The man seemed to perceive everything.

'You may go,' he said casually, but when I was at the doorway, he added, 'How are things with you and Cornelia?'

I stopped and answered with a bit more than a half-truth. 'Not what they were, I'm afraid. She met someone else while we were away.'

'That is a hazard of the lives we live. Sometimes a long separation will do that. I'm sorry.' He sounded truly sorry as if he thought it was his fault, and in a way it was. 'Remember though, Tychaeus will always be your son.'

'It's alright,' I was surprised I was trying to ease Caesar's feelings. I suppose if I had been in love with Cornelia I would have wanted to hurt him. 'We are still on good terms with each other.' Caesar nodded a dismissal, so I quickly left the room before he could say anything that would make me still more uncomfortable. As I walked toward my workroom it crossed my mind that he, in the past, affected to not even know Cornelia's name and yet, after a year in Hispania, he could remember it now.

Once again, my worries had turned out to be groundless. I was beginning to realize a lesson life teaches that you young men would do well to learn."

"What is that," I politely asked.

"The gods are difficult to fathom and the way they order the world is beyond the understanding of men. I have come to realize that the things we worry most about are almost never the things that bring us serious harm. The things that do the most damage to us and most seriously disrupt our carefully laid plans are the events we never see coming toward us. In fact, the old proverb is true; 'When the gods wish to punish us, they grant us what we pray for.'"

At that, Mela interrupted. "How was it possible to bribe the thousands of voters? That would take years to meet with them all!"

Polybius smiled. "You are, of course, right in that. It was not the actual voters who were given the money. No, it was the men who had a vast number of clients who were bought. They, in turn, persuaded their clientela to vote one way or another."

Polybius stifled his second yawn, so I suggested we return home and come back the following morning. Polybius readily agreed and asked that we see ourselves to the door, as his legs were feeling a bit weak. We said our goodbyes and made the return journey home.

LIBER XVII

Because our villas were so near each other, and the days were longer, Mela and I would sometimes spend entire days listening to Polybius tell the story of his life. This was a burden on my right hand, scratching notes for several hours a day. It was, however, more of a burden on the family slave I had arranged to carry the sack of tablets to Polybius' villa on the days we went there. He would then meet us late in the afternoon of each day, to carry home the sack full of tablets with my notes scratched into their wax surfaces. On this day, we arrived later, so I carried fewer tables and they were managed by Mela and me.

Castor escorted us up to the second floor balcony. Where Polybius greeted us and offered, as usual, refreshments. Today it was a dark wine and berries. After I reminded him where we left off, Polybius continued his tale. "The following day was much as the other days leading up to the election; the salutatio was followed by a trip to the forum to mingle with the voters followed by meetings with influential equites at the baths followed by a dinner party at the home of an influential patrician. Since Caesar announced he was seeking the consulship, I was required to go with him to social events such as that night's party. My function was to not only give him the names and particulars about people we met on the way to or from the party but to wait outside the triclinium, if the host allowed, or in the atrium of the home and gather any useful information from the household staff or the waiting slaves of other guests. It is surprising how much information one can piece together from the seemingly inane gossip one hears. After the party, it was Caesar's practice to walk home. Since he first settled on climbing the ladder of honor of Roman politics as his career, Caesar rarely traveled in a litter. He always said, 'a politician needs to be seen by the voters.' This was especially true now that he was seeking the consulship. On the walk home, we would discuss what we learned.

On that night, Caesar was strangely quiet, and when I tried to tell him what I learned he pressed his fingers to his lips to indicate he wanted me to remain quiet. I understood that he had heard the same thing I had and didn't want to discuss it where others might hear. Once inside the tablinum of the Domus Publica, he spoke. 'Tonight I learned the Optimate faction plans to unite behind Bibulus in his run for the consulship in an effort to block any legislation I might propose when I am elected. I'm afraid they are right in their belief that my efforts and his money will not be enough to get Lucceius elected as my co- Consul.'

'I heard the same, so it must be common knowledge.' I was feeling glum about Caesar's prospects. 'I also heard they think they can deny you the consulship altogether.'

'Well, that is up to Fortuna I guess, but I still like my odds.' Caesar seemed sure he would win. 'I also heard something disturbing. They mean to pass a law assigning to the Consuls of next year the task of demarcating the forests and woodland paths belonging to the state when they lay down their offices, rather than a province to govern. They mean to deprive me of any chance to win a triumph.'

'That will make it easier to prosecute you for the actions you took in Hispania.' I couldn't see much hope.

'We will talk about it more tomorrow. We both need to rest.' Caesar paused as if to say something, so I waited. 'When is the next open night in the schedule?'

'There are no free nights unless you want to cancel your private dinner with Servilia.' I thought it unlikely that he would cancel that, so I pulled the scroll containing Caesar's schedule from the bag still slung over my shoulder to check to see what else we could cancel.

'Get together with Demetrius tomorrow and make the arrangements to turn that private dinner into a party for nine. Make sure Servilia and her husband are on the list. I don't want to hurt her feelings any more than I need to.'

'Who else should be invited?' I asked.

'Make sure you invite Pompeius Magnus. Tell Demetrius to spend whatever he needs to make the party impossible for Pompeius to pass up. Invite Cicero too. I hear he spends these days practically sitting on Pompeius' lap anyway. Fill out the rest with interesting people.' Caesar was clearly planning something.

We parted ways, Caesar going to his sleeping chamber and me to mine. I blew out the oil lamp on the small table beside the bed and settled in when I looked up to see Caesar in his tunic standing in the doorway. I sat up quickly, asking, 'is there something else, Caesar?'

As I was about to stand, Caesar, waved me back onto the bed. 'I've been thinking, Polybius. Remember that conversation we had on the beach at Brigantium?' I nodded yes, but realizing he probably couldn't see that in the dark I started to speak. Caesar cut me off. 'I think you were right when you said the problems were too big for one man to solve. I'm certainly smart enough to do it, but I don't have the money or the influence to get past the Optimates. What do you think about two or three men joining forces?' I started to speak, but he cut me off again. 'Don't say anything yet. Sleep on it and tell me what you think tomorrow.' Without realizing, I witnessed the planting of the seed that would change Rome forever.

LIBER XVIII

The following morning, after the salutatio Caesar had to attend the final ritual of the Vestalia. As you know, on the ides of Junius the Vestal Virgins practice the ritual sweeping of the Temple of Vesta. While no man is allowed to participate in the actual ceremony, it is traditional for the Pontifex Maximus and the Flamen Dialis to observe the rites. It is vital that this most sacred ritual be carried out correctly, for it is widely understood that without the blessing of Vesta, Rome would lose the special relationship she has with the gods, and our empire would fall. This festival took most of the morning and was then followed by a sacrifice. The timing allows for the meat of the sacrificed animals to be ready in time for the midday meal, so, after he changed from the Pontiff's robes into the toga candida, Caesar and his associates were able to dine on lamb while sitting at a table in the courtyard of the Regia for all of Rome, but especially the voters on the way to the forum, to see. I, of course, being a slave, couldn't partake of the sacrifice, so I sat apart with the other slaves and we ate eggs, cheese, and olives for our meal. After the meal, I expected Caesar would go to the forum and speak from the rostrum. He normally made at least one and sometimes as many as three speeches from that platform each day while he was campaigning. Instead, he excused himself from his companions and asked me to follow him

148

into the Domus Publica. Once inside we went straight to the atrium where there were a couch and a chair placed near the fountain. Caesar sat on the couch and made a gesture indicating I should sit on the chair. I knew immediately this was to be a private conversation. When he didn't wish to be overheard, Caesar often chose to sit near a fountain; the sound of splashing water makes it nearly impossible for someone, standing at any distance more than a few feet, to overhear a conversation.

'Have you thought about what I said last night?' he asked.

I have, and I think you are right. Should you be elected, you will need to ally yourself with some powerful senators to make your consulship a success.' What I said was obvious, but safe. Anyone elected to high office needs strong allies to succeed.

Caesar frowned at me. 'That much Cato's barber could tell me.'

I felt a shudder when what he said brought back memories of that pompous man and my time as a slave in the Cato house. I shook it off quickly before Caesar could notice and gave him a more complete answer. 'I've also thought about who those allies should be,' I gave Caesar a small grin. 'You will need men of wealth and men of influence.'

'Go on,' he said, nodding.

'You'll need to use Lucceius for his money. You can bring in Crassus and a few others where your plans meet with their own interests, but Crassus cannot play a lead role.'

'Why do you say that?' Caesar seemed disappointed at what I'd said; as if it went against a plan he was already beginning to form. 'Crassus has invested more in my career than anyone else. At this point, he won't be denied a say in my consulship.'

'I say it because you mean to use Pompeius Magnus for his influence. Crassus will never work with Pompeius.' I said it with certainty.

'Why do you think that I've settled on Pompeius?' Caesar already knew the answer, but I believe he wanted to confirm how my thinking ran.

I smiled at him when I answered. 'I've watched you work for some time now. The sudden dinner party that Pompeius must attend, the fact that he has been added to your schedule for the day following the party, and the fact that we will be going to the bath on the Aventine two days after that, which just happens to be the bath favored by the great general, all tell me that you are courting him. I understand why you are doing so, as he is, right now, the most influential man in Rome. And, he will never work with Crassus and Crassus will never work with him. The men are the bitterest of enemies.' I paused, not sure if I should go on, but I knew Caesar must know everything I know. 'Yesterday, while you were meeting with Lucceius at the baths, when you sent his man, Marcus, back here with me to work on the list of influential equites you could bring together from both your clientele, I learned something that might change things.'

'What's that?' Caesar was genuinely curious.

'It will take divine intervention for Lucceius to be elected Consul. Cato has given his support to a plan for the entire Optimate faction to pool their resources to see that Bibulus is elected Consul instead. He has come to realize they will not be able to stop you, so they want Bibulus in place to block all your legislation.'

'What's the source of this information?' Caesar had a look of concern.

'Lucceius' nomenclator told me he overheard Bibulus, who was just drunk enough to forget to lower his voice, tell this to Decius in the atrium of Lucceius' villa while the two men were waiting to meet with his master.' I, without thinking, had lowered my own voice while saying it.

'Do you trust Lucceius man?' Caesar was irritated.

'I do,' I responded with a nod. I didn't tell Caesar that Marcus said this while we lay in each other's arms after making love. 'I also heard this from Cicero's man Tiro when we ran into each other two days ago, but I didn't give it much credence because he had it third hand as it were. Cornelia knows a man who works for the launderer who cleans Cato's togas. She is going to have him confirm it with Cato's slave today. I was planning to tell you when I heard back from her.' I also didn't mention that Cornelia was in love with her spy and that I was, on occasion, still making love to Cornelia. 'I hesitated to believe the story since Cato is opposed to any sort of corruption and it is counter to his character to endorse a plan to use bribery to buy an election. How do you suppose the others got him to back it?'

Caesar laughed. 'Cato is a magnificent hypocrite. His "old republican virtue" is a mask he wears to keep his support in the Senate. I suppose, by now, he has come to believe his own legend. I'll bet he justified supporting the drive to buy the election because in his mind it's in the public interest to stop me. Anyway, you are resourceful.' Caesar stood up and began to pace. 'So, what do you think about this problem?'

'I don't know just what to think,' I answered. 'I agree you need Pompeius for his influence, and you can bring him in by offering him legislation establishing farms for his veterans. The current Consuls have been blocking that. I also see why you think you need Crassus. If you cut him out after years of investing in you it will create bad blood, and you don't want him as an enemy. I also don't see how the two will ever work together.' I smiled weakly at Caesar.

Caesar spent a long moment lost in thought, watching the water splashing in the fountain. Finally, as if he came to a decision, he sat and leaned forward resting his elbows on his knees. Before speaking he looked around the room to ensure no one was listening. 'There is another reason I want both of these men on my side.' He said it in almost a whisper.

I leaned forward and waited patiently.

'I've spent my life in Roman politics and I've studied all the players. In all that time, I've never met any man more dangerous than either of these two. They are both where they are today because they will stop at nothing to achieve their ends. Pompeius wanted glory, so he was loyal to Sulla and did his bidding. In those times of terror during the proscriptions, he stained his hands with so much blood he was given the nickname "the young butcher." For his efforts, he was rewarded with great commands. His genius for organizing armies led him to win greater glory than any Roman in history. Now he wants to be accepted as a leader, perhaps the leader, of the political world.'

Caesar once again checked for interlopers by looking over his shoulder. 'When Sulla marched on Rome that first time and was defeated, Crassus was with him. He too dreamt of glory and the defeat of his patron was hard on him. He fled to Hispania when Cinna started to arrest the supporters of Sulla. When Cinna died (84 BC) Crassus joined the Sullan faction gathering in Africa. When Sulla returned from the east at the head of his army, Crassus joined him. Crassus was given command of the right wing in the Battle of the Colline Gate and it was through his success there that Sulla's victory was ensured.

'Crassus' genius seems to compel him to make money. When Sulla instituted the proscriptions against his enemies, Crassus had a role in making the lists and more importantly, in hunting down the men on the list and delivering their heads to Sulla. The man who delivered the head was allowed to keep a significant portion of his estate. On more than one occasion, Crassus convinced Sulla to add the names of men whom he had learned the whereabouts of, so he could sweep in and kill the man for his fortune. In the end, he went too far when he added the name of a man without Sulla's approval. After that, Sulla never again fully trusted him and he was, for the first time, passed over by Pompeius. But, his efficiency in capturing and killing men, often-innocent men, laid the foundation for his fortune. Now, Crassus wants to earn the military glory Pompeius was able to, time after time, snatch from him and at last be recognized as a general as great as his rival.

'Both of these men are too dangerous to have as enemies, so I've always made it my policy to remain close to each of them. They will each, in his own way, try to pit us against each other. Crassus will try to set me against Pompeius and Pompeius will try to set me against Crassus. Pompeius lacks political experience so he will be easier to control, but Crassus is the more dangerous of the two.'

Caesar paused. 'So, Polybius, you can see my dilemma. I must find a way to bring them together while letting each man think he is using me to achieve his own ends. If I bring others into the mix, it will complicate things even more. I want to keep the number of men involved as small as possible. As you know, too many cooks spoil the stew, so the main players must be Crassus and Pompeius.'

I didn't see how it could be done, but I knew if any man in Rome had the intelligence and political savvy to bring those two bitter enemies together, it was Julius Caesar.

'Let's go,' Caesar said, moving toward the front of the house. 'I want you to continue working with Lucceius' man. Give him the impression I believe he will be elected. I don't want to lose his support or his money before I'm elected Consul. Also, as quietly as possible, arrange a meeting with Crassus.'

'Where should the meeting be,' I asked.

'His villa in the Alban Hills, I trust us to be able to visit him with little noise, far more than I trust him to do the same coming to see me.'

With that, we stepped out into the sunlight to be among the men who would elect Caesar to the Consulship. As we walked toward the forum, Caesar seemed to be lost in thought, greeting voters without his usual enthusiasm, prompting me to lean in and say to him, 'Remember, Caesar you need to be here, with the voters. What's troubling you?'

Caesar shook his head and smiled. 'Thank you, Polybius. I was just thinking how in Cato's mind the public interest always coincides with his own interests, and how more often than not, his own interests seem to involve destroying me.'

While Caesar was on the rostrum making a speech I had not only heard ten times before but had helped to write, I went over to the Curia to see if any of Crassus men were waiting under the portico for the start of the Senate's session. It was there I was able to request the meeting. Within the hour, the man found me near the steps of the rostrum and told me the meeting was on for the

next day. The timing irritated me as it would mean rearranging

Caesar's schedule and canceling another assignation with Servilia,

but I was certain this was important enough that Caesar wouldn't

be upset with me about it.

LIBER XIX

The Crassus villa was magnificent. The home now belongs to one of the Metelli and the years have stolen some of its luster, but it is still a wonder to behold. I sat in the atrium, a few feet from Crassus' man, some distance from the tablinum door that we each furtively looked at when we thought the other wouldn't notice. We spoke of small matters, me pretending not to know what the meeting concerned, and him pretending not to care. Near the end of the meeting, voices were raised, or more precisely, the voice of Crassus was raised, but Crassus was a man of many secrets, so years before he had hung heavy tapestries on the walls of the room to muffle any sound from inside and the door was thick. The shouting was followed by a brief period of quiet before the door swung open and Caesar strode from the room. Before I could react, he was walking past me and I had to collect my bag and hurry after him.

In the courtyard of the villa, we both immediately got into our litters to begin our journey home. To disguise the fact that it was Caesar visiting Crassus, I was obliged to ride in a litter so I wouldn't be recognized. I was a little uneasy about slaves having to carry me, but I enjoyed the journey much more than if I were walking or even riding on a mule. Our bearers and litters belonged to Crassus and were attached to one of his houses in the city. We were obliged to rise before the sun and, wrapped in cloaks, make our way in the dark to Crassus' house on the Palatine. By first light, we were already at the Carmentalis gate and out of the city. We didn't stop until we were at the six-mile marker from Rome. I was grateful, since I needed to relieve myself, and wanted to see the slaves rest a bit. It was here that Caesar and I had a chance to speak about the meeting. I couldn't wait for him to bring it up, so I started the conversation while helping Caesar adjust his toga. 'I heard shouting. I'm guessing it didn't go well?'

'It went as well as I expected. I was able to get Crassus onboard by giving up on Pompeius.' Caesar seemed not at all disappointed or concerned.

'But, you said you needed Pompeius. I think you might need him more than you need Crassus.' I was concerned about him. 'After all, he is by now, nearly as rich as Crassus. If he hadn't rewarded his veterans so royally, he would be even wealthier.'

'When we get back to Rome, we will head straight to the bath on the Aventine, where I will meet with Pompeius and get him to agree to work with me without Crassus.'

'I thought you said you need them both.' I was now more concerned.

Caesar clapped me on the back, playfully pushing me toward the litters. 'I need them both, together or not, to ensure my election. After I'm Consul I will need them working together if I'm to accomplish anything. I can't afford to have either of them as an enemy, and if I choose to work with one over the other that will be the situation. I'll also need them both on my side to ensure I'm not dividing my time between 'demarking woodland paths,' and facing trial the year after I'm Consul. One way or another, I'll figure out how to get them to work together with me. They're reasonable men with more to gain by this arrangement than they have to lose. I'll find a way to persuade them. Until then we make them each think I'm just using the other until the election.'

'That is dishonest.' I knew how naïve I sounded as soon as I said it.

'Politics, like war,' he responded mildly, 'depends mostly on deception and good luck. I'm hoping Fortuna still favors me and will supply the good luck. It is, however, always up to the general to supply the deception.' With that, we were climbing into the litters and the slaves were approaching, so we could no longer speak candidly but just before the bearers lifted our litters Caesar leaned over from his to mine and said with a wink, 'I hope you still have connections with the goddess. If she favors you that will help me.' I couldn't tell if he was being impious or if he was serious, but it occurred to me that if he did believe Fortuna favored me, he would never willingly sever my connection to him.

Later that day, in a relatively short meeting with Pompeius Magnus, Caesar was able to bring the general over to his side and ensure his election to the consulship. When he announced this in a strategy meeting with his top associates there was a collective sigh of relief followed by cheers and clapping. Characteristically, it was Aurelia who brought the group back to earth with, 'Let's return to work. This election hasn't been won yet, and anything can happen.' At that formidable woman's suggestion, the group, including her son, did get back to work.

One day after the ides of Quintilis (July 16) the Senate voted on the Proconsular assignments for the consuls of the coming year once they leave office. This was highly unusual as these decisions are never made until well after the election and always involve negotiations with the Consuls who will take up those assignments. It was not at all unexpected when the Optimates browbeat the rest of the Senate into assigning Caesar and his co- Consul the task of demarcating the forest and woodland paths on public land, or some such nonsense. Caesar chose to use this law to his advantage and made speeches in the forum telling the people that the Optimate faction was so afraid of the support he had with the plebs that they would do anything to stop his election."

I was a bit annoyed that Polybius gave so little to that historic meeting between Pompeius and Caesar, and I revealed my irritation with my tone, when I asked, "Before you go on, can you tell us more of the meeting at the baths? After all, wouldn't you consider that the day the Triumvirate was formed?"

Polybius sighed. "One rarely realizes the significance of seemingly mundane events even if they have a great impact on the world. Battles and elections we notice, but the thousands of choices that lead to those great moments are seldom recognized. You use the term Triumvirate, but that is a word only used years later to describe what was conceived that day. I didn't know what was discussed until after the election when Caesar set his associates to the task of quietly building support for the plan he had described to Pompeius that day at the baths. There was, however, one exchange between the two that I was present for that day. As Pompeius was taking his leave, Caesar stopped him. 'There is one more thing, friend.' Pompeius turned back. Caesar continued with, 'since Auletes has attached himself to you as your client, once I'm elected Consul, I'd like you to invite him to Rome to discuss his situation.' Both men smiled conspiratorially before Pompeius nodded and turned to leave. In those days when a Roman used the Greek word for flautist as a name, he was always referring to the reigning pharaoh of Aegyptus. It was to be some time before I realized the significance of that brief exchange."

"What was the plan," I asked. Sometimes Polybius' tendency to meander toward the point was a source of frustration.

"To understand the plan you need to understand the politics of those years."

I glared angrily at Mela when I saw him roll his eyes. He was far more interested in hearing of battles in distant provinces than in the Curia. Polybius noticed our silent exchange and smiled. "My young friend," he said, nudging Mela with his foot, "to appreciate the exciting parts of my story you will need to learn the patience required to endure the background to the story. Your brother is quite right. I should have provided the information you'll need to make sense of things. Homer was only able to start his story with the rage of Achilles in the tenth year of the war with Troy because his audience knew what had come before." Polybius leaned over to pick up his wine cup indicating he was going to provide a long explanation of things, but he paused as he brought it to his lips. "Not that I'm comparing myself to Homer." After taking a gulp of wine, before setting the cup down again, Polybius stared for a moment into the wine in his cup, lost in thought. He blinked twice, breaking the spell the muse had placed him under, and setting his cup down added, "but, now that I consider it, the events that followed were every bit the stuff of epic poetry. Someone should write poetry of those events. Prose cannot do Caesar's life justice."

"At any rate," Polybius said, leaning back and shutting his eyes, "You shall hear of the politics of those days. Without a doubt Caesar had influence. He was, after all, the Pontifex Maximus and a triumphant general, in spite of the fact that his triumph had been snatched from him. He had great influence, but the first man in Rome was, without a doubt Pompeius Magnus. Pompeius had won greater victories than any other general in the history of Rome. Many compared him to Alexander the Great, and Pompeius did everything he could to build on that myth. Looking back, many wonder why he didn't simply seize control of the government of Rome and have himself made dictator, but

Pompeius was made arrogant by his success and could see no reason to subvert the constitution to that degree. He was confident he could get what he wanted through the use of more conventional illegality. He was also confident he could raise an army anytime he needed one. This was true at that time. Unfortunately for him, he deluded himself into believing it was true nearly ten years later. By then, it was too late. Pompeius returned to Rome the day before the nones of Februarius during the consulship of Valerius and Niger (February 4, 61 BC). He refused the many splendid honors offered him by the Senate and only requested he be allowed to postpone his triumph until the end of Septembris of that year. He needed the extra time to plan the most lavish triumph Rome had yet seen. He also wanted the event to coincide with his birthday.

Pompeius was widely expected to seek the consulship, but he had spent his life up to that point fighting the enemies of Rome and not his own political enemies, so he had little acumen for politics. He was content, for now, to use his influence to have a man named Lucius Afranius, one of his most loyal subordinates in the war in the east, elected Consul for the following year. He intended to wait until that year to confirm the political settlement he had made in the provinces in the east. His lack of political skill, however, caused him to miscalculate the level of jealousy his success engendered among his fellow senators. In those days, it was not enough for a man to succeed; he also needed to see others fail. When Pompeius arranged to have a law introduced confirming all of the actions he took in settling the provinces in the east, after the war, he discovered the strength of the opposition to him. His great success had humiliated many proud men. First among them was Crassus. Pompeius first humiliated Crassus when he returned from Hispania many years before to assist in the war against the rebel slave, Spartacus. Crassus had the war all but won, when Pompeius swept in and dealt the final defeat to the rebel army at Sena Herclae (Senerchia). He then took full credit for ending the war. Another influential senator Pompeius had turned into the bitterest of enemies was Lucius Licinius Lucullus. This remarkable man was to lead the Optimate opposition to Pompeius' settlement of the east and more importantly, the law providing for the settlement of Pompeius' veterans on farms in Italy. Pompeius knew how dangerous dissatisfied soldiers could be.

Lucullus and Pompeius had been rivals since they both served in Sulla's army, but while Pompeius was favored by Sulla with extraordinary honors and commands, Lucullus rose in politics in the more traditional way. He achieved the consulship in the same year as Caesar's uncle on his mother's side, Marcus Aurelius Cotta (74 BC), and while Consul he successfully defended Sulla's reorganization of the constitution.

After his consulship, Lucullus drew Cisalpine Gaul as his Proconsular command, but after the Proconsul of Cilica died, he used his influence to have his command transferred to that province. He too craved great military glory and he wanted a command in the east so he could lead the war against King Mithridates VI. Lucullus, for nearly seven years, commanded with great energy and skill in the war against Mithridates and others. On his arrival, he was able to relieve Cotta who was under siege in Bithynia and he then raised a fleet and defeated Mithridates' navy to gain command of the coasts. Lucullus then, avoided a pitched battle because he was wary of his enemy's superior numbers, especially Mithridates' famous cavalry forces. At last, Lucullus defeated the king's forces in a decisive battle at Cabiria.

Rather than pursue Mithridates and capture or kill the king, he conquered the kingdom of Pontus, at last bringing some semblance of order to the east but allowing Mithridates to flee to the kingdom of Armenia. Lucullus made a noble attempt to rein in the greed of the tax collectors in Asia, but failed at this, bringing himself enmity from the senators in Rome who were their silent partners. He then demanded the king of Armenia turn over Mithridates, provoking a war. In a series of successful campaigns, Lucullus decisively defeated the Armenians.

During the winter of his sixth year in the province (68-67 BC) Pompeius could no longer take Lucullus' string of successes. Pompeius paid Lucullus' brother in law, Publius Clodius Pulcher, whom you already know from the Bona Dea scandal he would become famous for years later, a sizeable sum to foment rebellion among Lucullus' troops. At that time, Clodius was still officially a Claudius, but we will get to that in due time. Even before it was official, he preferred the plebeian spelling of the name. Clodius was already feeling he had not been rewarded sufficiently by his father in law and was easy to turn. He was able to start a mutiny among the legion he was serving with that emboldened other legions to, in turn, mutiny."

Mela was once again interested in the story, with talk of war and mutiny, so in his excitement, he interrupted. "Why did Pompeius want Roman legions to mutiny?"

Polybius was patient. "Quite simply, Mela, out of jealousy. Pompeius saw Lucullus' success as a threat to his own dignitas and he wanted the command in the East for himself. It reached the point where the legions would only promise to defend their positions and they refused to obey the commands of their general. The Senate had no other choice but to appoint a new Proconsul, and the most experienced and most popular man available was Pompeius Magnus.

Pompeius' malice didn't end there though. He had arranged for his friends in the Senate to deny Lucullus a triumph. The opposition was so strong that Lucullus' triumph was delayed by nearly three years; during that time he was forced to live outside the boundary of the city, successfully stalling his political career. I believe it may have been his example that caused Caesar to see the futility of trying to seek the consulship in absentia, forcing him to give up his own triumph. Lucullus retired to a life of luxury at that time. He had amassed a great fortune in the East, and he spent lavishly. Indeed, his gardens just outside Rome were so grand they are still regarded as a great marvel. Lucullus' life of luxury led the stoic wit Tubero to call him Xerxes in a toga. Even this Pompeius couldn't leave alone, publishing an epigram where he referred to Lucullus as Xerxes in a dress.

It was said at the time, the only reason Lucullus maintained any interest in politics was to oppose Pompeius, and he did indeed become much more active in the Senate on the return of Pompeius from the East. At any rate, when the sweeping law to confirm Pompeius' settlement in the east was proposed, Lucullus led the opposition. Lucullus demanded each particular of the law be debated separately in the Senate; especially those parts touching on matters that varied from the decisions made by Lucullus himself during his governing of the Eastern provinces. He was supported in these matters by the very influential Metellus Celer who until recently had been brother in law to Pompeius, and the former Consul Metellus Creticus. Even Cato and Crassus worked together to oppose Pompeius' settlement. His man Afranius had little more political skill than Pompeius and faced with the opposition of the powerful men united against the legislation, he was unable to have either law pass. All this came to a head, as it were, in the month of Junius. Caesar was able to secure Pompeius' support by convincing the politically naïve general that there was no hope for the law that year but that he, as Consul, would do whatever it took to see it pass the following year. Pompeius took the bait. With the support and the clienteles of both Crassus and Pompeius Magnus, there was no doubt that Caesar would be elected. On Election Day, the only suspense was supplied by the election of his co- Consul. We of course couldn't afford to worry about that. Aurelia made it clear that we were all to take nothing for granted. It was our duty to work as hard on election day as we did throughout the campaign and to not be complacent or distracted by other concerns, so that is what we did. Caesar's election was announced first, shortly after midday. The vote was so heavily in his favor that it was decided early. As soon as Caesar's election was certain, we took a few moments to celebrate and then all set to work getting the remaining tribes to cast votes for Lucceius. The extra effort did no good, however, as Bibulus, with the support of the Optimates, defeated him rather easily. That night, Caesar hosted a torchlight dinner for his closest friends, once again on the enclosed courtyard of the Regia. We celebrated well into the night, leaving worries about Bibulus for the following morning. That night, Cornelia came to my room and we made love. My heart wasn't in it, but for a young man, the heart is seldom the organ in command when it comes to matters of sex. I knew I would probably never have an opportunity to be intimate with Marcus again, so I made love to Cornelia with a vigor borne of that frustration. Our son slept on a blanket on the floor in the corner of the room. I was surprised our passion didn't wake him, but he was at an age where he would sleep through an earthquake. Afterward, as we lay together, I told

Cornelia of my intention to buy the freedom of both her and our son, allowing them a chance at happiness. She swore to me she would not let Tychaeus forget me, but I knew that would be nearly impossible. Caesar made it clear that he intended to hold onto Imperium. The only way that would be possible was for him to be appointed Proconsul of a province. I also knew he wouldn't be content with a province such as Macedonia that was peaceful and settled since he also craved the sort of glory that can only be won through war. I knew Caesar would take me far from Rome, and my son would grow up thinking of the launderer's assistant as his father. I resigned myself to that fact and was content knowing he would grow up free.

LIBER XX

There was surprisingly little for me to do in the months between the election and the start of Caesar's term as Consul. I focused on getting up to speed with the lives of anyone who mattered. It is astonishing how quickly marriages are arranged and dissolved and how often men disown and adopt sons. Much had changed in our year away from the city and I needed to make necessary adjustments to my memory villas. I was also occupied with religious matters, as Caesar saw his position as Pontifex Maximus as a useful tool for remaining in the minds of the people. In all, the months between Quintilis and Januarius were most pleasant. In spite of hours spent each day on political maneuvering, lining up the support of various praetors, Aediles, and most importantly, Tribunes, and several futile attempts to get Crassus to warm to the idea of working with Pompeius and Pompeius to warm to the idea of working with Crassus, Caesar was much more relaxed. He was able to spend more time with Servilia and Marcia, his other mistress, giving me more time to spend with my own family. From time to time I thought I might be falling back into love with Cornelia, but each time I was able to remind myself that it was the experience of having a family that I loved and not the mother of my child. I was also able to remind myself that as a slave I couldn't ever truly have the type of family I wanted to give my son.

Three days after the ides of Decembris (December 13th) the Saturnalia festival began. I remember being awakened to the smell of smoke and the sound of a woman screaming. I rushed out of my cubicle thinking the domus was on fire. I nearly ran into Cornelia, Tychaeus in her arms, as she ran from the doorway of the cubicle she shared with another slave woman and her child. The screams had stopped and had been replaced by laughter, so we followed the sound to the kitchen, where we found Aurelia and Julia sitting on the bench holding hands and laughing. Both Cornelia and I stood mutely in the doorway not knowing what to make of it when both women slipped to the floor and between giggles began to apologize profusely. Finally, Aurelia said to me, 'the morning meal will be a little late master. Julia forgot to open the flue and she burned the meat.' With that, Julia jabbed her grandmother in the ribs with her elbow and the two women began to laugh again. Aurelia added, 'I'm afraid we're not very good at this.'

I looked over at Cornelia to see that her look of surprise had been replaced by a broad grin. It was only then I remembered it was Saturnalia and we had the next few days free from labor. Not knowing what else to do Cornelia and I made our way to the atrium where we sat on the edge of the impluvium and watched our baby son lean over the side and splash in the water. It was then that Caesar came out of the tablinum, wearing a slave's tunic and smiling broadly. With mock seriousness, he said, 'the other slaves don't know how to cook very well, so I've prepared some dried meat and figs. Would you like to eat here in the atrium or in the garden?

'The garden, I guess,' was all I could think to say, and Cornelia and I with Tychaeus toddling between us made our way to the back of the domus. A long table and chairs had been set up with enough chairs for all the slaves of the house. Some of the other slaves were already seated and Demetrius, also dressed in a slave tunic was going around the table with two pitchers, filling the cups with wine or water. We sat, both forcing smiles and watched as the other slaves came in, taking their places at the table all the while joking, laughing, and singing. In recent days there had been some unspoken uneasiness between Cornelia and me. I assumed it was because I would soon be buying her freedom, but twice in the past few days I had tried to bring the topic up and twice she shook her head and said nothing was wrong. Cornelia and I spoke of trivial things as I watched her pick at her food. The meal turned into quite a feast after two freedwomen attached to the Pontifex Maximus' service took over the cooking duties but Cornelia ate and drank little. After the meal had ended and the household slaves sat around the table enjoying their leisure as Julia and Aurelia cleared the plates, Cornelia handed Tychaeus to the woman sitting beside her and walked rapidly across the garden toward the latrine. I got up to follow, but Marcia who worked with Cornelia in the laundry room grabbed my arm and when I looked at her in irritation she simply shook her head 'no' and followed that with a nod toward my seat indicating I should sit down again. I pulled my arm free and walked to the latrine. When I got there, Cornelia was sitting on the bench beside one of the pots with her head in her hands.

'Are you ill?' I asked. I was truly concerned for her.

'I'm fine,' she said forcing a weak smile. 'The wine made me feel a little nauseous.' Cornelia stood and slid past me in the doorway, saying as she did, 'it's time to get dressed, Caesar will be waiting for you.'

I took Cornelia's hand and stopped her. 'Cornelia, please talk to me.'

She shook her head and looking at the floor said quietly, 'there's nothing to talk about.' With that, she walked toward the women's dressing chamber to wait her turn while Aurelia, Julia, and the free women of the household dressed the slave women.

I made my way toward the rooms where the men would be dressed. Since I was his nomenclator, Caesar made a point of dressing me personally, and this made me a little uneasy, but this year I felt it even more. We were nearly the same height by then, so I noticed Caesar had laid out one of his own long-sleeved tunics and a fine woolen toga with the purple stripe. We were going to the forum to watch slaves make ribald speeches about their masters, telling jokes that at any other time would, at the very least, earn a beating. I slipped out of my slave tunic and stood still as Caesar slipped his tunic over my head. When he began to drape the toga over my shoulder, adjusting the first fold, I stopped him. 'Caesar, may I do it myself?'

Caesar laughed. 'It is almost impossible to get a toga to hang right if you do it yourself, master.'

'Then can you send someone else in to do it?

Caesar laughed again. 'Don't you trust me to do it right?' He then turned serious when he saw I wasn't laughing. 'What's wrong Polybius?'

'It doesn't feel right, you dressing me and waiting on me,' I answered quietly.

'It's Saturnalia! You should enjoy it.' He started to adjust the fold that had slipped. 'You let me dress you every other year.'

I stopped him again. 'This year is different. You're different.'

'I'm different?' He seemed surprised.

'Maybe not different, that's the wrong word.' I paused to collect my thoughts. 'I see you differently. I've seen you as a conquering general. I've watched you govern a province. And now, you are a Consul elect of Rome. Maybe you are different.'

Caesar sighed. 'I'll send Demetrius in. But, we are going to get drunk together today!'

Feeling awkward wearing a toga, I made my way to the other side of the domus. I wanted to say goodbye to Cornelia and our son since I knew I wouldn't be returning home until after he was asleep. I found her alone in her cubicle. When she saw me coming through the open door she quickly dabbed away tears with a small linen cloth she held. I stopped just inside the doorway. 'I came to say goodbye to Tychaeus. He'll be asleep when I get home.' I paused. 'You've been crying.'

She waved me away with the cloth, avoiding looking in my eyes. 'Don't worry about me, it's nothing.'

I thought about turning to leave, but I didn't. 'Cornelia, you must tell me what's bothering you! Neither one of us will have any fun in the next seven days if you don't. I'm your friend, please talk to me.' I sat on the bed next to her trying to not let the toga slip.

'You look funny,' she said, finally smiling.

'You do too.' She was wearing one of Julia's dresses and her face was painted with cosmetics. 'Now, don't change the subject. I'm not leaving until you tell me what's wrong.'

She looked at the floor and said quietly but with an edge to her voice, 'I'm pregnant you idiot!'

I was shocked. I don't know why I hadn't considered the possibility. We still made love on a regular basis. It then occurred to me that I might not be the father of the child. 'Is the child mine?'

Cornelia punched me in the arm. 'Of course, it is,' she hissed.

'I'm sorry,' I stammered. 'I just thought maybe....'

'Sextus and I have not yet had sex. The baby is yours.'

We sat quietly for some time as I came to fully understand the situation. 'Who have you told?' I asked with more urgency than I intended.

'Maia,' she answered.

'Just her? Was there anyone else?' I realized this would put my plan for their freedom at risk.

'Just her. Why is that important? I would have told you first, but I thought you'd be angry.' She had stopped crying.

'Don't tell anyone else. I'm not even sure I have enough money yet to buy you and Tychaeus. I know I can't buy three.' I then leaned over and hugged her.

Cornelia hugging back began to softly cry again. 'You're not angry?'

Breaking the hug I looked in her eyes. 'You've smudged your cosmetics. No, I'm not angry. I've got to go, but remember don't tell anyone about this. We can talk about it when I get home.'

Playfully pushing me away she said, 'we'll talk about it tomorrow. You'll be drunk when you get home.'

LIBER XXI

The relative calm of my life changed dramatically when Caesar swore the oath of the consulship in the Temple of Capitoline Jupiter on the first morning of Januarius. The same morning he presided at the first meeting of the Senate for the new year, and at that meeting, Caesar made a gracious speech telling the Senate that each member needed to be willing to work with every other member in the interest of the people of Rome. Caesar even promised to work together with Bibulus, his colleague in the consulship. He was very careful to address the concerns of the Optimates. He stated outright that he would propose no measure to that august body that would damage the interests of any member of the Senate, and he was careful to keep this promise. Of course, since the Optimates were set to oppose him at every turn, he found it impossible to present any legislation to the Senate after his initial introduction of the lex agraria. The session ended early so everyone could go home or to the baths and continue plotting against each other.

Caesar held a meeting of his closest associates to adjust the strategy they had developed in light of Bibulus' victory. It was during this meeting I came to fully realize how closely Caesar held his own counsel. From the questions asked and the direction of the conversation, it became apparent that the only people in the room who knew about the arrangement Caesar had made with Pompeius Magnus were me and him. Even Crassus, who was sitting on Caesar's right enjoying the victory almost as much as if it was his own, seemed to not understand the machinations that were happening under his nose, as it was. The only plans being made during this meeting were plans to cement relations with useful magistrates lower on the ladder. Caesar needed Tribunes to work with him, for he knew he would need their veto power were he to outmaneuver the Optimates in the Senate. When he proposed Antonius approach Publius Vatinius, even Crassus raised his eyebrows, while bluntly stating, 'that man's an extortionist. You will bankrupt yourself buying his cooperation, and you need to make money this year. I'd like to see some return on all I've invested in your career.'

Caesar proved that day that he was no longer content to regard Crassus as his superior. He always believed he was more intelligent and more capable than the man, and now he intended to prove it. 'If you go along with me, Crassus, you'll make a bigger return than you ever imagined. Vatinius is worth every denarius he demands.' It was a pity for Crassus that he too didn't sense the change in their relationship.

'Why do you say that?' Antonius asked incredulously. 'I agree with Crassus,' he said, adding, 'this time.'

'Vatinius has bronze balls,' Caesar answered calmly. 'Just look at what he's done in the twenty-two days he's held office.'"

Polybius leaned over and picked up a piece of cheese. He held it out as far as he could and when he still couldn't identify it by sight he brought it to his nose and inhaled deeply. "My senses fail me. Can either of you young men tell me what sort of cheese this is?"

Mela quickly identified the cheese as from Gabalis (Gévaudan) and then seizing the opportunity said, "Now you must tell us what Vatinius had done."

Polybius took some time chewing the cheese savoring the taste of it; he sometimes said taste was the last of his senses that continued to work properly. Finally, after a sip of wine, he answered, "quite simply, he stood up to Cato and the other Optimates. Tribunes assume office on the Lux Mundi (December 10) and the very next day he introduced a series of bills that Caesar had already bought in anticipation of the possibility of losing the election. One bill concerned the composition of juries. When Cato, in a speech to the Senate said he would never allow such a bill to become law and, more importantly, the gods would never allow it, Vatinius took to the rostrum and in a speech to the people made it clear that even the gods wouldn't stop him from representing the interests of the Roman people. He bluntly stated he would take not the slightest notice of the alleged omens the Optimates were always observing as a means to obstruct votes on legislation they objected to. I remember that speech particularly well, since Caesar and I wrote it the night before Vatinius delivered it.

The rest of the meeting involved making the determination as to who was to act as the go-between with which praetor or Aedile or the members of the Senate who were with the Populares. At the end of the meeting as Caesar was seeing everyone to the door and watching them, one by one, either walk down the Sacra Via or in some cases, be carried along the road in a litter. At last, Crassus was the only one left in the vestibule. I was just near enough to hear him say, 'Gaius, I'd like a word with you. I've heard you've been talking with Pompeius and I need to know what that is about.' It was unusual for Crassus to refer to Caesar by his praenomen.

'I'm glad you stayed until last.' Caesar's tone was conciliatory. 'I wanted to talk to you about just that.' Caesar turned and led Crassus by the arm back toward the tablinum. I caught his eye, raising my eyebrows questioningly, causing him to give me a slight nod, so I followed the two men. Once inside, they both took seats and I moved with my tablet and stylus to the stool in the corner where I tried to be invisible. Caesar poured wine from the pitcher into two fresh cups and slid one across to Crassus.

'I have been talking to Pompeius. I need his support.' Caesar was speaking in the most reasonable tone.

'You need my support more.' Crassus was firm.

'I need the support of both of you and I'm asking you to promise yours.'

'I will never work with that man!' Crassus' tone was rising and looking around to see if anyone was listening he remembered I was in the room. 'Can we talk in private?' he said to Caesar while staring at me.

Now it was Caesar's turn to be firm. 'Polybius stays. Nothing will be written down.' With that, I set my stylus and tablet on the floor beside me. I spent the rest of the time looking at my hands or my shoes, focused on committing every word to memory so I could write it down later. Caesar softened his tone. 'Marcus, we both know I can get nothing done this year if you oppose me.' Crassus nodded, so Caesar continued. 'We also both know if Pompeius opposes me the result will be the same. I can ask you to step aside and do nothing this year, but that would be an insult and that wouldn't advance your own cause. There are things we each want, and by working together, the three of us can achieve what we desire.'

Crassus grunted a muffled chortle. 'I am the richest man in Rome. What I don't have I can buy. What can you and Pompeius Magnus get me.' He overemphasized the 'Magnus' and sneered.

Caesar remained reasonable. 'You cannot buy everything. Pompeius has wronged you, that much we all know. He overshadowed you and stole your glory at every opportunity. Your strategy now seems to be to prevent him from doing it again, but that will not rub out the past. What is done is done, and to get what you want you need to achieve at least as much as he has, if not more. You're fifty-five years old.'

Leaning back in his chair, Crassus corrected him. 'Fifty-six.'

Caesar ignored him and continued. 'You can oppose Pompeius and run out of time to have the opportunity for the success you so want. Working together, I will see that all three of us have that opportunity. You know the Senate is jealous of each of us and won't allow any one of us a great command. Pompeius may be able to force their hand one more time by appealing to the people, but the world is very different now that Hispania and the east are pacified, and the Senate feels less threatened by the enemies at our borders and more threatened by its own enemies in Rome. The Optimates will stall and delay until you're dead and I'm in exile.'

Caesar paused to let Crassus absorb what he said. Crassus responded less harshly. 'What do you propose?'

Caesar was ready for this. 'I propose nothing short of the three of us working together to take control of the republic. Then we will get what we want; what we need.'

I was shocked by what I heard, but I sat passively as if the two men were talking about the weather or the quality of last year's vintage.

'If we do that, it will mean the end of the republic.' Crassus sounded almost sad.

'The republic is nothing more than a shadow of what it was anyway.' Caesar didn't sound sad. 'Think about what I've said, my friend. I will convince Pompeius that it is in his interest to work with you. I'll get him to agree, and I will ask you both to swear, as I will, to make no important political decision without the consent of each other.'

With that, this most important meeting was over. As Caesar was walking with his hand on Crassus shoulder toward the door, I had already picked up my stylus and was committing the words I remembered to a more permanent form. Later that night I would put pen to parchment and record the meeting in a more lasting way. I still have that document after all these years. Perhaps upon my death, I'll leave it to you, Lucius.

Later that night, just after putting my writing tools away, I approached Caesar as he sat at the table in the tablinum reading the transcript of his conversation with Crassus. 'Master, can I speak with you.' I almost never called Caesar 'master,' and this put him on guard.

With a look of concern, he asked, 'what is it, Polybius.'

'There's something important I'd like to talk to you about.'

Caesar set down the parchment and gestured for me to sit in the other chair. I took a breath and continued. 'I'm not sure if I have enough money, but I would like to buy Cornelia and Tychaeus. The sale of a slave attached to the Domus Publica requires the consent of the Consul and the Pontifex Maximus. You are now in a position to grant that permission. Cornelia's position is easily filled by others and our son contributes nothing to the house, so it would make sense to sell them both. Cornelia has already arranged a place to live, so you will not need to support her.'

I intended to go on with much more in the same vein when

Caesar cut me off with a wave of his hand. 'Save your breath and your money, Polybius. I have no intention of selling either of them.'

My heart sank. 'Why not master? It would mean little to have them gone.'

'You are being disingenuous with your arguments,' Caesar answered. 'Cornelia has a level of expertise I have rarely seen in a slave launderer. What she does may not be a widely appreciated function, but it is important. And, your son, based on what I know of you and what I've already seen in him, promises to grow up to be a very useful man someday.'

His words devastated me. 'May I go now, master?'

Caesar ignored me and went on. 'You worked as hard as anyone preparing for my election, and that put me in a position to grant your wish. I'm not going to let you buy Cornelia and your son to just give them their freedom. Draw up the necessary documents and I'll grant them both their freedom outright. You need not buy them. You get very little thanks, Polybius, so consider this a gift from me.'

As low as I was feeling I rose even higher. I sat there beaming, when Caesar stood up, saying, 'what are you waiting for? Draw up the documents and we'll submit them in the morning. Go.'

I jumped up ready to run when Caesar stopped me by laying his hand on my shoulder. 'I must say, it's very noble of you to wish to buy the freedom of Cornelia and your children just so they can have a life with another man. I'm not sure I would do the same.'

With that, he sat back down and started to re-read the transcript. As I turned to go, his words struck me. Caesar had said 'children' when he spoke. He not only knew Cornelia had plans to live with another man, but he knew she was pregnant. This shouldn't have surprised me, as nothing remains secret among slaves, but few masters take such an interest in slave gossip.

The following morning I ran to Cornelia's cubicle so I could tell her the news. Needless to say, she was overjoyed. I wished we had more time to celebrate, but I had to begin my work day. Still, it was one of the sweetest moments of both our lives.

LIBER XXII

The following morning was the start of the Compitalia festival. At sunrise Caesar, dressed in the robes of the Pontifex Maximus, followed by Aurelia and Julia and all the members of the household including the slaves, filed out into the Sacra Via to stand before the Domus Publica. Some of the slaves were grumbling because the morning was cold, and Cornelia was in an irritable mood because she had stayed awake well past dark helping the other slave women prepare the woolen figures and the balls of wool to be presented to the goddess. I, on the other hand, felt honored to be part of the ceremony. I have always been pious and to this day I take religion very seriously. I was a little troubled by the way Caesar seemed to hurry the process of placing the statue of Mania, that most terrible goddess of the dead at the doorstep, and following his lead everyone else felt the need to rush things. I paused as I presented my ball of wool to hang at the door and said a prayer for all the dead and those who would die this year that they would have a pleasant stay in the goddess' realm. After our little ceremony, most of the household went into the domus, but Caesar, Antonius, Salvius and a couple of other men, and I made our way to the Regia where the other Pontiffs and their slaves met us. From there we proceeded a short way down the Sacra Via to where it crossed the Argiletum to make the sacrifice of honey cakes to the Lares of the city. We were met with the plebeian and equestrian neighborhood magistrates, each wearing the toga praetexta. As you no doubt know, for this festival, it is slaves who assist with the sacrifice since the Lares always take great pleasure in the service of slaves. Traditionally, slaves have a day of liberty similar to those days of the Saturnalia, but in reality, this is only offered to the slaves of those who are not engaged in any public business. Since public business is held on this day, my staff of secretaries and I were obliged to attend the Senate with Caesar. It was on this day he presented the lex agraria.

The day after that, following the salutatio, we walked across the forum, the seven lictors clearing a path to the Carmentalis gate. Once the lictors passed through the gate they exchanged the fasces with the ones wrapped around the axe. Having crossed the Pomerium, Caesar's lictors now carried the symbols of supreme Imperium; that is, the right to inflict the death penalty. Our destination was the censor's office in the Villa Publica, where we filed the necessary documents granting my family's freedom. I recall the intense feeling of accomplishment I had at that moment, but my personal concerns were only allowed a short amount of time, as greater things were in the works. While leaving the censor's office we quite by chance encountered Crassus. This chance encounter had, of course, been carefully planned. Crassus made a great show of postponing his business so he could walk with his friend the new Consul. As we passed the temple of Spes just outside the gate we, again quite by chance, encountered Pompeius on his way to the temple of Fortuna and Caesar and Crassus decided to join him in making a sacrifice. After the sacrifice, which was too perfunctory for my liking, Caesar, Pompeius, and Crassus met in the antechamber of the temple and swore an oath to abide by the agreement Caesar had worked out and what the world now refers to as "the First Triumvirate" was born. Later that month they would meet again in the Temple of Capitoline Jupiter and confirm the oath, but this is the day the agreement was made real and the agenda they had planned was set in motion. Immediately after this, the three men went directly to the Curia to await a quorum of senators. It was not long before the requisite number of senators was in attendance and Caesar began the meeting. After the traditional prayers, without addressing unfinished business from the previous session, Caesar proposed a most ambitious piece of legislation. I was excited and feeling a bit light-headed as I awaited his signal. With a nod he let me know I was to bring him the scroll with the text of the lex agraria. I knew the law by heart as I had copied out its many revisions as Caesar, Crassus, and Pompeius hammered it out during the month prior.

'Today,' Caesar began in a loud clear voice that echoed off the walls of the Curia, 'I propose a law that will benefit every citizen of this great city. Today, there are countless Romans without the means to feed and shelter their families. Today, there are countless more who are able to find shelter in only the most dangerous and unhealthy conditions. It is not the fault of these good citizens that they cannot provide for themselves and their children. When these citizens of Rome rise up and riot it is a natural response to the shame and humiliation we lay on them. Men want to serve a purpose and there is no greater service than service to Rome. We need to allow these idle men longing for purpose, to work for their city, and what nobler work is there for those who have served their time under Roman arms or have not yet been called to do so than to work the land and provide for fellow citizens. I have heard members of this body heap blame on these citizens, calling them lazy idlers and leeches, but it is not their fault. No, the fault lies with us, the cities fathers, for neglecting our children. We need to provide the means for the poor of Rome to be self-sufficient. It is good that we provide grain to the poor so they have their daily bread, but this is a bandage covering the festering wound. Free grain only saps the men of the spirit that makes Romans great. Our fathers, fathers tilled the soil and provided food for not just their own tables, but for the tables of the craftsmen and merchants of Rome. Now our daily bread is made from grain imported from Sicilia or far off Aegyptus when vast tracts of land lay uncultivated right here in Italia.' There was more in this same vein, designed to show the moral necessity of the law he was about to propose. After his carefully constructed introduction that had a good number of senators nodding and murmuring in agreement and another large portion scowling and shaking their heads, with the majority, shifting nervously on the benches, Caesar laid out the meat of his law. He had been careful to address all the concerns of the previous agrarian laws that the Senate had found objection to.

As he presented the bill, all land in the province of Italia was to be made available for distribution excepting the land in Campania, which he proposed Rome keep because of its excellent quality. A commission of twenty of the most excellent men, so that many might share the honor, with a committee of five within this group conducting most of the work, would be elected by the people to oversee the purchase and distribution of the land, and Caesar was very careful to exclude himself from eligibility to sit on the commission so there would be no hint that he intended to prosper from this law. Caesar further proposed that only land that was voluntarily offered for sale would be purchased not at the arbitrarily reduced prices previous laws had proposed, but at the value the land held at the most recent census. Past laws had incurred the rancor of senators by insisting an investigation be made into the legality of land ownership. For years, wealthy senators had been encroaching on public land and expanding their vast farms by quietly moving the boundaries onto land belonging to the state. Caesar now proposed there would be no investigation as to the rightful ownership of any land that was already occupied or being farmed. The colonists were to consist of Pompeius' veterans of the eastern wars but with the majority to be selected from the list of Roman men who had families with three or more children. The grants of land were to be inalienable for twenty years, overcoming the objection that the new owners would simply sell the land and return to the city. Previous laws of this type were objected to on the basis of a lack of funds to make the purchases. Caesar proposed in his law that the land would be bought using the treasure Pompeius had captured from the cities of Magna Graecia and the ample proceeds still coming in as tribute from Pompeius' eastern conquests. When this part of the law was read out, all heads turned toward Pompeius, expecting him to object, but he simply sat very upright, solemnly nodding in agreement.

There was a long silence punctuated by the echo of a random cough or the sound of the shuffling of feet following the reading of the law. The silence was broken when a slave standing near me along the wall dropped his tablet and stylus with a loud clatter. This acted as a sort of signal for the men to start talking among themselves. Caesar had planned for the start of this informal discussion and he loudly asked for decorum in the chamber. It took some time to get the senators' full attention again, and when he did, Caesar finished his remarks. 'It would seem you all want to discuss this matter, and it is only right we debate a law of such importance, but it is proper that we do it in a fashion that lends credit to our deliberations. Therefore, I will call each of you by name and ask you to voice your criticism of my proposal. I give you my word I will adjust or, if necessary, strike out any clause to which you object provided you can state a sound reason for your objection, which I may have overlooked. My man will record your objections and they will be published tomorrow.'

With that, Caesar signaled me to step forward to record the objections of the senators as he called on them one by one. In spite of my discomfort standing before the Senate, I had to smile at the way Caesar had stressed the word "published," putting the Optimates on notice that the people would read and hear of their objections. I stood poised to etch the objections into the wax of my tablet, one by one; starting with Crassus who as an ex- Consul was first asked his opinion, followed by Pompeius. Each, of course, gave an enthusiastic endorsement of the law. As for the rest, the majority of the senators who were not closely aligned with Caesar, Crassus, or Pompeius, either said they had no objection at this time or silently shook their heads. Cato rose to his feet and said that while he had no objection to any particular part of the law, he didn't feel that it was a good time to introduce any innovations. While it embarrassed the Optimates, not a single member of the Senate could find cause to object to the law, as everyone agreed that something needed to be done about the problems caused by the multitude of idle men, women, and children choking the streets of the city. As the last senator's name was called, I showed my blank tablet to Caesar, prompting him to dismiss me with a nod. With that, Balbus rose to his feet and moved that the matter be put immediately to a vote. This was followed by several objections, not of the bill, but on fine points of procedure. Finally, a motion was put forth to adjourn the session and postpone a vote for two days. This proposal was carried more as a result of the discomfort many members were starting to feel at the prospect of the session being dragged out until sunset. With that, the session was over and I stood watching Caesar as he stood on the low platform watching the members of the Senate file out the large door of the Curia. At last, it was just Caesar and his closest associates and the slaves standing in the empty chamber.

The next day, Caesar mounted the rostrum in the forum and, without mentioning the law he had proposed, made a very elegant speech outlining for all who would listen, the seriousness of the problems caused by too many people with too few jobs living in Rome. As expected, the speech was very well received and much talked about. When Caesar seemed to be at the end of his speech, his voice rose again with passion and he described the law he had proposed the day before. From the crowd in the forum came an enthusiastic response. He carefully argued that his proposed law would address each of the serious ills affecting the city. At several points, his speech was interrupted with cheers and chants from the people in the forum. When the enthusiasm was at its peak, Caesar turned toward Bibulus who had been standing off to the side of the rostrum deriding Caesar's speech to a group of his supporters and invited him up on the platform to give his opinion of the law. Bibulus, who was already more than a little drunk, was never good at handling crowds, but he realized it would give a very bad impression if he refused to speak to the people, so he reluctantly mounted the steps and stood beside Caesar on the rostrum.

Bibulus would have been better off if he had declined to speak, as all he could do was to repeat the opinion Cato had given in the Senate. 'I oppose no particular of the law my colleague proposes, but this is not the year to introduce any new innovations.' His voice cracked with nerves.

Caesar addressed his fellow Consul, but in a voice that was meant for the crowd. 'What will it take to gain your support for this law the people so desperately need?'

The crowd went wild, shouting and stamping their feet they called on Bibulus to consent. For some time, Bibulus continued to try to quiet the people with calming gestures and soothing words that could not be heard above the shouting. All the while Caesar continued to try to persuade Bibulus to support the law.

As mobs of people will, the crowd began to act more as one being. Someone shouted out in Latin, firmo lex, calling on Bibulus to support the law, and others picked up on it. When Caesar saw what was happening he began to make sweeping motions with his arms, causing his toga to slip down around his waist. With each sweep of his arms he shouted 'firmo lex,' and soon the entire forum was chanting along with him. Bibulus was sweating profusely and finally shouted 'enough! As Consul I demand you hear me!'

Caesar quickly quieted the people to allow Bibulus to speak. The forum that just a short time before was filled with the din of the crowd was now nearly silent. I recall a dog barked in the distance as Bibulus, red with anger wiped the sweat from his brow with the edge of his toga. His voice shaking, Bibulus shouted to the crowd, 'Even if every man in Rome wants this law, you shall not have it this year!' With that, he stormed down the steps of the rostrum and was swept away by his supporters and his lictors.

Caesar conducted no public business on the following day (January 4), instead, he chose to focus on private financial matters with Demetrius. He very much needed to finalize an investment in a tax-farming company. Since patricians couldn't engage in such business practices, like most members of the Senate Caesar had a trusted freedman act as the official investor in the firm. In his case, Demetrius stood as proxy for much of Caesar's private business dealings. The day spent without public appearances also gave the people an opportunity to talk about and form opinions of Caesar's agrarian law. Although he didn't publicly list the particulars of the law in his speech, he made certain the details of the law he proposed leaked out into the sea of public opinion.

LIBER XXIII

The next day a meeting of the Senate was called and it was moved that the Senators vote on Caesar's proposed law. Before the vote was called though, Cato moved that all other pending business from previous sessions be discussed and voted on. The Optimates were, of course, able to drag these matters out until the session ended due to the sighting of a bad omen by one of the Tribunes in the pay of their faction. Caesar remained patient for several more meetings of the Senate, and each time one or more senators would stand and make a heartfelt speech assuring the Consul that his decree would be passed this session, but each time another excuse was found to postpone the Senate vote. Things finally came to something of a resolution fifteen days before the calends of Februarius (January 15). Caesar was growing quite frustrated with the tactics of the Optimate faction and it had become apparent to him that they were delaying the vote until the following month when Bibulus would hold the fasces and they would be in a better position to direct events.

The evening before, I was instructed to dispatch boys to the homes of Pompeius and Crassus insisting they arrive early for the Senate session that morning so they could meet with Caesar. Caesar and I arrived first and he was waiting in one of the anterooms in the curia when first Pompeius and then, a short time

196

later, Crassus arrived. They each left their slaves on the portico and I led them into the room together. By now the two men had grown accustomed to my attendance at their meetings and neither offered any objection when I followed them in and shut the door.

Caesar was pacing when we entered the room. 'They are going to delay until Februarius.'

Crassus sat on the marble bench along the wall. 'We shouldn't be here. If they hear we're meeting they will suspect we've made an arrangement.' He looked glum.

'It's too late to care about that now.' Caesar was angry, but controlled his voice, with its tone rising but not its volume. 'We need to act and we need to do it now.' It was at that point I noticed Caesar was rolling three dice in his left hand.

'What can we do?' Crassus asked, tilting his head up and leaning forward.

'If they try to block the vote today we bring it to the people.' Caesar continued to pace.

Pompeius spoke for the first time. 'I agree with Caesar. At some point, they'll realize we've entered into an agreement. Why not now?'

'Even if we put it to a vote by the plebs, Bibulus will be watching the sky for omens and he will block it.' Crassus said. 'What do we do then?'

'Ignore him. Ignore them all.' Pompeius said in a matter of fact voice.

'My feelings exactly, my friend.' Caesar said, tucking the dice into a fold in his toga and placing his left hand on Pompeius' shoulder.

'They won't sit down for that.' Crassus was warming to the idea. 'We will have to expect there could be violence.'

Pompeius answered him. 'I've brought more than twenty thousand veteran soldiers back from the east, and they want farms to live on. If there is violence I need only to stamp my foot and they will be at our backs.'

'Then we are agreed,' Caesar said, 'today I try to force the vote and if they try any of their tricks I put them on notice. If the vote doesn't happen today we take it to the plebs tomorrow.'

'Agreed,' the other two men said in unison.

With that Caesar nodded to me and I opened the door and stood to the side to allow the three men to pass out into the main hall of the curia. From where I stood I could see Bibulus had arrived and was standing talking with at least ten of the Optimate senators. They stopped talking and eyed the three men suspiciously as they split off from each other, Caesar to his place as presiding Consul and the others to their own men in the Senate. A short time later, Cato arrived with several more senators and Bibulus immediately joined him and they had a whispered, but very animated, conversation.

Once again, Bibulus moved to discuss the lex agraria. Caesar, with less patience than he had on previous days, began to call on members to discuss their objections to the law. Several members of the Optimate faction made long speeches on the glory of Rome and the greatness of her citizens, avoiding the point entirely. When it came time for Cato to speak he launched into one of the variations of the same speech he had already given twice in two previous sessions. 'My fellow distinguished senators,' he began. 'As you know, I am a man of principle and while I find no particular fault with this law the Consul has presented to us, I believe it is in the best interests of the Senate and People of Rome to make no innovations of this magnitude this year. On general principles, I believe we need to adhere to the system that has served our city well since the days of our ancestors and take no steps beyond what has worked so well for so long.'

From past experience, Caesar knew this would lead to a long history of not only the city of Rome but of Cato's distinguished family. This speech was intended to delay the vote by hours and force an adjournment due to darkness before it could be called. Caesar had had enough of this and said so, cutting him off. 'Senator Marcus Cato, we have heard this speech before!' Cato stared dumbly at him, temporarily stunned by the breach of senatorial procedure. Caesar continued, his voice rising even more. 'We are the fathers of Rome and we are neglecting our children. We must call a vote on this matter!'

Cato looked at Caesar and regaining his composure answered him. 'So you have said before. It seems I am not the only one who repeats himself when speaking of matters he thinks are important. Please, Consul, respect the rules of this house and allow me to continue.' I was watching this exchange with great interest since I knew Caesar would not back down today.

'No you may not continue! If you say another word I will have you dragged to the Carcer if need be.' With that, he signaled to the chief lictor standing at his place along the wall, and the man moved forward with two other lictors following him.

Caesar had most likely expected Cato to have a Tribune veto the Consul's order, but Cato was too keenly aware of his reputation as a righteous defender of virtue so he simply said, 'I can see you intend to make a mockery of our hallowed traditions and ignore the ancient procedures of this body. I will not fight you. I will remove myself to prison because I respect the Imperium of the Consul, however unfit the man who holds that office may be. With that, he turned and walked toward the door. Once the Senate returned to order, the debate continued with Caesar calling on the next man, but one by one several of Cato's supporters rose and left the curia. Caesar had clearly not expected this and grew angrier at each departure. Finally, he shouted at the last man to make his way down from the benches. 'Marcus Petreius! You ignore your duty and walk out of here before the session is adjourned?'

Petreius was the man who led the forces that cornered and killed Catilina. He had, up until this time, been sitting on the fence. It was clear now that he stood firmly with the Optimates. He turned and faced Caesar. 'I prefer, Consul, to join Marcus Cato in prison rather than remain here with you.'

The Senate was in an uproar and it was clear there would be no vote that day, so after spending a good deal of time bringing the Senate back to order, Caesar said in a loud, clear, and very controlled voice, 'I have gone to great trouble in this matter. I have made you the masters and the judges of this law, so that if any part of it did not suit you, it should be remedied here in this chamber and should not be brought before the people; but since you are not willing to pass even a preliminary decree, the people shall decide for themselves.' With that, he ordered Cato's release from prison and adjourned the session, however, the damage was done and Cato had scored a victory over him. Unfortunately for Cato, he hadn't realized that Caesar had already planned for the eventuality that the Optimates would obstruct the vote in the Senate.

On that same day, Caesar began publishing a record of the official proceedings of the Senate and the popular assemblies. This official record is still, to this very day, issued twice each month and posted and read out in the forum. Caesar wanted to establish this practice, so each of his acts that was intended to help the people of Rome would be known to everyone, and each attempt to block those acts by his enemies in the Senate would also be known to all. As one of the first items on the agenda for that first meeting of the Senate was the Consular slaves that were to be allowed to attend Caesar and Bibulus in the Curia or the temples where the Senate met. There have always been official slaves owned by the state in the name of the Senate and People of Rome, attached to the various magistrates to assist them in their official duties. As the importance of the Consulship declined since Augustus established a monarchy, this number has steadily grown. In those days there were six state-owned slaves attached to the Consul who were allowed to attend him in meetings of the Senate, in addition to as many personal slaves he could convince the Senate to allow him. Most new Consuls try to have the number be as large as possible to enhance their own authority, but Caesar didn't wish to fight his first battle over something quite so trivial, requesting only five personal slaves. I was, of course, on that list, so in addition to my other duties, I was to oversee a staff of four clerks attached to the office of Consul to compile the information and compose the official record.

LIBER XXIV

Servilia's husband was away from Rome on business so, on the pretext of visiting Aurelia, she was able to come to the Domus Publica. As usual, Caesar and his lover dined alone in the triclinium and then retired to a chamber Caesar had set aside for lovemaking, where they spent more than an hour behind the heavy wooden door. After that, Servilia did actually visit with Aurelia and Julia in the garden while Caesar and the three women played a game of dice.

It was late in the evening when Servilia left and Aurelia and Julia retired to their rooms.

After seeing Servilia to the door and safely into her litter, Caesar returned to the garden where he sat at the table, seemingly lost in thought. I couldn't sleep, so with nothing else to do, I found myself a cloak and one for Caesar and went out into the garden. I found Caesar casually rolling the dice, picking them up, and rolling them again. He didn't hear me come up in the shadows behind the lampstand, so I shuffled my feet, causing him to look up. 'I've brought you a cloak, Caesar. It's getting cold.'

Caesar had removed his toga and wrapped that around his shoulders, so he really didn't need the cloak but, just to be polite I suppose, he stood and replaced the toga with the woolen cloak, throwing the unused toga over the back of one of the chairs. I helped him fasten the clasp to secure it. He rolled the dice once more and then looked up at me. 'Sit, please,' he said while gesturing to the chair.

'Would you like more wine?' I asked, feeling strangely sorry for him. He had just been elected Consul and spent a very pleasant evening with his family and the woman he loved. I couldn't understand why he seemed so troubled.

'More wine will only cause me to wake up before sunrise, needing to piss.' Caesar smiled while he continued to watch the dice as he rolled them across the board.

I knew from experience that Caesar's invitation for me to sit meant he wanted to use me to think through some idea or other that was troubling him, so I sat quietly, with patience. It didn't take long for him to stop rolling the dice and begin to speak. 'I've become Consul. I should be satisfied with that. I've reached the top of the ladder. I can simply do nothing all year and it won't change that fact.'

Caesar paused, so it was time for me to offer the counter-argument. 'There are things the people need and you're now in a position to help them.'

'Anything I do with be opposed by Cato and his faction. They've already demonstrated they are willing to use any means possible to accomplish this. Look at what they've done to block the necessary laws to settle Pompeius' veterans and to prevent my triumph.' Caesar once again picked up the dice and began rolling them around in his hand.

'What are the most likely means they'll use to stop you?' I asked.

'Cato has already shown his capacity to talk for hours, forcing the Senate to adjourn without a vote,' Caesar said this with a smile.

'Then you can take your legislation to the people and let them vote in the Comitia, directly for the laws.'

'And,' Caesar countered, 'The Optimates will stop the people from voting by finding ill omens at every turn."

'You are the Pontifex Maximus,' I countered.

'That means nothing. They have the other Consul on their side, and even a priest can't prevent Bibulus from watching the sky and observing the flight of the birds. I can't legally overrule him.'

I shook my head and said, 'if the old proverb that tells us the voice of the people is the voice of the gods is true, I wonder what god was speaking when the people elected Bibulus as your co-Consul.'

'Whichever god it was, he is certainly not making it easy for me,' Caesar said with a sigh.

I was at a loss. 'Do you have any weapons at hand to counter these measures?'

'No, unless you count the ill will of the plebs. But, my enemies will also be able to sway public opinion. The people can be fickle, and there are more men of influence in Cato's faction than on our side, and they have a great number of clients among them.'

I could tell Caesar had an idea, but he wasn't yet ready to put it into words, so I went on. 'Pompeius and Crassus both have a vast number of clients. Pompeius has his veterans too. They need to get them here for the votes, but that won't do any good if the votes are canceled by bad omens.'

Caesar began to roll the dice around in his hands again, before finally casting them onto the board. 'I can ignore them.' He said this quietly but forcefully. 'I can ignore their omens and I can silence their long-winded speeches. I'm the one with the Imperium.'

'Wouldn't that violate the constitution?' I asked. 'Wouldn't that mean certain exile next year?'

'Not if I can hold onto Imperium,' he answered. It seemed as if a cloud had passed. Caesar had come to a decision.

'How can you do that?' I asked him, 'when they've promised to have you demarking woodland paths next year. They'll never give you the kind of Imperium that will keep you from standing trial.'

'Then,' he responded, 'I'll just have to take the Imperium for myself.'

I had come to expect Caesar to take chances, but I never expected him to go this far, so I asked the question to which I already knew the answer. 'How will you be able to do that?'

He rose to his feet signaling it was time to retire for the night before speaking. 'I guess I'll just have to violate the constitution a little more.'

That night was the last night I spent with Cornelia. It was both bitter and sweet. She waited up for me, and though I was tired, we talked about the good times we had and made love in a slow and tender way. I was especially touched when she promised she would save her money and buy my freedom. Of course, we both knew that could never happen. We then drifted into a deep sleep. I thought I had slept late, when, through my closed eyelids I could see bright light as if the sun was already high enough to have reached the small window near the ceiling. Then I felt a finger brush my cheek. Instantly, I realized this was another visit from Fortuna. I opened my eyes to see her beautiful face and her intense eyes staring at me. She stood silent as I sat up, and even then she didn't move or speak. I didn't think she would say anything, but as soon as I was about to speak she said in her musical voice, 'Do not fear the future, Polybius. There will be times, both difficult, and easy. There will even be times that are tragic, and glorious. My hand is always on the rudder.' With that the light faded and she was gone. It took me some time to fall back to sleep.

LIBER XXV

The year of Caesar's Consulship seemed to move at the pace of a chariot race. There were times I was quite literally breathless, running between the curia and Caesar's various contacts among the lesser magistrates. Fortunately, by this time, I only needed to personally deliver the most critical information. I had on my staff a very fleet-footed boy who did most of the actual running. There were so many important political decisions made that year, decisions that affected the whole of the world, as Rome was and is the world's center. Once Caesar made the decision to disregard the constitution events became easier to manage but more dangerous.

I recall a discussion I had with Caesar one evening just after his decision to move against the Optimates and make a political stand. We were working, as usual, me at my writing desk and Caesar reading dispatches from the provinces. Myron, my secretary was going to fetch a fresh lamp and the other man had excused himself to go to the latrine, leaving Caesar and me alone. Boldly, I asked him, 'how many more fronts can you fight on in this war with the Optimates? Sooner or later you may find yourself plunging from the Tarpeian Rock.'

Caesar paused in his reading and considered the matter. 'As long as I keep the plebs on my side, I'll never be taken up to the Rock by an angry mob, and the Senate would never vote such a punishment without the backing of the people.'

'How can you be so certain?'

'With few exceptions, the Senate is composed of cowards. They know their decisions become precedents and someday they too could suffer the same fate. No, the worst they will do to one of their own is to banish him to a dismal little island somewhere. Those we must worry about are not my enemies in the Senate, but my friends. Success can make friends turn, and only the gods can protect a man from those closest to him.' With that, Myron returned with the lamp and Caesar returned to his reading and me to my writing.

I was surprised at the ease with which Caesar was able to convince Crassus and Pompeius to abandon the constitution, but in looking back I've come to realize this should not have been unexpected. Both men had long considered themselves far above others, and both had lived through and prospered as a result of Sulla's dictatorship. I suspect they each fancied they were using Caesar and the other to become the sole and supreme master of Rome. Unfortunately for them, Caesar had a military and political genius far superior to theirs, and while he was their junior partner in terms of experience and wealth, Caesar was the Consul and held Imperium, allowing him to direct events.

That day, just before sunset, Caesar formally called for a contione to be called for two days hence. By working well into the night my staff and I were able to produce enough copies of the announcement to have the news posted in every part of the city and all the towns within a half day's walk to the city. In several places, it was even arranged to have the news read aloud by men trained in elocution."

With that, Mela interrupted. "I've heard about the contione, but I really don't know what it is." I was surprised by his admission of ignorance on any matter.

"In those days the contione still meant something. Now they are only called when the emperor wants to make a show of respect for the 'republic.' A contione was a meeting of the people with the sole purpose of educating the citizens on the particulars of a law they would soon be asked to vote on. In the early days of the republic, the senate was only meant to act as an advisory body to the Consuls, but later on, they became the source of legislation and the ultimate arbitrators of whether or not many laws were good for the citizens. With the legions of citizens living in Rome, it became impossible for the plebs to gather and vote for or against most of the laws that were needed to govern and bring order to a growing empire. As the republic faltered and died, the contione served as a means of stepping around the wishes of the senate and Consuls. It was rare, indeed, for a Consul to call for one, but there had never been a situation where the Consul and his powerful allies were in such direct and irreconcilable opposition to the Senate.

Foolishly, the Optimates didn't, at first, take the contione seriously. Caesar and his allies in the Senate were able to make the speeches from the temple steps to the crowd gathered in the forum with the Optimates merely watching from the distance and laughing at the display. They didn't believe Caesar would make much of an impression on the plebes and they trusted on the strength of their own clientele to blunt the effect of these meetings. They also knew that they could use ill omens to delay the vote until the following month when Bibulus would hold the fasces and strengthen their position against Caesar. What they didn't count on was Caesar's severe, yet elegant use of the Latin language as a powerful tool of persuasion. They also expected the vote to be called for the next day. Instead, Caesar called for another and then still another contione. In all, four contiones were called before the Sementivae began. The Sementivae have also fallen by the wayside, as it were. They were festivals in honor of the sowing of a variety of crops. A way to implore the gods for good harvests. Caesar called no senior magistrates to speak to the people at these meetings. After Bibulus had shown his disdain for the will of the people he left no opportunity for the Optimates to make amends. Instead, he called senior senators who supported the law. This was the first real indication that Caesar had entered into an arrangement with Crassus and Pompeius, as they each spoke in support of the lex agraria. In a carefully staged demonstration, Caesar worked the crowd to beg Pompeius to see that the bill he supported become law.

Pompeius always loved to hear the people shout his name and

he basked in their adulation. Finally, he stepped forward and quieted the crowd. Turning toward Caesar he said clearly and loudly, 'Consul, the people of Rome and my veteran soldiers need this law. You have my absolute support in the Senate and you have my word, should anyone take up the sword to oppose this law, I will take up my shield and my sword to oppose him!' The crowd went wild.

On the final day before the festival, Caesar called for the vote to take place six days before the calends of Februarius. Since the plebes were not obliged to work during this three-day festival, there was ample opportunity for them to gather in the taverna and streets to discuss the law. The festival also drew many people in from the outlying areas of the city, making them available for the vote. Since the slaves were also not obliged to work, it became nearly impossible for the opposition to mount much of a public campaign against the lex agraria. I and much of Caesar's staff of slaves working on 'political' matters voluntarily continued to work. For most of those under my supervision, the willingness to work was not purely out of respect for our master but was motivated by my making it clear that those who didn't choose to continue working would be transferred to very unpleasant positions in the ranks of Caesar's growing numbers of slaves. I also pointed out that Caesar had recently made the purchase of some copper mines and these mines were currently short of workers. I was, in large part, motivated by my admiration of Caesar but, like a dark cloud overhead, I was always aware that should Caesar fail in retaining Imperium, I would face torture to provide evidence against him.

Four days before the calends of Februarius (January 27) was marked as the day for the vote to take place. That morning as Caesar was being shaved, I reported the status of his plans to him. The vote was to be taken early, so we were to be under the portico of the temple of Castor and Pollux just after sunrise. This location was chosen for the vote as there was more room at that end of the forum and we were expecting a large turnout. 'Have we heard from everyone?' Caesar was calm; I was not.

'Calvinus was the last to report. Everyone is in place,' I answered.

'Good,' Caesar replied. 'What about Pompeius' men? Did his veterans bring their swords?'

This alarmed me. Before answering, I looked Caesar in the eye and then looked sideways at the man shaving him. This slave was new, and I didn't know him.

Caesar smiled. 'At this time, it matters very little who hears of our plans. Either all goes well, or we will need to use force. Cato must realize we've planned for this, so either way, the fact that I've placed armed men in the forum will not be a secret for very long.'

I was still uncomfortable. 'Yes, Caesar, the men are all in place.' Since before dawn, Caesar's supporters had been moving into strategic points in the forum. It was important the Optimates not block the roads on the north and east sides of the forum, as these were the places where most of the plebs would enter. To see this wouldn't happen, Pompeius had arranged to have his veteran troops station themselves at the key points and at the Vicus Tuscus at the south end. Many of these men had swords or daggers hidden in their togas and breastplates under their tunics. Others had short clubs tucked into the folds of their togas. To demonstrate his loyalty to Caesar, Marcus Antonius had volunteered to wear a breastplate and carry a sword. For a member of the senatorial class to do so could mean death were he to be caught. Caesar thanked him but told him to leave his sword at home.

As the slave wiped Caesar's face with a damp cloth he asked me, 'how's the crowd?'

'The forum in nearly full, with more coming.' Caesar didn't want to arrive too early, as he wanted as many voters as possible to hear his final speech.

There was nothing left to do so I went to the vestibule to change into my street shoes. I should have found something to busy myself with, as the time seemed not to pass as I waited for Caesar to come from his dressing room. I fidgeted nervously and debated whether or not I should visit the latrine. Finally, Caesar came across the atrium and met me at the vestibule. 'Are the lictors at the door?' he asked.

'Yes, they are,' my voice trembled a little. 'You're not wearing a breastplate?'

Caesar patted me on the back and smiled. 'Don't worry, Polybius. All will be well.' With that, he looked around to see that everyone was present. Once he became Consul we rarely stepped out the door with fewer than ten freedmen and slaves in attendance.

When the door slave opened the door a cold wind blew in giving me a chill and we stepped out into the street and were quickly surrounded by supporters to the sides and back and lictors in the front. It was a short walk from the Domus Publica to the temple nearby and we were very soon mounting the steps with the lictors lining themselves up before them. Just a short time after we arrived, one of the boys posted to observe events at the west side of the forum pushed his way through the crowd to report that Bibulus had mounted the rostrum and reported seeing a bad omen in the early morning sky. When I relayed this news to Caesar he leaned toward me with a smile and gesturing with his free hand out at the noisy crowd below, shouted, 'I'm sorry, Polybius, I can't hear you over the voice of the people.'

The crowd was larger than expected and from our vantage point on the platform, we could see more voters streaming into the forum, so Caesar didn't wait long to begin his speech. After giving the order for the voters to separate into their tribes and waiting for a decent interval for them to do so, he immediately started to speak. He once again explained how the dire problems of poverty and unemployment were hurting the city. In the middle of his speech, I noticed a ripple, coming from the west end of the forum, in the sea of people. As the ripple moved closer I could see the lictors clearing a path. Moving forward I caught Caesar's eye and with a slight nod of my head, I directed his attention toward Bibulus and his supporters as they made their way to the temple. In a prearranged move, I signaled to a group of runners stationed at the base of the temple, and the boys moved toward the back of the temple where they could run around to the various places the veterans were posted and alert them to possible trouble. As the lictors parted the crowd at the bottom of the steps, we could see that along with Bibulus and his attendants, were Cato and three Tribunes. The Tribunes were clearly there to veto the proceedings, but as this could only be done before the proceedings began it would be illegal to stop it once the voters had separated into tribes.

Bibulus slowly made his way up the steps and stood at Caesar's side. 'My colleague has chosen to join us,' Caesar shouted to the assembled crowd. 'I hope he has come to lend his support and not his opposition to the right of the people to decide.'

Bibulus scowled. 'I have not changed my opinion in the slightest.' He said much more after this, but nobody could hear his words over the roar of the crowd. While speaking, Bibulus signaled down to the Tribunes indicating they should join him on the temple steps, but the crowd of veterans posted at the foot of the steps crushed together in front of them preventing them from pushing through. I feared someone would do violence to the

Tribunes, but the disciplined veterans merely held their ground and even prevented members of the public from moving in on the men. As the crowd moved in toward the steps the Tribunes were forced further back and the situation soon became chaotic. The crowd rushed forward with many of the armed veterans in the front, moving up the steps of the temple. I grabbed Caesar by the arm and tried to pull him back but he shook me off. I wanted to run, but I stood by his side. Caesar had faith that the veterans, several of them men of rank, could control the violence. Clubs were drawn, but I didn't see any blades as Caesar took three or four steps backward pulling me by my tunic, allowing room for those who made it up the steps of the portico to push Bibulus to the marble floor before dragging him to the steps where he was roughly pushed, causing him to roll down. After the initial group made its way up the steps Caesar's lictors and several veterans blocked anyone else from mounting the platform. At the base, I could see the crowd surround Bibulus' lictors and, overpowering them, beat them with fists and clubs and finally seize their fasces, which were pounded on the pavement until they smashed to pieces.

Bibulus, in an attempt at heroism, scrambled to his feet and barred his neck while pointing up at Caesar and shouting, 'I would rather stain this proceeding with my blood since it is clear I will not be allowed to stop him!' The crowd mocked this attempt at heroism, as a basket of dung, which was conveniently at hand, was dumped over Bibulus' head as the crowd jostled him.

Rocks were thrown and a few of Bibulus' supporters were hurt as they made their retreat. One of the Tribunes was injured by a rock, a crime that is punishable by death since the person of a Tribune is sacrosanct, but because it wasn't known who threw the rock, nothing came of it. Cato stood his ground in the melee, shouting at the crowd until he was hoisted up by two of Caesar's supporters and carried behind the temple and dropped to the ground.

Order was soon restored, and Caesar announced that it was time to begin the voting. As the lines formed, Cato came back with his toga tied in a bunch around his waist, bare-chested since he never wore a tunic, except in the very coldest weather. He continued to shout invectives at the voters, but it didn't take long for him to realize he was having no effect, so he stormed off the way he came. The vote was taken and the bill became law by a wide margin. By midday, we had retired to the courtyard of the Regia where Caesar spent the rest of the day receiving the good wishes of the voters."

The day had been quite warm and as the sun rose it grew even warmer. I could see Polybius was beginning to feel more discomfort than I would wish on a man of his years, so I asked if he would prefer Mela and I leave for the day.

"Thank you for noticing my discomfort, Lucius. Rather than leave, I have a better idea."

What his better idea turned out to be was a visit to the small private bath attached to his villa. I had been there before, but not since he added a new upgrade. When I had been to his bath it was just the standard bathing tub, but sometime in the last few months he had had a shallower tub installed, so he could, with assistance, have an easier time getting into and out of the water. A combination of hot and cold baths was a perfect way to end the day.

LIBER XXVI

It was three more days before Mela and I would visit Polybius. The hot weather persisted and our father felt it best we let Polybius rest and remain cool as best he could. When we did rejoin him he picked up his story where he left off.

"Good afternoon," he said in greeting, "let us resume the story with Caesar's victory over the Senate. After the vote, on the very next day, the last day of Januarius, there was a meeting of the Senate. Caesar made a gracious speech in which he announced that he wished Bibulus well in the next month when it was his turn to have the fasces. The bill that had become law in yesterday's Comitia vote was then read out to the Senate, including the clause that each senator was to, within five days, swear an oath to support and uphold the law. This caused a murmur of discontent on the side of the hall where most of the Optimate faction had stationed themselves. Bibulus, in turn, made a rambling and slightly slurred speech filled with invectives against Caesar and demanding the Senate grant him dictatorial power so he could restore law in this time of 'civil unrest.' When he finally finished his speech, Bibulus looked expectantly around the hall assuming one of his supporters would make a motion for the Senate to vote on the measure. There was silence. The previous day's events had frightened many of the senators, leading them to hold off on making any move against Caesar, Pompeius, and Crassus, until they could see which way the winds of public opinion were blowing. The leaders of the Optimate faction realized this and didn't want to be embarrassed by having such a proposal voted down. After a long silence, Bibulus began to rail against the cowardice of the Senate and announced he was feeling ill and was retiring to his home until the Senate had 'grown a backbone.' The rest of the meeting was taken up with mundane public business until one of my secretaries returned and stood to wait by the door. It was customary for the Consul to announce his intentions for the month he was to hold the fasces, and since Bibulus had left without doing so, Caesar had sent the slave to his home to ask Bibulus his plans. When Caesar saw the young man standing in the doorway he turned toward him and asked, 'what does my co-Consul report will be his agenda for the month of Februarius?'

The man stepped forward and in a clear, loud voice said, 'The Consul Marcus Calpurnius Bibulus reports that he will be watching for omens.'

Caesar observed the formalities, having his lictors walk behind him every other month, but Bibulus didn't return to the Senate for the remainder of the year and was scarcely seen in public. In fact, the only public appearances he made were to mount the rostrum and report that he had seen various omens, which technically invalidated any legislation that he disapproved of. By Martius, the joke was circulating that the Consuls Julius and Caesar were leading Rome.

After the dramatic victory over the Optimates, I hoped, in vain, that things could return to normal. I was still handling Caesar's religious duties, scheduling the lictors, as well as supervising my staff of secretaries and organizing the material to be published in the forum. This was all in addition to my regular duties as nomenclator. With his elevation to the Consulship, Caesar met with individuals from every part of society in and around Rome and from the provinces. I needed to know as much as I could about these men, and sometimes women, so he could appear to know them. I was getting little sleep.

That same day after the Senate meeting and a light mid-day meal, Caesar went to the baths for a prearranged meeting with Crassus. Now, of course, a trip to the baths involved more politics than ever before and it was not until the cold bath was complete that any prearranged meeting could take place. As Consul, it was impossible for Caesar to have his bath without being petitioned for favors or being bothered by sycophants who merely wanted to tell their friends they conversed with Julius Caesar. We had so much work to do that even a trip to the baths involved traveling with a legion of slaves. In addition to his barber and bathers, Caesar and his friends were followed by secretaries, translators, (there were constantly representatives of King Ptolemaeus of Aegyptus asking for a meeting), copyists, and the bearers who carried what seemed to be half the contents of my work cubicle with us. On some days we brought along a large-bodied deaf and mute slave to stand in the doorway and prevent anyone from entering a private meeting room. Boxes of scrolls and manuscripts too important or sensitive in nature to send along in advance were carried behind us. An entire cartload of supplies was sent in advance and left waiting on the street near the bath. This included worktables, boxes of blank scrolls and sheets, writing tools, wax tablets, and food for the staff. Caesar's associates also brought along smaller staffs of slaves.

I was making a good deal of money at this time. Without asking, men would slide coins across the table where I worked in the courtyard of the bath and request an appointment or a consideration, and these payments were substantially greater than the ones I earned when my master was a praetor or a propraetor. Most masters allowed their slaves to keep only a portion, if any at all, of the money earned in this way, but Caesar allowed me to keep whatever I was given. His only stipulation was that I not solicit money from any petitioners and give the same consideration to men who came to me empty-handed. My work area had been prearranged at each of the three baths Caesar divided his days between. He now only attended baths with courtyards large enough to accommodate his retinue while still allowing space for citizens to exercise or relax. The tables of my staff and I were always set up in a corner near a small private meeting room. On this day, some two hours after first arriving, Caesar and Crassus, both naked save the linen wraps around their waists made their way to the private meeting room. Crassus was shivering a bit as the day was quite cool, but Caesar never seemed to mind the cold. I followed behind with a wax tablet in hand and took my usual place on the stool in the corner. The mute slave stood in the doorway and the lictors took their places to prevent any unplanned intrusions.

'We've known each other for too long, my friend.' Crassus was in a good mood. 'I've run out of small talk.'

'I agree. Gossip doesn't suit either of us, but the important things we need to talk about must not reach Cato and his lapdogs. How did that man ever rise to such prominence?' Caesar's question was one I often asked myself.

'Let's do business, I've got two more meetings after this one.' Crassus was ready to get to the point. 'Pompeius has what he wanted now we need to get ours.'

'You no doubt want your investment returned,' Caesar said. 'If everything goes as planned, I'll pay you back the full amount before the year's out.'

'And my profit?' Crassus smiled, seeming to know what was coming. 'I assume you're working on some legislation that will benefit my purse...and yours? Your man Demetrius is investing heavily in the publicani.'

Caesar smiled too. 'Demetrius is a free man. How he chooses to invest his money is no concern of mine, just as the investments of your freedmen are no concern of yours.'

'We are in agreement. But, that law was stillborn in the Senate last year. What do I get now?'

Caesar signaled me to get wine from the sideboard. 'Isn't it enough that you'll be elected to the committee overseeing the land distribution. That's got to be worth quite a bit.'

'Pompeius gets that too. What do I get that he doesn't?' For Crassus, the competition with his rival was at least as important as his profit. I suppose that's the way it is when a man has more money than he can possibly spend.

'You will get the lex publicanus and you will get it before Martius is out.' Caesar was firm.

'You are dreaming, Gaius. The Senate won't hear it again and if they do they won't even allow it to come to a vote.' Crassus' good mood was fading fast.

Caesar set his cup on the table between them and stood up to pace across the small space the room afforded. 'I don't intend to bring anything but the most inane nonsense to the Senate while

I'm Consul. I'm putting Vatinius to work. He'll propose the laws we want and they'll be put to the people.'

Crassus looked skeptical. 'I'm sure there will be ill omens on the day of every vote.'

'I'm going to ignore them, as we agreed, and have our people see nothing but good when birds cross the skies. Don't worry about your profit. We'll both get rich before this year ends.'

'I'm already rich,' Crassus said, standing. 'I must admit, I'm a little wary about this strategy of ignoring the omens.'

Caesar asked, while resuming his seat, with complete seriousness, 'Have you found piety, Marcus?'

Crassus answered him in character. 'Not piety, but rather practicality. If you choose to ignore every ill omen Bibulus reports it will provide the grounds to invalidate everything we accomplish this year. The attacks will start on the day you are no longer Consul and unless you have a very strong ally elected to succeed you, there will be no way to stop them.'

'Let's not worry about next year for a while longer,' Caesar answered him. 'If we stand together, we will be able to prevail.'

Crassus looked skeptical. 'I must get dressed now, as I have to attend to a real estate transaction.'

With that, the meeting was ended. After Crassus had left Caesar too rose from his seat. 'I'm not certain I have his full support, Polybius. Keep your eyes and most importantly your ears open and learn what you can about any other plans Crassus may have.'

'I'll try, Caesar, but as you know, Marcus Crassus keeps secrets well.'

'And,' added Caesar as we walked out into the courtyard, 'arrange a meeting with Pompeius as soon as you can.' The meeting was arranged for the following morning after each man had attended to his salutatio. Pompeius was now spending most of his time at his home on the Aventine. Unfortunately, that was one of the few meetings Caesar excluded me from."

Polybius paused to adjust the pillows around him. In the course of his talking, he had slid lower on the couch so it became nearly impossible for him to sip at his wine. I took the opportunity to retrieve a fresh wax tablet and ask why the publicani were so important. When he was, with Mela's help, again comfortable, Polybius took another sip of wine. "Today we think of the publicani only as functionaries of the emperors, as it were. But, in the days of the Republic, these wealthy equites were in a position to make vast fortunes for themselves and those who invested in them. Crassus acted as the patron of the equites who held the tax collecting contracts for the province of Asia. In those days, the right to farm taxes for a province was auctioned off, usually for a term of five years. The payment of the taxes to Rome was considered a loan until the contract expired and at that time Rome would pay the publicanus his interest on the payments. The real money to be made was in the practice of allowing the tax farmers to keep any amount in excess of the amount of their bid as profit for themselves and their patrons. Unfortunately for Crassus' clients, in their zeal to secure the rights to the lucrative province of Asia they bid too high and were disappointed by the size of the fortune they made. Rather than a large fortune, they wished to make a very large fortune. Two years before, Crassus had supported a bill to reduce the amount of their bid by one fourth. Through Cato's efforts, this law was postponed for several months before it became such a nuisance it was easily voted down in the Consulship of Silanus and Murena (62 BC).

A slave came into the room at that moment and whispered something in Polybius' ear, causing Polybius to frown. "Tell him to come back tomorrow," was all he said, dismissing the man. While I was curious as to what was the matter, I did not ask, and Polybius did not offer an explanation.

"Now, where was I?" Polybius settled himself against the large cushion as I reminded him of his place in the narrative.

"Yes, the meeting with Pompeius. I must mention what happened the night before that meeting. On the way home from the baths Caesar asked to see the scroll with the schedule for the month. At the beginning of the year, I created a calendar of days for each of the months. I always carried the current one with me and every night I updated it with any appointments that were added or changed. I still have my man Valens do this for me. After reviewing the calendar, Caesar handed it back to me saying, 'send a boy to Celer and cancel today's meeting with him. Move the meeting with the Aegyptian ambassadors to the day after next. Set aside time for me to show them the sights.' I immediately set the fastest boy off to cancel the meeting.

When we returned to the villa Caesar went directly to Aurelia's suite where he found her weaving. When he entered the room he shut the door, leaving me standing in the atrium. After nearly an hour with his mother, Caesar came to my work cubicle and sticking his head in the doorway said, 'when my daughter returns from her bath, have the doorman send her to see me. I'll be in the tablinum.' I could not at all understand what this had to do with Crassus' actions, but I knew it was significant.

Later that evening I managed to 'accidentally' run into Julia. Her suite of rooms was on my way to the passage that joined the Domus Publica with the Villa of the Vestals. I now made the nightly pickup of any communication from the Chief Vestal to the Pontifex Maximus, since that ancient woman had developed a condition that prevented her from walking. I sat on a bench in the atrium until I saw Julia and a slave girl step out into the portico of the atrium. I then began to casually walk toward the back of the domus. Naturally, I stopped to talk to my master's daughter as we were nearly the same age and had always been on friendly terms. During our brief conversation, I managed to jokingly suggest that it was odd that Caesar would schedule a meeting with his own daughter. Had Julia been a man she would have been a master politician. Even as a child she knew when to hold her counsel and had the natural ability to dissemble when the situation called for it. Her answer, therefore, was surprisingly candid. 'We both know, Polybius, my father is destined for greatness, but his destiny requires those near to him to play their parts too. I'm more than happy to do what I can to help him.'

She was careful to avoid being specific in what she said. I suspect she was testing me to see what I knew of the matter. My response was equally vague since I couldn't imagine how Julia could help Caesar's political ambitions. A twenty-year-old woman hardly had the power to advance a man's career. 'Are you truly happy to do what he requires, or is this simply proper filial devotion?'

'Why can't it be both?' was her response.

I brought up the matter with Cornelia the following morning. Since the launderer's shop where Cornelia and her new husband worked was just a short distance away, I was sometimes able to spend a short time with my son before returning to the domus in time for the salutatio. I carried a small sundial with me that told me the hour, so I had to limit my visits to sunny days. Cornelia and I would sit on the bench in front of the shop and talk when the morning was not too cold. While bouncing my boy on my knee I would tell Cornelia about the events in my life. I was somewhat selfish in this since I considered my life to be vastly more interesting than hers we rarely talked about what had transpired with her. She never seemed to mind, since she was able to catch up with some of the gossip in the Caesar household. After running down the doings of our extended slave family, I moved on to Caesar's meeting with Julia. I rhetorically posed the question that had been troubling me since the previous day. 'Julia has no political influence. How could a twenty-year-old girl possibly help Caesar?'

Cornelia laughed and shook her head.

'Why do you laugh at me?'

She leaned forward and kissed me on the cheek while taking Tychaeus. She could see it was time for me to leave. 'You are probably the smartest man I know, but sometimes you seem as stupid as an ass.'

This would have hurt me had it come from almost anyone else. 'What do you mean?'

'The daughters of ambitious patricians are very powerful tools to advance their father's causes. Think Polybius.'

With that, the answer came to me but I was still a little puzzled. 'But Julia is already betrothed to another.'

Cornelia smiled. 'Marriage arrangements can be unmade as easily as they can be made. It would seem to me Julia may be marrying someone else.'

'Who could she possibly be marrying? She seemed happy about the match.'

Cornelia smiled again. 'I'm not well versed in the lives of the mighty families of Rome; that's your job. I do know, however, Julia has a strong attraction to older men.'

'You must say nothing of this to anyone!' I was afraid of the difficulty that would arise for Caesar, but especially for me, if this story began to circulate throughout the city and the source of the story was traced back to me. I wanted to continue the conversation, but the shadow on the sundial I set on the ground beside the bench was already past the mark where I usually left. I had to run back to the domus. My mind raced as fast as my feet and as I tried to imagine the most advantageous match for Julia my mind continued to return to a single name: Pompeius Magnus. If this was the answer I knew Caesar was risking alienating Crassus entirely.

I had, alongside all my other work, been attempting to learn the rudiments of the Aegyptian language. Before leaving Hispania, Caesar asked me to write Demetrius asking him to procure an Aegyptian translator. The man he found was quite expensive, and not at all useful for anything but translating. I thought this an extravagance at the time, assuming the purchase was made on a whim, but it soon became clear that Caesar foresaw that sooner rather than later, Aegyptus would need to come under the Aegis of Rome. As you no doubt recall, not too far in the distant past, Caesar had taken the stand that Aegyptus was already a possession of Rome, having been left to the Senate in the will of Ptolemaeus Alexander. His view then was that the current king only needed to be convinced by a Roman army he was happy to lead. Now he was looking toward a diplomatic union. Caesar realized it would be more advantageous to be awarded a province to govern after his year as Consul, closer to Rome, and not someplace where his lines of communication could be interrupted for many days at a time by rough seas and bad weather, so he no longer wanted to lead an army to Alexandria. At the same time, he didn't want to let that glory go to anyone else, so he wanted the Aegyptus question to be answered before he left office. It was essential that the affairs of that strange land be put in order because grain from Aegyptus helped to feed many of the Roman provinces of the east. The series of rebellions against the royal family and the wars they fought against each other created an unstable position in the east. In spite of the instability, the Senate refused to address the question, assuming any interference in Aegyptian politics was likely to lead to an expensive war.

Orestes, the Aegyptian slave obtained by Demetrius was a curious man. He was past midlife and quite lazy. In his youth, he had been a scribe for the Ptolemaeus who was the ruler of Cyprus and brother to the Aegyptian Pharaoh of the same name. The man committed some small offense and was sold into slavery by that unstable ruler. Having once held a position of importance at a royal court, Orestes was never able to adjust to life as a slave. Since he was lazy and weak, and his only asset was his skill with the Aegyptian language, he passed through the hands of a series of masters who used him for special assignments and then tried to rent out his services to those needing a translator until they realized he was costing them more in food and upkeep than he was bringing in. He had a congenial personality and the pleasant face of a plump baby. It was these characteristics that no doubt kept him from being beaten into some sort of usefulness by a cruel master. Caesar too had little use for the man. Since I couldn't stand to see him sit idle I would often use him to translate parts of Caesar's library into the curious pictures that form the written language of the Aegyptians. This served no real purpose but kept the man busy. When I had some spare time, I would insist he teach me the Aegyptian language. From time to time, Caesar would go to him and ask him to teach him an Aegyptian greeting or a useful phrase. He would also question Orestes at length about the family relations of the Ptolemies.

The talents of the man were finally put to good use just after the celebration of the Lupercalia." At this point in his story, Polybius paused to go to the latrine. He rang a small bell to call one of his men to assist him as he shuffled down the hallway. When he returned, he was followed by a slave carrying a woolen cover that the slave arranged over his feet. "For the past year or so, I sometimes feel cold in my hands and feet, even in the warmest weather. I've heard it said that men die like trees, from the top down, but I seem to be the exception to this observation; I am slowly losing my life from my extremities inward."

At that, Mela quite surprised me. Leaning close toward

Polybius, he quietly said, "would you like us to go, Polybius, so you can rest." I think the tender way he said it surprised and embarrassed even him because his face reddened when he caught my eye.

"Polybius laughed. "I'm quite all right. If you boys left me alone with every ache and chill, we would never get to the end of the story." Leaning back on the cushions, Polybius closed his eyes as he did when he wanted to remember clearly days long past. "Now, Lucius look at your notes and remind me where I left things."

"The Lupercalia."

"Quite so. You boys have probably witnessed the Lupercalia several times, and you Lucius may be asked to participate this year. The year of Caesar's Consulship was the first time I actually witnessed the festival close up, as it were. Only the slaves of magistrates are allowed near enough to really see what is happening, and in the year of Caesar's praetorship, I was suffering a fever and spent those three days at home under a blanket. This particular year, the weather was quite cold. There was ice where the water had collected between the paving stones of the streets and onthe steps up the side of the hill, making the walk to the windswept south end of the Palatine a bit treacherous that early morning. The festival is a very old one dating back to the time of the founding of the city itself. It has been said that the festival derives from the Greek festival called the Arcadian Lycaea, but this is nonsense. It is merely a coincidence that our two cultures have a festival involving wolves. The festival dates back to a time when the people of Rome scarcely knew of the existence of Arcadia, having only heard of the place from contact with traders in the Greek colonies dotting the coast of Italy. Originally shepherds, to honor Faustulus and the she-wolf he discovered suckling the infants, Romulus and Remus, celebrated the rites. The duties of the shepherds were transferred to the Luperci, the so-called "brothers of the wolf." This corporation of priests was divided into two collegia made up of members of the families Quinctiliani and the Fabiani. Now, of course, there is a third collegium made up of members of the Julii in honor of the god Julius. As Pontifex Maximus and Consul, Caesar was required to stand as witness to all the important rites associated with the festival. I, therefore, was required to stand in a roped-off area nearby with the secretaries and nomenclators of all the other magistrates and priests who were either witnessing or participating in the rites. It was events like this that helped those slaves in my position to form bonds with each other. By meeting regularly like this we were able to form a sort of informal collegia of our own. On that frigid morning, I tried to gather useful information from the other slaves. Of course, as often as not, the men in my position would misinform each other in the service of our masters.

The festival began with the chief of the Luperci sacrificing two male goats and a dog. Two young men, one of the Fabii and one of the Quinctilii, were led to the altar with much ceremony. Now, of course, both are members of the imperial family and the others merely observe the rite. These young men had their foreheads marked with the blood from the sacrificial knives, which were then wiped off with a woolen cloth soaked in goat's milk, after which the two young men were expected to laugh most heartily. I think the cold may have taken some enthusiasm out of their ritual laughter. I have many times heard more heartfelt laughter when viewing the lowest comedies performed by the worst actors on the streets of the subura. I really felt sorry for the Lupercanii that day, as they were each allowed only a single goatskin as clothing. These rites all took place then, as they do now, at the sacred cave on the south side of the Palatine near where the imperial palace now stands. Legend tells us this was where Faustulus first found the twins. In those days, the cave was just that: a cave. Now its walls have been tiled with beautiful mosaics and its roof has been carved into a dome. The sacrificial fires provided some heat for those close enough, but I was grateful for the woolen cloak I brought along. While the animals are roasting for the sacrificial feast, the Lupercanii cut strips from the skins of the goats. As it takes until midday to roast the sacrifice and prepare for the sacrificial feast, most of the observers either go to their homes or carry on with other business, only to return to the site for the feast and the rites that follow. After the feast, young men of senatorial rank strip their clothes off and are each given two of the thongs, bound together, that the Lupercanii cut from the goat skins. They then run up and down the streets of the Palatine and the area around the hill striking anyone they encounter with the bands, all the while laughing. The streets are usually lined with young women because to be struck by one of the revelers' shaggy goat thongs is considered most lucky and a sure way to ensure fertility and easy pregnancy. Fortunately for the young men, the sky was clear and the sun warmed the day nicely by the time the sacrificial feast had ended.

For over an hour of the time between sacrifice and feast, Caesar met with Pompeius in a small chamber in the nearby temple of Apollo. I was excluded from this meeting. When Caesar returned to the street, he signaled me to come to his side. In a low tone, he said to me, 'clear my schedule for tomorrow morning. I have a meeting with the pharaoh. After the feast, we need to go home and prepare. Send one of the boys to find Demetrius and have him get the villa across the river ready to receive a king.'

I leaned in toward Caesar, and said in almost a whisper, 'Less than a day is not much time to prepare for a king.'

Caesar smiled and whispered back, 'that's alright, Auleutes isn't much of a king.'

I rarely questioned Caesar's instructions, but this time I said to him, 'wouldn't it be bad form for the Consul to leave before the runners start?' I said this for purely selfish reasons; I really was looking forward to seeing dozens of young men lined up naked before us as they received the sacred thongs. Caesar agreed, and I was able to watch, for nearly an hour, the naked bodies of the young men."

I was curious as to why the Pharaoh of Aegyptus was in Rome. Polybius smiled. "Aegyptus was ruled by the descendants of Ptolemaeos, the great general who helped Alexander conquer the East. For most of its history, the family was at war with itself. Various members of this family often appealed to Rome for assistance in their petty wars."

He continued. "The following morning after the salutatio we set out for the villa on the far bank of the Tiber River. Since all Rome was celebrating the Parentalia festival, no magistrate could conduct public business, freeing up the Consul to spend some leisure time at his villa. We left the house on foot, the way being cleared by the lictors. Once we crossed the river, Caesar climbed into a litter Demetrius had arranged to have waiting for him. I was assigned an ass to ride immediately behind the litter. We had been in the villa just long enough for Caesar to have a slave wash the dust from the road off his feet and dress him in the Consular regalia and hurry to the silver and ivory chair that was set out in the atrium of the villa, when the door slave announced the arrival of Pompeius Magnus, Imperator, and former Consul. In what sounded almost like an afterthought, the slave then announced the client and friend of Pompeius, Pharaoh, Ptolemaeus Neos Dionysos Theos Philopator Theos Philadelphos, king of Aegyptus. Caesar rose to embrace Pompeius most heartily. To an outsider, it would have been easy to believe the two men hadn't seen each other in a decade, rather than the previous day. After an impolitely long interval of small talk, Pompeius took Caesar by the elbow and said, 'come and meet my client, Ptolemaeus from Aegyptus.'

Caesar approached the king of Aegyptus as if he was of no more importance than a Greek grain importer. The pharaoh, surrounded by six members of the Aegyptian embassy and nearly twice that number of slaves waited, staring impassively at Caesar as he approached. It was obvious he thought he would be greeted as a great king, but Caesar never considered foreign kings to approach a Consul of Rome in dignitas or in authority. In Caesar's mind, the pharaoh was no more than a wealthy and interesting client of Pompeius.' Caesar knew that he, as Consul of Rome had the power to raise the pharaoh up or break him.

The king was a rather short, rather fat man with a lined face and hair that was died unnaturally dark for a man of sixty years of age. He wore Greek dress died purple and trimmed in gold, Caesar looked him up and down, from his face to his leather boots died purple, and back up again, resting his eyes for a moment on the king's diadem. He then met his eyes and said, in Greek, 'you are the one they call the flute player. I am Gaius Julius Caesar, Consul of Rome.'

Ptolemaeus' lips tightened at the words 'flute player,' but he kept his composure. 'I know who you are, Consul, just as you know who I am.' The pharaoh was clearly having trouble hiding his indignation.

'Yes,' Caesar said coldly, 'and you come to Rome, looking for my assistance.' With that, Caesar turned and arm in arm with Pompeius led the king and his embassy toward the garden behind the peristyle at the back of the house. Not knowing the proper protocol, I hung back with the Aegyptian slaves. Caesar, without looking back, said in a loud clear voice, 'come along Polybius. The pharaoh has his scribes, and I will need mine. We must have an accurate record of this meeting.'

In the course of the next hour, or perhaps less, sitting beside a bubbling fountain, Caesar and Pompeius sold the pharaoh of Aegyptus his own throne for the staggering sum of 6000 talents ($375,000,000), by guaranteeing in the name of the Senate and People of Rome that Ptolemaeus was the sole and rightful pharaoh of Aegyptus. Caesar was suddenly quite wealthy. The 'gift' from the pharaoh was, to be precise, transferred by letters of credit to Pompeius as the king's patron as an expression of gratitude. Pompeius immediately signed over half the amount to Caesar to express his gratitude for the Consul's intercession in the matter. Until the law was passed, the two could not draw on the line of credit. The law ensuring the king's right to rule over Aegyptus, the famous lex de rege Alexandrino, was to never be presented to the Senate, being enacted over the sputtering of the Optimates, less than one month later, like almost all Caesar's legislation of that year, in the Comitia. As the meeting ended, Caesar turned on his considerable charm and began to talk to the king as if he was an old friend. I was surprised how he had the king laughing at a joke as the three men retired to the couches in a heated pavilion at the rear of the garden where a meal of exotic waterfowl was ready to be served. I was left behind with two other slaves to record their negotiations with the Aegyptian embassy as they haggled over the purchase of grain.

LIBER XXVII

The rest of Februarius was occupied with getting allies, including Pompeius and Crassus elected to the commission tasked to distribute the public land to the poor families of Rome and to Pompeius' veterans. The only other legislation of any note passed at this time was a series of laws regulating the actions and the tribute paid by client kingdoms and principalities. Caesar also passed a law that had been proposed at the beginning of his term, allowing for greater challenges to jurors. The law regarding the challenges of jurors was widely understood as a warning to any who might be considering bringing him to trial when his term as Consul ended. True to what he told Crassus at the start of the year, Caesar did this through the use of Vatinius and each of these laws was passed in the Comitia against the wishes of the Senate.

At about this time I noticed a cooling in Crassus' relations with Caesar and while working late with Caesar one night, I asked him about it. 'It's nothing. He's just disappointed that he didn't get a piece of the lex rege.'

'Why didn't he?' I had wondered this before but never asked.

'He chose not to get involved. He didn't think it would pass. Besides, to pay for his throne, Auletes borrowed money from some of the men who borrow money from Crassus. He stood to gain from it either way, though I'm sure he would like to see the money he lent out, come back to him twice.'

'Well,' I sighed, 'I hope it's nothing, but I've been going over the vote totals for the lex rege and they don't add up as they should.'

'What do you mean?' Caesar came to my side of the table to look at the sheet with my columns and numbers for the votes from each tribe.

'The agreement was all three of you would work for this vote, correct?'

Caesar nodded as he shifted the sheet of papyrus closer to the oil lamp.

'Crassus has his greatest influence in these eight tribes, and carries a lot of weight in these three as well, but probably not enough to tilt the balance if the Optimates worked together.' As I said this I pointed out the places where Crassus should have guaranteed the votes in favor of the law. 'The law was voted down by these three tribes,' I said pointing out three of the tribes that Crassus had the most influence in, 'and very close in this one.'

'But four of Crassus tribes delivered big. Two were nearly unanimous.' Caesar studied the numbers carefully and then added, 'but by then the vote had already been decided in our favor!'

I nodded in agreement. 'Had the vote been close when it was the turn of those tribes to vote, it could have gone very differently. During the vote, I noticed Crassus' men working those tribes as hard as they worked the first to vote, if not harder, in spite of the fact the votes didn't matter. I think they may have been urging the men to vote for the bill so it would look like Crassus had pushed for it when he held back his support in the early voting.'

Caesar rubbed his face thoughtfully. 'Ask around. Discreetly though, as I don't want nothing to become something because we are prying into Crassus business. The less I know of how you gain your information the better. I need to be able to claim ignorance if you are discovered.' Caesar went back to his side of the table and to the dispatch, he was reading.

I welcomed this turn of events. Outside of the many hours I needed to be by his side, Caesar generally let me set my own schedule. As long as I got all my work done, he left me alone. This new assignment gave me one more reason to slip out for an hour or more during the day. Since first working with Lucceius man, we had a regular meeting time, three days each month, at Lucceius' house on the Palatine. Lucceius almost never visited that home and the door slave could be bought quite cheaply. Unfortunately, I was frequently required to attend to other business and had to send the man a note of apology. I felt he was getting irritated at my frequent cancellations, so I welcomed one more reason to be away from Caesar. I also used it as an excuse to visit the laundry where Cornelia worked; I would play with my son while gathering any information she might have learned by overhearing gossip, or more directly, from the slaves who patronize the place. Also, it was exciting to spy on Crassus.

Throughout the years I have found that the character of a man leaves its impression on his entire household. As Caesar was a man who put a premium on civility, his slaves, for the most part, also valued civility. As Caesar was decisive, those who worked for him were also decisive. Crassus was a very greedy man. He was greedy for money and he was also greedy for honors and the accolades of the public. This was not at all unusual among the senators of that time. Since the second Punic War, and the expansion of Rome's dominions to far off places, great wealth had been flowing into Italy and Rome. Indeed, this is still the case. Easy money and greed go hand in hand, just as opportunities for conquest and the lust for glory do. As a result of this character trait, Crassus' slaves were also trained to be greedy and were easy to bribe. Since Crassus almost never allowed a slave to buy his own freedom, they almost always spent the money as soon as they got it, buying little luxuries that their master chose to overlook because it saved him money. If a slave buys an expensive meal at a taverna, he will certainly eat less of his master's food that day. If he chooses to buy himself a pair of fine shoes, it saves his master the need to furnish footwear and makes it appear he dresses his slaves well. Several of Crassus' slaves were also easy to find. As you already know, Crassus made a fortune in real estate speculation. When a fire would break out in the meaner sections of the city, the closer of two of Crassus' freedman would rush to the scene with his slave brigade of fire-fighters and haggle with the owner of the insulae as the flames consumed the building. The higher the flames rose, the more the price dropped. To make this system work, Crassus had a dozen or more slaves, all healthy young men, whose only job was to move about the subura and the poorer sections of the Viminal and Aventine hills and watch for fires. Once a fire was spotted, they would run to the closer of two insulae; one at the base of the Aventine and one on the slope of the Viminal, where the freedman and his fire-fighters could be found, often playing at dice or exercising in the courtyard. Each team was so large they displaced the space normally taken by four or five shops. It was said that if a fire went unnoticed and the freedman wasn't alerted in time to negotiate with the owner, the entire team of 'spotters' would be beaten.

It was a simple matter to make the acquaintance of one of these boys since my man Myron was on friendly terms with him. What was more difficult was to learn anything useful from him. I arranged to be standing on the corner where the street of the stone masons meets the street of the metalworkers. I was talking to one of the men who had taken a break and ran to the nearby fountain, when the boy, named Linus, walked by. This area was a prime location for these young men, as the metalworkers were frequently starting small fires and occasionally they would get out of hand and spread to the insulae above the shop. After the initial small talk, it was a simple matter to return to the district on the two following days. On the second day, I went to purchase door hinges. On the third day, I returned with the story that I bought the wrong size for my master. It was at the third meeting that I suggested it would be useful for Caesar to learn who Crassus was dealing with.

Linus seemed uninterested until I suggested my master might be willing to pay for good information. Money was not a difficulty, as Caesar allowed me access to a purse of coins to pay for miscellaneous expenses. It was then Linus told me about the daily meeting the spotters had with the freedman in charge of their area. Each day they would meet before sunrise and discuss the events of the city. Religious festivals, weather, and politics all had an impact on where and when fires were most likely to break out. The boy also told me that the freedman always had a copy of Crassus' daily schedule so he could send someone to fetch Crassus should he be needed. I told him I would pay well for a copy of that schedule each day. Linus assured me the man was careless and often left the schedule lying on his worktable. He said it would be a simple matter to copy the meetings onto his wax tablet. Each of the spotters carried a wax tablet to note the exact location in the event he was too exhausted to lead the team back to the site. For this, they had all been taught a crude sort of shorthand writing that would make it easy to copy the information.

All went according to plan for three days. Each morning when Caesar was either at the Senate or in the forum on public business I would slip away for a short time and exchange a couple of denarii for Crassus' schedule. On the third day, as I copied the notes from his wax tablet to mine, I stopped at the last entry and looked up at Linus. 'Are you sure you have this right?'

He looked irritated. 'Yeah. I copied it down just like it said. Is there a problem? I get my money even if you don't like what it says.'

I nodded and handed him an extra coin. 'No problem,' was my reply.

As I walked away I felt a little sick. The last name on the list of people Crassus had scheduled meetings with was 'G Julius Caesar.' This was a meeting I knew nothing about, and I was fairly certain Caesar didn't either. The meeting did happen later that day. At the end of the Senate session, Crassus asked Caesar if he could have a word. In spite of the cool weather, I had been sweating throughout the session and my state of agitation was nearly unbearable when Crassus looked me in the eye before leading Caesar by the arm to the small meeting room at the side of the curia. The meeting was brief and Caesar left the room looking as if nothing out of the ordinary had happened. I clutched at this straw and for that brief time chose to believe it was nothing to worry about, but as I followed Caesar out onto the portico of the curia, I could feel Crassus eyes on my back. I also knew in my heart Crassus wouldn't have listed a brief meeting at the end of the session on his schedule if he hadn't meant it as a warning for me.

On the walk home, I asked Caesar about the meeting. All he

would say is, 'we'll talk about it at home.'

When we arrived at the Domus Publica I wanted to find some busy work far away from Caesar, but I knew I must face what happened, so as soon as I changed into my house shoes I went into the tablinum where Caesar was standing looking out at the fountain in the back of the house. I shuffled my feet to let him know I was there.

Caesar spoke without turning around. 'Crassus tells me you have been paying one of his slaves for his daily schedule. I told him I knew nothing about it.'

My voice caught and I had to repeat the first word as it came out so softly. 'What...what should I do?'

'Stop,' was all that Caesar said.

I was disturbed by the conversation. 'Is that all?' I asked. I could see Caesar nod so I turned to leave.

As I crossed into the atrium, Caesar called me back. When I returned he was pulling the chair out to sit down and read through the draft of the daily report my boys had compiled for publication the following morning. 'Crassus is not to be trifled with. This is my fault. I set you to this task and whatever happens, is my responsibility. Remember that. Bring me whatever information you gathered after everyone else is asleep tonight. We can go over it then.'

That night by the light of a single oil lamp, Caesar and I pored over Crassus' schedules for the three days' worth of information I had obtained. Most of his meetings were mundane business, but meetings with two men stood out. On the first day, Crassus had a meeting with Cicero in the early part of the day and then met him again at the baths that afternoon. The second and again on the third day, Crassus met with young Gaius Scribonius Curio. I thought the meetings were unusual but didn't see much significance, however, Caesar did. 'Crassus is playing both sides. Curio will be running for one of the open Aedile positions. Crassus will be backing him.'

'What do you mean?' I was still in the dark.

'Curio is Cicero's man. He is lining up support against us, to use later in the year, or perhaps next year.'

Hearing that, I was reminded of something. 'I saw Cicero having his midday meal with Curio at the taverna near the temple of Saturn the same day Cicero met with Crassus.' What Caesar said made sense, but I didn't understand Crassus' motives. 'Why would he be planning to move against you?'

'I'm not sure. Maybe he's covering all the bets. Maybe he wants to get posted to a province where he can win a triumph and he doesn't want Pompeius or me to cast a longer shadow. For men like Crassus, it isn't enough to succeed. Others must also fail. And, for many years he has been able to buy pretty much anything he wanted. The one thing that has eluded him is the great campaign where he could best Pompeius. I'm sure now he's also afraid that I'll achieve great success as well when I get my province next year.

And, I no longer owe him any money. I'm out from under his thumb.'

I went back to the metalworker's street the following morning with the intent of paying Linus a final sum by way of apologizing for any trouble I may have caused him. It made me sick to think that he would probably receive a beating for his troubles, but I consoled myself with the knowledge that it was he who was being disloyal to his master and he was aware of the consequences of his actions. I looked around but the boy wasn't anywhere to be seen. As I turned the corner onto the street where we met, I felt a hand on my shoulder. I stopped in my tracks, expecting the worst. I turned slowly looking up into the eyes of the freedman in charge of the fire brigade. 'You're lookin' for your new friend?'

I said nothing. I could feel the blood drain from my face and I felt as if I would faint.

'He ain't gonna be comin' back.'

Still, I stared blankly, trying to focus my mind.

'He wanted you to have this.' With that, the man thrust out his big hand.

I instinctively reached out to take what he offered, and he pressed a stylus into my hand just before he turned and walked briskly around the corner into the crowded street. I just as quickly walked the other direction. It wasn't until I was under the portico of the basilica that I stopped to look at the stylus. It was the same type as the spotters carried; a short wooden one with a brass tip.

This one, however, was stained with what appeared to be blood. Several days after that the body of a young male slave was discovered trapped in the grate where the great sewer empties into the river. He had been beaten severely and then stabbed several times. It was assumed he was a runaway from outside the city since nobody had reported a slave, matching his description, missing. The skin had been cut away at the spot where the identifying tattoo is frequently inscribed, so the matter was dropped. It was apparent that what Caesar had at first said was nothing, had indeed become something as a result of my interference. When I learned the news from Cornelia on the walkway in front of the laundry shop I had to quickly thrust our son into her arms so I could turn into the street and vomit.

I said nothing to Caesar about the discovery of the body, but somehow he knew. That night after everyone else had gone to sleep I met briefly with him to review some changes to his schedule for the following day. After the meeting, as I was packing up my stylus and tablets, Caesar reached over and laid his hand on mine, stopping me. I looked up and met his eyes. Caesar paused a moment before gripping my hand tighter and saying, 'what happened to that boy is not your fault. The fault is mine. Marcus is a dangerous man and we are playing a dangerous game. I'm sorry for putting you in the middle of it.'

I looked down at our hands on the table, mine under his, before speaking. 'I was not nearly as discreet as I should have been. I underestimated the situation but I've learned my lesson and it won't happen again. I'll keep my eyes and ears open, but I won't do any more than that for now.'

Caesar nodded and released my hand. In spite of his reassurances, I didn't sleep well that night.

Caesar was angry with Crassus and with Cicero, but he dared not show it. He had to let Pompeius know what was occurring, but he needed to do so in a way that would not cause the two men to have a public rift. Pompeius was not nearly as adept at the delicate art of public pretense as most of his peers, but with Caesar's guidance, he played his part well. Both Caesar and Pompeius acted as if nothing happened. I was blamed for being over-zealous in protecting my master's interests and for now, all was as it should be. I'm sure Crassus assumed he had duly warned his political partners and they were both put in their places. It was this turn of events that convinced me that for all his abilities, Crassus could be quite the fool. Now that I think about it, maybe it is because of a man's abilities he is sometimes able to turn himself into a fool. Crassus, and later Pompeius, like many men of wealth, influence, and power convinced themselves that they could master any situation.

Originally the plan was to have Pompeius and Crassus share the Consulship the following year. This would have almost certainly guaranteed that all of Caesar's acts would be confirmed. Now, with Crassus' good faith in question, Caesar and Pompeius let it be known that the Consuls would be Gabinius and Sulpicius. Crassus evidently heard the news from Cicero. Pompeius knew he couldn't do anything more to publicly humiliate Crassus, but he took Cicero's betrayal to be more personal. For nearly two years Cicero had been cultivating Pompeius and the two had become fairly close. I was present when Pompeius warned Caesar that he was looking out for a way to damage Cicero politically. That opportunity came in late Martius. Gaius Antonius, Cicero's colleague in the Consulship four years prior, was brought up on charges. Cicero chose to defend the man, confident in his good standing with Pompeius, Caesar, and Crassus. If Crassus had warned him that Caesar was aware of their dealings, he made no indication of it. Antonius had been accused of the usual misconduct during his term as Proconsul of Macedonia. Pompeius and Caesar chose not to oppose his prosecution and they even worked against him. They expected Cicero to understand their actions as a warning for him to remain neutral to their political dealings. They even privately hinted to him that if he sided with them they would see that he could have a say in selecting the magistrates for the following year. Cicero, however, was proud of his reputation and didn't want to be seen as working with Caesar and Pompeius to subvert the constitution. On the morning nine days before the calends of Aprilis (March 22), in his closing speech in defense of Antonius, Cicero was not at his best. He was suffering from a cold in his head and looked tired and distracted during his speech. This is probably why he briefly moved away from the planned text of his closing defense long enough to bemoan the state of political affairs at Rome. It was clear that this was meant as an insult to Caesar and Pompeius. Caesar was a man of mild disposition and not easily roused to anger, but when he was he acted quickly and surely. Sometimes, he acted too rashly, and this was one of those times, but perhaps Caesar's true genius was his ability to extricate him from those situations and find himself in an even better position. Cicero spoke his misguided words in the morning. By the eighth hour, Antonius had been convicted and was preparing to go into exile and Clodius was being transferred to plebeian status. The latter was plainly illegal, as even Caesar would tacitly admit by claiming no recollection of the event, but for a time it caused a real sensation.

Mela, acting in his usual tactless way, interrupted Polybius. 'Why was Clodius punishment for what Cicero said?'

Well, Mela, I don't think you were in attendance when I explained to your brother the events that are now referred to as the Bona Dea scandal. Lucius can relate this part of the story to you on your walk home today. What I will say is that Publius Clodius Pulcher became a major political power in those years and he did so in the most unconventional way. Clodius was born a Claudius, from one of the most ancient and noble branches of that ancient and noble clan. In his youth, he began to refer to himself by the plebeian spelling and pronunciation of his nomen and insisted everyone call him Clodius.

Clodius was a cousin to Caesar's lover, Servilia, but the members of the patrician families were all related to each other in some way, even more so than they are today. Perhaps that's why they seemed inordinately preoccupied with the crime of incest; many of their relationships were straying dangerously close. As a young man, Clodius served under his brother in law, the rightfully famous Lucius Licinius Lucullus whose gardens are still a wonder to behold. Lucullus became fabulously rich from the booty he collected while conquering the east and after being forced into political retirement on his return to Rome, he spent lavishly on villas, gardens, and public works. At any rate, Lucullus held the command in the east for five years and had great success in his campaigns. His mistake was in not keeping abreast of the mood of the Senate at Rome. After defeating Mithridates in battle, rather than pursue him and finish him off, Lucullus completed the conquest of Pontus and added a new province to the Roman sphere.

Unaware or unconcerned about the debate going on in the Senate over whether he should be replaced in his command by a general who would bring an end to the wars in the region, Lucullus continued his steady but slow conquest of the east. Mithridates fled to the protection of Tigranes, king of Armenia and Lucullus used this as an excuse to provoke a war with that kingdom and he defeated Tigranes in battle, but by then it was already too late in the year and he needed to move south to his winter headquarters. The morale of his troops was already poor, as many of the men felt they had been shortchanged when the spoils of war had been divided up and they wanted to end the campaigns as much as the leaders of the Senate in Rome. Pompeius, who wanted the eastern command for himself, saw this as an opportunity and bribed Clodius to foment rebellion in the legions. Clodius was quite successful and Lucullus was recalled and Pompeius was sent to replace him.

Upon his return to Rome, Clodius needed powerful protection as a result of his treason and the fact that Lucullus had discovered that Clodius had been carrying on a sexual relationship with his wife who also happened to be Clodius' sister. This was incest of the most serious kind. All right-thinking people would believe only incest with one's own mother to be a more serious crime. I have heard that the long arm of Pompeius may have stretched toward Rome and offered some protection as well. Clodius realized that at age twenty-seven it was time to settle into a more respectable life. He married Fulvia, the daughter of the wife of Licinius Murena, a cousin to Lucullus. Murena was quite influential and was able to provide temporary protection for Clodius and he was not yet prosecuted for any of his crimes. Two years after returning to Rome, Clodius was once again serving in a province. This time he went to Gaul as a member of Murena's staff when he was posted to that province. The following year he returned to Rome to see Murena, his protector elected to the Consulship and he thought he was safe for one more year, however, he found himself dragged into the Catilina conspiracy. At first Cicero, the senior Consul accused Clodius of being involved with Catilina's plot to overthrow the government, but by forging close ties with the Optimates and assisting Cicero in uncovering the plot he became a trusted confidant to both Consuls. In fact, Cicero came to trust him enough to allow him to join the group of young nobles and equites that acted as his bodyguard at this time.

Confident in the powerful protectors he had surrounded himself with, Clodius made a stupid and rash move. Clodius was always sexually adventurous and began an affair with Caesar's wife Pompeia. This led to the Bona Dea scandal and charges were finally brought against him. The most Caesar could do to help him is to deny any knowledge of the affair, which he did, so Clodius reached out to Pompeius who ignored him, and Cicero who turned on him. Cicero was in a position to lie in support Clodius' alibi that he was not in Rome on the night of the Bona Dea scandal, but because he wanted to forge closer ties to Lucullus and Pompeius, Cicero told the truth and Clodius' conviction was assured. In a last desperate measure, Clodius turned to Crassus and struck a deal to support him in his political aims if the wealthy Crassus would buy his acquittal. This Crassus did with lavish bribes to the jurors.

The end result was that Clodius became a confirmed Populare

and the sworn enemy of Cicero and as it would later turn out, of Pompeius, though no one suspected he would turn on the great general since he seemed to focus all his hatred on Cicero. Clodius was a Quaestor serving in Sicily during the Consulship of Silanus and Murena (62 BC) and on his return in the year of Caesar's Consulship, he once again made it known he wanted to renounce his status as a patrician and be adopted into a plebeian family so he could become a Tribune. Like everything else in Rome, while such a move was possible, it involved a strict legal formula and serious religious rites, so it should have been a long and involved process, but when Cicero made is ill-conceived remarks during his closing speech at the trial of Antonius, Clodius became a pleb that very day.

There was a certain young man of the Fonteius clan who was willing to become Clodius' father for the right price. For some time Clodius had been fishing around for someone to lend him the money. Three days prior, he had been able to tell Caesar he had found the money to buy the transfer. Caesar saw no reason at that time to sanction the move, though as Consul and Pontifex Maximus he was in a position to do so, so Clodius was looking for another loan to use to give Caesar a reason in the form of a bribe. That morning, after three days of rain, the sun was shining brightly and the weather had begun to warm. I recall standing on the portico of the curia at Caesar's side listening to Cicero's speech. The old curia was positioned in such a way that it was quite easy to hear an orator in the forum and since this was an important trial that drew large crowds, the arguments were all being made from the rostrum. The acoustics of the forum and the hush of the crowd when Cicero was speaking allowed us to hear every word. Both Caesar and I already knew the text of Cicero's speech as I had obtained a copy from Tiro the day before, so we were both surprised enough to look at each other when he strayed from the text. A mere five or six sentences later, he returned to his original speech, but the damage was done. I looked over at Caesar and could tell he was trying to control his anger. Through clenched teeth, Caesar said to me, 'have someone find Pompeius. I want to meet him at the Regia now.'

'The Regia?' I wasn't sure I had heard him right. 'And, what about Marcus Crassus?'

'Crassus is out of town.' By the way, Caesar said 'out of town,' I knew Crassus was making himself hard to find. Caesar was already making his way down the steps when he said, without looking back, 'yes, Polybius, the Regia.' I quickly gave instructions to three of my staff and sent them off in different directions looking for Pompeius. I had to run to catch up with Caesar's group as it made its way through the forum. Without the benefit of his lictors to clear a path I and the remainder of my staff had to force our way through the crowd. I heard Cicero, just for an instant pause and lose his place in his speech when Caesar and his group of followers disturbed his audience as they passed. As we neared the Regia I sent my remaining two staff slaves who were with us that morning off to the Domus Publica to make the arrangements for refreshments and fresh tablets for note-taking to be brought to the Regia. In a short time, I was with Caesar in the courtyard of that ancient home of the Pontifex Maximus.

It wasn't long before we could hear Pompeius' arrival. While he held no official position in the government of Rome, and therefore had no lictors, he didn't let that stop him from acting as if he did. I could hear his unofficial bodyguard bellowing 'make way for Pompeius Magnus,' while clearing a path for him and his followers. The large group that came with him was left to mingle with Caesar's group in the courtyard and the street as we went into the Regia itself.

Pompeius greeted Caesar with, 'why are we meeting here?'

'If you concur, we are not meeting as senators, but rather as Pontifex Maximus and auger.' There was no small talk today. 'I trust you heard Cicero's speech?'

'I was having a snack at the taverna in the basilica. Yes, I heard him.' Pompeius was clearly as angry as Caesar.

Caesar was pacing. 'I realize I can't do anything about Cato and Bibulus and their people, but I'll not stand for our own allies trying to straddle the fence. I've had it with Cicero and the others trying to play both sides. The man's not running for anything, so why in the name of Jupiter does he need to kiss the unwashed feet of the mob?'

'What do you propose?' Pompeius was at the table munching a bit of cheese. I watched him gesture to the man to put a little more water in his wine. This was serious business.

Caesar paused and looked at me. 'Polybius, can you clear the room? I want it to be just us four, he said pointing at Pompeius' man and me. I did as I was asked and when we were alone, Caesar noticed Pompeius' secretary trying to scrape a clean spot on the surface of the wax tablet. With a quick movement of his hand, he indicated I should lend him one of my fresh ones.

Caesar then began to speak. 'Clodius wants to be Tribune, and that will have both Cato and Cicero pissing blood. He can't become a Tribune unless he becomes a pleb first. He's found a man willing to adopt him. I say we should make it happen.'

'When?' Pompeius continued to pick at the cheese plate. 'It must be soon.'

'Why not today? I will be the priest and you will be the auger. We both have the necessary qualifications.' Caesar was nothing if not decisive and that was how it was decided.

The rest of the meeting was about the logistics of getting all the principals together in the same place. As the meeting was about to break up, I felt I needed to point out a couple of important facts. 'I'm sorry Caesar, but there may be a problem with your plan.'

Caesar looked annoyed. 'You're not going to tell me it's illegal are you, Polybius.'

'Plainly, Caesar it will be illegal to get this done today or any other day. Clodius renounced his patrician status at a meeting of the plebs last year, but the Consul refused to recognize it because the proper rites had not been observed, and the Consul was his own brother in law.'

'Yes, I know this.' Caesar looked vexed, Pompeius looked amused, and his man looked confused, but I forged ahead.

'As I understand it, the man who plans to adopt Clodius is many years his junior. Our laws require a man reach at least thirty years of age before he can adopt and he must demonstrate that he has tried and failed to produce a natural son. Fonteius, as I understand it, just turned twenty and I doubt he is done trying to produce children. Also, the situation requires a careful examination of the circumstances by the College of Pontiffs. And, the whole thing must take place before a meeting of the Comitia Curiata. This can't all happen today. At least three market days' notice is required before the Comitia can even meet.'

Caesar was firm. 'Nowhere is the Roman constitution carved in stone. There is not even an official listing of all the Roman laws. Our constitution has always been flexible. Pompeius, here held his first Consulship fourteen years before he was eligible, so don't tell me this thing can't be done today. Round up the curial lictors and have them meet here in two hours; they can act as the assembly. Get three or four of the pontiffs here as well. And, have someone find this man Publius Fonteius and tell him the Consul Caesar says he is about to become a father. Let's get moving. I want this all done in the next two hours.'

We left Caesar and Pompeius and were both on our way out the door, already discussing how we would divide up the tasks, when Pompeius stopped us. 'Perhaps someone should fetch Clodius, as well.' Clodius' adoption and his emancipation were complete less than three hours later.

After the adoption, before Clodius could return home and celebrate his new plebeian status, Pompeius and Caesar attached a very short leash to his collar in a brief meeting in the vestibule of the Regia. I was not invited to the meeting but, as I was finishing up some work nearby, I could plainly overhear much of what was being discussed. I was at a disadvantage, as I had the pontiff Manlius discussing an upcoming religious festival in one ear and Pompeius' man trying to tie up the loose ends of how we would announce and publish the adoption in the other. What I did hear was Pompeius say firmly, 'When you become Tribune, have no illusion about who you belong to. You will not use the position to strike at Cicero!' I also learned that Clodius was to be offered an ambassadorship not to the lucrative kingdom of Aegyptus as he had hoped and as Crassus had promised him earlier in the year, but rather to Tigranes, king of Armenia. I watched as Clodius' mood darkened, and as he left the Regia, he was clearly furious at Pompeius and Caesar. After all, Clodius' reason for becoming a pleb was to be elected Tribune with the goal of attacking Cicero.

Two days after the ides of Novembrisr in that same year and

with the help of Caesar and Pompeius, Clodius was elected a Tribune of the plebs. He proved to be a bigger nuisance than Caesar ever imagined, and the legality of all his acts was to be questioned for years to come, as the legality of his adoption into a plebeian family was highly suspect, but that was in the future.

It was strange to watch a sort of game being played between the three men who continued to meet and discuss any political moves they were to make, as they were bound to do nothing which all three didn't agree to. Crassus always acted as if nothing was amiss when he met with Caesar who was in a greater position to influence politics, but both men knew they were secretly working to undermine him. Pompeius and Crassus were always outwardly friendly and agreeable to each other, while everyone knew they each detested the other and subtly tried to encourage Caesar's suspicions of the other's disloyalty to their pact. By the nones of Aprilis (April 6), it was apparent Clodius had also been bought by Crassus and was working against Caesar. Clodius was a loud boastful man, and would often speak of the arrogance of Caesar in the way he flaunts the constitution in carrying out his acts as Consul and the need for a man like Crassus to take the lead of the Populares. For the time being, he was quiet about Pompeius' involvement in government affairs and seemed to forget the flagrant violation of the constitution that made him eligible to run for the tribunate, but Clodius was more adept at popular agitation than he was at sound reasoning. Foolishly, Clodius told Cicero that he was seeking the tribunate so he could undo all Caesar's acts as Consul. Cicero passed this information along to Curio, and Curio passed it along to Antonius who then told Caesar. Marcus Antonius enjoyed being the center of attention and when he knew something others didn't, he could never keep it to himself. One evening, while sharing an oil lamp, Caesar leaning over and reading dispatches from the provinces and I planning the schedules of the pontiffs for the next several days, Caesar sat back in his chair and sighed.

'What's wrong, Caesar?' I asked.

'I can't concentrate. It's time we send Crassus a message that we can work without him. He must be reminded he needs us at least as much as we need him.'

'Is it true?' I asked. 'Does he need you?'

Caesar shook his head. 'I'm not sure, but I hope he still thinks he does. We need to act now before he strengthens his position.'

'You've already given him what he wanted. How can you make your bond with him any stronger?' As always, I was genuinely curious to see Caesar's genius at work.

'I can't, so I plan to strengthen my bond with Pompeius.'

I was tired and therefore less cautious and I let a one-word question slip. 'Julia?'

Caesar smiled and shook his head. 'You're getting very good at this, Polybius.' I'll talk to her tomorrow. Find us a propitious day later this month or by the nones of next month. Did you happen to notice if my mother is still awake?'

'I think I heard her girl Helena reading poetry to her a short time ago.' I pointed toward Aurelia's suite with my pen. Caesar rose from his chair and headed in that direction as I went back to my work.

LIBER XXVIII

A few days later, as the meeting of the Senate was set to begin, Caesar rose from his curial chair and waited patiently for the room to come to order. 'I have an important personal announcement to make concerning my family and I wanted you, my esteemed colleagues, to hear of it from my lips before it is published and posted in the forum. We will be celebrating a wedding four days before the calends of Maius (April 28).' Thinking I knew what was coming, I had been rubbing a smudge of bird shit from the tile in front of me with the toe of my shoe. When Caesar said the date, my head snapped up. I couldn't believe he got the date of his daughter's wedding wrong! The date had been set for the day after the calends of Maius (May 2). I tried to catch his eye while shaking my head. Caesar turned and looked at me as I silently mouthed the correct date to him, hoping he could read my lips, but he only winked and smiled and turned back to the now attentive house. 'On that day, the daughter of Calpurnius Piso Caesoninus and I will be married.' The side of the house occupied by the Populares broke into applause, while the Optimates grumbled and scowled. Crassus simply glared at Caesar. Needless to say, I was stunned.

After the house returned to order, Pompeius rose from his seat on the bench. 'I would like to be the first to congratulate the Consul on this happy news.' Caesar nodded at Pompeius, who continued. 'I too have a wedding to announce. Gaius Caesar has been gracious enough to allow me to marry his daughter, five days after he marries the daughter of Piso.' At that news, the entire house broke into an uproar. I watched as Crassus turned and stalked out of the chamber. Little real work was done that day, and the session was adjourned shortly after it began.

We waited to see how Crassus would react and we didn't need to wait long. Within days, the reason for Crassus' meetings with Curio became evident. Young Curio had great influence among the next generation of senators and he was using it, and Crassus' money, to stir them up against Caesar and Pompeius. Young men generally do not need to be directly bribed. Curio was able to stir up trouble by having much more wine than water in what he served at his elaborate parties. He always made sure the discussion stayed on topic and the topic was always politics. Curio was clever enough to never frame the public discussion as Populares against Optimates, but rather as Caesar and Pompeius against republican government. Since each of these sons of senators he was trying to influence was at the age when he was contemplating his own rise in politics, it was easy to convince them that having two men hold all the power in the republic would make that impossible. Crassus was a master manipulator of opinion. By creating a campaign against Caesar and Pompeius through the sons of senators he was able to create a much wider public discussion of the situation. The young men had little influence on the political views of their fathers, but they were able to influence the family clients who were not important enough to earn a place at the salutatio. It is amazing how quickly seemingly idle talk in the forum or around a fountain, and anonymous scribbling on a wall can infect the collective mind of the mob of Roman citizens. Against my advice, for the time Caesar chose to ignore what he called idle chatter.

While Caesar ignored the gossip against him, he did increase the pace of his legislative agenda. He used the occasions of the weddings to, at least temporarily increase his and Pompeius' popularity. Pompeius marriage to Julia was celebrated in high style, as it was her first marriage and Caesar wanted to make it memorable. His marriage to Calpurnia was much less lavish but still drew large crowds of well-wishers. In the days immediately after the weddings, through Vatinius, Caesar introduced the lex Campana, his second agrarian law, the law ratifying all Pompeius' acts when he governed the provinces in the east, and the lex Vatinia de Imperio Caesaris. It was very clever the way Caesar handled this situation. I was present when he discussed the topic with Balbus, Demetrius, his sister Julia, and Aurelia one evening in late Aprilis, just before the marriages. The meeting had been ostensibly about the wedding plans and involved a much larger group of associates. While marriages are a private family matter, the wedding of a sitting Consul naturally becomes a very public and very political affair. After most of the group had left for their respective homes, those remaining retired to the garden in the back of the Domus Publica. Over wine, fruit, and cheese, the talk continued on a much more casual level.

Balbus posed the question that had been on my mind all evening. 'Shouldn't your marriage be at least on the same scale as Pompeius'? You are the Consul, Gaius.'

Aurelia answered him first. 'Julia is a young girl and she should have wonderful memories of the day. The gods know Pompeius can afford it.'

Balbus smiled and said to her, 'I can see where your son gets his skill at politics.'

Smiling back, Aurelia asked with mock innocence, 'whatever do you mean?'

'You answered the question for him, without answering the question. Julia and her new husband can have a wedding that rivals that of a Hellenistic king and queen, and the Consul's wedding can be just as grand. After all, I've heard he recently came into a large sum of money and he can't have spent it all buying Vatinius' support for his laws. The people would love it as well.' Balbus was playful in his response, and I knew, because this group of friends were comfortable enough with each other, the talk would remain friendly. Had there been others in the room it would have quickly become much more heated.

Demetrius spoke up to bolster Aurelia's side. 'Perhaps the Consul feels that it would be unseemly to have a lavish wedding since this is his third time at it.'

Finally, Caesar joined the talk. 'Have you all forgotten that I'm still here? I'm sitting right here!' We all laughed at that, but when the laughter subsided, without losing his smile, Caesar's look became more serious. 'We know each other well, Balbus, and you know I don't do anything without thinking it through first. There is nothing I can do now, and probably for the rest of my life that doesn't have political implications.'

Balbus nodded and said, 'and that's exactly why I asked the question. The people might come to think you are merely Pompeius' puppet and he holds the real power.'

After a pause, Caesar said, 'I will tell you my reasons, but what is said here stays here.' With that, Caesar looked over his shoulder to see if anyone was nearby. We were alone. 'You're right. People might come to think Pompeius has me on a leash. I hope they do.' I noticed that Balbus and Demetrius both raised their eyebrows, but Aurelia didn't seem the least surprised. Caesar went on. 'Bibulus publishes scathing pamphlets nearly every day. He has reminded the public of every indiscretion I've ever been accused of since I became a man. He wants to paint me as a second Sulla. That is why I had Vatinius propose the law confirming all Pompeius' acts in the east alongside the land law. I want to give the impression I needed to trade his law for his support of my agrarian law, and I wanted to make it clear that the agrarian law is only meant to address a serious social problem.'

Demetrius followed Caesar's thread. 'You want everyone to

think Pompeius is the second Sulla they need to worry about. I suppose you also hope that nobody notices that by colonizing all of Campana you acquire tens of thousands of new clients.'

Caesar nodded. 'For now, at least, I'm content with everyone, including Crassus, believing I dance to Pompeius' tune, at least until I can secure Imperium for the next few years.'

Balbus answered, 'you will need to have strong support for any law that gives you that much power. Half the Senate wants to see you stand trial next year. They want you destroyed.'

Caesar nodded. 'That's why I put through legislation that benefited Crassus and Pompeius first. That's why I pushed legislation that is popular with the people. In order for the Optimates to succeed in destroying me as a politician and as a citizen, they must, at the same time, have all my acts as Consul invalidated. I've built a wall of support with these laws. Pompeius, Crassus, and the voters have a very real interest in seeing my acts as Consul confirmed. That can't happen if I'm put on trial and sent into exile.'

I was surprised not a single member of the group questioned Caesar's plan for securing Imperium 'for the next few years.' It was traditional for Proconsular Imperium to be awarded for a year at a time and only extended in a time of crisis. As it stood right now, the best the Senate was offering Caesar was the supervision of cattle pastures after his year as Consul. At that time I understood clearly that Caesar did intend to become a second Sulla, but with much less bloodshed. Later that night, alone in my room, I thought about what he had said some years earlier. 'Sulla was a political illiterate for resigning his dictatorship.'

The agrarian laws were immensely popular among the plebs. The overcrowding of the city had reached an intolerable level, and Caesar was able to make a clear case that the opposition of Bibulus and the Optimates was purely personal and that they were morally in the wrong. Once put to a vote the law passed easily in the Comitia. Caesar used his boost in popularity to then have Vatinius propose the lex Imperio, giving him Proconsular Imperium for five years. Earlier in the year, Caesar set his aim toward Illyricum as his province, as that would keep him close to Rome, but since there was no current crisis in that part of the world it would make it difficult to gain a longer term as a Proconsul. But, the situation changed more toward his favor and it seemed to me he did indeed have Fortuna on his side.

The Gauls had for centuries been a source of trouble for Rome. After winning Hispania from Carthage in the Punic Wars, Rome needed a secure land route to those provinces and southern Gaul was taken as the province of Narbonensis. The peace and security of that province and the province of Cisalpine Gaul was essential to the security of Italy and Rome itself. To secure the peace, Rome had established treaties with some of the more cultured tribes that bordered the Roman provinces. As you will recall, three years earlier, after being bribed by Catilina and his coconspirators, the

Allobroges, a fairly civilized Gallic tribe living in Transalpine Gaul on the border of Cisalpina had revolted against Roman rule. This revolt was put down by the propraetor Gaius Pomptinus the following year, but when Catilina stirred up the Allobroges, it had been like poking a beehive and the other tribes in the area had also been stirred to unrest. The tribes that had treaties with Rome wanted to enjoy peace as much as we did. By having access to ports like Narbo and Massilia, these tribes could enjoy, through trade, the luxuries of the world and the prosperity it brought. Many of the border tribes had become quite wealthy through trading wine with their less civilized neighbors to the north. The troubles in Gaul had led to a series of visits by embassies of the allied tribes, including Diviciacus, one of the princes of the Aedui who had been a personal acquaintance of Caesar. You will hear more about this remarkable man later, but for now let us just say he was one of the best-educated and most cultured of Gauls and had become, through a series of visits to Rome, a friend to many of the leading senators. During Caesar's term as propraetor of Hispania Ulterior, Diviciacus visited Rome, staying in Cicero's home, to plead for Roman protection against the Sequani, an aggressive and warlike tribe bordering their territory on the east. As a result of his charm and eloquence, Diviciacus secured the commendation of the Roman senate for his and other allied tribes to the protection of whoever might be the governor of Narbonensis.

LIBER XXIX

On the surface, things remained peaceful, but the Sequani had formed an alliance with the Arverni, another warlike tribe bordering the Aedui on the west, placing them in a very precarious position. Still, the threat of Roman protection kept the peace. Secretly though, these two tribes had also enlisted the aid of Ariovistus, a barbarian prince from Germania, on the far side of the Rhenus River. In payment for his assistance, Ariovistus demanded the Sequani cede nearly a third of their land to him, allowing him to establish a Germanic kingdom in Gaul. This action, in turn, roused the Helvetii to action. The Helvetii were a tribe of Germanic origin that had migrated across the Rhenus some half century earlier. Since they had already left their ancestral lands in Germania and had no ties dating back to antiquity in the lands they now occupied just north of where Cisalpina and Narbonensis meet, they were persuaded by one of their princes to look for better lands to the west. Of course, this was taken by many to simply mean they planned to conquer the territory of the Roman allies before Ariovistus could do so. Any mention of the movement of Gallic tribes stirred a profound fear in the hearts of Romans. In spite of the fact that more than three centuries had passed since a Gallic tribe had descended on Italy and sacked Rome, people were still terrified of the Gauls. In addition to fear of the Gauls, there were still living people who could remember the time when the Teutones and the Cimbri clashed with Roman forces less than fifty years before. On that occasion, Rome lost over 80,000 soldiers and Italy itself was threatened. These cultural memories had a profound effect on both the Senate and the people. The Senate had to do something to allay the fears of the people, so in Martius of the year before Caesar's Consulship, the Senate voted to have the two Consuls draw lots for the provinces of Transalpine Gaul and Cisalpine Gaul and decreed that legions should be recruited without regard for any exemptions from service. Lucius Afranius drew Cisalpine Gaul and Metellus Celer won Transalpine Gaul. At the same time, three senators were sent as ambassadors to the Celtic tribes to persuade them to not join with or assist the Helvetii. These ambassadors did their jobs well, and for a time the situation improved, dashing Celer's hopes of winning a triumph. As it turned out, Celer never even saw his province, as he was prevented from leaving Rome by the decree of a Tribune, and while the Senate wrangled over that, Celer met an untimely death in Aprilis of the year of Caesar's Consulship. At the time, it was widely believed that Celer was murdered by his wife. She had the reputation of behaving in a rather debauched way, and it was said she desired to kill her husband so she could indulger he lust. I met the woman once, and I certainly got the impression she had a very forward personality, but she did not strike me as a murderer.

At any rate, Caesar saw this as an opportunity. He wanted to demonstrate to the Senate and People that the Gauls still posed an immediate threat. This was made more difficult when a dispatch from the propraetor Pomptinus arrived from Transalpine Gaul in Maius, announcing his defeat of the Allobroges. Of course, Caesar had political allies in Narbonensis and indeed one of Pomptimus' military Tribunes was secretly informing Caesar of what was going on in the province. Because of this, Caesar knew the 'decisive defeat' reported in the dispatch was merely a tactical retreat on the part of the enemy. I remember well the day the dispatch from Pomptinus arrived, as it was just a short time after the secret dispatch from Carolus, Caesar's man in Pomptinus' fort in Gaul had arrived. Caesar, Balbus, Antonius, and Pompeius were working in the Regia, as Calpurnia was hosting a 'ladies night' in the domus. Caesar had just finished reading the report from a client in Narbonensis when he broke the seal on the scroll sent by Pomptinus. He burst into laughter on reading it, with its lofty language and a request to the Senate to award him a triumph. Handing it to Pompeius, he ran his fingers across the side of his face. 'That man at the baths didn't do a very good job with this shave. I'll need to have my man redo it.'

Pompeius read the dispatch carefully and then reread the first report. 'The man is an ass,' he finally said, handing the scroll to Balbus.

'Yes,' Caesar agreed, but this isn't his doing. 'He's in the pay of somebody, and I'm guessing it's Bibulus. He wants Transalpine

Gaul for himself next year.'

By this time, I was comfortable enough, and well enough informed, to join the conversation without being asked. This always surprised Pompeius' man Milo as he never had this freedom. 'If I may say so Caesar, there is a greater purpose to this.' Caesar nodded at me. 'Bibulus certainly believes the Senate will award him the province of his choosing, as he has the backing of Cato and has no need to resort to this sort of thing unless he believes the threat of war might cause the people to award the province to you if the matter is put before them. The greater purpose is to deny you any chance of gaining a province.

Balbus agreed. 'Polybius is right. They mean to keep you here in Italy. I would force him to prove the numbers of dead and captured are accurate.'

'For now,' Caesar said, 'I'll question the facts, but I won't put up too much of a fight. The Senate will no doubt want to immediately vote a thanksgiving to Pomptinus. I'll not stand in their way on this one. Let it leak out that I intend to have Illyricum as my province.

At this point, I must point out two things, as I have just now brought them up. Caesar was once again mentoring Marcus Antonius, and his relationship with Calpurnia had turned out to be, at least up to this point, a happy one. He continued to see Servilia, every few days, but he got on well with his new wife and a genuine friendship that would later bloom into love, was developing. Calpurnia was an intelligent and savvy woman, very like Aurelia in her own way, and didn't seem to object to Caesar's dalliances with other women. As a point of fact, Servilia was attending the very dinner Calpurnia was hosting that evening we were forced to work in the Regia. As for young Antonius, I asked Caesar later that evening as we walked across the street to the Domus Publica, why he was again keeping him close. Caesar's answer puzzled me at the time, but I was later to learn how correct he was. 'I see something dangerous in that young man, and I like to keep the dangerous people on my side.'

True to expectations, the Senate voted a thanksgiving to the propraetor Pomptinus the following day.

While it was never proved, but long suspected by Caesar, Crassus didn't stop with rousing the public against us. Two nights before the Ides of Maius (May 13) Pompeius arrived unexpectedly and unannounced at the side door of the Domus Publica. This door was only used to bring supplies in through the kitchen and was constantly kept bolted and barred from the inside. There was however a small window in the door where the kitchen slave could check the identity of the person on the other side. About two hours after sunset the door slave who manned the front door of the Domus came to me. 'There is a strange man at the door, saying he has a message for the master. He says it's most urgent.' The doorman was very agitated. 'He looks like a tramp from the street, so I tried to send him away with a shake of my club.' With that, he shook his club at me. 'He held his ground and asked me if I could read. When I said no, he smiled and said that was a good thing and he offered me a silver coin to bring this here note to you.' He showed me a small scroll with his other hand. 'He knew your name, Polybius, so I figured this was really something.' With that, I took the scroll and followed the man back to the front door, being careful to remain three steps behind him. When he opened the door and looked around he turned back to me with a puzzled look on his face. Scratching his chin he said, 'He ain't there no more. What's the note say?'

'Shut the door and lock it, please.' At this point, I was nervous as well. Once the door was bolted and barred, I slipped the string that was wrapped around the scroll off the small piece of papyrus. The note simply said, 'go open the kitchen door. Now.' I was intrigued by the cryptic message but what really caught my attention was the handwriting. It appeared to have been written by Pompeius. Caesar had not been feeling well and had gone to bed early, but I felt this was important enough to wake him. I went to his chamber off the peristyle and drew back the curtain. I didn't need to wake him.

Without opening his eyes I heard him say rather crossly, 'what is it now?'

'I'm sorry Caesar, but this seems urgent.'

'It better be,' he said swinging his legs over the side of the bed and rubbing his face. I stood there dumbly until he snapped, 'well, what in Dis' name is it?'

'I'm sorry, but a strange man delivered a note. It's not signed, but it looks like it was written by Pompeius.'

With that, Caesar got up and took the note from me as he stepped into the peristyle looking around for a lamp. I quickly ran over to the stand near Calpurnia's chamber and took one from the stand just outside her door. I couldn't run back for fear I would extinguish the flame, but shielding it with my hand and walking as quickly as possible I was able to meet Caesar halfway. I held the light while he read the note. With that, he quickly walked back into his chamber and emerged with a dagger, before moving just as quickly toward the kitchen. Oddly enough he stopped briefly by a mirror that hung on the wall near the triclinium to check his hair. I can't imagine in that dim light he could really see anything, but it was a habit of his. I followed Caesar into the kitchen and stood behind him as he opened the shutter blocking the window in the middle of the door. I noticed Caesar stood back and to the side to avoid anything that might be thrust through. 'Is anyone there?' he asked.

From the other side, in a hushed whisper, I heard Pompeius say, 'it's me. Now open the damned door!'

Caesar moved his face to the window and looked out, but he couldn't see much, so while blocking the door with the bulk of his body he took off the bar and drew back the bolt, opening the door just enough to look out. He quickly pulled the door open allowing

Pompeius, wrapped in a dark cloak and carrying a sword in his right hand to push his way into the room. Caesar quickly shut and bolted the door behind him. 'What are you doing here?' Caesar asked in a surprised tone.

Pompeius turned and looked at me, but said to Caesar, 'are you two never apart?'

I answered him before Caesar could speak. 'With all respect sir, the note was sent to me.'

Pompeius scowled. Let's go somewhere and talk. Not where anyone else can see me. With that, he looked at me again. Caesar led him to the nearby triclinium with me following when we entered the room Pompeius scowled at me again and said, 'I'd rather we speak alone.'

'I trust Polybius,' Caesar said, matter-of-factly.

'Right now, I'm not sure I do,' Pompeius answered.

I was hurt, and I'm sure it showed, but I turned to leave when Caesar said. 'Polybius please draw the curtain and come sit on one of the stools. When I looked I noticed he was staring crossly at Pompeius. I'm certain if Pompeius would have asked without insulting me, Caesar would have had me leave, but by questioning Caesar's trust in me, Pompeius had also insulted my master.

Pompeius sighed and took a seat on one of the couches. Caesar sat too and I sat on one of the stools. Looking at me, Pompeius said to no one in particular, 'this is of the utmost secrecy.'

'Out with it,' Caesar said.

'Okay, here it is. I ran into Bibulus today.' Pompeius paused.

'So? My co-Consul chose to come out of his house. He was no doubt scanning the sky to see what the birds are telling him about my actions.' Caesar was irritated by all this.

Pompeius realized he needed to get to the point so he did. 'He found me as I was heading home from the bath. He had one of his lictors pull me aside and into, of all places a public latrine on one of those little out of the way streets off the Vicus Longus. He obviously had his men clear the whole street, so we were quite alone. Standing in the middle of the latrine, he told me there was a plot in the works to kill me!' Then, as an afterthought, he added, 'and you too.'

'Did he tell you who is planning to kill us?' Caesar didn't show any surprise but took on a look of cool calculation.

'He wouldn't give me any details. He just told me to watch my back. And yours.'

Caesar rose to his feet and began to pace. 'Polybius, do you have a tablet?'

I reached in my bag and found one that I could quickly scrape clean, as Caesar went on. Let it be known that I'm feeling ill and cancel the salutatio tomorrow. Make a list of the household slaves you trust most and get a list from them of the slaves they trust least. Send someone to get Demetrius and Balbus first thing in the morning. Not a word to anyone else. While I'm home sick, I want you out, discreetly, seeing what you can learn from your contacts outside the house.' It was only then he turned to Pompeius. 'Figure out who your most trusted veterans are, but remember if anyone is going to do this, it will probably be someone close to us. I also want you to get us some weapons. Come back tomorrow after your salutatio, and don't see anyone alone.'

Pompeius nodded and rose. 'I can take care of myself, but for now, I need to get home. We can talk more tomorrow. We need to figure out why Bibulus would warn me of an assassination plot. I would think he would prefer to have us both dead.'

Caesar, speaking to both Pompeius and me, said quietly, 'Ask around, discreetly, if Crassus is also a target. If he isn't, we may have a bigger problem.'

I stepped out first, looking around to see if anyone was watching before pulling the curtain back for Caesar and Pompeius. As Caesar held the door open for Pompeius, he rested a hand on his shoulder and said quietly, 'Make sure my daughter is protected.'

With that, Pompeius pulled up his hood and embraced Caesar. I could hear him whisper hoarsely, 'They will have to kill me before they get near her.'

Why indeed would Bibulus warn Pompeius of a plot? That was the question. As it turned out I was able to get some information that may have provided a rationale for Bibulus' actions after meeting with Tiro the following morning. We still met from time to time to sell each other information. Since Cicero wasn't as active in politics as he had been, it was more to exchange gossip rather than trade in any useful information, but that morning I had an agenda. We had a standing meeting for the morning before the ides of each month, unless there was public business that kept us apart. We would meet at a certain corner near Cicero's domus in town and take a stroll down the street. Cicero, and therefore Tiro, had just returned from one of his villas south of Rome, and they only had a few days before they were set to travel again. In that turbulent year, Cicero chose to spend much of his time outside the city. I arrived first and was sitting on the fountain wall waiting for Tiro. I recall the morning was a bit chilly for mid-Maius and I regretted not bringing a cloak. Tiro approached and I was anxious to walk off the chill I was feeling.

Tiro started with some inane gossip about some senator's wife, when I cut him off, as I was on a mission to gather real information. 'I have heard there may be a plot against the Consul. What have you heard?'

Tiro smiled and looked at me sideways. 'There are two Consuls. Which one are we talking about?'

'I don't really have time to play this game, Tiro. So, name your price and tell me what you know.' I untied my purse from my belt.

'Three denarii.' Tiro named a price at more than three times what we usually exchanged and I didn't argue. I just handed him his money and nodded.

'I have heard, and this is just a rumor, that there is a plot.' Tiro stopped and looked around to be sure no one was listening.

In my impatience, I said, 'Yes, I know that much. Why is Bibulus warning Pompeius who he must know would warn Caesar?'

At this, Tiro looked surprised. "Pompeius warned Caesar himself?'

'Yes,' I answered him. 'You didn't know?'

'I'll lay it all out for you, as far as I've been able to piece together from what I've heard and what I've read in Cicero's letters. Bibulus doesn't fear Caesar. In fact, he thinks Cato and he will be able to get everything he's done and will do this year undone by having them all declared invalid. They both do however fear Crassus and Pompeius and they were very surprised to see those two agreeing on anything, much less working in concert with Caesar. They were hoping to create suspicion between them and drive them apart.'

'Is Bibulus just making it all up, or is there really a plot? And,' I asked pointedly, why would this warning cause Pompeius to suspect Crassus' I was as confused as ever.

'Because, either the plot will happen, or it will be foiled.' Tiro was speaking in almost a whisper now. 'If it happens, Cato's faction wins. If it is foiled, those involved will almost certainly reveal that they are in the pay of Crassus. Pompeius will come out on top, and he will owe Bibulus a debt of gratitude.'

I made one further guess as to Bibulus' motive. 'It would also come out that Bibulus was aware of the plot and if one or the other survived, and if he didn't warn them, he would face charges in court.'

'There is another possibility,' Tiro added, looking at me with an expression that was very close to pity. 'You're too young, Polybius, to have lost so much of your innocence. It just may be that Cato and Bibulus believe it would be a very great wrong to assassinate a Consul of Rome, or anyone for that matter, to achieve political aims. They truly do respect the Roman constitution and would like to see it preserved. Please give that some consideration.'

I smiled at him. 'Maybe you're right Tiro. I'll give it some thought.' I quickly hurried home to tell Caesar what I had learned.

At the meeting with Pompeius that morning, it was determined that they needed to mend their fractured relations with Crassus. He was too powerful for them to move against, so the only thing to do would be to put him in a position where he placed more value on both of them alive rather than dead. Caesar asked me to arrange a meeting between the three for the next day. What was said at that meeting, in a private room at the baths, I do not know. Crassus made it clear it was to be just the three of them in the room and Caesar didn't say a word about it afterward."

With that we took a break for a quick, late lunch. We dined on fruit and some small game birds that Polybius' sons had captured in their snares. Rather than continue his story after our meal, Polybius said he needed a nap and invited us back the following morning.

LIBER XXX

The next morning, after the normal pleasantries, Polybius asked me to use my notes to refresh his memory. After I read back what I had last written, he settled into the pile of pillows on his couch. "Quite so, now I remember. Caesar had returned from his meeting with Crassus and Pompeius. I did not know what the meeting was about, but I soon pieced together some clues. The very next day, after this meeting, Caesar began a very public campaign to increase his popularity with the plebs. He began to frequent the tavernas and baths in the lower quarters of the city. I thought this was rather bold, with the threat of assassination hanging over him, but he said it was necessary. He never went anywhere without a dagger in his tunic belt, unless it was into the Curia or a temple and his lictors were kept especially close to him as well, but he didn't take any other special precautions. About this time I started the practice of keeping one metal stylus with a very sharp point at the ready, should I need a weapon. I continued that practice for the rest of my days with the Caesars.

The popularity campaign culminated in a magnificent party. Quintus Arrius, one of Caesar's erstwhile rivals for the Consulship had, upon losing, immediately become a strident supporter of the Populare cause. Around this time his father had died, which was in no way unexpected, as the man was very old and had been ill for some time. As it turned out, his death helped Caesar's cause. Arrius hosted a very lavish funeral banquet and invited the city. The banquet was held at the temple of Castor and Pollux because the area in front of the temple was the largest open space within the city walls.

The banquet was timed to coincide with the Rosalia Festival (May 23), so tens of thousands of roses adorned the temple and the hundreds of tables that had been set up for the feast. Caesar made it a point to advertise for workers among the unemployed plebs for the hundreds needed to build tables and decorate for the festivities. During Caesar's Consulship he, as often as was practical, would pay the unemployed poor to do whatever temporary jobs the city needed doing. It appeared to me that every Pleb in the city turned out for the feast, with large queues forming in anticipation of getting a seat at one of the tables. Cattle, pigs, sheep, and goats were roasted by the hundreds and bread, fruit, and vegetables were piled high on every table. Hundreds of slaves from the households of Caesar's supporters were pressed into service to bring food and wine to the guests. Caesar and his companions, including his new father in law Calpurnius Piso, and his new son in law, Pompeius Magnus, attended dressed in the tunics of the working class and would from time to time make speeches from the steps of the temple and shower the crowd with a handful of candies or coins.

The mood of the entire city was lifted and the banquet made the voters very much inclined to back anything Caesar or his supporters proposed. The following morning, the Tribune Vatinius proposed the lex Vatina de Imperio Caesaris, a law that would give Caesar as his Proconsular command Illyricum and Cisalpine Gaul. The law also would allow for Caesar to command three legions with the Senate providing for their maintenance, and the command was to extend to no less than Martius of five years hence. The law excluded the Senate entirely, except for the payment. Caesar was to have the authority to appoint all the legates for the provinces, including the two that would hold magisterial authority. The required Contiones were immediately scheduled and the vote was held just before the nones of Junius (June 4). With the support of Pompeius and Piso, and apparently, for reasons I didn't at the time understand, with the behind the scenes support of Crassus and his vast clientela, the bill became law, much to the chagrin of Cato, Bibulus, and the rest of the Optimates. Bibulus had, of course, reported ill omens that should have canceled the vote, and Caesar had, of course, ignored him. Caesar had secured his Imperium.

Cato at this time tried a new tactic and put pressure on his son in law Bibulus, to persuade the staunchest Optimates to stop attending the Senate entirely. This created a very new situation for Crassus to deal with, as there was no real opposition to Caesar's and Pompeius' power. Crassus on the surface remained friendly to the other two, but his great fear was that Pompeius would once again overshadow him and, behind the scenes, he worked to prevent that. For a man of such great success in business and politics, it amazed me even then to think he didn't notice the real threat to his power was Caesar. At this time, almost no one saw the potential of Caesar. This was probably because his achievements didn't display his abilities, but rather the way he went about reaching his goals did. Caesar trusted in his good fortune, or perhaps I should say the goddess Fortuna, but it was his ability to make quick and sure decisions that took advantage of whatever came his way and his willingness to take calculated risks whenever the rewards would be greater than the result of doing nothing. Caesar now realized he could pass laws in the now more compliant Senate without resorting to the Comitia. This was first demonstrated when it came time to fill the seat left vacant by the death of Celer. Pompeius made the motion that the province should be added to the two others awarded Caesar and the motion became law with almost no debate. This province was however awarded, as was traditional, for one year only and would need to be renewed. The compliant senate also, at Caesar's prodding, recognized Ariovistus as a friend and ally of the Roman people.

LIBER XXXI

Cato, using Bibulus as his mouthpiece began to publish 'edicts' in the absent Consul's name and having them posted in the forum alongside Caesar's publications. He also began to publish any snippet of conversation his spies could overhear that would make Caesar look bad. That is why it was reported and is still believed that Caesar 'announced' to the Senate that having reached his goal he would now leap upon his enemies' heads. This was, in fact, something he said, but it was said to a few friends and was intended as a joke. These publications were of two kinds. Some of them were laws proposed by Bibulus that Caesar and Pompeius were reported to have rejected, suggesting they were thwarting the constitution. The majority, however, were scandalous and obscenity-laced accounts of the personal behavior of the two men. I always suspected Crassus, probably through some agent of his, had a hand in this too, since one of the postings suggested Caesar, during his Aedileship, went behind the back of and tried to double-cross Pompeius, and another reported Caesar's affair with Pompeius' then-wife, Marcia. Many of the scandalous accusations against the two men were accurate, but one was, I am entirely convinced, a complete fabrication that had started in Caesar's youth and continued right up until his death, and that was the scandal with the king of Bithynia."

I wondered if Polybius would address this point, as he had mentioned he would many visits earlier. I had even discussed this story with Mela and this caused him to sit up and take notice when Polybius mentioned it. Unfortunately, or perhaps intentionally, as he liked to tease us with the most salacious parts of the story, Polybius needed to take one of his frequent walks to the latrine. When he returned and settled in again, he seemed to forget where he left off.

"Anyway," he started in, "Caesar didn't take the bait that was being dangled in front of him, but Pompeius did."

At this, Mela sat up again. "Excuse me," he said more pointedly than he intended, "you didn't finish what you were saying before."

This caused Polybius to smile. "I beg your pardon," he answered. "While I don't believe gossip is important, I suppose it is what a good biographer relies on to keep his audience's attention.

The king of Bithynia." Polybius sighed and shook his head, repeating, "The king of Bithynia. Of all the men I ever knew, I would say Gaius Julius Caesar had the least physical attraction to his own sex. He was powerfully drawn to women, both young and old, and never expressed, to my knowledge, sexual interest in a man. At any rate, one of Bibulus' edicts brought up the old scandal. In the edict, Cato, through Bibulus, described Caesar as the 'Queen of Bithynia. He went on to further say that Caesar was a man, 'who once wanted to be fucked by a king, but now wants to be one.' This was an old bit of gossip that got its start before I was born when Caesar was a young man serving on the staff of Marcus Minucius Thermus. Caesar, who was then nineteen years old was sent on a diplomatic mission to King Nicomedes of Bithynia. The king enjoyed the company of young men and had a reputation for making lewd advances to them. Caesar took rather longer than expected to finish his work in the kingdom, which fueled speculation, but it was only later when he volunteered for a second mission to try and secure the assistance of Nicomedes and his fleet in the war with Mithridates that the rumors took hold. A fantastic tale was concocted that became more elaborate and detailed with the passage of time. In this story, Caesar had joined in the fun at a banquet of the debauched favorites of Nicomedes, all attractive young men and boys. At this party it was said that Caesar, wearing a purple silk shift, acted as cupbearer, playing the part of Ganymede to Nicomedes' Zeus. It was also said that near the end of the banquet when there was far more drinking and far less dining going on, the royal attendants led Caesar to the king's bedchamber where they became lovers. This story was even repeated by Cicero who claimed to have heard it from a group of merchants who were present at the party, but the story is absolute rubbish."

Mela, taking a sip of wine, asked Polybius outright, "how do you know it's not true?"

"How does one know anything that has not been personally

experienced?" Polybius sighed. "One must study the facts and determine what the evidence indicates is most likely. As I've stated earlier, those of us who are attracted to our own sex learn to recognize each other. We can tell at a glance, no doubt picking up on unspoken clues, who is like us and who is not. Of course, this is certainly not foolproof, but I must say I never once detected any of the signs in Caesar. What I did have a chance to witness was Caesar's lifelong pursuit of women. I saw him carry on multiple affairs with high born Roman matrons and low born wives and daughters of barbarians and I watched him fall in love with the Queen of Aegyptus, but never once did I see him touch a man or boy in a sexual way."

Mela wouldn't let up, and his persistence began to make me uncomfortable. "But, how do you know Caesar didn't try it once with the king and decide he didn't like it?"

Polybius seemed unfazed. "The most important thing to do when determining the truth of an event from history is to compare all the available versions of the events and determine what makes the most sense. In this case, based on what I knew of Caesar, I chose to believe another story of what transpired in Bythinia."

"What was that story?" I interjected. "I've only ever heard the scandal."

"I base what I believe on the explanation for Caesar's stay in Bythinia I heard from Caesar's own lips. One evening, while lingering before a campfire after having a little too much wine, I became bold and somewhat impertinent in my speech, much like young Mela here." With that, he gestured toward my brother who at that instant was lifting his cup to his lips. Mela's face quickly reddened as he set his cup on the table. "It was just Caesar and me sitting and staring as one does into the dying flames of the fire. Everyone else had gone to his tent. Earlier, we had been discussing Caesar's career and of course, his service in the diplomatic mission he was sent on during that war came up. The relaxed atmosphere of a campfire and the strong wine prompted my boldness. 'Caesar,' I said, 'what really happened in Bythinia?' I immediately regretted what I'd said when I saw a frown mar Caesar's previously contented expression.

'You too Polybius?' Caesar looked disappointed.

'I'm sorry. I was out of line to ask such a thing." I quickly added, 'Please forgive me.'

Caesar sat staring into the fire for longer than I expected before speaking and the silence made me even more uncomfortable. I was about to ask leave to retire when he looked over at me, drawing my gaze to his. 'I will tell you the truth, but you must tell no one, as I have made a promise to take the secret to my grave.' I gave Caesar my word. After a pause, he said, 'I fell in love with the queen of Bithynia.'

This didn't surprise me at all. By all accounts, the queen was much younger than the king and only about ten years older than Caesar. 'Why don't you just tell people the truth? The king has been dead for so many years now, who will care?'

'The queen will care,' Caesar answered, 'and I think our daughter would care.'

This did shock me, but it made sense. One time Cicero interrupted a speech Caesar was making in the Senate in defense of Nysa, the Bythinian princess and listing his own personal obligations to the royal family, by shouting, 'enough of this. We are all familiar with what he gave you, and what you gave him in exchange!' Nysa was visiting Rome at this time, and I had the opportunity to meet her. I hadn't noticed it when we met, but in reflecting on what Caesar admitted to me, I realized she closely resembled him, especially her intense dark eyes.

LIBER XXXII

But, we have strayed from our original subject. The edicts Bibulus had been posting began to have an effect. Politics of today are much less messy than in the last years of the republic. Today it is necessary to please only the Augustus and those surrounding him. In Caesar's time, it was important to keep the teeming masses of Roman citizens happy, and this was nearly impossible to do. By and large, people are stupid and gullible. A very small proportion of mankind does all that is important or creative and the rest merely follow the lead and do the work. In Republican politics, a month was like a lifetime. The whims of the masses could be easily swayed and ground that seemed solid a few days prior turned to quicksand. Perhaps a more appropriate metaphor, though one you boys might not understand, is that of a frozen lake. I recall one time in Gaul when a nearby pond froze over. For days I was able to enjoy the experience of walking on its slippery surface, but one day after the weather began to warm a bit, I found myself feeling the ice crack beneath my feet. As gingerly as possible I tried to make my way back toward the shore, but alas, when I was but ten or fifteen feet away, the ice around my feet broke into several pieces sending me into the frigid water. Fortunately, the water was only chest deep at that point and I didn't die that day. That is what the political situation was at that time. Before the end of Junius what was being published by Bibulus began to be scrawled on the walls of public buildings and small groups of men and women would shout their disapproval as Caesar made his way down the Sacra Via toward the forum. Curio, sometimes from temple steps and sometimes even from the rostrum itself, began to openly attack Pompeius and Caesar and their supporters. Clodius began to do the same, but most of his poison darts were aimed at Cicero.

Caesar's popularity was on the wane, while Bibulus' star was rising. His popularity seemed to reach its lowest point in Quintilis (July). When, as was customary for the Consul, Caesar entered the Circus for the stage performance portion of the Ludi Apollinaris, he was met with silence from the audience, but when Curio entered a short time later, he was greeted with a tremendous ovation.

A few days later, Gaius Scribonius Curio, father to the young agitator, paid a visit to Pompeius to warn him of an attempt on his life, naming Vettius as the would-be assassin. Apparently, Vettius had, because the younger Curio was stirring up so much public enmity toward Pompeius and Caesar, assumed he would be keen to assist in the assassination. Curio was, however, not willing to go that far and reported the news to his father who then reported it to Pompeius. The following morning Vettius was called before the Senate to explain his role in the plot. At first, Vettius denied everything. This prompted Libo, a close ally of Crassus to move that Vettius be released since there was no evidence linking him to any plot. I happened to look over at Crassus as Libo was speaking and saw that he had a look of satisfaction on his usually gruff face.

This motion was about to be put to a vote when Pompeius' man Florus moved to have the Senate guarantee that Vettius would not lose his life if his testimony results in the Senate finding him guilty. Caesar, as Consul, asked Pompeius as the target of the plot if he had any objection. When he didn't, it was put to an immediate vote and passed. With that, Vettius, whose testimony sounded much rehearsed, began to name a list of distinguished men, including Servilia's son, Brutus. When he spoke that name, Caesar's face showed anger for the first time that day, as he too looked at Crassus. This, of course, prompted me to look toward Crassus again. The look of satisfaction was gone, but he didn't appear overly distressed. When Vettius sounded as if he was straying from a rehearsed script though, and the list of names grew, I noticed Crassus' scowl return and from where I stood I could see the vein in his forehead pulse. Vettius ended his list of conspirators with the Consul Bibulus, saying he was the instigator of the plot and the dagger Vettius was to use in the murder had been handed to him by Bibulus' nomenclator.

This caused quite a stir in the Senate, with Cato rising to his feet to accuse first Pompeius and then Caesar of being behind an invented conspiracy. After the Senate came to order again, it was decided Vettius would be taken into custody for carrying arms without the senate's authority, giving Bibulus an opportunity to tell his side.

On the following day, we rose early and just after sunrise crossed the forum to pay Vettius a visit in prison. With his lictors and I waiting outside, Caesar spent nearly an hour alone with the man. After that, he had Vettius brought to the steps of the temple of Castor to, under interrogation by Vatinius, repeat his allegations to the assembled people. There was a sizeable crowd, as Caesar had me post notices of the assembly throughout the city immediately after the Senate meeting was adjourned. Vettius' account varied in several significant ways on his second telling. While Bibulus was still named as the author of the plot, Lucius Lucullus who was standing for the Consulship and Lucius Domitius Ahenobarbus, a candidate for praetor, were named as well.

Ahenobarbus had at one time been a supporter of Pompeius but had started to take an active role opposing the governance of Caesar and Pompeius. Vettius made no mention of Cicero, but he did name Gaius Piso who was betrothed to Cicero's daughter. Brutus' name was, of course, omitted from the list leading Cicero to later joke that a night had passed between the first and second naming of the conspirators. Later that same day Bibulus made one of his rare public appearances to declare from the rostrum that he had warned Pompeius of the possibility of assassination in mid-Maius and asked rhetorically, why would a man warn his political enemy of a plot in Maius only to involve himself in another not two months later? No mention was made of Caesar being a target. Vettius' second version of the conspiracy was, of course, an attempt by Caesar to sully the reputations of the Optimate faction to weaken their chances in the upcoming elections. While the plot was real, and Caesar suspected it was Crassus behind it, Bibulus' supposed involvement was a clumsy attempt by the desperate Vettius to deflect blame from himself and the real author of the plot, while the testimony that Lentulus and Ahenobarbus were part of it was Caesar's invention.

Caesar's action had an effect and the thin ice of public opinion began to crack again, and the Optimate slate for the magisterial elections seemed to be losing ground. As a result, two days later, Bibulus, or more likely Cato using Bibulus as his instrument, directed that the Consular elections for the following year be postponed until October. It was, no doubt, hoped that the delay would help the Optimate candidates Lentulus and Ahenobarbus in their attempts to be elected, since the furor swirling around the assassination plot would have subsided. Caesar was of the mind to have Vettius tell his story loudly and often, and Pompeius seemed to agree, resulting in Vatinius' creation of a special court where those accused could stand trial.

This prompted Crassus to invite the two to a private meeting. I was never quite sure if I was given all the information as to the events of the latter half of that year. Often when Caesar met with Crassus, I was excluded from the meeting. Crassus never did trust me and it was at his insistence that I was left out. Caesar explained to me that he made this simple concession to Crassus to keep his goodwill. After this particular meeting where heated words, that I could hear though not clearly understand, were exchanged between the men, Crassus left quickly, and clearly in an angry mood. Two days later, and just one day before Caesar sitting as judge in the special court that was to interrogate Vettius, the man was found choked to death in the well of the Carcer, where the most dangerous prisoners are held. The matter was promptly dropped.

The remainder of the year Caesar spent shoring up the political support he would need to have back in Rome when he began his five years as a Proconsul and in educating himself on the situations of his provinces. Late into each evening Caesar and I would spend hours poring over histories and reports of the two Gallic provinces and Illyricum. The days were spent in political maneuvering with an eye toward the future. The three men ruling Rome no longer made any pretense that they were not acting in concert with one another and would meet openly to discuss policy and make plans. One such meeting was called by Caesar to be held in his villa on the far side of the Tiber for the day after the ides of Quintilis (July 16). A few days before, there began an outbreak of fever in the subura and many of the senators retreated to their homes outside the city. Others chose to remove themselves fifty miles or more, but Caesar felt it was important for him to remain near Rome. This meeting was perhaps one of the most important meetings of Caesar's life, for with this meeting he solidified his control over Rome and set in motion events that none of us could foresee. On this particular day, I was working in my cubicle just off the tablinum. Caesar walked into the room so quietly I didn't hear him enter, so I don't know how long he stood in the doorway looking at me. Finally, I happened to glance up and seeing him there startled me and caused me to involuntarily jump in my seat.

'I'm sorry,' Caesar said. 'What are you reading? You seemed fairly engrossed in it, so it must be interesting.'

This made me smile. 'Not at all interesting, but it is something I must do.'

With that Caesar came and looked over my shoulder to see I was studying a list of merchants from Illyricum. The censor's office kept lists of all the most prominent traders and merchants for tax purposes, and I was trying to update my information on the prominent people in the provinces we would be moving into. Caesar didn't need to be told why I had been studying the list, but he did ask me, 'Which province are they from?'

'Illyricum,' I answered. 'I'm moving from east to west.'

'Switch it around. Start with the two Gauls, and learn those first.' This told me that we would be spending our first year in Gaul. However, at the time I didn't think we would be spending all our time in Gaul, and far more of it than anyone foresaw. 'I actually came in here to tell you something,' Caesar continued.

'When Crassus arrives for the meeting he will want you to leave the room. Don't.'

'Licinius Crassus will not allow it,' I said.

Caesar was firm. 'Crassus doesn't own this home and he doesn't own you or, for that matter, me. Make sure you have a good supply of tablets to take notes.' With that, he left the room. I was secretly elated. I craved knowledge of the events of those days, and I loathed being left out of discussions.

An odd thing happened at that moment. I was sitting quietly thinking about how events were unfolding when I felt an invisible finger brush my right cheek. I immediately looked around the room, but I was, of course, quite alone. It was then I heard the soft and musical voice of Fortuna. 'Now, it begins in earnest,' was what I heard, as clearly as if she was standing over my shoulder. This was the first time the goddess every visited me while I was awake.

When Crassus arrived it was Demetrius who showed him into Caesar's tablinum. Caesar rose to greet him. 'I hope you don't mind that I asked you here before the others. There are things we need to discuss without them.'

Crassus nodded his agreement and took one of the many seats that had been arranged around the room. The large table that normally dominated the tablinum had been removed to the atrium and had been replaced with several chairs and three smaller tables. 'Polybius,' Caesar said, 'please draw the curtain.' I did as I was asked and returned to my seat.

Caesar started the discussion. 'We haven't been getting along well, Marcus, and I mean to mend the rift if you are agreeable.'

There was an uncomfortable silence during which Crassus stared at me. Finally, he spoke up. 'The boy should leave.'

'No,' Caesar smiled and answered mildly. 'Polybius stays.'

'I'm not comfortable with that. Frankly, I don't trust him.' Crassus was studying his fingernails, clearly reluctant to start an argument so soon into the meeting.

'I trust him,' Caesar answered back in the same mild tone, 'and if you don't trust him you don't trust me. I want a record of what is said in this room, and he is the best man to accomplish that.'

Caesar sat back and waited through another uncomfortable silence when at last Crassus spoke again. 'Fine. But, mark me well, if any word of what we say here leaks out, this slave of yours will sorely regret it!' This made me think of the poor young man who was stabbed and dumped in the sewer and I felt a little ill.

'I can assure you if word leaks out it will not come from Polybius.' With that Caesar stood up and leaned forward looking Crassus in the eye. 'And, my friend, if anything were to happen to Polybius I too will regret it, and I don't take misfortune lightly.' Caesar never raised his voice but the way he said the words were chilling. I could see even Crassus was unnerved. With that, Caesar lightened the mood by walking over to the sideboard and taking cups down from the shelf. 'This wine is excellent. I think you'll enjoy it.' He poured first Crassus and then me a cup of wine.

'Now, as I was saying, I hope you are agreeable to what I have to say. I aim to repair our relations because frankly, I will need your support here in Rome when I leave for my provinces. What do you want in exchange for that support?' Crassus seemed surprised by Caesar's directness and seemed at a loss for words. Prompting Caesar to add with a smile, 'surely you've thought about this, Marcus.'

Crassus looked at his fingernails again. 'I will wish to choose the Consuls for next year.'

'I can't do that,' Caesar said taking his seat again. 'I've already promised it to Piso and Gabinius, but you can choose for the year after. I'll fix it with Pompeius. Four years from now I'd like you and Pompeius to be the Consuls, so when I return to Rome I can watch your backs when you leave for your own provinces. But, you can have a say in all the magistracies for the two years in between. What else?'

Crassus seemed subdued by Caesar's attitude. I had never seen him behave this way with the man. Finally, Crassus spoke up again. 'You won't like it, but there is something I must insist on.'

'What is it?' Caesar smiled, spreading his hands before him. 'I'm willing to compromise.'

'I know you think we need Cicero's support. I've heard you offered him a place in our coalition again. I don't know why you'd do that after he snubbed you when you made the same offer last year, but I've always thought you were too forgiving. I want him gone.'

'What do you mean by 'gone?'' Caesar asked, leaning back in his chair.

'I'd like him thrown from the Tarpeian Rock, but I'm sure I won't get that, so I aim to see him banished. I'd also like you and Pompeius to make up with Clodius. I thought it was rather rash of you two when you made him a pleb. If you'd asked me I'd have advised against it, but you didn't ask me. Now that he is a pleb he will be a Tribune, of that I'm certain, and I want both of you to stop denying the part you had in it and let me use him. If you insist on Piso as Consul for next year, when he wins I want to use him to go after Cicero too. Crassus then sat back in his chair and waited for Caesar's answer, but he didn't need to wait long.

After a brief period of consideration, Caesar leaned forward across the small table and said with a smile, 'done!' And then, leaning closer still and looking Crassus in the eye he added, 'on one small condition. Crassus leaned back showing his discomfort in having Caesar lean in on him both figuratively and literally.

Crassus paused for some time before asking, 'what is your condition.'

'It is a small condition,' Caesar responded. 'After we made Clodius a pleb, Pompeius and I thought we owned him. Somehow, though, you managed to snatch him from us.'

With that Crassus smiled. 'I didn't steal him, you threw him away.'

Now Caesar smiled. 'The embassy we offered him?' Caesar shook his head with a sigh.

'That was more of an insult than an embassy.' Crassus was chuckling. 'Clodius is a wild dog, but he is not easily fooled. He expected to be given something lucrative, like a posting to Aegyptus to negotiate the squabbles of that volatile family. Now that would be a situation that could make a man's fortune. Instead, you offered him the position of errand boy to a petty little king.' Of course, he was ready to piss blood after that. And he wanted to piss that blood all over you and Pompeius. After that, it was easy to buy his loyalty!'

'Of course, you're right.' Caesar was being very conciliatory now. 'I want him back though. I won't stop you from using him to go after Cicero, though I really do like the man, I want him for my purposes.'

Crassus laughed again and took a gulp of wine. 'I can't give him to you. The best I can do with a man like Clodius is to set him free. You'll have to cage him again yourself if you want him. Let me use him for Cicero and he's yours if you can get him.'

'Then we have a deal, said Caesar. After both men raised their cups to each other, Caesar added, 'if there's anything else you think of, let me know. I'm willing to be more than reasonable. All I ask of you is that you work for me and not against me. I don't want any of my acts undone while I'm in Gaul and for the next few years we need to figure out how we can all hang on to some sort of

Imperium to keep from being banished ourselves.' With that, Caesar rose and walked the few steps to Crassus who also rose and the two men clasped hands on their renewed, if uneasy, friendship. Then, before breaking his grip, Caesar pulled Crassus toward him and hugged him and kissed him on the cheek. 'I've always liked you, Marcus, more than you liked me.'

Crassus broke the embrace and laughed heartily. 'If you keep that up you might make me cry!'

Once he returned from walking Crassus to the door, Caesar said to me, 'Set up an appointment with Clodius. No, make it an official summons from the Consul.'

I must have looked rather dubious when I said, 'What makes you think he will obey your summons.'

Caesar answered. 'Clodius is smarter than everyone gives him credit for. He'll come. When he's Tribune he can ignore the Consul, but that will be another man's problem.'

A short time later the room began to fill up as the others invited to the meeting began to arrive. There was Aurelia, of course, Balbus, Vatinius, Demetrius, Antonius, and four or five more. For the next few hours, this group plotted how best to have Caesar's candidates elected to the various offices and what to do if they didn't all win. It was well into the evening when the last man went home and Aurelia retired to her side of the house. Once again it was just Caesar and me, so we moved out into the cooler air of the peristyle and sat in the dark looking at the stars.

After just sitting quietly for a while, I broke the silence. 'I want to thank you for what you did today, allowing me to stay for the meeting with Crassus.' I truly was grateful.

'He needs to know you're not going away, and he needs to know I trust you.' Caesar sounded tired.

'Still,' I continued. 'Marcus Crassus has proven himself to be a dangerous enemy. It appears he is willing to do whatever it takes to protect his interests.'

'You are referring to Vettius.' Sometimes it seemed as if Caesar could discern my thoughts.

'And the slave boy,' I answered.

'I have always known the man's character. It is hubris that causes him to think he can do anything he pleases. I wanted him to be made aware that while that may be true of his relations with others, it is not with me. My financial debt to him is cleared and he must understand we are now on an equal basis.'

'So it's Gaul we go to first?' I already knew the answer but I wanted to change the subject.

'It's the best chance for glory. I need a triumph and I will need to win the Consulship again. I can't just stay home and write letters and treatises on philosophy like Cicero.'

I knew he was right, so with that, I asked leave to go to bed. I would need to transcribe my notes the following morning, so I needed to be awake before the sun. Before I left him I asked him a question that without my knowledge would change my life.

'Caesar, can I ask you for something?'

Caesar had walked with me into the tablinum and was already reading one of the documents from a pile of recent dispatches from Gaul. He looked up from it as an answer. 'Could I get a slave literate and fluent in the Celtic language? I want to learn their language before we go.'

Caesar nodded and went back to his document as he took a seat. 'See Demetrius tomorrow. We probably have someone useful working at the villa in Massilia. If not I'm sure he can find someone.'

As I walked to my bedchamber I smiled to myself. It occurred to me that Caesar didn't believe Crassus was his equal, and he certainly didn't believe Crassus was his superior.

After I snuffed out my oil lamp I lay on the bed looking at the shadow of the tree branch that the moonlight cast onto the ceiling of my chamber. It was a warm night and, being outside the city, the shutter was open. I reflected on the fact that I would be leaving my children for at least five years and I resolved to spend as much time, while still in Rome, as Caesar's busy schedule would allow, getting to know them. I didn't want them to forget me in my absence. The following morning, after transcribing my notes, I tracked down a slave named Aristus who Caesar had acquired in Hispania. This man was renowned for his ability to paint the most accurate likeness of a person and I wanted him to paint my portrait so I would have something to leave with my two sons. Of course, I had very little time to sit for him, but we managed over the next few months to have the portrait completed. The next time we are at my villa. I will show it to you and you can get an idea of how I appeared as a young man. After arranging for the portrait to be painted I found Demetrius as he was leaving his morning meeting with Caesar and gave him my request for the slave I needed.

Demetrius smiled an odd smile and with a wink said, 'I think I have just the right man for the job. He works with the overseer of the villa in Massilia. He handles the transactions with the locals when they procure supplies for the place. I'll get back to you.' I was pleased with the ease with which he complied, but I was a bit puzzled by the way he said he had 'just the right man,' with a wink. I dismissed it though and went about my business.

At any rate, I digress. The rest of the year was much less eventful but still included some important moments. Pompeius tried to shorten the leash he had Clodius on to keep him from doing anything stupid before the election, and Crassus, while not actually supporting Caesar seemed to accept the fact that Caesar was in a superior position with guaranteed Imperium for the next few years, so he didn't actively oppose him. In spite of the best efforts of the parties involved, the vocal opposition to the alliance of Caesar, Pompeius, and Crassus had taken on its own life and would ebb and flow in intensity, but did not ever disappear. This was even true after Caesar left for Gaul. I believe that is one of the reasons Caesar looked to the rapid and complete conquest of Gaul.

He knew the support of the people was essential to his retaining Imperium, and nothing he did would cause his popularity to rise as much as the conquest of a long-feared enemy of Rome."

At this point, I felt I needed to interrupt Polybius. "From what I have read of those times, Caesar's conquest of all of Gaul was the result of a series of unanticipated hostile actions on the part of the tribes of the region. Everyone seems to agree that he was just reacting to circumstances as they arose. Are you saying he had planned it from the start?" I realized I sounded incredulous, and thought my attitude might insult Polybius, but it caused him only to laugh.

"The author's you have read were deceived into thinking that Caesar was simply reacting to events." Polybius was clearly amused by this.

It was Mela who brought up the question that was poised on my lips but I thought might be too much an expression of doubt. He asked, "what about Caesar himself. He seems to imply it was not his intention to conquer Gaul. If that had been his intention why didn't he move all his legions to that province when he set out?"

"Ah," Polybius responded while reaching for his wine. After taking two or three sips he went on. "You have both read his commentaries on our years in Gaul. I can tell by your question, Mela, and by the expression on your brother's face. It's easy to take seriously that those words were exactly what we said they were:

reports from the field of action. The truth is the main purpose was to present Caesar's actions and motives in the best possible way. This was, of course, easy to do as the man was a brilliant general and his deeds were great. I'm quite certain that had he lived a few years longer those lands beyond the Persian Empire may have fallen under Roman sway." Polybius' face took on a distant, wistful look as he said this. He took another sip of wine and continued. "The fact that no one today believes the conquest of Gaul was his intention from the start is because so few who were alive at that time knew it was what he wished to do. And that, my young friends, is due to a suggestion of mine. During a conference in Quintilis (July) of the year of Caesar's Consulship attended by the small group of men who would become his closest military advisers in the coming year, Caesar announced his intention to conquer and annex all the lands between Italy and the ocean to the north. Sometime in that meeting, it was Labienus who brought up the best way to publish the information. Caesar was leaning toward having it included in with the daily acts we were posting throughout the city and everyone seemed to be nodding agreement.

Somehow, through a change in my demeanor or expression, Caesar divined my disagreement. 'Polybius seems to be the only one in disagreement with this plan.' He looked at me with a smile on his face, but a curious intensity that told me I must respond.

'I'm not a military strategist. In fact, what little I've seen of war frightens me. I'd rather not comment.'

Balbus was about to continue with the discussion, assuming that was the end of the matter when Caesar raised a hand to indicate we weren't finished. 'It's true you have not yet proven yourself as a military strategist, but I have come to trust your opinion on political matters, and how we make my intentions for Gaul public is a political question.'

I was pleased that he would say he trusted my judgment in front of Balbus, Labienus, and the rest, and that gave me the courage to speak what was on my mind. Looking at Caesar and avoiding the stares of the others, I said simply, 'I wouldn't publish this at all. In fact, I would make everyone in this room promise to not speak of it to any who is not present here and now. That is my thought on the matter.'

I heard a snort from one man, and out of the corner of my eye I could see Balbus was shaking his head, but Caesar wouldn't let the matter drop. 'Why?' was all he said, and then he waited as I collected my thoughts.

'It seems to me, and these men might disagree, that if you announce such grand intentions for the years after your Consulship when your term is barely half over, it will make you an easy target for an accusation of hubris. It will excite the derision of those who believe you cannot accomplish all that you say you will and the jealousy of those who believe you can. Either way, you will have both groups working against you to see that you do not succeed.' Since Caesar was listening intently and I had gained the attention of the rest of the men, I was emboldened to continue. 'In fact,' I went on, 'I would never say that is your intention. From what we know of the tribes of Gaul, they will present a multitude of pretexts to provoke your intervention in their affairs. I would let out, at each step of the way, that you were only doing what was right and necessary to protect the citizens of Rome.' Having no more to say, I stopped talking and sat through an uncomfortable silence while everyone considered what I'd said and waited for Caesar's reply.

Finally, leaning back in his chair, Caesar said, 'for now we say nothing. Not a word to anyone outside this group. We'll consider this again, but until we once again meet, I want you all to think about what Polybius has said but share nothing of this meeting with anyone else.' With that, the meeting ended and I was never aware that the matter was again discussed as a group, but it was the policy Caesar adopted.

Less than a month later, in Sextilis (August), Caesar attempted to remedy one of the grave ills that he said was eating away at the strength of the Roman Empire. Everyone agreed that the provinces, won through the superior arms and the superior culture of Rome, existed to be used for the benefit of Rome. If this were not the case, why would the gods have allowed them to fall under the sway of Rome? Roman dominion lifted the less civilized up and gave them a culture and learning it would have taken them centuries to attain on their own. This no one disputed, and it is still clearly true today."

I couldn't tell if Polybius was being facetious or was serious, so I interjected, "there may have been some Greeks who disagreed."

Polybius took a sip of wine and smiled with a nod toward me. "Yes, perhaps some fools from that part of the world may have disagreed, but they were merely resting on their laurels as it were. They believed that since they had conquered Ilium centuries before Romulus built the mud hut he called home they were the cultural superiors to Rome, but Roman arms corrected their misguided thinking. Some Aegyptians probably felt the same since they could look daily on structures their ancestors had built more than a thousand years before the founding of Rome, but by this time their ancient dynasties had been replaced by the Ptolemies and they had begun to look like any family playing the sort of disputes that interrupted the Cara Cognatio feast only on a worldwide scale.

Anyway, my young friend, you cause me to digress from my point. I was talking about a serious illness that was infecting our empire. The city was run as a republic, but the provinces were, in essence, run as petty kingdoms. The kings had been replaced by Proconsuls, but they were often even more despotic than any king. You see, a Proconsul or propraetor only served for a year, therefore he had no need to keep the people he governed happy. He also had often run up enormous debts in his rise to his lofty place. This naturally led to a situation where governors saw the appointment to a province as a means to steal back the fortunes spent on climbing the political ladder and to put others into their debt by enriching them as well. Caesar meant to change this.

In Sextilis he introduced the Lex Julia repetundarum that limited the number of "gifts" a governor could accept and required him to balance the province's accounts to the Senate's satisfaction or answer for any malfeasance in court upon his return. He also used this time to strengthen his political support by having Vatinius, using the Comitia, pass a law to strengthen the colony at Comum (Como) in the heart of Transalpine Gaul. Caesar actually directed the town center be moved when the nearby swamp was drained and the population was increased by nearly five thousand new colonists. This, of course, increased his clientela but more importantly added to the pool of new recruits for the legions. Technically, the town had Latin status and therefore its people did not have full Roman citizen rights and were not eligible to vote or serve in the army, but Caesar got around that constitutional nuisance in his usual fashion; he simply ignored it and throughout the remainder of his Consulship and his extended Proconsulship treated the people as Roman citizens. In fact, he treated all the people of Cisalpine Gaul as Roman citizens whether or not that status had been legally granted to them.

To avoid any immediate trouble in Gaul, Caesar opened negotiations with Ariovistus. Ariovistus was said to be a most remarkable man. For a barbarian, he demonstrated both political skill and a strong military mind. If you remember from our discussion of the news from Gaul, some eleven years earlier, in a war fought over the control of trade routes between Transalpine Gaul and the barely civilized interior of the land, the barbarian tribe called the Sequani took sides with another tribe, the Arverni against a third tribe called the Aedui. The Aedui were considered friends of the Roman people, but their appeal for help was not heard by the Senate. The Sequani, in what would turn out to be a most foolish decision, accepted the aid of Ariovistus, a prince of the German tribe the Suebi to help them in this war. Ariovistus and his army crossed the Rhenus (Rhine) River and helped them defeat the Aedui. What the Sequani hadn't planned on was that the Germans would stay on the west side of the river. Ariovistus, flush with victory, deprived the Sequani of one-third of their territory and was demanding one third more as more of his people crossed the Rhenus while ruling the people with a level of oppression that bordered on slavery. This situation, of course, was of great concern to the Senate as it impacted the stability of a very profitable trade with the province of Transalpine Gaul. Through the use of inspired diplomacy and expensive gifts, Ariovistus agreed to be less oppressive to the Sequani, forgoing, for now, the demand for more territory, but more importantly to keep the peace in Gaul. Caesar did this by persuading the Senate to recognize him as king of his tribe and as a friend of the Roman people. While this went against the long-standing treaty that Rome had with the Aedui, Caesar simply didn't want a war to break out before he was in command

of the legions that would fight it.

LIBER XXXIII

By the time the elections for the magistracies were held in October, Caesar's political position was much strengthened, and in spite of the best efforts of the Optimates, his choices for Consul and most of the other positions were elected. With his father-in-law, Calpurnius Piso, and his close ally, Aulus Gabinius, as Consuls and the support of Pompeius, and to a lesser extent, Crassus at Rome, Caesar felt, at least for now, secure enough to focus on Gaul. Unfortunately, he could only plan for the future, as he was not yet Proconsul. At this time he assembled his staff of legates. To build his staff, Caesar conducted a series of interviews with potential legates. Some names had already been decided on, but the selection of a legate was not made solely based on a man's military ability. His political strength was often the deciding factor. One meeting I found particularly sad was the meeting Caesar had with Cicero. I hadn't particularly liked Cicero since my dealings with him during his Consulship, but I liked his man Tiro and knowing Crassus' plans for him, I felt sorry for them both when Cicero turned the offer down. Caesar could not tell Cicero of Crassus' plans but he came close when he saw him to the door after the interview.

Clasping hands with him, Caesar looked Cicero in the eye and said, 'I do so wish you would reconsider, my friend. You have powerful enemies here in Rome and I think your political future might be made safer if you spend some time in a province.'

Cicero, not understanding Caesar's intent, simply shook his head and answered, 'I've made my decision. My no is final.' With that, the two men parted.

Four days before the ides of Decembris (December 10) Clodius took office as Tribune. His election was as certain as anything can be in this world. He had the full support of the three men who were the effective masters of Rome. Caesar and Pompeius were quite concerned about their waning popularity among the plebs and they meant to use Clodius as their tool. Having set the precedent of sidestepping the Senate and ruling through the Comitia, they were both well aware their opponents could do the same in an attempt to undo everything they had accomplished in Caesar's year as Consul.

As soon as we were certain of Clodius' election, Caesar and what was by now a very large group of slaves, freedmen, political associates, clients, friends, and lictors all set off for the Aventine Hill. It was traditional for newly elected Tribunes to make a sacrifice at the temple of Libertas on the Aventine on the day of their election and Caesar wanted to 'accidentally' meet up with Clodius. Caesar had already, in his role as Pontifex Maximus, attended the sacrifice performed by the priest of the goddess earlier in the day. Our official reason for returning to the temple was to partake in the feast that would follow. Caesar was already reclining on the couch that had been set out for him when Clodius arrived. Leaving his followers outside in a group on the steps of the small temple, Clodius, as impious as ever, spent just a short time sacrificing at the altar. It took him more time to wipe the blood from his hands than it did to perform the ritual. I could witness this from my vantage point in the area reserved for slaves behind the feast and between the temple and the road. I said a silent prayer to the goddess asking her to forgive the impiety of the men elected to steer the ship of state. This was, of course, one of many prayers I muttered or said to myself that day. The Lux Mundi was always a sad day for me then. Another tradition is for all the former slaves who had been freed that year to come to the temple and make a small offering to the goddess in thanks for their freedom. It put me in a gloomy mood to see all the smiling and laughing faces of those who had attained the freedom I so painfully longed for. I was cheered to see Cornelia, carrying our infant son and leading Tychaeus by the hand, among a cluster of freedwomen making their way along the road. She had, just a month earlier, given birth to a second boy. I called out to her and waved, but in the din of the festival, my voice was lost.

Caesar's voice was however heard by Clodius. I could see but not hear Caesar stand up as Clodius came near and wave his hand above his head. I began to move forward to assist Caesar in getting Clodius' attention when I saw the man stop and look around and notice Caesar. By this time I was only a few feet behind Caesar's couch and could hear him say, 'Tribune Clodius! Would you care to join in the feast? I think I can get you a couch.'

To which Clodius declined. 'I am going to celebrate my election with a much-deserved bath. Would the Consul care to join me?'

To this, Caesar heartily acquiesced. 'I've had more than my share. I think I'll leave some for the others to enjoy and will take to the baths. Are you going to the one here on the Aventine?'

I had to smile, as this was all just so much theater for the senators and wealthy equites surrounding them. This meeting was something that had been planned by Caesar three days prior. He would not have been foolish enough to reveal the plans he had for Clodius before his election to the tribunate was certain, but he wanted to meet with him and set things moving as soon as possible after the votes were tallied. As was usually the case with meetings held at the baths the men enjoyed their exercise and bathing before retiring to a private room. It was then, as I waited on the benches lining the exercise area I first met the man who was to teach me the Celtic language of the Gauls. Demetrius came in with a group of men, and when he caught sight of me he walked quickly across the grassy area nearly getting hit in the head by a ball that was thrown between two naked young men I had been watching exercise. Four of the six men who had entered with him followed behind.

'We've been over half the city looking for Caesar.' Demetrius sounded convincing as he said this though I knew this too was just so much more theater. It was he who suggested the meeting place for its convenience to the temple of Libertas. 'I've got a small real estate transaction that needs Caesar's seal on it today or we will lose the deal.'

I had risen to my feet and greeted three of the four men in the group but didn't recognize the slave standing behind the others, looking at the turf at his feet. 'Who's this?' I asked Demetrius. In spite of his loose tunic, I could see the young man had an appealing physique; not too thin, but not yet gone to fat as so often happens to slaves who work as scribes. I knew his role because I could see the ink stains on his fingers and was for an instant self-conscious of the ink on my own hands.

Demetrius smiled and answered, 'he's your man if you want him. This is Lucterius. I have plucked him from obscurity as a keeper of household records for the Villa Julia of Massilia to come to Rome and teach you his native tongue. Now, you get to know each other while we go find your master. You can decide later if we keep him or send him back beyond the Alps.' With that Demetrius and the three freedmen in his company rushed off across the exercise yard leaving me to get acquainted with my new language instructor. Once the other men were gone, Lucterius looked first in their direction and then at me. I nearly let out a gasp. He was quite handsome. In his own unique way, he reminded me of my old friend, Gaius Vitrius. It wasn't so much in his features, but rather in the way he smiled. I almost expected to see the gap in his teeth that I remembered from my old friend.

'My name is actually Loctravos, but every Roman feels the need to make it sound more Latin, so I've grown used to having two names.'

I must tell you I was smitten. My heart was beating rapidly and I was feeling a bit light-headed. I had to remind myself that in all probability this young man didn't share my attraction for members of the masculine sex. 'I also have two names. My mother named me Tychaeus, but I am now known to the world as Polybius.' I couldn't help but smile back as I tried to focus my attention on my would-be teacher. It wasn't long before I began to suspect that Lucterius and I were alike in our attractions. For no reason I could name, I was sure of this by the time Caesar returned with Demetrius, Clodius, and several other men. I'm not certain I made any sense during our conversation that filled the time the others were gone, but Lucterius didn't indicate anything seemed amiss so I just continued to babble, conscious of my beating heart and half wondering how he couldn't hear it thumping away in my chest.

Demetrius and the men he arrived with were the only ones dressed. The rest were wrapped in the linen cloth provided by the bath. I was sorry to leave my new friend, but it was time to work. Demetrius assured me with a wink that Lucretius would be waiting at the Domus Publica when we arrived. When Demetrius winked, I made the connection to when he first mentioned this young man. Demetrius chose him because he knew of my attractions and was setting me up for romance. I was embarrassed and had to turn away to avoid him seeing me blush. I immediately picked up my bag and gave Lucretius a nod that was more formal than I would have liked. I stood for a moment watching him walk out behind Demetrius and his group until I heard Caesar calling my name. I had hoped he hadn't called too many times before I heard him.

I have always had the ability to concentrate on the business before me, but this day it took an extra effort. The other men went off to the exercise yard while Caesar, Clodius, and I walked down a narrow cool passage. I was relieved by the coolness as it helped me focus. I remember studying the intricate black and white pattern on the mosaic floor as a means to take my mind from the young man I just met. Several paces down the passage we came to a small unadorned private room. I'm sure it was chosen for its heavy wooden door. There was a slave waiting in the room but at our arrival, he silently slipped out and made his way down the hall. Once we entered, Caesar shut the heavy door behind us and slid a stool against it, indicating with a gesture that I was to sit there. I understood immediately this also meant I was to listen for any activity on the other side. I was disappointed there was no wine or even water; I was parched.

'I've always supported you, Clodius.' Caesar got right to the point.

'When our interests aligned,' Clodius responded with a wry

smile.

Caesar smiled back. 'There was a time not too many years ago when I should have become your enemy, but I showed clemency. Any other man would have tried to destroy you, yet here we are.'

Clodius looked almost repentant when he said, 'I'm sorry about that. You know I am, but I assumed you didn't love her.'

'That's all water under the bridge,' Caesar answered, 'I didn't love her, but you should never have put me in that embarrassing spot, especially not then. Sometimes you behave like a perfect ass.'

Clodius only shrugged. 'As you say, water under the bridge. What can I do for you now?'

There was a chair for him, but Caesar didn't sit. He began to pace back and forth across the small room. 'You can tell me your plans for your year as Tribune and we can see exactly where our interests align.'

'I will tell you one thing I plan to do that will not make you happy. We have a mutual friend that neither of us would like to disappoint. He wants me to go after Cicero.'

Caesar dismissed this with a wave. 'Marcus can have what he wants. Just do it after I've left for Gaul. What else?'

'I plan to lift the ban on private clubs. The craftsmen can benefit from the associations.'

'Bullshit,' Caesar said. 'You want to organize them into voting blocks. I don't really care if you lay the foundation for your future, but I won't openly support you on this one. What else?'

'I'm not sure how you'll feel about this, but I plan to put a law in front of the plebs lowering the price of grain once more. I know what you're going to say, Rome can't afford it at the current price. You're going to say we are almost giving it away now, but we've got huge revenues coming in from the east and the people are suffering.'

'Another Lex Frumentaria. How cheap?' Caesar was to the point.

'Four.' Clodius was also to the point.

'You plan to drop it more than two asses?' With that Caesar shook his head no.

Clodius rose from his seat. If I don't, there's no point. The people don't want us to give them partial relief. It's four, or nothing at all, and I mean to see this done.'

Caesar laid a hand on Clodius' shoulder and led him to the corner of the room farthest from the door. 'Then it's nothing at all,' he said.

Clodius scowled and moved to walk back to where he started when Caesar stopped him. 'You misunderstand me, my friend. I want it to be nothing at all. I'll support it and I'll support it publicly if you propose a law giving the grain away.'

Clodius laughed. 'You're joking!'

'I'm serious. Just do it before the end of the year so I can back your plan while I'm still Consul.'

With that, Clodius understood, and so did I. 'You really are worried about the rabble turning against you.'

'You're a pleb now, Clodius,' Caesar answered with a grin. 'You shouldn't talk about your people that way. Just make sure you do what you can to protect me when my year is up. Are we in agreement?'

Clodius grasped Caesar's hand and leaned in and kissed him on the cheek. 'We are,' he said. 'Now if there is nothing else, I'd like to go for another dip in the caldarium. This room is chilly.'

I stood to open the door but stopped when Caesar added, 'Just one more thing. Clodius stopped at the door and turned back prompting Caesar to continue. 'It's not for me, but rather for Pompeius. Personally, I don't care at all, but he would like you to find some way to embarrass Bibulus.'

'With pleasure,' Clodius answered and then he nodded at me to open the door.

LIBER XXXIV

Clodius put his Lex Frumentaria before the plebs the day after the ides of December (December 14) with the intention of calling the vote during the height of Saturnalia when the poor were in high spirits and had the license to poke fun at their leaders. For the Caesar household, Saturnalia was particularly festive. As Consul, he felt the need to set an example and outdid his usual generosity and geniality toward his slaves and freedmen. On the day slaves were allowed in the public baths, the Caesar household and that of Pompeius joined together at the baths on the Aventine for a great party. Caesar even invited Cornelia and my children to our home for two full days.

It was during this time that I really got to know Lucterius, and I realized we were falling in love. He was more reluctant, and we showed our affection through hand holding and kissing, but the real intimacy developed when we shared personal details about our lives and related our pain as well as our past joy.

The last day of the year was cold. There had even been a thin crust of ice on the water in my washbowl in the morning. After the salutatio, we all donned cloaks in preparation for making our way to the forum for the traditional oath to the gods on laying down the symbols of Caesar's office. Aurelia joined us that morning and I was even able to bring Lucterius along without question. After the oath, Caesar made a modest speech of thanks to the people of Rome and then, almost as an afterthought thanked the Senate, to which the crowd laughed and cheered. Caesar and his band of supporters joined Pompeius' sizeable following just to the south of the rostrum. It was strange to see his lictors, now without the fasces over their shoulders suddenly mingling with the others in the group. I was to Caesar's left and a bit behind him when I saw Pompeius nod his head toward Clodius who could be seen beside the steps to the rostrum. 'Our friend didn't come through with my request,' Pompeius said with a sour note in his voice. Upon the rostrum, Bibulus had just taken his oath and was waiting for the crowd's attention before making his speech.

I couldn't see Caesar's face, but I could hear the smile as he spoke. 'The year is not yet done.'

Pompeius scowled and turned to walk away when Caesar stopped him by gripping his arm. 'Stay and watch Bibulus' speech. I think you might like it.'

'I'm sure I won't like anything that fat little prick has to say.'

'Trust me on this one.' Caesar turned his head and gave me a wink. Pompeius reluctantly turned back to watch the start of what promised to be a long and dull speech from Bibulus.

Bibulus stepped forward. I could see he looked almost sober. 'People of Rome," he shouted in a firm clear voice. Pompeius shook his head in disgust, and first, there was a gasp and then a loud murmur of excitement and expectation from the crowd.

Clodius had stepped onto the platform next to Bibulus. Bibulus stopped speaking and turned and glared at him. When the crowd was again quiet, Bibulus began again. 'People of Rome.' His voice sounded a bit shaky as he looked over at Clodius.

When Bibulus paused, Clodius stepped forward and in a loud, firm, clear voice announced, 'as Tribune of the plebs, I forbid Marcus Calpurnius Bibulus to address the people at this time!' Clodius then took a step back. Pompeius burst into laughter and let out a whoop. I had never yet seen him so happy. Standing to my right I heard Aurelia say, 'Shameful,' but when I looked over at her I could see she too was stifling laughter. I looked behind me at Lucterius and smiled at him as well, so we could share in the moment.

Bibulus stood sputtering at Clodius. 'You, you, you can't do this to a Consul addressing the people of Rome!' Bibulus actually stamped his feet.

'I can,' Clodius said loudly yet mildly. Besides, citizen, you are no longer Consul. You have laid your office at the feet of Jupiter before the Senate and People of Rome.' With that, the crowd cheered. Bibulus stood stamping and sputtering for a time and then with an obscene gesture at the assembled mass of people stormed down the steps of the rostrum.

Caesar turned and leaned in toward Pompeius, and shouted over the din of the people, 'I knew you would enjoy his speech, Gnaeus!' Pompeius could only wipe the tears of laughter from his eyes.

For a time, Caesar thought it would be best to take up private life. By rights, he could have proceeded immediately to his provinces, but he felt the need to remain in the city until he could determine how well his allies were guarding the rear. That was his expression, not mine. When another senator asked him when he intended to go to his provinces, Caesar reminded the man that the entire point of his Proconsulship was to win military glory, and one cannot campaign in the winter. We returned home that day as an illustrious Consulare and his nomenclator, with no more fanfare than any other prominent member of the Senate. Later, Caesar dined with a few close friends on couches set up on the courtyard of the Regia. I took the opportunity to take a private meal with Lucterius on the balcony of the Domus Publica. I have always liked balconies. For reasons I don't understand, most people, as they go about their daily lives, rarely look upward. A balcony is a place where one can do almost anything in plain view while not being observed. The most illicit thing I did that day was to steal a kiss from Lucterius. I suppose I should admit it was more than one kiss.

The following day Caesar played his part in the Agonalia festival. Caesar, as Pontifex Maximus took part in the ceremony of presenting the figs and the jars of honey to Janus. As has usually been the case, both sets of doors to the temple were open. It was a long-established practice to only close those doors when Rome was at peace, which had only happened twice in our history. Since my youth, it was closed twice more during the reign of Augustus, as he brought peace to the world. As you know, this is a day when gifts and presents of money are given to family members, so when we returned home Caesar and his family had a meal of bread and honey and exchanged gifts. I was surprised when I was sent for, and even more, surprised when Caesar gave me a small sweet cake and a small purse of coins.

Later that day I asked for leave to visit my children. Before I left the domus, I privately presented a gift of a few coins to Lucterius in honor of Janus the god of new beginnings. The remainder of the coins I gave to Cornelia to hold for my sons until they were old enough to make use of money.

LIBER XXXV

Caesar didn't have to wait long to see how well his allies were able to protect him. In spite of the best attempts of Crassus, Pompeius, and Clodius to influence the doings of the Senate, the first two by pressuring their own trusted allies and friends, and Clodius from outside with threats of veto, on the third day of Januarius Caesar's enemies went on the attack. The Optimate faction had managed to elect two praetors, Gaius Memmius and Lucius Domitius, and they proposed that the Senate open debate on declaring all Caesar's acts as Consul to be invalid. This would naturally be followed up by a trial based on the supposed illegality of Caesar's acts. The legal foundation for this was Caesar's own declaration, when he first proposed the agrarian law, that he was willing to submit the law to the judgment of the Senate. Three days were spent debating the agrarian law. On the third day, Caesar was monitoring the debate with a group of friends, not from the benches of the Senate, but rather from a table outside a taverna across the forum in the Basilica Sempronia. By all reports the first two days had been nothing but humiliation for Caesar, with the Consul Calpurnius Piso not calling on him to speak, allowing him to only suffer in silence as the verbal abuse was thrown at him by the Optimates. Caesar saw no reason to attend the Senate on the third day of debate and chose to enjoy the sunny day. Because we were in public, I was relegated to sitting on the stone block in the sun just outside the roof of the portico and I felt it would be inappropriate to join in the conversation in that company, but I was able to listen, and it was my task to read the dispatches from the steps of the Senate. Caesar had had me arrange to have runners posted on the portico of the curia to regularly report the progress of the debate. I couldn't for my own life understand it, but I didn't dare ask why he took this extraordinary step.

I was grateful then when Balbus asked the question that was on my mind. 'Why are you so worried, Gaius? They're debating just your first act. If they spend days squabbling over everything you did for the past year, it'll be the next year before it comes to an end. If I were in your shoes, I'd just stay home and search for omens. You can do that since you're Pontifex Maximus.'

Caesar was about to answer when a runner came up and handed me a wax tablet. I gave him a fresh one and sent him back to the Senate. Caesar looked at me with a calm, but concerned expression and asked, 'what is this one?'

'It's nothing,' I replied.

Caesar looked at me and said crossly, 'just read the damned report and let me decide what's important.'

Dutifully, I stood up and read, 'the senator Gnaeus Pompeius has asked to be excused from the session on account of a sudden illness. His request was allowed.'

'Shit, this cannot be good,' was all Caesar said. I then noticed he reached into the fold of his toga and took out his three dice he frequently carried and began to roll them around in his hand.

I didn't dare ask, but Demetrius did. 'What does it mean?'

Caesar merely stared at the curia lost in thought, so it was Balbus who answered. 'The reports we've been getting can only tell us what's said in open debate, but a lot of the real business is happening in the conversations among the senators themselves. This can only mean something important is about to happen.'

All eyes were looking at Caesar as he stared at the curia, lost in thought. In just a moment he came out of his reverie and turning toward Balbus, calmly said, 'you asked why I'm worried about them debating just my first act? The answer is simple. If they can declare my first official act illegal, the precedent is set. A motion will be put forward to declare my Consulship to be invalid and all my acts illegal.'

With that, we all looked toward the curia, and soon enough we saw Pompeius coming down the steps and out of the shadows, followed by three slaves and four equites. Pompeius was walking about as fast as a man can walk without it being said he is running. Caesar rose and walked out into the sunlight to meet him in the center of the forum near the Lacus Curtius. The two men walked back toward us, deep in conversation. When they reached us, Caesar did not sit down. 'Very soon it's to be put to a vote, and after that, I'll be summoned.' Turning to Balbus he said, with a nod to the taverna's proprietor who was leaning on the counter, 'pay the man what we owe him and then catch up.'

With that, Caesar and Pompeius began to walk rapidly down the length of the portico, causing everyone else to hastily down the last of their wine and quickly follow them. I was the last to leave, having the necessity of organizing my tablets and packing up my writing supplies, so I needed to run to catch up. When I reached Caesar and managed to catch my breath enough to speak, I asked between gulps of air, 'Where are we going, Master?'

Caesar just looked at me as he walked and said, 'To assume my Proconsulship!' I couldn't help but think of the day just over a year prior when I followed Caesar into the city when he gave up his triumph to announce he was running for Consul. We followed the street between the basilica and the temple of Saturn out to the Carmentalian gate. Caesar stopped for just a moment at the gate and looked back into the city before turning and marching through the portal.

This was, of course, just a legal formality. There was almost as much of the city outside the gates as there was inside, but Caesar had technically left Rome and therefore assumed the Proconsulship. Once again, after a lapse of just three days, Caesar had Imperium. Once outside the gate, I was reminded that I didn't always know all of Caesar's plans. The eventuality of leaving the city had been anticipated and Demetrius had already prepared the villa on the far side of the river for an extended stay. The documents that we had prepared more than thirty days before, granting Vatinius his status as legate had been signed and sealed and his escort and slaves were already waiting for him at the villa as were his wife and two daughters. He was to leave the following morning for Cisalpine Gaul. What his instructions were from then on, I had no idea. I didn't even know whether or not we would be leaving. I was reminded of the way we left Rome for Hispania and worried I wouldn't have an opportunity to say goodbye to my sons. Fortunately, Caesar had planned to remain just outside the city until he could determine the best course of action. Word must have spread quickly that Caesar had left the city, for shortly after we arrived in the villa the Tribune Lucius Antistius appeared at the gate asking to see Caesar. Once inside the atrium of the villa, Caesar greeted him cordially. 'Antistius my friend!' Caesar raised his hand in greeting but was careful to stand far enough back to not touch the man to avoid any possibility of being accused of striking a Tribune. Pompeius and the Tribune Manius who had come with us stood by to act as witnesses to the exchange.

Antistius was cold. 'I am not on a social visit. Gaius Caesar, I summon you to appear at once before the people's court in Rome.'

Caesar simply shook his head and said, 'No.' He followed this up with, 'I'm sorry you made the trip all the way out here. Can I offer you something to eat or drink?'

Antistius was clearly surprised by this response and asked, 'No?'

With this, Manius stepped up and said, 'It is my judgment and that of the other elected Tribunes that Gaius Caesar cannot be compelled to attend your court, as he has assumed the Proconsular Imperium and has left Rome on official business as directed by the Senate and People of Rome.'

Antistius was clearly frustrated but he realized he had been beaten. Before turning to leave he said, 'You cannot avoid Rome forever.' What none of us knew then, was that it would be nearly eight years before Caesar would again cross the Pomerium to enter the city again.

Caesar's standing on the legal technicality of having left Rome in an official capacity was an elegantly simple solution to the immediate problem. The Optimate faction couldn't possibly ignore the constitution in order to prosecute a man for ignoring the constitution.

For now, Caesar and his enemies were locked in a stalemate, but soon Caesar would launch a counter-offensive. That evening Crassus came to the villa with Clodius and three other Tribunes. The meeting lasted late into the evening forcing all the men who attended to spend the night at the villa. In the morning we all rose early and set the plans that had been decided on the night before in motion. Caesar and I immediately began to compose a speech that would soon be divided into three speeches against Memmius and Domitius. The following day, on the nones of the month (January 9), Caesar, Crassus, and Pompeius began to play their parts. Clodius went into the city with clear directions and a much heavier purse. I was present to record all that Clodius said, as his three masters were apprehensive that their man might stray from the path they laid out for him. While many of the senators were making their way to the curia, Clodius mounted the rostrum and gave public notice of two laws he was proposing to bring to a vote. He chose this time because Caesar wanted this to be the topic of discussion in the senate meeting that day, distracting the Optimates from discussing his Consulship and serving as a warning. The first law had the Lex Vatina that had awarded Caesar his Consular province by popular vote as its precedent. Clodius proposed that the Consuls for the current year also be given their provinces in the same way and with the same generous allotment of funds. The money was to be diverted from Aegyptus and three other provinces.

With the second proposed law, Clodius took aim directly at Cicero. He proposed a law that was merely a restatement of the law used by Caesar more than four years earlier in arguing against putting the conspirators in the aborted attempt by Catilina to usurp the government to death. Clodius proposed a law that would have any magistrate declared an enemy of Rome and face banishment should he execute or cause to be executed any Roman citizen without the benefit of due process of the law. This was, of course, understood by everyone to refer to Cicero's execution of the Catilinarian conspirators. I don't know whether or not Clodius was clever enough or organized enough to plan it, but Cicero happened to be passing through the forum on his way to the Curia at the very time Clodius made his speech. From my vantage point at the corner of the second-floor balcony of the Basilica Aemilia, I had a clear view of the forum. Cicero had stopped at the back of the crowd and was listening intently to Clodius' proposals.

When Clodius had finished speaking of this second law, Cicero didn't wait to hear any more. Rather than proceed on to the curia, he turned back the way he came. I later learned that he immediately went home, removed his senatorial insignia, put on his toga of mourning, and began writing letters to friends to organize a campaign against the law. The first law effectively rewarded the Consuls, as every man would prefer to not have his provincial appointment decided by jealous rivals in the Senate, and they both wanted the unusually large purse that came with the appointments, it also removed the threat from the Optimates that they could be policing the pastures and country lanes the following year. The second law not only distracted the Senate and silenced Cicero, but also served as a warning that an investigation of one Consulship could open the door to an investigation of the Consulships of all the living ex- Consuls who comprised the most powerful group of senators.

Cicero for his part didn't sit idly by. His associates organized demonstrations against the law. As a countermeasure, and against the wishes of Caesar, Clodius had his gangs of young equites and their clients use violence to break up the demonstrations. Several times a near-riot broke out, for once a mob begins to act as one creature, it is impossible to control, not that Clodius had any inclination to control the violence he instigated. During all this, Crassus was busy buying property that he picked up cheaply as a result of the fires that broke out in the violence. I'm fairly certain he had agents placed in Clodius' mobs with instructions to start fires. What made things worse for the people was that the riot itself frequently hindered the work of Crassus' fire brigade and caused several blocks to burn down before his man could buy them.

For his part, Pompeius removed himself from the city to his villa in the Alban hills some thirteen miles to the south. Caesar, meanwhile, tried to influence things from outside the Pomerium. On the first day of the festival in honor of the birth goddess Carmenta (January 11), knowing many of the shops would be closed and public business was not allowed, Clodius called a meeting of the plebs to be held in the Circus Flaminius. This spot was chosen because many people would be attending the races later in the day anyway, and because this venue was outside the city walls allowing Caesar to attend. The two Consuls spoke first, mourning the constant partisanship of the Senate that distracted the city fathers from the urgent issues they needed to address. Piso and Gabinius, in their speeches, spoke of their disgust at the killing, a few years before, of the Catilinarian conspirators without trial. Also during his speech, Piso issued a Consular edict forbidding the wearing of mourning for any reason but a family death or a state tragedy. When Caesar rose to speak he took great pains to sound reasonable and measured in his views. He wanted to appear to the people as the level headed and clear thinking opponent of rabid partisans who opposed him for no better reason than personal interest and personal enmity toward himself. When Caesar spoke of the deaths of the Catilinarian conspirators, he reminded the people that he was the only senator to oppose the summary executions, but also that he didn't think it right to create a law to punish Cicero now, in light of the fact that almost the entire Senate supported him in the executions or remained silent. Cicero, for fear of violence, didn't dare visit Caesar, but he did send friends, all prominent members of the Senate, to Caesar, Crassus, and Pompeius. Caesar merely used this as an opportunity to remind Cicero he had tried to help him before but was rebuffed and now as a Proconsul attending to the business of the empire he had no say in the day to day workings of the Senate that he couldn't attend. Pompeius also took the line that as a private citizen his hands were tied but, in his usual fashion, he took it even further. He said that Cicero should refer the matter to the Consuls and if they can persuade the Senate to declare a state of emergency and grant him an extraordinary Imperium, he would be glad to take up arms on Cicero's behalf. Crassus simply refused to see the emissaries of Cicero, 'out of regard for Caesar.'

All of this took some time, but I was not allowed to sit idle. For much of the day, I was acting as the eyes and ears of Caesar in the forum, while Balbus and Antonius were keeping an eye on things from inside the Senate. While I was in the city, Lucterius was working with Balbus on organizing the supplies for six legions. This was the first indication I had that Caesar was planning to raise two more legions. Lucterius was a sorcerer when it came to mathematics. Most calculations he could do without resorting to an abacus or wax tablet. I myself have never been very proficient at mathematics.

During the evening Lucterius would teach me the Celtic language. This was something of a pleasure for both of us as we were both in love with the other and relished any time together.

Clodius had to call the requisite Contiones to present his proposed laws before a vote could be called. The first vote was for the law to grant the provinces to the Consuls. This was on the last day of Januarius, for fear the Optimates would find a way to block it. This caused the law that would be used to banish Cicero to be delayed until the middle of Martius. The first half of Februarius is, as you are probably aware, filled with days that are deemed too unlucky for public business. The Lupercalia that effectively prevented the calling of the Contiones until the end of Februarius and early Martius follows these days. Finally, the vote was scheduled for the day before the ides of Martius (March 14). Cicero, to forestall the public humiliation voluntarily went into exile two days before the vote was taken, taking a ship to his villa near Pompeii. When the law was voted on, it was coupled with a sentence of banishment for Cicero for 'acting outside the laws as established by the Senate and People of Rome,' making it official. When I told Caesar of the outcome of the vote, he looked up from his reading and after a moment of thought said, 'I don't know why Cicero didn't see this coming. He should have taken my offer and become one of my legates. Even without my protection though, he could have ignored the whole thing from the start taking the view that he and everyone else had heard and would heed the warning.' Had he done that rather than making it essential that the law is defeated in the voting, he could have easily persuaded Caesar to have Clodius withdraw the proposal.

On that same day, a dispatch from Gaul set into motion the final preparations for our departure. It had been known for some time that the Helvetii, a people of barely civilized wild men and women, had been intent on moving the whole of their tribe to the west of Gaul. Their reason for the move was stated to be a desire for greater space, which was, at least in part, no doubt true. But, that would only provide a rationale for moving the surplus population of their tribe. This proud people wished to keep their tribe together, but that would be impossible if they were to remain in their current home. Ariovistus and his Suebian army were applying pressure to the Helvetii with stepped-up raids on their herds and farms. Since the Helvetii had already all but decided on a full-scale invasion of the lands to the west, this new development added the push to the already present pull of the rich lands of central and western Gaul.

I remember clearly the arrival of the dispatch from an agent of Caesar's whose stated business was to trade wine, newly arrived from Italia at the port of Massilia, to the tribes to the north of Roman Gaul. This was, however, just a side business. His real source of income derived from selling information to influential men in Rome. For the past year, he only dealt with Caesar. Caesar received the scroll from a messenger just as he saw the last of his clients to the door at the close of his salutatio. Standing in the atrium he broke the seal and stepped into the center near the fountain to catch the sunlight as he read the small cramped script. When he finished reading, Caesar said, to no one in particular, 'at last.' Holding up the scroll again, he reread a portion of the message and then turned to me. 'Find Balbus and bring him to me. I'll be getting a haircut.'

Balbus had, for more than a month, been staying most nights at Caesar's villa. His country home was too far away for daily commerce with the city and since he had assumed the post as legate he too was barred from crossing the Pomerium. I found him in Caesar's library and told him of the dispatch. He too sighed and said, 'at last. Let's go.'

With that, we joined Caesar in his suite where his barber was plucking his eyebrows into a perfect evenly matched pair. Caesar didn't dare move his head but instead looked at Balbus in his reflection in the mirror set on a stand before him. 'Find Veilinus and bring him here.' Caesar used the Latinized form of the Celtic name.

Balbus looked confused. 'Is he in Rome? I thought he'd sailed home.'

Caesar smiled. 'He's gone no farther than Ostia.'

I should tell you, that Veilinus was a lesser Celtic chieftain who was the go-between for Caesar and Ariovistus. I knew the name but had never met the man. Balbus left immediately, leaving me standing there watching the barber pluck stray hairs from Caesar's left ear. 'Do you need me, Caesar?'

Caesar winced as one hair fought hard to remain attached. 'You know, Polybius, men are cursed in an odd way. As one grows older, the hair you most want flees from you, while new unwanted hair sprouts up in the oddest places. Do you trust your man Lucterius?'

'Yes, I do.' As soon as I said it, I hoped Caesar wouldn't ask what my trust was based on since I had no solid reason other than an infatuation. I was grateful he didn't ask.

'I'll want him there to translate what might be said by that wild warlord and his men in their Celtic tongue. Tell Lucterius to not speak though, I don't want him giving himself away with his accent.' With that Caesar waved a dismissal. I was at the doorway of the room when he said, almost as an afterthought, 'have the boy Marcus transcribe your notes when we are finished.'

'Marcus?' I asked incredulously. 'I can do it myself.'

'No, Polybius, I want Marcus to do this job.'

I smiled at Caesar's reflection. 'I suppose then you'll need him to retrieve something from the Domus Publica.'

'You are clairvoyant,' Caesar smiled back. 'Why don't you send him for the map of Gaul, the reliable one, not the other?'

'We have that one here already. I brought it six days ago when I went into the city.' I spoke before I'd carefully thought about the request.

Caesar leaned forward to more closely examine his reflection and answered, 'he doesn't know that.'

Marcus was an excellent clerk, but he was one of the most indiscrete men I'd ever met. He gossiped more than the women in the vegetable market. At one time, I suggested Caesar sell him, but he informed me that such people come in handy. He was most often used to compose birthday greetings and party invitations, as he had a wonderful script, but his real usefulness was only truly employed when Caesar wanted a piece of information spread throughout the city. I set Marcus out to copy a treatise on the cultivation of the olive to keep him busy until Balbus could return with Veilinus later that day.

LIBER XXXVI

Since it would be some time before they returned from Ostia, I asked leave to visit my family in the city. I found Lucterius and invited him along. I wanted him to meet my children and their mother, since I had a strong feeling we would soon be leaving Rome. We had a nice time that afternoon. Cornelia was grateful for me to take the boys for a while. Lucterius and I brought them to a small garden near one of the fountains and played with them as if we all four were children. The boys took to Lucterius quickly and he seemed to take to them as well. As we walked home, I explained to Tychaeus that I might have to go away for some time. I wasn't sure he fully understood me until he began to cry when I told him it could be a long time before I would see him again. This made me sad, but I knew this day would come and accepted it like a stoic. It was that day I delivered the portrait I had commissioned into Cornelia's care and left instructions as to how we could regularly exchange letters through Aurelia. I neglected to mention that Cornelia was learning to read and write and appeared to have become quite proficient at both. That was one great advantage to the times we lived in. In days not long before it would have been impossible to communicate so readily from the far off provinces, but one of the lasting effects of the advance of Roman arms is the wonderful network of roads the legions built as they moved across the world. During our whole stay in Gaul, unless we were fighting in the remotest wilderness, there was a nearly constant flow of information to and from the city. I imagine these same roads will still be of use a thousand years from now. When we returned to the washing shop with the boys, I knew from the length of the shadow on the pavement that it was time to go. As fathers have done for millennia on parting from their families, I charged Tychaeus to be good and take care of his mother. With hugs and kisses, we left.

As we walked back Lucterius seemed both nervous and excited about going to Gaul. 'Caesar is an odd man.' Lucterius said.

'What do you mean?' I was truly puzzled, as I never thought him to be odd.

'I mean as a master.' Lucterius said this quickly thinking no doubt I may have been offended. 'He treats you almost as if you are his freedman and he treats me as if I belong to you. You didn't even need to ask him if you could bring me to the city.'

'I'm afraid he trusts me probably more than I deserve, but Caesar is a good man and he likes to see the best in people. Once he told me that while he realizes there must be slaves, that it is indeed part of the natural order of things that the vanquished belong to the conqueror, there is a natural dignitas that all men have, including the enslaved, and if a man doesn't give it away, as some do living extravagant lives or losing themselves to their vices, it cannot be lost or taken by another. Therefore he treats even slaves decently; that is unless he catches the slave in betrayal.'

'Would you ever betray Caesar?' Lucterius didn't look at me when he asked the question, pretending to be taking in the sites of the city.

I didn't look at him when I answered, looking at the pavement in front of me as I walked. 'If Caesar is correct, and I believe he is, and we all have a natural dignitas, mine is such that it stirs in me a strong urge for freedom. This urge from time to time ebbs as the tide does, but never entirely leaves me. I'm never quite comfortable, and I don't believe I ever will be until I'm free.' We were both aware that I didn't exactly answer the question. We crossed the bridge in silence. Once on the other side of the bridge, the city seemed to change character with the spaces between buildings growing. Today, of course, there is no difference in the character of Rome on either side of the river, but that wasn't true then. I took advantage of a copse of trees we passed to pull Lucterius aside and into the shade for some kissing. We had little time to spare, so I made up for that with greater passion. Our talk was much more playful for the rest of our walk home.

Perhaps an hour after we returned to the villa, Balbus arrived with Veilinus. We were alerted to their arrival so everyone was ready for the meeting. Lucterius and I were at the ready with our tablets and styli, Caesar was casually discussing with Demetrius a play he had recently seen and Marcus was in a cubicle well within earshot copying the text on olive cultivation when Balbus brought Veilinus and two other men into the tablinum.

Caesar immediately stood and forgoing a greeting, snapped, 'What in the name of Dis is going on in Gaul?' He dramatically tossed the scroll with the news onto the table for emphasis.

Veilinus looked obsequious. 'There is some unrest, I'm told.'

'Some unrest?' Caesar raised his voice a bit more. 'I have a report here that tells me the Helvetii are planning to move through Roman territory, and they are planning to do it very soon.' He emphasized the word, Roman. 'I am told they have burned their villages and abandoned their fields. Why am I just hearing of this now? Shouldn't you have told me about this?'

'I did not know,' Veilinus stuttered a bit as he said it. "And, I'm not sure I believe it.'

'I pay you to know this sort of thing.' Caesar pretended to be controlling his anger.

Stupidly, Veilinus turned to one of his companions and began speaking in Celtic.

Caesar let this go on for just a short time before saying sharply, 'Please keep this discussion to either Latin or Greek.'

With that, all three of the Gauls began to rapidly talk over each other with wild looks and wild gestures. "That's enough!' Caesar barked, but the men continued until Caesar slammed his hand on the table with a loud bang, causing everyone in the room to start. 'Why,' Caesar asked, 'did you not report this to me?' Caesar's voice was calm, but his glare was chilling.

Veilinus took on an expression of meekness. 'Perhaps your

sources are better than mine.'

Caesar sighed. 'You, Veilinus are supposed to be my source of information from Gaul, and I pay you well.'

'It would seem,' he answered cagily, 'I am not your only source, and all I am saying is perhaps your other source is better, or perhaps that information is incorrect. As I told you before, The Helvetii will not make a move this year. They are planning a migration for the next spring. I have always provided you with solid information in the past. What makes you trust this other person over me?'

'Perhaps you're right.' Caesar sounded most reasonable. 'You have always been trustworthy, so perhaps you're right. Go with Balbus and update him with everything you know. With that, the three men followed Balbus out of the room. I gave Lucterius a nudge and nodded in their direction indicating we should follow. For nearly an hour Balbus sat with the three men over an ewer of wine and interrogated them on the politics of every tribe that bordered Roman lands. Lucterius did well, pretending to look bored each time the men spoke to each other in Celt. Once they resumed speaking in Greek, we would each pick up our stylus, but while I wrote what they were saying, he would write what they had said in their native language. It is common, in business transactions to use two or even three clerks to write what is said to ensure an accurate accounting, so the Gauls suspected nothing. At the end of the meeting, Balbus invited the three men to spend the night at the villa, but they declined, claiming to have important business in Ostia in the morning.

After the meeting, Balbus and Lucterius immediately joined Caesar and me in the tablinum. Before joining them, I walked over to the cubicle where Marcus was working and told him to take some time to stretch his legs and get some food or visit the latrine. As soon as he was gone Caesar spoke to Balbus. 'I really don't care what they said in Greek unless you think it's something we don't already know.' Turning to Lucterius, he said, 'I need you to remember everything they said in your language.'

This caught Lucterius off guard but he quickly regained his composure. 'In this room, they were talking so fast and all at once.'

Caesar reassured him. 'I don't need the exact words, but tell me what they said as best you can remember.'

Lucterius looked down at his tablet and turned it over and sideways before finding the right notes. 'The one called Velinus was upset that you had the report. He said it was to have been delayed. The other two were blaming each other for not stopping it.'

There was more in this vein and the discussion would have gone on longer if Caesar hadn't said, 'put it in writing. I'll read the report later.'

Just as we were leaving, Lucterius looked down at his tablet and stopped, turning back to Caesar. 'Master?' Lucterius was timid and hesitant.

Caesar looked up. 'Hmmm?' he murmured, distractedly.

'One thing was strange. When they talked about the Helvetii mustering their forces they repeatedly referred to Dvmani and the half-moon.

'What of it?' Caesar asked.

'Your report says they will muster three days before the calends of Aprilis. That's the twenty-ninth day of Martius. When I did the calculations based on the moon, their date is the twenty-fourth day of the month.'

'Are you sure?' Caesar seemed surprised.

'They repeated the date three times and I've checked my calculations twice.' Lucterius was firm this time, 'I am sure.'

Caesar's face suddenly flushed and he slammed his fist down on the tabletop causing his wine cup to topple and spill. 'Damn them to Dis!' He sat red-faced and fuming for a moment before looking to me. 'Get everyone together, we've got work to do.'

I knew it wasn't a good time to question Caesar, but I felt I must. 'It's almost sundown. Do you want to see them tonight or should I call them for tomorrow?'

Caesar glared at me. 'If they can be here in the next hour I want to see them tonight. Send some of the boys out to gather them here. Have the bigger men act as escorts. Arm them with clubs. Get word to Crassus and Pompeius that it is imperative I meet with them tomorrow.'

Timidly, I asked, 'What does this all mean?'

Caesar sat red-faced and staring straight ahead, and then looking up he said, 'it is a deception plotted by someone to make me look bad. I will be portrayed as idling just outside Rome while the province I was charged with is overrun by Gauls. There's a chance though to turn this around and make me look like the hero, but we must act now.'

With a nod I turned to leave, tugging on Lucterius' sleeve to pull him along. Before I could reach the doorway, Caesar stopped me. 'Polybius?' His tone was milder. I turned and looked back at him. 'Have the messenger tell Pompeius to bring my daughter with him and arrive as early as possible. Before you go to sleep tonight, find some time to write to your children. You won't be able to see them again for some time.'

I nodded. 'Thank you, Caesar, I've already said my goodbyes earlier today but it would be nice to send them a note. I had a premonition this would happen.'

Less than an hour after sunset most of Caesar's circle had assembled. In a brief meeting lit by torchlight in the garden behind the villa, Caesar explained the situation and announced we must be prepared to leave the morning after next. We would be traveling fast and light; the baggage would follow us later. I silently prayed to Fortuna I would be favored with a manageable horse as the meeting broke up with each man sent on his way to do his part to prepare for our journey. As we walked into the villa from the garden, I said to Lucterius, 'I hope you can ride a horse.'

He smiled and shook his head in pity for my naiveté. 'I am from Gaul and my father was a warrior of the Helvii. I rode my first horse when I was five or six years old. It has been over ten years since I was allowed on a horse, but I think I'll remember how it's done.'

Having grown up in Rome I tended to forget there was a world outside the city. I laughed and looking over my shoulder leaned in for a quick peck on Lucterius cheek. 'Then you can finally teach me how it's done, as I'm terrified of the beasts!'

My task was to round up my staff of clerks. For the next two or three hours, I took dictation from Caesar as he paced back and forth composing letters to various agents in Gaul and orders commandeering supplies and arranging lodging along the way to make our trip to the province faster. As soon as I finished transcribing the message in shorthand on a wax tablet it was sent to one of the clerks to be transformed into a readable copy. Lucterius was kept busy translating several of the documents into the Celtic tongue.

It was past the middle of the night when Caesar called a stop to our work and allowed me to send the clerks to bed. Unlike me, Lucterius was unaccustomed to this sort of late-night work and he discreetly squeezed my hand under the table and whispered goodnight as he sleepily shuffled off to bed. I joined Caesar and Balbus in the garden where the night porter had set out wine and fruit. I desperately wanted to join Lucterius, but until Caesar gave me leave, I stayed with him. Caesar wearily laid down on one of the couches in the garden and Balbus took another while I sat on the nearby bench. After the porter had left, Caesar beckoned me to him as he propped himself up on one elbow. 'Bring your wine,' he said. I did as instructed and came before him on his couch. 'I want you to lie down at the end of this couch. Don't argue the point, Polybius. You deserve it more than Balbus and look at how he lounges.'

Without opening his eyes, Balbus growled, 'you were too busy composing letters to see how hard I worked today. You didn't have to go all the way to Ostia.'

As I took my place at the end of the couch, Caesar teased Balbus. 'That's just the sort of thing a Proconsul has legates for. If you were not up to the job you should have declined.'

Balbus snorted a laugh. 'We'll soon see who's up to his job.' Of course, none of us doubted Caesar's ability.

We all three lay back on the couches. For my part, I contemplated what the next few days would bring. After a long silence, Caesar said to me, 'you've decided on the staff you'll bring?'

'I settled on the final list just today,' I answered.

'You're bringing Lucterius.' It was a statement, not a question.

'Yes, I think he will be useful. He has taught me his language well, but I'm not ready yet to handle all the nuances of the Celtic language.'

Caesar's eyes were shut, but his mind was still focused. 'I agree,' he said, 'he will be useful.' Then he added as an afterthought, 'you two are good together.' I always wondered how much of my life Caesar observed and chose not to comment on. After a pause, he said, 'I'm going to miss Calpurnia. I've grown very fond of her these last few months.' I didn't know whether or not to connect that comment with the previous one and I was too tired to trouble my mind over it. We lapsed into silence again and I had drifted into that place between wakefulness and sleep when I was roused by a nudge from Caesar. 'Balbus is snoring, so that must mean it's time for bed.'

I gratefully shuffled into the villa and to my cubicle. At the house in the city, Lucterius slept in a cubicle with the other clerks, but with more room available here at the villa, we had a cubicle to ourselves. I made this arrangement without consulting our master, but Caesar always left these things up to me. Our cubicle had the luxury of a door, so Lucterius and I slept in the same bed. I tried to not wake him as I entered the room, but I heard him mumble, 'is it morning?'

'Go back to sleep, love,' I whispered, 'we have a few more hours.' With that I slipped off my tunic and let it drop to the floor and slid under the wool blanket beside him, pressing my body against his back. With that, I was asleep.

I thought I was awakened with a start, sensing a glow in the room. All at once I knew it was Fortuna. I rolled away from

Lucterius to face the light-filled room. Fortuna stood near the door, bathed in light. I threw off the blanket and sat up. I wasn't afraid of waking Lucterius; I'd learned from her past visits that this experience was for me alone. I didn't speak, knowing she would talk to me in due time. 'You think less about freedom, Polybius,' she said at last. Sadly, I knew she was right. 'But today, you felt that itch again. Let it go and trust me. You will be free one day, but there is still much work for you to do. Working for divinity elevates you above the free, this you must know in your heart.' At the time I thought she was suggesting that my work was for her, but years later when I stood and watched the Senate vote divine honors to Caesar, this visit came back to me and I realized for the first time she was referring to Caesar. She seemed to fade into a mist and disappeared as the light dimmed to darkness. I found myself sitting on the side of the bed with just the sliver of moonlight that came in through the crack between the shutters lighting the room. I lay back down but it was some time before I could sleep. I was grateful when Lucterius rolled over in his sleep and slid his arm across my chest, as Gaius would do so often in my summer of freedom.

LIBER XXXVII

I awoke with the sun. I quickly washed my face and made a trip to the latrine. On my return, Lucterius had already left the room. I was nervous and excited as I've always been at the prospect of long travel. Caesar was already awake, writing a letter to Servilia. I felt sorry for him that there was no time to visit her. I'm certain she would have divorced her husband and married Caesar had there been any hope her brother Cato would consent to the union, but that was clearly an impossibility. I had little to do that day. My function was to remember everything and use the information I could recall to help my master organize things. That work had all been done. Today was left for the men of action to carry out those plans. Lucterius still had translations to make and this would take some time as he was careful in his work and strove to provide as clear and exact a rendering as possible. With little real work to do, I volunteered to run errands in the city. My first stop would be Servilia's house where I would deliver Caesar's letter. From there I would place my own letter to my children into Cornelia's hand. After that, I had planned to make a stop at the Titus copy shop in the hope of visiting my old friends and I would round out the visit to the city with a trip to the Domus Publica to accompany Aurelia to Caesar's villa. What I was able to learn that day was that my secretary, Marcus fulfilled his purpose. Everyone I encountered was talking about the movement of the Helvetii, but as Caesar had hoped, the story had grown with each telling and now people actually believed that Gauls were on the verge of invading Italy.

I was able to visit the Titus domus and see my old friends. It made me sad that so many of the slaves from that time were gone, but Lydia and Alexander were still there. I was especially sad when I thought about my mother.

When I arrived back at the Caesar domus, an old slave named Corus was on the step of the Domus when I approached, and he ushered me in. I learned that Aurelia was making final preparations, so I took the opportunity to walk around the house and take it all in. I wanted a memory of the place that wasn't populated with all the people I needed to recall. As I was studying the fresco in my sleeping cubicle I heard movement behind me. Turning, I faced Aurelia. 'You seem sad, Polybius.' She said it with concern.

'I will miss Rome. But, I guess I'm just as excited about the journey. Five years is a long time.' I realized I was sad.

'You can write to us, and I assure you my son will not be able to avoid involving himself in politics. I'm also sure you will return to Italy several times.'

'The future is so uncertain. The little of war I saw in Hispania was enough for a lifetime. And, I will miss my boys.' I was being very candid, almost to the point of appearing disloyal.

'I too worry about my son, but it is his place in this world. Gaius

Caesar has achieved much, but I'm certain he is destined for true greatness. He must do this, and it's your place in the world to help him. It's time to go. Tomorrow is the Quinquatria. I'll consult an astrologer and write to you to tell you what the future holds.' She smiled, but the crease in her brow betrayed her own concern for the future. With that, we moved out to the street together. There was a retinue of twelve slaves to act as escort and guards. Aurelia traveled in a litter and I walked beside her. She kept the curtain open so we could converse along the way. The day was bright and sunny, but off on the horizon to the northwest, I could see clouds gathering. I reached in my bag and found my lucky die and carried it in my left hand.'

When we arrived, Pompeius, Crassus, and Clodius were meeting with Caesar behind the closed door of the tablinum. Caesar took the arrival of his mother as a signal to break up the meeting and escort the others into the atrium. I heard him say to the three men as they came into the open, 'I'm counting on you. I don't care how flimsy the pretext, at the first opportunity we need to get Cato out of the city.' With that, he greeted his mother with a kiss. Aurelia greeted Pompeius with affection, Crassus with politeness, and Clodius with a nod and a glare. She wasn't as forgiving as her son and she could never overlook the Bona Dea scandal. Clodius quickly said his goodbyes and made for the door and Crassus excused himself saying he had a business transaction to attend to, but Pompeius remained with the family as he was

Caesar's son in law. They moved out to the garden where Julia was waiting. Caesar invited me to join them, but I asked leave to join Lucterius for a riding lesson he promised me. By the end of the day, I was proficient enough to not embarrass myself on the journey. That evening, everyone retired early, as we would be up before the sun. Lucterius and I made love that night, as it was clear it would be some time before we would have any privacy.

We were awakened by the night porter well before the sun rose and as I threw off the blanket, I felt a damp chill in the air. It had rained the night before and now there was a lingering mist. When I stepped out into the atrium I could feel the moisture cling to my skin. Slaves were already piling cloaks on a long table that had been built the day before for the specific purpose of organizing our few supplies. It seemed as if all the villa's slaves were already up and working and I could smell our breakfast cooking in the kitchen. It was Caesar's belief that we needed to be fortified for the journey so he ordered a lamb to be roasted the night before. Caesar would have preferred pork, but as it was within the nine days preceding the Hilaria festival, pork was prohibited. I met Demetrius on my way to find Caesar and learned that he was already at work. As we entered the tablinum I found Caesar at the table writing out final orders. The plan was simple. Caesar, his legates and Tribunes, and a handful of slaves were to depart immediately and travel as quickly as possible to a small town with the Celtic name Genava (Geneva) where the Rhodanus (Rhone)

River exits a great lake that is formed where the river widens for a time. This was the place where Roman territory met the land of the Helvetii and it was a wild and unsettled place. This town is now a city thanks to Caesar's foresight in establishing his fort there, but the town we were traveling to was little more or perhaps a little less than a trading outpost. We were to travel so lightly that we were not allowed a change of clothing or even tents to sleep in. I was not looking forward to this journey. Caesar rose to shut the door as we entered the tablinum. He greeted me with a nod and a smile. As he picked a key up from the table and rose from his seat turning to the strongbox on a stand behind him. When he opened the box he took out two purses heavy with coins. He then spoke to me for the first time. 'You tell me you trust your man Lucterius, so I trust him too. I want you to divide this money between you. I've already given each of the men their share to carry. We'll be riding through some pretty unsettled territory and in the event bandits ambush us, I don't want to lose all our money. They won't think slaves will be carrying bags of coins, so they likely won't look for any in your things. If we are attacked, we split up. After a decent interval, we can find each other again by listening for the whistles. You are to give two short blasts with this.' With that, he handed me two small whistles and the bags of money. I must have looked terrified as Demetrius and Caesar both laughed and Caesar clapped me on the back.

'What if they want slaves if they can't get any money?' I

swallowed hard as I said this.

'Any bandits we meet won't want to be encumbered with slaves to guard. They'll be after coins and nothing more. Don't worry about it. It's just a precaution. Besides, most of us will be carrying swords.' Caesar's words were not very reassuring. Turning to Demetrius he handed him the key to the strongbox and said, Take care of the place for me.'

Demetrius reached out and touched his arm, answering, 'I always have.'

Before shutting the strongbox, Caesar reached in and brought out a smaller box. When he laid it on the table and opened it, I saw the dagger I had taken from the dead priest in Hispania. Caesar had had a new sheath and belt made for it. 'Wear this under your cloak.'

I felt slightly sick when I came to realize the dangers of this journey. I convinced Caesar to bring Lucterius with us to act as an interpreter, but I did so for selfish reasons and now for the first time I thought of the danger I put him in. I found Lucterius in the inner courtyard, lacing his riding boots. I gave him one of the bags of coins and told him what Caesar had told me. Looking around to be sure no one was listening, I said to him, 'this will be dangerous. You don't have to go; I can tell Caesar you are ill. You'll be safer following in the baggage train.'

Lucterius smiled at my concern and reached out and grabbed the back of my head pulling my face to his. After this brief but passionate kiss, he touched my cheek and said, 'The world is full of dangers, and I think we're better off if we face them together.' I was about to protest, but Lucterius had already turned away and was walking quickly toward the door.

By the time the first dim light began to penetrate the fog, the men were all gathered near the fountain in the outer courtyard with some of the men bickering over which of the horses they were each to ride. The horses had been chosen for their strength and speed, so it really didn't matter which horse one was given and we would go no more than a few hours before we were to change horses and continue our journey. A cold mist hung over everything and as I looked down toward the city I couldn't even discern the river through the fog that hung over the landscape. I was both nervous and excited as I pulled myself onto the horse I was given, and followed the others as they walked their horses a couple of times around the courtyard getting a feel for the animal. On Caesar's word, we all made for the gate and a new phase of life began for both Caesar and all who were associated with him.

I did not realize it at the time, but the conquest of all of Gaul had been set in motion."

EPILOGUE

Now, my friend, Nicarcus, I must leave off at this portion of the story of the life of Julius Caesar. I am continuing to compose the rest of this biography. Caesar was one of the greatest men in the history of the world and his life demands to be recorded. I am grateful to have heard his life's story told by his closest confidant. However, I must send this biography to you in installments. His life was too large to be set to parchment all at once. I will send to you the next chapters as I, with the help of my secretarial staff, am able to render the events of Caesar's life into a complete narrative.

I pray that the gods are good to you and those you love.

Lucius Seneca.

For a richer reading experience and to see updates about the sequel to Nomenclator Initium and Nomenclator Imperium, visit nomenclatorbooks.com. There you will learn more about the Roman world at the time of the Nomenclator series of novels.

I hope you have enjoyed Nomenclator Imperium. If so, please write a review at www.goodreads.com and watch for the sequel.